K. Morris Carroll

Second Thoughts

Published by: ThreeZeroMedia

Cover Design by: Christopher A. Brown

ISBN-13: 9780974059143

Distributed by:
ThreeZeroMedia
threezeromedia.com

K. Morris Carroll
Second
Thoughts

ThreeZeroMedia

Prologue

Your life really does flash before your eyes when you die. I've always heard that but never believed it to be true. Out of all the wonderful moments in my life, my wedding to the man of my dreams, the birth of my son, seeing him walk across the stage to receive his diploma from high school, his acceptance to Howard University, my own graduations, my success in my chosen field, why does this have to be the last thing I see?

I can't wake up.

That's because dead people don't wake up, stupid.

They don't have to listen to the likes of you either.

Then maybe you're not dead. God is good, even though you don't deserve it. Maybe He's giving you a second chance again.

Maybe. Oh please, maybe. But what if I don't do any better this time than I've done before?

Don't think about that right now. Just be grateful that you're not dead.

Maybe.

Simone was rolling over beneath the thick, warm feather comforter and extra blankets when the alarm went off. Or was it the cell phone? Did it really matter at this point? Whichever it was, it interrupted her most pleasant dream. She couldn't remember what it was, but it was good. That Cheshire cat, shit eating grin was spread across her face to the extent that another Wednesday morning wasn't looking that bad right now. *Hu-uummmpp Daaaaay!*

"Hello?" she whispered into the air.

"… 97.3 WNPW, National Public Radio…"

"Good morning to you too," she replied, snickering softly. All of her friends could not understand why she listened to that mess when some good ole gospel or R&B would get your blood pumping first thing in the morning. *White people tell each other things when they think we are not listening. Try it sometime. You will be surprised at what they say.* Her friends just looked at her and shook their heads. It is Simone after all, what do you expect? Then they'd give her that, *we love you girl* look, and keep rolling.

She sat up in the bed and looked around for some hint that might help her to remember what she had been dreaming about. Nothing. Just the spacious bedroom in the new house that she and her husband moved into about two years ago. Actually, it would be a year and eight months on Sunday if anyone was keeping track, which they weren't at this point. Despite all that had happened in that year and eight months, Simone was feeling pretty good this morning and desperately hoped that the day would still feel as good at the end as it did at the beginning.

She reached for her robe and carefully placed a toe on the hardwood floors as if she were checking the temperature before committing herself to placing both feet out into the real world. After careful consideration, she got back into the bed. Nothing pressing today. Department meetings tomorrow, no client appointments, and the one mediation scheduled for this afternoon had to be rescheduled due to conflict for one of the participants. There was still a little bit of time left before the court date, so it was all good. But there was something she had to do this morning. What was it?

The cell phone started to serenade her with Etta James and she remembered immediately.

"Hello," Simone croaked into the phone.

"Good morning, baby. You sound like you are still in bed."

"Having a hard time getting myself together this morning. How are you doing?"

"I'm good. Talking to a beautiful lady this morning. Trying to anyway. Did I call too early?"

"No, I just forgot that I'm picking up Maia this morning. So, thanks for waking me up. I was about to cover my head and call it a day." By this time Simone was up and on her way into the bathroom. She put the phone on speaker and started her morning ritual.

"Maia is excited. She has something to tell you."

"Why didn't she tell me last night?"

"It is a surprise, so she thought she'd wait, dramatic effect and all. You know ten-year-old girls. What are you wearing right now?"

"My skin… and that's going to remain that way if you don't let me get myself together."

"That sounds good to me. Send me a picture."

Suck of the teeth and roll of the eyes followed by a giggle. *I do love this man.*

"I will be there on time," Simone said through the whir of her Professional Care toothbrush.

"Call when you leave the house so that she'll be at the door and won't keep you waiting."

"I'm taking today for me. A little Simone time sounds real good to me right about now," she said as she turned to start the shower.

"Is that the shower I hear? Let me wash your back."

"Don't you have work to do or something? That's what they pay you for. I'll call when I leave the house. Okay?"

"Okay."

"Bye bye."

"Bye pardner."

Simone looked in the mirror and cast her eyes down as she saw the girlish grin on her fully-grown woman face. And it's not an ugly face either. *Oh, please. When are you going to get over it? Just because your mother said what she said a million years ago, you're still acting like it's a big deal. Grow up girl. You are loved. Men stop and look twice, be honest, sometimes three times. You're no Halle Berry, but who is? Not everybody needs to be. You are you. 'Nuff said.*

She finished dressing and set the house alarm. Walking out to the metallic pearl Volvo parked in the drive, Simone reached into her pocketbook and pulled out her cell phone. When she was settled in the driver's seat, she connected the Bluetooth and smiled as she backed down the driveway. *Safety first.* Simone drove through her neighborhood to the connector that led to the city. She enjoyed the drive every morning because it gave her the 'me' time that she so relished. It also gave her time to test out the efficiency of her new ride. She traded in the 5 series BMW her husband felt that she needed. "It complements my 750, don't you think?" he had said. Somehow, she wasn't in the mood to be an accessory anymore. "I like this. It's me. Understated, but in control," she said to herself as she signaled for the off ramp towards downtown. *It's about time you realized that. Took you long enough.* She reached for her iPhone and asked Siri to do her thing.

"Hey, I am on my way."

"Cool, I'm walking Maia to the door now."

"I'm sitting at the light---" Simone looked in the rearview mirror as she waited for the light to change. *Why isn't this car slowing down? Can't they see the light is red?* The sound of metal hitting metal reverberated through the phone along with the sound of Simone's scream. The car jolted forward into the path of a minivan full of uniformed kiddies on their way to private school. More crunching metal, squealing brakes, and terrified screams.

"Simone, Simone! What happened? I heard that from hear!"

"Daddy, Daddy, what was that? What's wrong?" Maia looked up at her father's face and saw nothing but dread.

"It's okay, Princess. Go back inside. Take the phone and dial 911. Do it now!"

People gathered on the sidewalk to stare at the twisted vehicles tangled in the middle of the street. A few were trying to direct traffic until the police, fire trucks, and paramedics arrived. One woman was at the Volvo's driver's side window talking soothingly through the glass to Simone letting her know that help was on the way. The children and the driver of the mini-van slowly tumbled out of the vehicle, shaken but not badly hurt. The driver of the car that had plowed into Simone wasn't so lucky. The car was a much older model something or other that was built before airbags were standard equipment. With no airbag or seatbelt, the driver had not stopped as suddenly as the car. The man, or bearded woman, had continued to travel through the windshield and on to what was left of the hood of the car. The distant sound of sirens grew ever louder as the police, ambulance, and fire trucks raced to the scene. Approximately five minutes had passed since the sound of the first crunch had occurred. The efficiency of the first responders to emergencies in the downtown area of the city was impressive. It had always been that way but since the threat of terrorist attacks had invaded the hearts and minds of city officials everywhere, the response time for kittens stuck in trees or young black men in hoodies had decreased significantly.

"Anyone know the victims? Check the cell phones for ICE numbers. Get that stretcher over here!" A paramedic barked orders to whoever was closest to him as he jumped out of the ambulance. Bystanders pulled out cell phones and started recording the events in case something went wrong, got really exciting, or could be uploaded to YouTube, or sold to the local TV affiliate for the nightly news.

"We're gonna need the Jaws of Life on this one. She's alive. That's a miracle. Anybody know this woman?"

The voice of another paramedic could be heard from the spot where Simone's trunk used to be. "This one doesn't need it, that's for sure." The paramedic moved her hand away from the neck of the bearded man spread across the hood. And walked toward the front of the Volvo to see how she could help.

A deep voice rang out from the crowd that had gathered on the street. The voice was breathless from sprinting the distance from the office buildings a half block away.

"Simone Dyson. Her name is Simone Dyson. Is she going to be okay? I'm riding with her to the hospital."

"Sir, if you can step back so we can do our job. The ambulance is over there. We'll get her out and get her to the hospital. Tell the driver you're riding with her, okay?" The paramedic looked to the fireman standing nearby with the Jaws of Life. "The husband?" The fireman shrugged his shoulders as he started to move toward the twisted wreckage of what used to be a new vehicle.

"I guess judging from the size of the rock on her finger. Poor guy. Looks like he's about to die himself."

"Yeah, love will do that to you, you know?"

"Yeah, let's get her out, okay? If anything happens to her, we'll have to resuscitate him too."

Jason held Simone's hand in both of his as they rode to the hospital, sirens blaring. It was unbelievable that with the damage to the cars that she wasn't seriously injured. Volvos. They really do live up to their reputation. Smart woman. *Beautiful woman.* Jason called his boy Mike to make sure Maia was safe and had a ride to school. Mike assured Jason it was all good but that Maia wanted to come to the hospital to make sure that Simone was going to be all right. Jason smiled and tried to sound like his confident self.

"She's good. Everything is going to be okay. No problem. Hold down the fort. I just want to make sure these fools do their job. Got to keep an eye out, you know?"

As he looked down on Simone's bruised face, he hoped that he wasn't talking out both sides of his. She didn't look too badly bruised right now, but he knew that by tomorrow all the trauma and swelling would start to show. *But at least there will be a tomorrow.* The blare of the sirens slowed and then stopped completely. *That must mean we're at the hospital. Thank you, Jesus. I'm not a real praying man, but I know when things are out of my hands. Please God, help. I don't know what else to say.* The paramedics opened the back of the ambulance and unloaded the stretcher.

"Careful guys, please be careful," Jason whispered.

The paramedic, who closely resembled the black guy from one of the CSI TV series, heard Jason's plea and quietly leaned close to him and said, "Don't worry, man. We got her. We got her. Gonna take good care of her for you. She gonna be all right. Won't let nothing happen to your wife, man."

Jason opened his mouth to speak but the Emergency doors rushed open and two doctor-looking people came dashing toward the stretcher. They helped push Simone inside, checking vital signs and jabbering a mile a minute about available rooms, IVs, milligrams of this and that. Jason followed as closely as they would let him, trying to see what they were doing.

"Excuse me, sir? Sir? Yes sir, you."

Jason stopped and looked around to find the mousy voice that was addressing him. "Did you ride in with the victim?" Now he saw the body attached to the mousy voice. *Minnie Mouse with a weave. I wonder if her man's fingers get stuck in all that when he tries to run them through her hair. Mercy.*

"Sir, did you ride in with the victim? I need some information please, to register her so that we can start treatment," squealed Minnie.

"Sure, what do you need? I'll tell you what I can." Jason muttered as he tried to figure out which door they took the stretcher through.

Name?"

"Simone Dyson."

"Could you spell that please?"

"S-i-m-o-n-e D-y-s-o-n."

"Middle initial?"

"R."

"Date of birth?"

"June 7, 1977."

"Type of insurance?"

"Aetna of Illinois… and that one with the duck."

"Address?"

"3725 Madison Court."

"Any known allergies?"

"Just to bees. She swells up like a blowfish. It's ugly. She doesn't have an Epi-pen or anything. I think she should though but what do I know?" Jason rattled off everything that he knew about Simone. He surprised himself that he could answer so many questions about this woman. This woman he has known for how long now? This woman who changed his outlook, his goals, his life. When he had answered all of Minnie's questions, she smiled at him with a new sense of respect. *Dag, I wish I had a man that loved me like that. Look at this dude. Those eyes. When he mentions anything about her…those eyes just shine. Dag, I need to find me a man like THAT! Better get my weave tightened this weekend.*

Jason sat for what seemed like an eternity. The walls and ceiling blended into each other to form a sea of drab. *Why do they do that in hospitals? Keep you calm if the news is bad?*

"Hello, there. I'm Dr. Ansula. I am treating Mrs. Dyson." The doctor stuck out his hand. Jason gripped it firmly.

"Is she alright? Can I see her now?"

"The Missus is going to have a complete recovery. It is a good thing that her vehicle is highly impact resistant. If she had been driving something else—well, the results would have been very different. A few contusions and possible concussion. We will keep her a few days to make sure everything is healing correctly." Dr. Ansula flipped through his chart and tapped it lightly. "Yes, please come this way to her room. She is settled and calling for you. Well, the words aren't quite clear because of the medication, but the intent is," he smiled.

Jason thanked the doctor and took a deep breath before he opened the door. He wanted the first thing Simone saw to be a strong and confident face to let her know that he was there and that everything was going to be just fine. He swallowed hard and unconsciously put his hand to his right eye before realizing he had done it. But when he opened the door, her head was turned the other way and her eyes were closed.

They gave her something to relieve the pain. That's good. She needs to rest. She'll see me when she wakes up. He pulled the straight back chair close to the bed and sat down. He gently picked up her hand and held it in both of his, just like he did in the ambulance. Only this time he held it to his lips for a while. *Thank you, God. See you got me praying twice in one day and it ain't even over yet. Really, I mean it. Thank you.* Jason swallowed hard trying to keep his emotions in check. He was a man after all and shit like this doesn't really call for silly emotions. Just deal. No biggy. But under the cool façade, he was shaking like a leaf and holding on to Simone's hand for dear life. Not hers, his.

The sun started to fade from the sky and Simone still hadn't awakened from her drugged sleep. Jason had relented and let go of her hand long enough for the nurses to check her vital signs a few hours ago. He had called Mike on his cell phone that he shouldn't have been using in the hospital.

"You know I got you covered, man. I picked up Maia from school and we had one of those extra large chocolate sundaes her momma says will rot her teeth. Then I took her to soccer practice. I'll pick her up if you need. Gimme a buzz later. Chevy and Sly are on their way to the hospital. I guess word is traveling now. Expect peoples soon enough. How's Moni?"

"Damn, she hates it when you call her that."

"Then don't tell her I call her that. She wouldn't know if you hadn't told her in the first place. You know I would never say that to her face," Mike quipped.

"I know that's right. She's sleeping, which is good, right?"

"Yeah, help her get her strength back. When she wakes up, tell her I asked for her." Mike hung up and Jason took a deep breath, feeling a little better at Mike's positive words. The hum of the machines seemed to grow dim as a clamor started to increase out in the hallway. Through the door, Jason could barely make out the words. It sounded like two people disagreeing, no, arguing.

"No sir, I'm sorry but you can't enter right now. Only one visitor at a time."

The squeal of Minnie's voice rose an octave as she tried to sound forceful.

"Mrs. Dyson already has a visitor. Her husband has been with her all day."

The door to Simone's room opened abruptly. A man entered with Minnie following close behind. "I am her husband," said the man. *At least on paper.*

Minnie's head tilted to the side as if yanked down by the weight of the synthetic hair. Pulling her head back towards center, she looked at the man, before she glanced at Jason. "Well, then who is that?"

Jason stood up to face the door. "Hello, Greg."

"Hello, Jason."

Neither man made any effort to shake the other one's hand or give a black man 'hug you like I got your back' hug or a good dap. Jason's jaw tightened ever so slightly under the surface, but Minnie saw it.

"Thank you for keeping my wife company today. I was out of town on business, but I am here now."

Minnie had really good mousy ears under all that hair, and she could have sworn she heard Greg growl as he finished speaking.

"As you should have been a long time ago. She's going to need attention over the next few days. It's good of you to get away from your important business but it's not necessary anymore."

Minnie looked from one man to the other. *No love lost here. Wonder if this is what I think it is? Can you spell triangle? What have you done, girlfriend?*

"Well, I am here." Growl. "So, thank you for helping out." Growl. "I can handle it from now on." Growl.

"That's good to hear that you're able to step up and do what a husband should. Too little, too late, I'd say. I'll be going now. But I will be back tomorrow and for as long as Simone needs me. That's what friends do."

You can be my friend all you like. Girl, I don't know you, but you got it going on up in here! I was upset 'cause I had to work today and miss my soaps. This is all that, the bag of chips and the drink, super-sized. I gots to get my hair done. And get me some of this kind of action! Minnie stepped back a few half steps to let Jason pass. She took a deep breath to pull in the scent of his manliness as he walked by. She could have sworn that she stumbled slightly. *Too much man? Never…*

"Thank you for all you did today. I know Simone would thank you too, if she could. See you tomorrow," he said as he glided out the door.

Yes, you will. Minnie watched him walk down the long corridor. Long, slow, confident strides. Like a man who knew what was what. Or at least that is how it would appear to anyone who didn't know what was running through Jason's mind right then.

If I walk slowly, I'll be near her a little longer. Lord, how did I get here?

Chapter **One**

Two years ago.

Children these days. If I acted like that when I was her age, Momma would have tore my behind up. Would not have been able to sit for a week. *Maybe two.* How did they get this way? The child is sixteen years old. Dresses like she's thirty. Talks like she's forty and probably knows more about life than I do.

That really doesn't take that much.

Hush.

I'm just saying...

We are not talking about me right now.

Maybe we should be. You are the one at home alone in that big behind house every night because your loving husband is loving someone else.

Didn't I tell you to hush? Whatever he feels for her isn't love, I'm pretty sure of that.

Well, whatever it is it made him move away from you, didn't it? Come on girl, you need to face it sometime. Holding your breath waiting for him to make up his mind is going to leave you unconscious as you hit your head on the floor. And you've done that how many times now? Just file for the big D word and get on with your middle-aged life. Do something useful—have a crisis or something.

I'm not telling you again-hush.

See that's why he dogs your sweet ass. You are too nice. Too forgiving. Too understanding. You should have worn her ass out, both hers and his too. But noooooooo. You go and wait patiently for him to decide what is best for him. Sickening.

If I had listened to you, I'd probably be in jail.

And divorced. I'm not seeing the problem.

Hush.

Simone was on her way out of the high school after visiting her mentee during American Education Week. The one week out of the year that most parents take the time to visit their children in school. Maybe that's all they can handle. God bless the teachers. Now that's a thankless job. Trying to get the best out of other people's children when their own parents can't even do it. On the other hand, Simone had seen teachers do miraculous things with other people's children. She had sat in Ronjai's English class today listening to her read her poetry. The words resonated from her heart. You could hear a pin drop in the room as she opened her heart with her words. After she finished, a few parents were trying to wipe their eyes without anyone knowing. Ronjai looked at Simone as if searching her face for approval. She found what she was looking for. The two of them hugged right there in the classroom. The tears flowed between them.

"Oh, Miss Simone, you really liked it? I wrote that one for you."

"What?"

"Really, I did. When I was talking about the fresh air and gentle breeze that cleared my mind—that was you."

Simone didn't know what to say so she looked in the direction of the teacher and motioned to her that she wanted to leave the room with Ronjai. The teacher smiled her approval and the two of them walked out of the room hand in hand. They walked down the hallway of the new school. All you could hear was the sound of high heel shoes bouncing off the sparkling tile floors. Everything else would be quiet now for fifteen more minutes until the change of class. Neither the mentor or the mentee spoke for a while. Each thinking their own thoughts.

"You know, when we first met, I didn't like you," Ronjai said with her head facing the floor.

 "Really?"

"Really."

Simone knew that it was a good time for her to use her strategic listening skills to help Ronjai say what was on her mind and in her heart right now.

"When you say you didn't like me, help me to understand what you meant by that."

Ronjai lifted her head and cast her eyes to the left. She was thinking and remembering. "You were so laid back and smooth it seemed. Like nothing ever bothered you. Like you were above it all."

"Sounds like I seemed aloof and unapproachable."

"Yeah, that's it. And I wondered why I got the uppity wench for a mentor when Takiyah got the really cool homegirl with the nails, pierced nose and belly button, and skinny jeans."

"Looking for someone who was more suited to your expectations."

"Actually, looking for someone who wouldn't have any expectations. You wanted something from me that I didn't know I had."

"What was that, Ronjai?"

"You wanted me to see my own value. To see that I was worth more than I thought."

"Learning to appreciate yourself."

"Exactly." They walked to the courtyard at the front of the building and found a seat in the solarium. "You know when it hit me? The day you came to my house the first time to pick me up for the African festival at the university. Ty was selling his usual noise on the street, calling every female within earshot bitches and hoes. Then you pulled up and got out the car and I thought 'let's see how she handles being called a hoe. Bet she won't be so calm then.' But you got out and looked directly at him and he shut up. Just like that, he shut up. I couldn't believe it. Then you walked up to him and said, "Could you tell me where Ronjai lives, please?" just as quiet and he answered you back real quiet. Like he was a gentleman. Tripped me out. That's when I decided that I wanted to be able to do that?"

"What is it that you wanted to know how to do?"

 "Have people listen to me and treat me like I mattered. That's when I knew Takiyah could keep her homegirl…. I heard Takiyah's mentor is in jail for possession, by the way. I would rather have you." Simone smiled. How could Ronjai remember that? It was what, three, four years ago? *Wow. Hadn't thought of that for the longest time. Should I tell her I was scared to death? No, let her think I have it together. With age comes wisdom and all that stuff. Maybe six years from now, when she's a little older and wiser, we can talk.*

"Miss Simone, why are you smiling like that?

"Oh, nothing."

The two of them made plans for a weekend trip to Spellman University and hugged each other. Ronjai's grandmother was so excited that her baby girl was looking to go to college, she would let her go anywhere with Simone. This was a different Ronjai than she used to be. The bell rang as Simone walked out of the school. She heard Ronjai tell a young man that if he wanted her attention, he should learn how to talk to a lady and stop showing his drawers. Until that time, he could get to steppin'.

I think that I'll go see Dad on my way home today. I'll surprise him and stop at the bakery and pick up some of that heavy behind bread pudding that he likes so much. Don't know how he can eat that stuff. Don't have to rush home tonight, Greg is not going to be there. Again.

Simone raised her eyebrows and crinkled her lips at the thoughts going through her mind. Thinking that Greg could be unfaithful to her was unbearable. Sure, they had been through all that several years ago, but they had worked through it with tears and more tears, mainly hers, she thought. But that wasn't the case. Greg seemed to change girlfriends like other people changed their drawers. This was what? Number three? *Maybe four.* Simone wasn't sure, but she had her suspicions. She had hired a private investigator to prove to her that her suspicions were wrong or that her suspicions were right. It really didn't matter at this point, as long as she knew something for sure. Something definite.

Waste of your hard-earned money. I told you what was what, but noooooooo. You needed proof. Pictures, dates, times. How'd you feel when you got all that? Can you say broke?

It was worth it, so hush.

Hush, my ass. You're lucky I can't leave your naïve behind. Listen to me as I tell you for the hundredth time. Divorce his ass. You don't need his money. He doesn't contribute to nothing no how. You work every day, like a dog I might add. You don't need his drama. I am tired of you blaming yourself every night. Tired of listening to you wonder what you did or didn't do. Tired of you looking in the mirror and thinking 'what is wrong with me?' Tired, do you hear me? Hello? What, you got nothing to say? Fine. I can shut up too.

Good.

Simone left the bakery with a heavy bag filled with bread pudding and caramel sauce in two little side containers. She smiled to herself thinking that at least she could make one Dyson man happy. Sad. Stinking thinking, her sister would have called it. The thought of her sister was bittersweet. She really didn't need that right now.

She drove to 'Daddy Dyson's' while listening to love songs on her Sirius XM radio. Bad idea. Or really good idea depending on the frame of mind of the listener. Simone chose to be upbeat about it.

Pretending in her own mind that someone truly loved her like Larry and Luther and maybe even Prince (if she was feeling nasty). Right now, she was being adored, as only Prince could do.

She parked in front of the house and finished listening to the song. Wiping the tears from her eyes, she looked in the rearview mirror and smiled at her reflection. Not the 'I am so beautiful, look at me' smile but the 'I am okay inside, in spite of everything else' smile. By the time she walked to the front door, it was opening. A huge man, looking like James Earl Jones with a skunk streak of gray hair, stood there grinning at her.

"My beautiful baby girl, bearing gifts. How did I get so lucky? Come on in here."

Horace Dyson reached out and grasped Simone's elbow and escorted her into the house as though she were a visiting queen. Simone loved to visit the patriarch of the Dyson family. Since she had never met Mrs. Dyson, she always thought the Horace truly enjoyed a female presence in the house. "Turns a house into a home," he always said. "Wish my boys could understand that." The two went straight into the kitchen and sat by the sunny bay window. At this time of day, there was at least an hour or two of sunlight left and it shone its brilliant color directly on the table. Simone thought they were lucky it was late fall. Midsummer-- and they wouldn't be able to sit here. But right now, it was perfect. Horace retrieved bowls from the cupboard and dared Simone to mention how the bread pudding would affect her weight or her diet or anything else that silly women use as an excuse to starve themselves or get backdoor compliments on how they look. Simone wasn't the type to do either and Horace knew that. He also knew that she had no idea of how attractive she really was. Not many women could carry off her height, build, and posture and not become totally vain. She just seems to think that is the way God made her, so it must be just fine. God don't make no junk. *Praise the Lord! She is fearfully and wonderfully made. With a good heart too. My son's a fool.*

"Honey, you want some water or tea. I got some of that herb tea you like, and I got some of that soy juice stuff in the box, and..."

"Soy juice? I never heard of soy juice."

"You know, soy milk. It ain't been nowhere near a cow so don't know why they try to call it milk." Horace laughed at his own joke. So, did Simone. If she had to pick a perfect father-in-law it would have been Horace.

So how did he get such an idiot for a son? Hush. *Well, you know I'm speaking the truth. Speak the truth and shame the devil. That's what the old people say.*

And I say hush.

"Tea would be really nice, I think. I've got a little bit of time before I need to get home, so… yes. I would like some tea. Thank you."

What a lady. You would think she was at a fine restaurant ordering from a waiter with the napkin over his arm. I like this girl. She makes a good daughter. My son's a fool.

"So, how you been Simone?" Horace had his back turned to the stove as he asked but he could feel the hesitation in Simone's voice as she searched for an appropriate response.

"I'm good, Dad. Work is going well. We just got a federal grant to begin Alternative Dispute Resolution for frequent offenders to lessen the burden on the courts. I'm really excited about that. We start sorting through possible cases for mediation tomorrow. Hopefully, it will make a positive impact. Hopefully."

"That sounds really good but hopefully, your life is more than just work." *See, that's why I love her. She ain't gonna rat out that no good son of mine. Got to pry it out of her. Now that's a real lady. Girls nowadays would be boohooing and screaming all over the place. She just holds her head up and keeps rolling. My Beckie would have loved her.*

"Everything is fine."

Liar.

"Greg has been really busy lately, with the planning of annexing Heathfield and Allington. It keeps him pretty busy."

"In other words, he's not home very much. So that gives you time to sit with an old man and eat bread pudding," Horace said between spoonfuls.

"Dad, you know I always bring you bread pudding and I love visiting here."

Here's your big chance, tell him his son is an adulterous, lying, good for nothing idiot and that you're leaving his sorry black ass.

Hush.

The two sat silently for a minute contemplating bread pudding and familial fidelity. When is blood thicker than water?

When it's your daughter-in-law who's trying to keep things together or your son who thinks that the world is his oyster?

"When was the last time that son of mine came with you to visit?"

"It's been a little while, I think. Maybe a few months. I think it was warm out."

"Sounds about right."

Trying to change the subject, Simone asked, "So, how is Karl? Haven't heard from him lately."

He's a bigger idiot than his brother. "Climbing to the top of the force last I heard. These boys hardly have time to enjoy the lives God gave them 'cause they're so busy trying to be God's gift instead of being grateful for what they have. Don't get me started. I am sorry."

Simone reached out and gently laid her hand on top of Horace's. He mirrored the gesture by placing his hand on top of hers.

"Having sons is an awesome responsibility. If you don't do it right, that sets up suffering for future generations. Sounds biblical, don't it? The sins of the fathers and all that. But as I look back on it, it's true. Every single time. It's true. Case in point. There were these two brothers. One was a real pretty boy. Had been since he was a baby. Grew up to be a real lady's man. You know the kind I mean. Smile at them and they want to drop their panties for him—forgive my language Simone. Shouldn't talk like that in front of you but you know what I mean. Anyway, the other brother was quiet, smart, and kind. He went to high school, got his diploma, and started working on cars in his father's garage. The only thing pretty boy ever went through was the back window of some poor simple girl's house. Supposedly had two or three back door children that he never claimed or took care of. He got by on the kindness of women while his brother worked his way through night school and opened his own car repair shop in his neighborhood. Now, in them days black folks didn't have too many vehicles of their own, so the chauffeurs for the white folks brought the big cars to him for tune-ups and oil changes because they knew he did good work and charged a fair price. They would tell their employer a price, pay half that much and pocket the rest. The employer didn't care, even with the fifty percent mark up, it was cheaper than what the white repair shops charged. He made a decent living. He wasn't rich by no stretch of the imagination, but he saved up some money and bought a house and married a sweet lady that worked just as hard as he did. They saved up their money and had two boys of their own. Taught them the meaning of hard work and a good education. Put both them boys through college.

Meanwhile, pretty boy was doing what pretty boys do. Breaking hearts, making promises he couldn't or wouldn't keep. Running from jealous husbands, running from jealous lovers. Just running and wasting his life. Never saw him with the same woman twice. He would come to visit his brother on some holidays, all dressed up with some fancy looking lady on his arm. Always looking down at his brother for having a wife who was just nice looking and not 'hot to trot' as he liked to call his lady friends. His brother would just smile and say, "She's pretty and she loves *me*. That makes her beautiful to me. I can't do any better than that."

Years came and went, and the brothers were out of touch for a long time. Pretty boy was doing his thing. Family didn't mean much to him because he didn't have any that he was willing to be responsible for. The other brother though, saw both his sons graduate from college. Late one night, there was a knock on the door. One of the sons was home from grad school and opened the front door to see his uncle pretty boy standing there. He looked a hot mess. His brother came to the door and saw him and brought him inside without ever saying a mumbling word. Seems that pretty boy had lost what little he had and was getting too old for any woman to want to take care of him. He was old, alone, and had nowhere else to go, so there he stood.

The nice-looking wife made up the spare bedroom and she and his brother took him in and nursed him until he was back up on his feet.

About a year after that, pretty boy's brother had a heart attack while helping a neighbor work on the engine of his car. The funeral was the saddest thing a person could ever hope to see. There were people from all over the city that had been helped in one way or another. From them chauffeurs to school bus drivers to church folk to neighbors from all around. Crying, truly grieving over the loss of such a good man. Pretty boy stood back from everybody listening to everything that people were saying about his brother and probably thinking that he had never done anything but made fun of him and his love for his family and friends. After the funeral, pretty boy thought that his sister-in-law was going to put him out, but she didn't. She continued to take care of him until he died two years later. She and her two sons were the only people at that funeral. I remember thinking, "I want my life to be better than that. I want it to mean something." To have done something for somebody else. To make a difference. To truly love someone and be loved back.

Pretty boy was my uncle, Gregory Hurricane Dyson. My father was his brother. I look at my sons and see my father and uncle sometimes. That's right. Your husband acts just like his pretty boy uncle, and I just hope and pray that he comes to his senses sooner than his namesake."

Chapter Two

Jason was sitting at his desk rubbing his eyes as he looked at the files in front of him. Wouldn't it be easier to log on to the system and sift through the tons of misdemeanors and dropped charges electronically?

Tired eyes are tired eyes.

What are these kids thinking now days? The sound of that rolling around in Jason's head made him snicker. He could hear those same words coming out of his grandmother's mouth when Jason was acting like he didn't know his head from a hole in the ground. So many chances for things to have turn out differently. Moms tried so hard to do everything that she could. Grams was just as dedicated to making sure all four of her grandchildren turned out all right despite that fact that there was no husband or father in the house. Never had been. *Sure, I was a wild child for a while. But thank God that I came to my senses. There but for the grace of God…*Don't these kids get it? They are young black males in this society. They should know that means they've got a target on their backs. Look at Travon Martin, Freddy Gray, Michael Brown, Daunte Wright, Ahmaud Arbery…innocent brothers that lost their lives for no reason. How much leeway do they think they are going to get when they make poor, *no-- stupid* choices about their future and then here they are, another statistic in the criminal justice system. This one in particular. Tyreek Henderson. Seventeen years old, four months away from being considered an adult. Made it to ninth grade by the time he was fifteen, dropped out before he became a three-peat as a freshman. Now he spends his time organizing drug deals for someone older and wise enough to use someone young to be his street feet. *What's he gonna do with you in four months, young blood? You think he'll have your back when you hit grown? I don't think so.*

Tyreek's file went on and on. Petty larceny. Burglary. Possession of marijuana. Not enough for distribution. *Probably finished the transaction before he got caught.* Gang related activity. Juvenile court. Halfway house. Psychological facility for observation after episode during trial. *Gee, smooth move. Wonder who told him to do that?* No convictions. *He must think his shit don't stink at this point.* Released to custody of his guardian, Mrs. Henderson, his grandmother. *What would our children do without their mommas and grandmommas?* Now, here sat Tyreek's file in front of Jason. Last chance before the shit hits the fan for real. Hold for trial in four months or give him one last chance. Jason's office had just been recruited for a pilot program with the State's Attorney's Office to incorporate Alternative Dispute Resolution in an attempt to lighten the load on the court system. In terms of work and cost, ADR as it was called, sounded good but was it really feasible to take this type of offender and expect him to resolve his tendencies and conflicts through opening up in mediation and adhering to the agreement that is created? Yeah, right. *You got another chance, didn't you? If somebody hadn't stopped your ass that day and talked to you, who knows what would have happened? You saw what happened to--* Jason moved his hands from rubbing his eyes to placing his chin in his hand and looking out the window on to the street. *That seemed like so long ago.* It was. *Twenty-four years, to be exact.*

Sixteen-year-old Jason Copeny knew he was God's gift to the universe. In fact, in the secret recesses of his own mind, he loved that old cartoon Masters of the Universe because he always thought they were referring to him and him alone. There could be only one. Or was that some other old movie line? This particular day master of the universe had skipped school and made his way back home to lay up with Alay'ah for part of the afternoon. That, Jason thought, was all he needed. He thought her name was appropriate 'cause she would 'uh...lay ya' with a quickness. Did it matter? Not as long as he got his too. After he finished and put her out, he put his head under his blanket and planned to catch up on his beauty sleep. Who knows who or what the evening would bring? Deep into his pleasant dreams, one of the twins, was it Tisha or Tasha, was pulling on the blanket.

"Get up, we need some bread." It was Tasha. Definitely, Tasha. For the quiet, reserved twin she could be a pain in the ass.

"Get out," Jason groaned.

"Get up. Now. We need bread. There is no bread. How am I supposed to fix Byron's snack without bread?"

"Fix something else. And get out." Jason rolled over and pulled the blanket back up over his head. Patience. He was the king of patience. Wait long enough and they go away after awhile. All except Tasha. She truly was the Mistress of the Universe in so many ways. For twelve years old, she ran the house while their mother worked two jobs keeping bread on the table, which they were now out of. Tisha was too busy being grown, sneaking out windows, and running the street at night to be responsible or concerned with the well being of their little brother Byron.

"Boy, I said get up! Now! We need bread!" Tasha shouted and jumped on the bed. She started to punch the blankets, knowing that Jason was under there somewhere. He rolled over to grab her hands and caught a fist right in the eye.

"Damn, girl. What is wrong with you? Calling me boy, punching me! Are you crazy? You need to get out of my face, girl," said Jason as he scrambled to the corner of the bed rubbing his right eye.

"You need to get up! I'm not telling you again," Tasha spoke the words quietly now with the same tone her mother used when she had had enough. She folded arm over arm and cocked her head slightly

to the side as if Jason might not understand the English language as well as body language.

"Or what little girl? Huh? What exactly do you think you are going to do, Miss Thing?" He was now sitting up in the bed, leaning forward. Feeling like what he thought a man should feel like. Intimidator. Threatener. Controller. Unfortunately for Jason, Tasha didn't know anything about Jason's version of what a man should be. How could she? There had never been a man in the house to show her or her siblings what a man should or should not be.

"Or I'm telling Momma you skip school and bring that girl with the short skirts and too little shirts in the house when she's at work. Then I'm going to tell her that you leave the house at night when she is at work when she told you to watch us." The head tilted in the opposite direction. Translation—'Do you understand what I am saying to you?' Yeah, I understand. Females, that's why no man can stand ya'lls asses for more than an hour at a time. Fine, you wanna play? Here play this.

"All right. I'll go get some bread. But who is gonna pay for it? You got some money?" Check, Miss Thing. Top that.

"No, but you do. Under the bed in the shoebox. Somewhere around six hundred thirty dollars last time I checked. Now if you don't want me to tell Momma about that too, you'll get up and put some clothes on your nasty black behind." Head straight up now, arms still folded. Checkmate.

"How'd you know about that, T? Who told you?" Jason was sitting up experiencing the first symptoms of shock.

"Nobody told me. I saw you when you thought nobody was around while you were hiding it. I know you get it from that creep that hangs down the street." Tasha knew enough not to tell Jason everything that she knew. She didn't mention the fact that she had known about the money for the past year. She saw Jason putting the money in the shoebox one night after he snuck back in the house thinking that everyone was asleep. She had gotten up to go to the bathroom and saw the light on through Jason's slightly open door. She tiptoed to the door and peaked inside thinking she was going to catch her brother looking at dirty magazines or something. No, this was much

worse. Where did he get all that money and why was he hiding it? Tasha ran back to bed and pretended to be asleep.

Two weeks later, Byron needed money for the rental fee for his flute at school. He had asked Momma who said, 'sure thing baby' and forgot to leave the money on the table for him before she went to work. Bryon was frantic as any eight-year-old would be when promised something from the one person you can always count on. Tasha looked at the tears in his innocent eyes and remembered her brother's stash under the bed.

"Don't worry By. Momma must have left the money upstairs. I'll go check." Tasha ran up the steps and into Jason's room. She pulled out the shoebox and opened it up. Fives, tens, twenties, and hundreds neatly stacked. She counted out the twenty-five dollars that Byron needed and closed the lid and shoved it back under the bed. She closed the door and walked back down the stairs.

"See," she said holding out the money, "I told you Momma left it upstairs."

That was the first time that Tasha had taken anything without permission. Over the past year, she had decided that she or her sister or baby brother should not have to go without or worry their overworked mother when her no good brother stashed money under his bed and made no effort to help their mother with the bills or anything else. Calling himself the man of the house. If that's what a man does, no wonder Momma doesn't have one here.

"We need something to go with the bread too. So, you might as well get some groceries while you are at the store, so Momma won't have to go this weekend."

"And how am I supposed to get stuff back here?"

"Can you say cab? You can afford it."

"What else do you want me to get exactly?"

"You eat here too. Milk and something to go between the bread. If you can't figure it out, here's a list."

"Oh, you are good, little girl. Real good. I won't forget this, you

know."

"Good. So, I won't have to tell you again next week. Now get up and get dressed. You need to stop acting like a chump. You are such a..." Tasha turned around and walked towards the door.

"Such a what? You got so much mouth. You got something to say? Say it! Such a what?" Jason hollered.

She stopped and turned around. "Such an idiot. Probably just like our Daddy. Why do you think we've never met him? Whenever we used to ask Mommie about him she just looks like she could spit. You are probably just like him. Good for nothing." Silence. *"You might want to wash up. You stink."*

Jason pulled on the gym shorts that Alay'ah had pulled off earlier in the day. Throwing a hooded sweatshirt over his head with a pair of Nike Airs paid for from his stash. He grumbled all the way down the steps and out the front door. He grumbled and cursed now that he was out of the house, all the way down the street, rubbing his eye the entire time. Girl got a good hook. She'll be able to take care of herself. Wonder if Tisha can hit like that, too? Jason walked with his familiar bop away from the sunset. Just like a good anti-hero. Heroes walk into the sunset. Anti- heroes that get punked by their twelve-year-old sister walk away from everything they possibly can, including sunsets.

"Good evening, Mr. Copeny." The deep resonating voice came from the porch of the house as Jason passed by. Mr. William always spoke when he saw Jason. Always called him Mr. Copeny when he saw him. Like he's making fun of me. With his wannabe wrestler ass. Just 'cause he all big like that don't mean nothing. Still put a cap in his ass...

"Evening Mr. William," Jason grumbled, forgetting that he was still rubbing his eye.

"And what are you into on this lovely evening?"

If it's any of your business. "I'm going to Tally's to pick up some groceries so that Moms won't have to do it this weekend. She don't get that much time off. She shouldn't have to grocery shop." It made sense when he said it out loud. It made him feel better to know he was actually about to help out.

"Looks like you ran into something today, Mr. Copeny. Maybe you should have stayed in school this afternoon. Protection from things that you can't handle." Jason dropped his hand and looked at Mr. William. Who'd this clown think he was talking to him like that? Sure, he and his wife, Miss Sashi, used to watch him and his sisters and brother when his mother was at work but that didn't give this forty some year-old loser the right to talk to him like that. He was the man of his house and what did this guy know anyway? Jason had had enough today. First Tasha, now this. It's the last straw.

"Look old man. I don't need you all up in my business. You ain't my father."

"If I were, I would have straightened your young ass out by now. His absence has been a detriment to your development. Your mother works hard with you, but you need a father." Jason couldn't believe his ears. Who did this guy think he was?

"I can't believe you, man! Talking about my Pops like you know him or why he ain't around. You know living with a woman ain't no easy thing for a real man. He had his reasons. I'm cool with that. I'm fine." Jason's breath was coming fast and strong.

"You're gonna end up just like him. Missing in action. A statistic in child support files."

What the f—did he just say? Jason walked up the steps on to Mr. William's porch. Took a step up into Mr. William's face, huffing.

"Nigga, I should knock you out. You got no right to talk about him when you don't know him. You talking about my Pops like you know him or somethin'."

"Boy, as long as you have air in your lungs, don't you ever disrespect me or any other grown person. You hear me, boy?" Mr. William spoke real quiet, leaning forward slightly, making Jason take a step back.

"Don't call me boy, nigga." Before Jason knew what hit him, he felt a pain like he never experienced before. All vision left his left eye. When he opened the right one, he was noticing the splinters sticking

out of the planks in the porch's floorboards.

Maybe he busted my eardrum 'cause I can't hear nothing either. How did things end up like this? What the f---?

"Get up, boy. Here, take my hand." Mr. William stretched his hand down to Jason.

"I can do it."

"What'd you say?"

"I can do it, Mr. William." Jason pulled himself to his knees. He shook his head and slowly rose to his feet. He grumbled something under his breath as he rubbed his left eye--making him forget about his right eye.

"You say something?"

"Nah, I mean no. I just didn't like you talking about my Pops. That's all."

"Your 'Pops', like you know him."

"You act like you got some right to talk about him. I don't like it. I am his son, and I don't know him, so, how can you?" Jason sounded like he was whining, even to himself, but he couldn't help it. He didn't know what to think, what to say, what to do at this point.

"He's my brother."

The sound of firefly wings was all that could be heard on that front porch for the next umpteen minutes. Time stopped, and left Jason wondering how in the hell did he end up on the far side of the Twilight Zone on his way to the Outer Limits.

"Pick your lip up off the ground, boy, and get in the truck. You gonna need some help getting your momma's groceries home." Mr. William walked down the steps as if he expected Jason to follow behind him like a whupped-up baby who just found out that Santa Claus was really Daddy dressed up in a cheap red sweater and work boots. Actually, that would have been easier to digest right about now.

Jason walked to the midnight green Jeep Cherokee and opened the door. His hand was unconsciously trying to decide which side of his face to rub first. For the second time, the Mr. William side won out.

"Well, get in. I find it hard to drive with the passenger door open. Put on your seat belt, boy."

"Stop callin—"

"What did you say?"

"Nothing, Mr. William."

"That's what I thought." William started the engine and pulled out into the street.

"I just don't like it when you keep calling me boy. I ain't no boy." His hand shifted to the other eye.

"Then what are you then? You sure ain't no man, that's for damn sure. Your momma working herself to death putting food in your lazy mouth and keeping a roof over your head, so you can lay up with some big tittied girl instead of getting an education or at least a job. A legal job anyway."

Jason turned and looked at William with a look of surprise on his face.

"Don't go looking surprised, boy. Everybody knows about you and Miss Thing. And probably about the other stuff, too. Everybody but your momma. Nobody has the heart to tell her--although I should have months ago."

"How'd you know?"

"'Cause a man knows how to handle his business and no man takes a little girl in his momma's house for what you took that girl in there for. Little boys don't know how to act. Standing on street corners hustling for grown men so that when the police come, they haul your young ass away and they get another young fool to take your place."

"You don't know nothing about me, old man." Jason mumbled under his breath as he stared out the window as the scenery changed from houses to stores and factories.

"You don't know nothing about yourself, is what you mean. That's what's wrong with you. You don't know who you are. And for God's sake, I don't understand why Mim won't tell you nothing about your daddy. How you supposed to grow up to be a man when you ain't never been around one?"

"I know plenty of men. Always have."

"Oh really? Ever had one in your house? Paying the bills? Fixing what needs to be fixed? Getting up in the middle of the night when there's a noise? Talking to you? Playing catch with you in the backyard? Walking you to school? Whupping that ass when you mess up? Saying he's proud of you when you do good? Teaching you to shave? How to wrap it up so that no other little boy has to go through not having no daddy to raise him? Answer me that, boy." More firefly wings. "That's what I thought."

The Cherokee pulled into the parking lot of Tallys. William cruised the lot for a space. Wrong time of night for shopping. Most people stopping for something on their way home from work. Rotisserie chicken and Stouffer's Macaroni and Cheese. Home cooking at its best. A silver Altima backed out and William swung into the spot with a satisfied look on his face. He turned off the engine and sat as if waiting for something. Firefly wings.

"Tell me about my father." Jason whispered. "Please."

"Boy, I mean Jason, that's your mother's job. Mim has her reasons for keeping it to herself, I guess. Let her tell you. Haven't you asked her in all these years?"

"Yeah, I asked her. We all have at one time or another. She just looks at us like we got two heads and walks away. She really looks at me like that a lot lately and I don't know why."

"It's probably 'cause the older you get the more you favor him. I see you sometimes walking down the street and swear I see him all over again. You look just like him when he was your age."

"Is he dead?"

William huffed and curled up his lip the way people do when they are disgusted with the world. "No, last I heard he was in Massachusetts.

We don't keep in touch since our mother died couple years back. Your grandmother, Mariah Holder. She would have loved to see you and your sisters and brother."

"I have a grandmother?"

And uncles and an aunt and cousins. You don't know who you are. I just want you to know, that's all."

The words stuck in Jason's throat. No matter how much he wanted to hold them back, they bubbled and boiled within his chest until he had no control over them.

"So, tell me who I am. I—I need to know. You are my uncle, right? So, please, tell me what I don't know. That's everything, I guess. I mean, I don't know what I mean..." First the words, now the tears. Burning and boiling out of his swollen eyes. More than any one boy can stand. Maybe he's right, Jason thought. 'Cause if this is grown up shit, then, I'm not ready for it.

"There's three of us. Your father is my youngest brother. I got him by five years. You'd think that wouldn't make that much difference, but it was like a lifetime between us. As different as night and day. Or like your grandmomma used to say as different as a scorpion and an armadillo. One always lashing out and the other all closed up in his own shell."

"Which one are you?"

"What do you think?" Jason didn't respond. "That's what I thought. Jay was something else. Yeah, I guess he still is. I don't know what your mother saw in him besides his pretty smile. Mim always could see good in every person. She still does. She gave your father chance after chance to be a man and live up to his responsibility. I think she knew deep down inside that Jay was weak. Maybe she thought if she didn't take care of him the world would swallow him up. It's sad to say that your brother was weak but it's true. He just didn't want to be a real man. Smiling and coming and going as you please. That's why Mim never married him. Wanted him to get himself straight first. Still hasn't, I guess."

"His name is Jay?"

Jason, just like you. Your momma thought that Jay, seeing his firstborn son, might cause him to step into a man's shoes. A new life with the same name as his, how much more can a woman do to show her love for a man?"

Jason watched William as he gripped the steering wheel until his knuckles turned a lighter shade of brown. William's jaw grew tight, and Jason sat quietly, afraid to say anything to his uncle as the man's face went through a series of contortions as he thought about his brother and things that had transpired in the past. Must have been bad, Jason thought. What was my father like to piss this man off so much? He seems to get madder whenever he mentions Mom. Mim. That amazing woman, Mimulus Copeny. Even if Jason didn't want to admit it, his mother was truly something to wonder over. She had taken care of the family on her own for—well—forever. Just like William had said. Jason remembered being little and sitting on a beautiful lady's lap and a big man standing over them. It was William and his wife, Sashi. Jason remembered wishing that this was his family. A mommy, a daddy, and a little boy. What happened to make him hate William so much when he used to be his hero? Maybe that was it. William was his hero when what Jason wanted was a father. When he was old enough to understand that William wasn't, couldn't be his father, he got angry. Angry at William, angry at his mother, angry with the world. Then Mim had two more babies, the twins, then another. All these kids. Where did they come from? Jason didn't even know Momma had a boyfriend. He never saw her with a man, except William, when he came over to fix something that broke, and Momma couldn't afford to pay a repairman to come over to do it. After William would fix the stove, the sink, the toilet, whatever it was, Mim would always offer him whatever she had in her oversized, overused purse.

"You know I ain't gonna take your money Mim. It's no good with me. Never will be."

"Thank you again, William, as always. I'll bake you and Sashi a cake for the weekend. I know how you like that strawberry crème cake with the whip cream icing. Sashi puts it on that pretty crystal plate she has. You all will enjoy it."

"Yeah, Sashi will be grateful. She thinks the world of you, you know that don't you?"

"I think the world of her too. She's so lovely. Kind, sweet, devoted to you. You're a lucky man."

"True. She is a wonderful woman. But she's not you, Mim."

"William. Don't. Please."

"Mim, darling Mim. Sashi loves me, she does. And she knows that I love her the best I can. And I will never leave her. I think that she tries to make up to me because she can't have any more children—"

"William don't ..."

"I need to get it off my chest, Mim. For once I need to say what's on my mind. In my heart." William walked over to the kitchen table and pulled out a chair. Mimulus sat down across the table.

"When Jay brought you home that first time, I thought he finally did something right. I prayed he wouldn't mess it up. I saw something special in you and hoped that Jay would see it too. I tried to be a big brother to you, you know? But the more I saw you, the more my feelings weren't those of a brother. And when I found out you were pregnant and that Jay got arrested and sent up for three years for possession, all I could think was maybe it was for the best. I would have married you Mim. I loved you."

Mim stared at the tile floor and said nothing for a long time. William shifted in his chair thinking that he had said too much, hoping that he hadn't ruined the delicate friendship that they had built up over the years. Please Lord, don't let me have messed this up. I'd rather be able to fix her toilet than her never speaking to me again.

Mim broke the silence, "My father wanted to name me Abigail after his grandmother who raised him, but he died before I was born. My mother named me after a little yellow flower that can be used to calm people's fears and give them courage. She always told me that I could never do anything if I was filled with fear. So, naming me after the flower was her way of keeping me safe from fear and providing me with courage. She was like that, her and her flowers and roots and herbs and old-time remedies." She stopped speaking and went back to staring at the floor for a minute. William sat with his elbows on his knees, rubbing his hands together. After what seemed like an hour, she continued. "When I found out I was pregnant, I picked up the phone to call Jason. I was excited. I started to dial the number and realized the first person I wanted to tell was you. I hung up the phone and sat for the longest time wondering what I was doing. I knew I loved Jason but you--you were someone I would want to be a father to my child. I hoped that your brother would grow up and be more like you. True to my name, I made up my mind not to act like some whiny little girl. Accept your man the way he is, I told myself. It will all work out. I believed it deep in my heart but didn't know if I was ready to say it, so I waited. And waited. I fell asleep and when I woke up, the phone was ringing. It was Jason calling from jail. He had been arrested and was high as a kite. I had never heard him like that before and didn't know what to do, so I called you. It just wasn't the time to tell him about a baby. I realized that there was never going to be a right time to tell him."

"I saw it in your eyes that day. You looked so hurt, so lost. All I wanted to do was pick you up and take you home with me. But I had to deal with Jay's mess and when I was done, you were gone. Just like that, gone. Disappeared for two years, how'd you do that?"

"How'd you find me?"

William chuckled to himself. "Girl, it sure wasn't easy. I promised myself that if I found you, I was never gonna let you out my sight. You was working at that nursing home over on East Lexington and I saw you getting on the bus. I followed that bus 'til you got off it. You stopped at this house and went inside. I sat there and waited for you to come out. You came out with this big fat faced baby. He had to weigh a ton. He looked so happy to see you. Grabbing your nose and grinning like you were the only person in the world. It was a beautiful sight."

"So, you followed me?"

"Hell yeah, for about three months. I needed some of your momma's flowers, I guess. Too scared to say something to you. You looked like you were doing okay. Wanted to see if there was someone. You know someone helping you out."

"Some man, right? You thought there was some man laid up in my apartment with my son there?"

"Mim, I don't know what I thought. All I wanted to know was that you were all right. And if it took a man up in there to make sure that was happening, so be it. I just wanted you to be all right. Felt a little guilty actually. Wishing if there was somebody that it could have been me. Real brotherly love going on there, huh?"

"William, stop it. You aren't the type to feel sorry for yourself. You've been here a long time. You need to go home. Sashi is probably wondering where you are."

"She knows I'm here. She knows I'm coming home."

"True. How'd you meet her, William? She's so sweet. I wouldn't have expected her to ---to—"

William laughed a deep laugh that shook the entire kitchen. "Go ahead and say it. Notice a big loud mouth negro such as myself?"

"No...that's not what I meant. Well, sort of, but not really. I noticed you, why wouldn't she? Any woman would..." Her voice trailed off.

"She was kind to me and listened to my troubles after you disappeared. She was there for me when I needed her and she truly loved me, in spite of the fact that I couldn't love her the way she deserved. It was enough for her. I do love her. She makes me laugh and feel like I'm important and needed. Funny. The way she loves me is the way I always wanted to love you." William reached across the table and touched Mim's hand. He waited for her to pull away. She didn't.

Chapter Three

"Man, get your black ass up from there. What are you doing anyway? We should have been at the courthouse ten minutes ago," Mike fussed as he entered Jason's office without knocking.

"Please, feel free to barge in," said Jason as he lifted his head off his hands.

"Looking a little rough there, bro. Leela put it on you good last night or what?" Mike tried to joke with Jason about his wife but for some reason it always seemed a little stressed. Mike bit his lip and waited for Jason to respond.

"Man, why do I put up with your country ass?" Jason mumbled as he continued to look out of the window.

"But you didn't answer my question." Mike took that as a sign that he could keep ribbing his best friend.

"And I'm not going to. That's my wife you're talking about, not some shorty like what you hang out with." Jason rose from his chair, shaking his head as he loaded up stacks of files and shoved them in his imported leather briefcase.

"Yeah well, I don't look whooped like your old married ass does.

So, I'll stick with the shorty. If I had a shorty." Mike laughed at his own joke.

"Maybe that's why you ain't got one." Jason replied as he stood up and shut down his computer.

"Well, I been looking at you lately and something ain't copasetic. The only thing that can make a man look that damn bad is a woman." Jason said nothing, behaving like he didn't hear the last statement. With that, Mike knew it was time to stop. *I knew he shouldn't have married her. It's been eleven years and she still ain't changed. I shoulda said something then but he loved her. So, did I… at least I thought I did. Just let it go, let it go. Time heals all wounds, right?*

Mike stood by the door lost in his thoughts as he waited for Jason to get his coat and hat.

"Man, you know I appreciate your concern. You're my boy and all that. I just don't know sometimes. I been thinking a lot lately about how I got here. Shit, how *we* got here."

"Yeah, I know what you mean. Things sure coulda been different."

"That's what I was just thinking. That day when Mr. William beat my ass."

"He didn't beat your ass, he blinded it," roared Mike.

"Yeah, he did. Best thing that could have happened to me to be perfectly honest with you. I couldn't appreciate it then. All I could think was I wanted to bust a cap…"

"Excuse me, Mr. Copeny," a Barbie clone dipped in dark chocolate squealed, "You have a phone call."

"Take a message please, Mimi. I am late for court."

"Um, it's your wife."

Jason looked at Mike. Mike shrugged his shoulders. "Why didn't she call my cell?"

"She said she wanted to make sure that you were here," Mimi mumbled.

"Where the f--, excuse me. Where else would I be?" Jason's jaws clenched as he chewed the inside of his cheek trying to restrain himself. The tension was thick enough to cause a fog delay at O'Hare Airport. "Take a message, Mimi. I am late for court." Jason headed toward the elevator. Mike took a deep breath and smiled at Mimi.

"See, that's why I'm not married," mumbled Mike talking to no one in particular.

"So, what was that all about?" Mike asked as he strode extra long steps trying to keep up with a pissed off Jason.

"How the fuck do I know?" Jason said more to himself than to Mike.

"Well, she is your wife, man," Mike mumbled under his breath.

"At this point, you can have her," Jason retorted.

Already did. "Nah, thanks anyway. She is fine and all that but, um, I prefer to feel your pain from a distance," Mike said waiting and hoping that Jason might laugh at his joke. Just a little bit.

No laugh. No response of any kind. Just more determined footsteps past the elevator towards the stairs.

"Hey, man. You just walked past the elevator," Mike called to Jason.

"You go ahead. I'm taking the stairs. Need to cool off. Meet you in the parking garage."

"That's twelve flights of stairs, man."

"Yeah. That might help a little bit. See you in a few."

"Oh, I get it. Your football playing ass thinks you can outrun your anger by running down some steps like they are the opposing team."

"Nah, my football playing ass knows that running down some stairs is better than running into the courthouse mad as shit. That don't fly. You know what I mean? I got to let this shit go right now. I got a job to do, and I can't focus when she pulls shit like this. And she knows it."

"What's up with ya'll lately? You noticed I ain't been over much lately.

Leela always seems—I don't know—I don't mean no disrespect, but, whack lately. Like she bored or disgusted or something."

Now Jason laughed. *How would he know what she's like when she gets bored?* "So, it ain't just me. I thought I was losing my mind. Thanks, man. You know what? I'll meet you at the courthouse. The stairs ain't gonna cut it. I'll walk." *She must have lost her mind. Checking up on me—at work! I'm out here trying to keep a roof over her twice dyed head and she's sitting up there checking on where I am? She truly has lost her mind.* Mike's right. I'm glad somebody else sees it. It's like…it's like…she's smelling herself. *Or somebody else is smelling her.* Whoa. That wasn't cool to even think that about her. I know she was best friends with drama before we got married but it's been cool, sort of. Yeah, she needed attention like other people need air but that's just the way she was. *Is.* That would account for some stuff, wouldn't it?

Yeah, like the hair you pay for every three weeks. And the nails and toes. Who sees her little piggy toes in December anyway?

Don't be so hard on a sister. She just wants to look good.

Exactly. But for who? Sure ain't been setting your world on fire lately. Even I know that women don't have 'female problems' twenty-three days a month and fall asleep early the other seven. Your wifey is creepin'.

"Not possible," Jason muttered to himself as he faced the wind and weather of a brutal Chicago morning.

Why not possible? Mr. Legal Beagle. Check the facts and let a jury decide. 'Cause I think the hussy is guilty.

That's my wife you're calling a hussy.

If the name fits… Okay. Sorry.

That's better.

Mrs. Hussy.

Simone was standing in the Great Hall of the courthouse with her head lifted towards the sky. She loved to do this at this time of day in this particular spot. The midmorning sun shone through the stained-glass depictions of a blind justice and balanced scales on the third-floor landing. It didn't matter what the hawk chose to do on the other side of these walls, the sun always provided a warming, even loving caress to whomever was willing to stop from their mission long enough to appreciate it.

A loving caress. Sure, could use one of them right about now.

Hush.

What? How long has it been since you felt someone's arms around you? Months? How many? I can't remember. Should have written it on the calendar and celebrate it as a holiday or something.

Hush, I said.

I'm just saying. I know. Your friends hug you, Ronjai hugs you so tight you can't breathe, at church, Dad acts like a bear, but who gives you that man-woman, husband-wife hug? Huh? Need I say more?

No. I've got work to do. I don't have time to feel sorry for myself.

Neither do I. This isn't about feeling sorry, this is about being aware of what's real. It's about stating facts. Despite it all, girl, you are doing okay. Some affection would be nice, but it isn't stopping you from living your life. Enjoying this moment, this glorious sunshine. Appreciate what you have. It really is quite good.

Yes, it is.

Now let's get in here and do this.

Simone stood there an extra minute breathing deeply and drinking it all in, as if she could bottle it up and save it for when the darker moments tried to creep up on her. People rushed past, maneuvering around her as she stood there with her eyes closed. *Just one more second, that's all I need to get by.* That Marvin Gaye, Tammi Terrill song from way back in the day popped into her mind and she smiled a smile so magnificent that the sun came closer and kissed her so that she glowed with a brilliance that was hidden from mere mortals.

Except for Jason. He had just finished his power walk to the courthouse. Ten blocks in fourteen minutes.

Getting old, bro.

That's a blessing, actually. Beats what's in second place.

Ooh, optimism. The walking helped, I take it?

 Feeling better. Can't be angry when you're fighting the hawk. Too damn cold.

Look at that. An Amazon. In Chicago.

Jason took off his Kangal as he slowed his pace to admire the striking woman as she worshipped the sun and it responded to her praise. Sure, he's seen beautiful women before, known several personally during his lifetime, but she was somehow beyond that. The way her black hair was pulled back in a bun. Very simple. Like she didn't have anything to prove. It was all her hair too. Not everybody can wear their hair like that and not look like an old school librarian. It worked for her. Shows off her dark almost black eyes. *Mim calls them 'bedroom eyes'. The kind that will get you in trouble every time.*

He noticed a long tattoo running down the back of her neck. Looked like a dagger almost. *Will wonders never cease? She didn't look the type.* When he looked more closely, he realized it wasn't a tattoo but a scar of some sort. *Wonder what happened.*

Her face was pleasant enough. Except for the space between her brow. It was smooth as silk, but careful observation showed that that was not always the case. She probably wouldn't be on the cover of one of those fashion magazines Leela had strewn all over the house, or in a commercial for flawless perfection in a bottle. She looked too powerful for that. Her overall presence did cause everyone who passed where she was standing to step two or three feet away from her as they walked. It was an unconscious thing, Jason could tell, but it was if her aura provided some sort of shield from mere mortals. He smiled and watched her as she stood completely absorbed in her own moment in time.

Not a care in the world. Must be nice.

She must be what? Close to six feet of well-proportioned femininity in stocking feet.

Now add those three-inch heels. We're talking confident.

Jason laughed to himself, thinking about Leela. She always asks strangers in the grocery store to reach things on the top shelves for her because 'I'm just too little to get them myself.' She thinks it's cute. Lots of women do it seems. Like being needy is a good thing.

I bet Lady Amazon never asked anybody for anything.

Jason shook his head as if trying to break a spell cast upon him for seeing things that are forbidden.

She is amazing though, don't you think?

Yeah, I do.

Regal, even.

Yeah, queen of the Amazons.

Man, you're tripping.

After this morning, I need a diversion.

Well, you found it.

Simone, the newly crowned mighty queen of the Amazons, took one final deep breath to thank the sun for its ministrations and turned toward the spiraling marble staircase that led to the trial and mediation rooms. She saw a man standing just outside the ring of sunlight as it struck the seal of justice symbol painted on the floor.

Maybe he's a vampire or something.

Never saw a chocolate vampire.

Especially such a handsome, dark chocolate one. That would melt in your mouth real quick don't you think?

Hush. What's he staring at? Is my slip hanging? Shirt unbuttoned? What? She did a quick mental overhaul of her appearance and decided that she was decent. So, she looked at him. Truly looked at him.

Jason swallowed. Hard.

Damn. Did she hear me thinking? What is she thinking? I should have been more careful. She'll think I'm a stalker in the courthouse.

So, he tried to smile his best 'lovely lady' smile but what he smiled was an honest 'you have moved me' smile. He hoped she missed it. That she wasn't that observant. But when he saw her head tilt ever so slightly to the right and the dark space appear between her brow, he knew that she caught it.

She doesn't miss much.

I know. Goddesses usually don't.

Time to go, Simone thought. I'm thinking the wrong things. That's what happens when you talk to yourself too long. Things may not be right at home but looking at other men like you are a starving woman drooling at a buffet counter is absolutely not the way to handle it. I have to get my head on straight. I've got to sell ADR to these district court people. It's not what they are used to but it's in everybody's best interest, the court, the parties involved.

The jails.

Yeah, that too. Focus, girl, focus. If you show that you believe in it, so will they.

Yeah, we got powers like that.

Simone giggled to herself as she put her hand lightly on the marble railing and glided up the stairs.

When she reached Pre-Trial Room 3-103, she took a deep breath, held her head up and opened the door.

There's nothing I hate more than walking into a room of unfamiliar people. They look at you like you've got some incurable disease called tall. The Bible doesn't say "...And God created woman. Short. Petite. Tiny." Whatever word was popular at the moment. God created me and that means I am perfect just as I am. Help me, Holy Ghost.

Only thing worse is when you have to deal with an insecure short man.

Is there any other kind?

Hush.

The four men in the room all stood when Simone entered. She quickly surveyed the space and chose a seat at the round table.

Mental note. This won't work for mediation.

While Simone surveyed the room, the men surveyed her. Only one of them knew her, Sylvester Havens or Sly, as she affectionately called him. His parents were huge fans of Sly and the Family Stone, hence his name. It was a little disconcerting that he looked so much like his namesake, professionally attired. One of the men had the look of a lawyer, another the look of a lackey to the lawyer and the last had the look of a man who liked what he was looking at. Simone looked at Sly and gave a brief 'here we go' smile. He returned it and leaned forward to shake her hand.

"Hey, partner. It's all you today. Do your thang, girl," Sly said quietly while he held her hand a little too long. As usual. Simone didn't think anything of it after all this time. But Sly did. Constantly.

Does she even notice that I worship the ground she walks on?

She's married, fool.

Does her husband know that?

Sly had met Greg at one of those mandatory holiday office galas. He and Simone had talked about making an appearance long enough to get credit for being there and then leaving. They both agreed if one left, the other would as well. He secretly hoped that she might come alone and then he could ask her to have coffee or that herbal tea mess she liked at Starbucks before she went home. He knew that she wasn't the type for flirting or leading somebody on, but he just really enjoyed her company and wanted to spend a little more time around her before the holidays hit. But she showed up with her husband, the city's Chief Managing Officer, who he heard so much about in the papers and on the news. Simone only mentioned him if somebody else brought him up first. No photos in her office of the loving couple on vacation or in loving positions for photo ops. "That's my private life. This is work," is all she would say.

After meeting Greg, a deflated Sly knew his evening was going to be rather dull. The three of them sat at a table with three other couples and had appetizers and small talk. The women talked about what shopping they still had to do, while Simone smiled and shook her head in all the appropriate places and practiced her reflective listening skills.

 "Sounds like you're feeling overwhelmed and worried with the amount of shopping you have left to do and that you might not get it all done in time and that meeting deadlines is important to you?"

"Exactly! You understand completely. See Charles, I told you I'm not the only one."

Greg had left the table to refresh his gin and tonic and get Simone a San Pellegrino about twenty minutes ago. Sly started to wonder if he got lost or something. The bar was in the next room, not Sri Lanka. Sly excused himself from the table and went to get another Corona when he heard a now familiar voice near the men's room door.

"Yeah, baby. I miss you too. You know I am obligated to make an appearance. When I leave here, I'll drop her off at home and be right there." Low man laughter.

"I got something for you, too. It's worth the wait. See you in an hour or so." More man laughter. "You too."

Greg put his cell phone back into his pocket and turned toward the restroom. Sly stood there trying to pull his lip up off the floor.

That good for nothing—should I tell Simone or go out there and knock him out? She doesn't deserve this. Not her.

Sly went back into the gathering forgetting all about his Corona. He would have plenty of time to drink something stronger later on.

"Greg's not back yet?" he started.

"No. But he will be soon. I am sure he has other places to be tonight," she said quietly.

"Where else could be better than spending time with you? That would make me happy if I were him."

"Happiness is relative, my mother always said. I tend to agree with her."

Greg walked back to the table with a huge celebrity grin on his face. He placed his hand on Simone's shoulder and bent down to give her a perfunctory kiss on the cheek.

"Honey, why don't we blow this party and start one of our own," he said just loud enough for the others at the table to hear. The women looked envious, and the men looked played.

He gets to leave but we don't. And look at who he gets to leave with.

The men looked at their grief-stricken wives. Sly just looked.

Simone stood up and graciously said her goodbyes. Sly stood and walked toward her with outstretched arms.

"Where's my Kwanzaa hug? Wrap all six days into one," he said keeping his eyes on Greg.

Greg's jaw twitched and Sly could have sworn he heard a growl coming from him.

Growl all you want mutha—if you hurt her, I will kill you myself.

"'Bye Moni. You call if you need anything, okay?" Sly looked her in the eyes. "Okay?" He lifted his eyebrows to indicate that he was serious. Simone gave him her patented Mona Lisa smile.

"I will, I promise. But I am fine. Honest. I am always just fine," she replied.

Liar, liar. Set your husband's pants on fire.

Hush. Not now. Let me get out of here in one piece okay.

Okay. Then we set his pants on fire.

The court appointed lawyer made introductions for everyone in the room as if these highly educated, intelligent individuals were unable to speak for themselves. But that's what lawyers do—speak for others.

Who in this room can't speak for themselves and I can surely speak for myself.

Oh Lord, here we go. Get a grip, will you?

"And this is Mr. Michael DeVries. Appointee for the State's Attorney's office," said the lawyer.

"My colleague will be arriving momentarily. We had a few distractions and setbacks this morning that made his travel plans go south," Michael cleared his throat and glanced across the table at Simone.

Impressive and she hasn't even opened her mouth yet. Unusual for a woman. He snickered to himself.

Simone caught the glance. His colleague must also be his friend or else he wouldn't have his back like that. That's nice.

But it sounds personal or else why wouldn't he be more specific? Never let your personal mess get in the way of your profession. And what's he sneaking a peak at? You're batting a thousand today, girlfriend. Maybe it's the Chanel. Number Nineteen. Gets them every time.

Oh please, give me a break. I'm suffering from monkey mind this morning. Jumping here and there. Got to stay focused…

The mahogany door opened quietly and in stepped the handsome dark chocolate vampire from the lobby. His hat and coat were in one hand, briefcase in the other.

"Please pardon my lateness. I am Jason Copeny. Appointee along with Mr. DeVries, who I am sure you have already met." Jason hung his hat and coat on the coat rack near the door and quickly perused the table. On first glance he saw two familiar faces and the back of a woman's head. On closer inspection, that long glorious, scarred butterscotch neck belonged to the Amazon goddess from downstairs. How crazy was that? He took a deep breath to calm his nerves and chose the seat nearest to the window.

Smooth. Do you think she recognizes you?

He looked up once he had placed the files from his briefcase on the table. And saw Simone's dark eyes drift in his direction.

Yup. She recognizes you. Now she knows you're a stalker.

Simone sat patiently as Jason settled in. He shook hands with everyone in the room starting with her. His mother had taught him to respect women after all and at this moment it gave him the perfect opportunity to prove to himself that she was real. He stretched out his hand to her and counted off three seconds so that it didn't appear that he held on to it too long. Her handshake was firm. Her hands were warm and soft. For some reason that he could not explain, all he wanted to do was lift it to his lips and hold it there for just a moment. *One thousand two. One thousand three.* His brain told him to let go. His hand said hell no. He blinked back to reality and moved on, shaking hands with everyone else. *One thousand one. One thousand two…*

Her eyes followed his movements. Everything was very deliberate with him. She liked the way he entered the room. Taking charge of the situation. Offering no "I'm sorrys," but holding himself accountable and introducing himself instead of allowing someone to take that power.

This could be fun.

Please hush and let me work.

"Welcome, gentlemen and thank you for having the Alternative Dispute Resolution Commission here today to start our pilot program with the State. We are pleased to offer our services to the courts to relieve the burden on the judicial system and ultimately the burden on the correctional system as well. It has been a long road getting all the players to the table, but we are all here now." Simone's eyes shifted towards the window seat.

Was that meant for me? Jason thought.

"Shall we get started?" Simone asked.

Chapter Four

Greg sat at his desk in his spacious office in the new portion of the city's Municipal Hall with his back facing the massive oak door. Body language experts would say that he had turned his back on society to examine the world beyond the windows of his fourteenth-floor office. What's the sense in planning so hard if you don't plan in something for yourself? Greg was playing his favorite game-Master of All I Survey. This thriving metropolis. He plans its growth, manages its efficiency, and controls its fiscal soundness.

But you can't figure out how to get your wife to talk to you.

How did I get myself into this situation again? I love her but I need something…more. I need—

The office door opened and in sashayed Greg's chief executive assistant, Sheva Morales.

"Don't you knock before you enter your boss's office?" Greg asked without even turning around. He could smell her a mile away. Whatever the latest perfume rage was, Sheva was on it, or rather it was on her, like a walking scratch and sniff.

Truer words were never spoken.

"I wasn't entering into my boss's office, I was entering into my lover's office," she purred in her slightly accented Spanish Harlem voice. She had been working on complete eradication but some things you just can't work away without voice training, which Greg had been paying for, for the past year. She said that people didn't take her seriously because of the way she talked.

Maybe it was the one size too small skirts and two sizes too tight sweaters. But I digress.

"Shut the door or your mouth before someone hears you," he said firmly yet quietly.

What does she want now?

Greg heard the door close and lock as the sound of Sheva's four-inch F-me pumps clickety clicked across the hardwood floors.

"Ay, Papi. What's wrong with my daddy this afternoon? Whatever it is, I can make it all better."

"What is it, Sheva? I've got a lot on my mind and a lot to do before I can leave tonight." Greg turned around slowly only to find Sheva positioning herself on the corner of his desk.

Don't even try to pull the skirt down, it won't work.

She smiled at him as she's done hundreds of times over the past year knowing what usually comes next.

No stockings again today? Easy access.

Greg takes a breath and shakes his head as he looks past the juicy thighs to the floor.

"So, will you be home by 7:30? I can bring dinner, or I can just bring me? Which would you prefer, or do you want both?" she said as she slid closer to his chair.

Home? You mean that three-bedroom condominium that I'm paying an arm and a leg for? Home is where Simone is. What was I thinking?

Greg didn't answer so she leaned in closer so that he could get a better view of the two mounds of flesh struggling to escape the lacey push-up bra under the too small sweater. He gasped for air because the origin of the perfume was down there somewhere wafting its way into innocent victims' nostrils.

Well, this victim is not so innocent.

"Do you like it, Papi? It just came out. Assignation. I thought it was appropriate. What do you think?"

Fumigation might be better. "I think I need to get back to work. And so, do you," Greg said still not having looked her in the eyes.

"Has something or someone bothered you today? Because last night when I left, you were fine. I've been in a meeting all morning, and this is the first chance I get to see you today and you treat me like I'm not even here. You act like I'm your wife or something." Sheva jumped down from the desk on to her four-inch heels and tap, tap, tapped over to the window and turned to look at the back of Greg's chair. "What is it you want Greg? I do everything I can to show you how much I love you and all you do is… what? I've waited a long time for you to do something about our situation and here we are having the same old conversation again."

"Sheva, baby, we aren't having a conversation. You are. I moved out, didn't I? What more do you want from me?"

Hands fly to her ample hips. "What more do I want from you? You can't seriously be saying this to me?"

"There's no need for you to raise your voice."

"Why not? It is soundproof in here. We have proven that before now, haven't we? Now I need to keep my voice down? What do you want me to be? What do you want me to do? You tell me you want to be with me, but you won't divorce your wife. What? Is it cheaper to keep her or what?"

It's quieter, at least. Simone would never embarrass herself like this. She's a lady. Something she could teach you, among others. Greg remembered when he told her that he was moving out. Simone looked at him, then at the floor and asked if he needed help packing his bags. She turned around and went to the closet and pulled out the 'good' suitcases that she had purchased for their 'second honeymoon' trip to Costa Rica two summers before.

"These have more pieces, and your suits won't get so wrinkled." That's all she said.

Greg turned around in his executive ergonomic high back leather chair and looked at Sheva. Starting at her head and traveling to her feet. Didn't take very long. Even in heels, she didn't come up to Simone's shoulder. She probably weighed a buck eighty, as much as Simone but that extra ten inches of distribution space made a world of difference. Sheva's Spanish heritage encouraged people to see her as voluptuous and curvaceous. And she worked that from every possible angle. No lie, Sheva was attractive. Pretty face, amply endowed in all the right places but in five years… *You know Spanish women don't hold up all that well. Not like black ones. Black don't crack. Brown… well, I can see that it ain't gonna last too much longer. Already starting to sag around the edges. And she's barely thirty.*

Since Greg had moved into the condominium or the 'love nest' as Sheva called it, four or five times a week she had showed up at the front door in various stages of a Victoria's Secret fashion show. He always grabbed her and quickly pulled her inside, so his neighbors wouldn't see. Sheva always giggled believing that her mere presence caused such excitement in the well known, easily recognized, married man. At first, it was fun and exciting. Sheva must have read the how-to manual on wild sex as she sat in the parking lot of the apartment complex every evening. Oh, the places you will go… Dr. Seuss had nothing on Sheva when it came to imagination. It was fun, even adventurous at times, true, but that's all it was. You can play but so many videos games, hit so many whack a moles at a carnival, or listen to so many 'yes, yes, si, si!' before it gets old.

Eight months ago, it was old. But she kept coming… And coming… And showing up in the evenings. Greg was less enthused each day and did his best to show her, as he was too passive to say to her face what he really thought.

"It's time to go now. I need some rest." Then he would turn his back as if he had fallen asleep as men are expected to do. And he'd wait and wait, thinking that she would get the hint and leave soon. She would just spoon up behind him and snuggle until the morning light forced Greg to put her out before the trash collection and newspaper delivery awakened the neighbors and caught her leaving.

Greg tuned back into her diatribe at the part where she was saying, "… so when are you going to man up and say something to her?"

"What did you just say?" Greg's jaw tightened and Sheva saw it. "You want to repeat that for me?" Growl.

"I …I was just saying that… you said…. you would talk to her, and I've waited and waited... it seems like forever. I just want to be with you. In public, you know? I want to go out to dinner and to parties and public gatherings. It's just not right."

You're right about that. For the first time, Greg realized just how not right it really was.

"I am going to talk to her this evening." *If she'll let me.* "That's why I need to get this work done before I leave here today."

"Really baby? Really? I mean honestly? I knew you would. I knew it! What time should I come over tonight? We have to celebrate! I'll get a bottle of champagne. The really good kind. I'll be able to afford it now, won't I? So what time is good? Seven? Seven-thirty?"

"Not tonight."

"Excuse me?"

"Not tonight."

"Well—why not?"

"We will have a lot to discuss, Simone and me. It could take a while."

"Okay, so let's make it nine o'clock. No biggy. I'll call in late tomorrow."

"I said not tonight. Now I have work to do. I have something important to do tonight and I need to get ready. Shut the door on your way out."

He turned his chair back around and continued to gaze out the window. When the tap tap tap paused and the whoosh of the door closing subsided, he smiled at the beautiful sounds of silence. He took a deep breath now that the air had started to clear.

Chapter Five

Jason was feeling pretty good as he trotted down the marble staircase of the Courthouse. Much better than how he felt when he arrived three hours ago. *What a difference a day makes, three hours actually. But who's counting?* A pre-mediation meeting had been scheduled for first thing tomorrow morning between the Court representatives, Mike and Jason, and the ADR representatives, Sly and Simone. Jason was feeling like a teenage boy around the new girl at school.

"Very impressive, Mrs. Dyson." He thrust his hand out to shake hers in a more informal and hopefully relaxed way than earlier in the morning. "I know that I announced myself when I arrived, but I just wanted to say that I am truly looking forward to working with you. And Mr. Havens." Simone shook his hand firmly in as professional manner as she could muster. Jason noticed the firmness of the shake. *Like a man. Strong and confident. None of those weak woman can't touch your hand 'cause you might have fleas handshakes.* He also noticed the softness and the warmth of her skin for the second time today. Nice. *Let go.* "I am excited about tomorrow. Mike and I like to start the day with coffee and donuts. Caffeine, refined sugar, bleached flour, and lard. Perfect way to bless the morning. Would the two of you wish to join us? Name your poison."

"I am fine, thank you for asking though. Sly might want something.

He likes a good strong coffee in the morning." *Sly. So, it's like that, huh?* Jason felt the building wind fizzle out of his sails. Sly heard his name and turned from his conversation with Mike. The two of them were getting along like it was old home week at the frat house.

"Hey man, guess what? My man, Sly here, is a brother. Pledged at Grambling of all places. How cool is that? This is gonna work out real good." Mike said as he patted Sly on the back.

"Yeah, I think so too. Working with good people, doing the right thing. I got a good feeling," Sly said. Simone looked at the three black men surrounding her. Strong, fierce, determined in their convictions.

Handsome, tall. Did I say handsome and tall?

Nobody asked you.

Well, you should have.

Jason turned to Sly. "Mike and I are taking orders for a first-class continental breakfast. Coffee, donuts. Are you interested? Can't seem to get your colleague to go along with the program though."

"And you won't if she doesn't want to," Sly looked at Simone and grinned an 'I ratted you out' grin. Jason watched the exchange between the two of them and realized how close they were. Real friends. No benefits. Just two people who really appreciated the fact that the other was a part of their life. Jason felt a twinge of jealousy roll through him.

"Juice and tea are on the list of offerings as well. Bagel, muffin, scone, biscotti…" Jason continued. *Anything. Say anything so I can get it for you.* He couldn't believe his thoughts or his actions himself, but he was not inclined to stop. He just wanted to please her somehow. To do anything for her because—

"Okay, I really used to love those chocolate covered angel donuts when I was a little girl. I haven't had one in ages. That might be fun," she finally relented.

"And what would you like to drink with that?"

"Soymilk would be nice."

"Soymilk."

"Yes. Thank you."

Jason looked at Mike and then at Sly.

"She's serious, man. Just pick up a quart and she's set," Sly said.

Simone gave a downcast smile worthy of a five-year-old. She looked to her new cohort of brothers and shook her head. "Should be a lively meeting in the morning," she mumbled.

"Guaranteed," the three musketeers laughed, and fist pumped, and black man hugged before pulling out cell phones to exchange numbers.

Simone shook her head and excused herself.

Where are you going? They are still in there having fun and you're leaving?

Too much testosterone.

Great, isn't it? They are lucky you are going to be the one to keep them in check.

I don't think they are the type of men that someone else keeps in check.

Yeah, well, we'll see about that. It's going to be fun, fun, fun!

Simone gathered her coat and gloves and quietly walked toward the door, hoping they were too involved to notice her leaving. Jason had his back to her but watched her reflection in the windows. The shimmer of the sun on the glass made it appear as if she glided through the door.

Appropriate, he thought. *Goddesses would do that.*

He walked out the front door of the courthouse replaying the past three hours in his head. He was braced to fight the hawk again, but the hawk noticed the spring in his step and decided to reward the brother who put up such a fierce battle earlier in the day. Instead of punishing a brother, it invigorated him. So much so that Jason chose to walk back to the office instead of taking the public transportation or riding with overly hyped Mike. He felt good. He felt alive. He felt so good that he had completely forgotten about the events that started his day.

It's been a good day. I think I'll call it a day and take my files home and work from there. I want to be ready for tomorrow. It's going to be good. Chocolate covered angel. Yes, she is. 'Til tomorrow, goddess.

The drive to suburbia wasn't all that bad. Maybe it was because the rush hour traffic hadn't manifested itself on the Loop yet or maybe it was because Jason's thoughts were completely occupied with his ever so eventful day. Either way, the trip seemed almost enjoyable on this bright and sunny afternoon. To the west a dark line across the sky indicated a front moving in. That was off in the distance. Nothing that could mess up the rest of his day.

While he was wrapped up in his thoughts and laughing at Tom Joyner rant against Steve Harvey's defense of the new administration, his earpod beeped.

"What's up bro?" he answered.

"So… whadja think of Miss Thang?" Mike asked all too enthusiastically.

"That's Mrs. Thang to you. What are you asking for?" Jason replied, hoping that his out of control actions had been noticeable only to himself.

"She is quite the lady ain't she. You don't see 'em like that too often anymore."

"What's that supposed to mean?" Jason was breathing a little easier since it seemed that Mike's train of conversation was going down a different track.

"She ain't like them legal chicks we see every day. And she ain't like a baby's momma for sure."

"So, you're saying she's different."

"That ain't the right word." Jason could hear Mike wracking his brain. The noise was causing static in Tom Joyner's monologue. "My Pops used to call it class. You don't see that so much anymore. Least not around here. You know back in the day you would see those old movies and clips of Dorothy Dandridge and Lena Horne. Not just beautiful black women but ones that nobody would even think to mess with 'cause they got style and class. That's what Mrs. Dyson reminds me of."

Jason was quiet as Mike finished speaking. He agreed wholeheartedly. Mike was right. You didn't see that much around here anymore.

Especially in your house.

"You put some thought into that one, didn't you? How long did that take you to come up with that?" Jason was surprised that Mike was as serious as he was. This was a completely different side for his partner. Mike liked women as much as any man but had never seemed to put much thought into seeing their assets beyond the obvious. At least if he was on this particular train, Jason could ride his little red wagon in peace.

"Nah, it ain't all that man. She's just really interesting. That's all. Did you see how she looks at you. I mean, so serious. Like she can read you. Like she knows what you're thinking. It's scary you know?"

"Only scary if you think she can read ya and you're thinking shit." Both men laughed and that relieved the seriousness that was building up over the phone.

"Well tomorrow should be a change of pace, at least. Man, you cracked me up," Mike quipped. "When you asked about what she wanted for breakfast and she told you nothing. You should have seen your face."

"What?" Jason asked.

"What, my ass! You know what I'm talking about. You ain't used to a woman telling you no." Mike laughed. "When was the last time that happened?"

"Including today?" Jason asked. "Today." They laughed and talked some more about their expectations for ADR and what games they might want to catch if they could snag tickets once the NBA lockout was over. Jason clicked off his Bluetooth and put the phone in his pocket and he approached the huge sign –Brightwood on the Avon.

He signaled a left into his development and meandered down the winding middle middle-class neighborhood. New houses with short driveways. Jason always thought that you could distinguish middle middle-class neighborhoods from upper middle-class neighborhoods by the length of the driveways. Middle-middles were long enough to park your car and spit to the garage. Upper middles meant that you could drive to the garage and turn the car around to back it into the garage. His home was definitely middle-middle. It was nice though. He admitted that. In a nice neighborhood of wannabe mini-mansions. Petite mansions he called them. Five bedrooms for two adults and a child. Four baths, two of which never were used except by company, which was almost always Leela's family and friends. A den, a family room, a sunroom, a formal living and dining room, a deck, a patio off of the master suite and a partridge in a pear tree… *and an upper middle mortgage.*

Jason and Leela had purchased the house in the midst of the housing craze. Leela saw it as an opportunity to show everyone how upwardly mobile they were and how Jason was doing well enough in his career to support his family on one salary. She would never say that to him but he heard her when she talked to her family and friends. He had known her long enough to know what she was all about. 'Keeping up with the Copeny's' would be a new reality show if she had her way. And she usually had her way. The balloon payment on the mortgage won't come due for another three years but heaven forbid when the day arrived. Leela had said not to worry, he would have a promotion by then or open his own office. She would be right there to support him through it all. All he needed to be was a little more positive and think big. *Hard to do on a small- already- used- up-on- other-things income.* Leela felt it necessary to have all the trappings that go along with a mini wannabe mansion lifestyle. Designer furniture. On one income. Two cars. On one income. Jason could live with the furniture part, you've got to sleep somewhere but the two cars when only one of them worked every day was hard to swallow. He had a ten-year-old Navigator that was in perfect condition and paid for, which made it even more perfect. His mother, Mim, had given them her Honda Accord when Maia started pre-school at that private academy on the other side of nowhere. No car payments. That made it possible to buy the house and pay tuition to pre-school.

Once they were in it, Leela needed reliable transportation for her 'activities'. She talked about it and talked about it for three years and then decided that talking wasn't effective, so she cried about it. When the financial feces hit the fan and the nation needed bailing out, Jason thought it the perfect time to use the Cash for Clunkers incentive to upgrade the Accord. When he mentioned it to Leela she cried some more. After a box of Puffs with 'lotiony softness,' they went to the dealer and picked out 'something that they could afford on one income'. She cried and mumbled all the way home.

"…if you did a better job of managing our finances and seeing that things were paid on time, our credit score would be higher and we could have gotten a real car."

If you would get up off your twice baked Pillsbury dough girl ass and get a job, even in a pie shop, then you could talk to me about our finances. Jason took a deep breath and gripped the steering wheel tightly chewing a hole on the inside of his cheek. He could hear Mr. William's voice in his head.

"Don't give no woman power over you with her words. You do what's right and you never have to second guess yourself. She ain't the only pretty kitty in the pet store. Why you think they call it a 'pet' store? Just remember though, when you get ready to marry the kitty—pick the right one. 'Cause once you got it, you can't take it back."

You know that's right. Jason drove home to the mini mansion. The smell of new car wafting around his head. He kept seeing Leela sneaking peeks at him as if she were waiting for him to comment on her remarks. When he didn't say a word, she exhaled loudly and got out of the car. "I guess we can leave it in the driveway," she said. *Translation—leave it out so people can see the temporary tags and know that we got a new car.*

"Nah, it's new. Its first night here deserves to be in the garage."

She sucked her teeth and waddled up the front steps. *Dough is getting kind of lumpy back there.* Jason smiled to himself, pressed the button on the garage door opener and inched the shiny new Buick into its new home.

Tonight, the Navigator wasn't parked in its usual spot in the driveway. *I can't believe Leela drove it somewhere and put it in the garage. What's wrong with her today?* He unlocked the door and stepped into the foyer.

"Hey, baby. How was your day?"

He recognized the voice but wondered what extraterrestrial could be using his wife's body to produce it. Leela walked up to him with that sparkling smile that captured his attention twelve years ago. She stood on her tiptoes and kissed him on the lips. A slow, long, yet supposedly innocent kiss. Then she just stood there.

Pretty kitty has feathers hanging out her mouth. I would be very careful if I were you.

Jason always hated his inner voice because nine times out of ten it was right. And the tenth time, he just should have listened a moment longer. It would have been right then too.

"Would you like a beer, baby? I got some Corona today while I was out." Leela turned and walked toward the kitchen. Jason watched her little freshly pedicured feet slap the hardwood.

He walked into the laundry room to retrieve the key to unlock the inside garage door. It wasn't hanging in its usual place over the light switch.

"Where's the garage door key, baby? It's not hangin' up here."

Thwap, thwap, thwap. The sound of the little freshly pedicured feet grew louder as Leela ran to the laundry room door.

"What did you need them for?"

I live here, don't I? If I want to unlock a door, I should be able to unlock a door.

"I was wondering why you put the Navigator in the garage. Last time you tried to do that, you knocked the driver's side mirror off."

"That wasn't my fault. I couldn't see because the seat was too low and—"

"Yeah, so where is the key?"

"I want to show you something. Close your eyes."

Oh Lord, she's done broke my ride. I knew it. Can't have nothing. That's why she called this morning to tell me she trashed the Navigator.

Leela placed her hand over Jason's and unlocked the garage door. They stepped into the dark garage and she flipped on the lights.

The only sound was that of the fluorescent ceiling lights.

"Where's the truck?"

"At the dealer. Don't you just love it?"

"What dealer?"

"The Mercedes dealer downtown. Don't you love it? He said you could keep it overnight and come in the morning to sign the papers."

"Sign what papers?"

"The papers to buy the car? The ones you would have known about this morning if you had answered the phone at your office instead of having your feet who knows where."

"So, what you're saying is that you called me this morning from a car dealer while you were trading in my truck on a car we can't afford without asking me. Is that right?"

"That truck was ten years old and we're lucky he gave us anything at all for it. I made out like a fat rat. The trade-in value equaled the down payment so all we have to do tomorrow is pay the first and last months' lease and tax and tags. Done deal."

"And you called me this morning to tell me this?"

"And so that the Sales Manager could verify your employment to put it in both of our names."

"Because you don't work."

"J-baby, don't be like that. I got us a sweet deal. I work hard. And you can too after we put Maia to bed."

Meow. Pretty kitty, hard at work. Wait 'til I tell Mim and Mr. William this one. Nobody else would believe this shit.

"Get the keys."

"Sure baby. You're going to love the way it handles. Just like the commercials where their pulling into the driveways at Christmas. We'll be the first Christmas car on the block this year." Leela ran off to get her shoes and coat. She was back before Jason could blink.

"Here's the keys. I figured you can drive it. I can keep it during the day for my errands and you can drive the Buick to work so that we don't put all those highway miles on this one."

"We're taking it back."

"What did you say?"

"We're taking it back."

"J-baby, what are you thinking?"

"Don't J-baby me. We didn't talk about this. We can't afford this. You know that. This keeping up with the Jones ain't working. I can't believe you did this. Let's go."

"How can you say this? Everybody else in this neighborhood drives Lexuses and BMWs and Mercedes. Hell, there's even a Jaguar two streets over and we've got a Buick and a ten-year-old truck."

"And? Are those people paying our bills? Hell no. I can barely afford to pay our bills. It's hard out there and nothing is getting any cheaper and you sit around all day finding new ways to spend the money I make. I work hard to keep a roof over our heads and we don't need this. Let's go."

"Oh, so it's like that. Now it's my fault because I stay at home. I have lots of good I do in the community. Maia needs her mother home when she gets out of school. But noooooo. It's my fault you are so stingy with your hard-earned money. If I had known this..."

"If you had known what, Leela?"

"Nothing."

"Nah, don't stop now. You are on a roll. If you had known what?"

"If I had known it was going to be like this, I would have explored other options."

"And what's that supposed to mean?"

"Just what I said. This hasn't been a picnic you know. We are always broke, living from paycheck to paycheck. We can never get ahead. Maybe you should have thought about us more and saving the world less and got a career that pays something."

"Oh, like your boy, Todd? The love of your life who you gave up for poor broke hardworking me? Or were there some other options that you wanted to explore?"

"Jay, you promised you would take care of me and that we'd be happy."

"Yes, I did. And I've kept that promise. You have never had to do without anything that you needed and most of what you wanted. We have a beautiful daughter. Do you remember what we went through? Maia is fine. We have a roof over our heads, food in our bellies--lots from the looks of it-- friends, family, each other, I have a job, transportation. What else is it you need?"

"I don't know. But this isn't enough." At that moment, the tears started to fall in torrents. Jason stepped back and watched the hysterics grow into a full-fledged hissy fit.

Me-ow.

"When you finish, come get me, so we can take it back."

Chapter Six

Today is the big day.

Says who?

Says you. Who do you think is talking to you? Your lovely and very pissed off wife? She might never talk to you again after last night.

And?

Oh, so it's like that, huh? All she wanted was a brand-new car she can't afford on money she ain't working for, to ride her ever spreading ass around in and look cute waiting for her fat little fake fingernail, weave wearing friends to tell her how lucky she is to have a man who loves her so much that—

Okay, okay already, I get what you're saying, and I agree, okay? Now shut the fuck up! I got to get breakfast for everybody and I'm too tired to think straight.

Listening to Leela's crocodile tears all night and keeping a brother up when he gots to go to work in the morning.

Why do I put up with it?

Good question. Why do you put up with it?

Didn't I tell you to shut the fuck up?

Jason sat himself up on the sofa in the family room. He placed his head on his hands and leaned over and stared at the carpet.

I hate this carpet. What did the realtor call it? Wedgewood.

Baby blue. Looks like North Carolina's basketball uniforms.

I guess it's supposed to bring out the color of Leela's contact lenses.

That was last year. He looked around the room as if he was seeing it for the first time. Too much stuff in one space. A pool table, a plasma TV that took up one entire wall, the sound system that was invisibly wired into the walls to be heard throughout the entire house, a wraparound sofa and loveseat, a curio cabinet filled with knickknacks and cutesy critters, and pictures. Pictures of the family at home, pictures of family on vacation, pictures of Leela, more pictures of Leela and oh, the window-sized picture of the happy couple. Newly married, so much in love, hanging over the mantle. Not a book in sight. What did she say?

"This isn't the place for books. This is where we relax and have fun."

Jason shook his head and rubbed it at the same time. He took a deep breath and forced himself to think about getting up and going upstairs to get cleaned up for work.

I wonder if she'll start crying again when I walk in the bedroom. Probably never stopped.

Oh well.

That morning, Jason drove the Navigator into the parking garage at the District Court. He got out of the SUV and caught himself straightening his tie in the reflection in the glass of the driver's window. He chuckled to himself.

Laughter is like a good medicine.

I could really use that right about now, he thought as he gathered up his black Jack Georges belting leather briefcase with debossing, a gift from Leela to express his affluence and position. Seven hundred plus dollars before the debossing.

And hardly anything in my wallet.

All that money to hold criminal files.

And carry the donuts. Now that was criminal.

Another chuckle.

It might be a good day after all.

"Hey man. I was beginning to worry about you. Been calling you like a junkie looking for a fix. Why didn't you pick up?" Mike was standing at the elevator door when it opened on the third floor. "Sly and Simone got here about fifteen minutes ago. Seems they don't travel on CP time either. Sly is gonna hang with us this weekend for the game," said Mike as he turned around and headed down the thickly carpeted hallway. "She looks good today, you know."

"Who?" Jason asked.

"Who have I been talking about? I sure as hell ain't talking about Sly."

"Simone? I thought you would have gotten over that since our conversation yesterday."

"Oh, she's Simone now. I seen prettier but I ain't seen finer, you know what I mean? There is something about her that grabs you. If she wasn't married, I'd have to say a little something something to Miss Lady."

"Like a woman like that would pay attention to you," Jason shook his head and followed Mike down the hallway.

"Oh, and she would notice you? Please. I always knew you were stupid. You just got lucky with Leela. She must have been on the rebound or something. But Simone, nah… that's a different world."

They walked down the seemingly endless hallway rounding corners and passing conference and meeting rooms. Two black men on *this* side of the legal system instead of *that* side. Mike and Jason must have been thinking the same thing as they passed by the pre-trial rooms. Neither said a word as they continued to walk.

"What's up with you today, man? Something ain't copasetic." Mike looked at his best friend hoping for a response of some sort. They had known each other since back in the day, running the same streets as young bucks, sharing a dorm room in college and sealing the friendship when they both pledged the same fraternity. The two of them had done some 'stupid shit' as Mike liked to put it before Jason got married. And even before that. Stupid shit that ended up in somebody being dead…. Time passed and those that were still alive continued living. Mike was Jason's best man at the wedding that almost didn't happen because of some stupid shit that Mike had never shared with his best friend. Mike knew that Leela was at the bottom of Jason's troubles this morning. He knew firsthand that Leela was a piece of work and every now and then he thought that he should have told Jason just that before the wedding. Now it was too late. "You alright?"

"You ever wonder why people get divorced? I mean really wonder what causes two people who took vows before God to one day wake up and say what the fuck am I doing here?" Jason kept walking, head down like he was talking to himself. Mike wasn't sure how to reply so he kept walking too.

"I mean shit, man. I work my ass off and spend all my time trying to figure out what I am supposed to do to make this thing work and it's getting harder and harder to make any sense of it. You know what I mean?"

"No. I don't. I take it things got kinda fucked up last night."

Jason burst into laughter. A woman, looking like she stepped out of Lawyers Weekly, walking in the opposite direction smiled at the two well dressed professional looking black men. *If she only knew.* Mike knew that when Jason laughed out like that for no apparent reason, he was truly livid about something, the irony of which was lost on Mike. He wasn't sure what had happened at home, but he was sure not to ask. J would tell him when he was ready. *Or not.*

They reached the meeting room and stopped outside of the door.

"You up for this?" Mike looked Jason in the eye. They had known each other long enough to be honest.

"Hell, yeah. I'm good. This is just what I need right now to take my mind off things. Spending my day in the presence of a lovely lady with a brain will do me good right about now. Let's do this." Jason put his fist out and waited for Mike to reciprocate. "Thanks, man."

Chapter **Seven**

Simone looked up from her tablet as the door opened and Mike and Jason walked in. Sly stood up and walked over to them. Love was spread all around while she sat there and admired how beautifully all that testosterone was packaged.

Girl, you are in heaven today.

Oh, please, don't start. We are here to work, not play play.

You don't know the meaning of the word. Just enjoy your day. It's not like every day you have men to pay attention to you. Well, it is, but you don't know how to appreciate it. So, if it happens today, enjoy it. That's all I'm saying.

That's all, really? What a surprise. Nobody is here to pay attention to me anyway.

Really? Mr. Copeny is more than willing to pay attention. You saw that yesterday. He is beautiful, you know.

He is also married. Just like me.

How's that working out for you? No one is suggesting you marry him. Looking at him is not against the law.

It's not the looking. It's the thinking that's the problem.

Mike walked over to the table and shook her hand. She smiled up at him as he walked around the table and settled in a swivel chair. Jason walked toward her, and she felt a knot well up in her throat. He extended his hand and squeezed hers ever so slightly, then slowly let go. *One thousand one, one thousand two.* Nothing provocative. Nothing untoward. Everything acceptable but somewhere in her being she knew otherwise. He surveyed the table and settled on a seat next to Mike, right across from Simone. He looked at her and Simone could have sworn that his eyes brightened, and his shoulders relaxed. She lowered her eyes slightly and smiled.

"I brought breakfast for everyone today. Tomorrow it's someone else's turn. We've got orange juice, bagels, muffins, assorted donuts, and chocolate angels for you, Mrs. Dyson." Jason was so animated as he took the food out of his gorgeous briefcase.

I know he didn't buy that for himself. He doesn't seem the type.

Wifey. She must love her man. Do you know how much that cost?

Yes, I do. I looked at one for Greg for his birthday a couple of years ago.

But you didn't do it did you? Why not?

I'm not the type.

Everybody sat and talked and laughed over juice and sweet carbohydrates. Simone fingered her donuts and drank her soymilk.

"You're not eating your donuts, Mrs. Dyson. Is there something wrong with them?"

"No of course not, they are wonderful. I'm saving them for later. I'll be bouncing off the walls if I eat them this early in the day. Thank you for being so thoughtful." She didn't have the heart to tell him that he bought the wrong kind of donuts. He seemed so much better than he did when he first walked in with Mike. She liked vanilla angel with chocolate icing. He bought chocolate angel with chocolate icing.

See, his nose was so wide open he couldn't remember what kind of donuts to buy. See the effect you have on men? I told you.

"I'll have a bagel though. How are you doing this morning?" she asked trying to make small talk.

"Better now. Some days it's just hard to get started, you know?"

"Yes, I do."

"And you? You look like you are all ready to take on the world this morning," Jason said between sips of juice. He admired her black tailored suit with the very thin turquoise pinstripe and sheer jet brown stockings caressing long shapely legs ending in patent leather pumps with three-inch heels. Very powerful and intimidating if you were to read her too quickly. In reality, Jason could tell, it was not that way at all. Just a confidence about herself and her ability. She had nothing to prove to anyone. No one to impress.

What about her husband?

Fuck him.

"I am excited about the work we are starting here today. I've been imagining it for the longest time. We have the opportunity to change the way things are done in this state. This has the potential to set a precedent for the way criminal cases are conducted."

"You are very dedicated to this work, aren't you?"

"Very much so, I have seen what it can do. How it can change things for the better. I think all everyone wants is to be heard."

"I agree. I also believe that there are those who wish to be heard more so than others."

"That is very true. That's why mediation is such a powerful tool. It provides each person an equal opportunity to be heard, even if the other participant is, shall we say, more vocal."

"It sounds like you have a great deal of experience with it."

"Yes, I do. I speak from experience."

"Well, I am looking forward to seeing how this is going to work."

"And if you stick around for the duration, you will."

"Oh, Mrs. Dyson. I am going nowhere."

For a moment, Jason forgot that anyone else was in the room. Mike and Sly were still arguing over which sports bar had the best specials for the ball games since they couldn't get tickets at this late date that they were willing to pay for. Jason's full attention was on Simone as she talked about mediation empowering the participants and bringing about change in the way that people interacted with others and even how they felt about themselves.

She's magnificent. She truly believes in what she is doing—making a difference in the world. Not just draining the life out of it. Like—

"Time to get started," Mike's booming baritone interrupted Jason's thoughts. "Just for the sake of formality and since this is our first time together, let's set some norms. Breaks as needed, food as needed, and breaks as needed." Everybody laughed and agreed that they could set their own times for stretches and refreshment. Lunch around noon. They all decided that lunch out would be cool—maybe a little too cool because the hawk was flying low this morning. The Weather Channel was calling for snow and more snow followed by a blizzard. So, they would order from the kosher deli down 45th Street that delivered. That way they could get more done.

"Sound good to everybody?" Mike asked. The response was in the affirmative and the small group settled into work mode. Everyone pulled out their electronic devices. Laptops, tablets, iPhones, and assorted cell phones that weren't smart enough to put themselves on vibrate without some assistance. The men faced Simone as if she was about to make an opening statement in a court of law. They gave her their rapt attention.

"Well, gentlemen, we are about to do one of two things. Permanently change the lives of two young men forever for the better or change their lives forever for the worst. I am hoping and praying for the former because there are hundreds of prosecutors out there that can do the latter. Tyreek Henderson and Shamel Brittingham are scheduled for trial in 90 days. They are charged with 1st degree assault with a deadly weapon and are looking at the possibly of five to ten years if convicted. From what I have read so far-- and Mr. Copeny and Mr. DeVries will provide the details for us—both boys have lengthy arrest records but no convictions. I call them boys right now because Tyreek is not eighteen years old, yet. The problem that arises is that he *will* be in twenty-two days. That will make him an adult and that's how the prosecution wants to try them. As adults. The stakes are high. I don't think that these young men realize that the court doesn't play with adults like they do with juvenile offenders. Shamel is nineteen and has only been charged petty misdemeanors until now. If we can get them to agree to mediation before trial and they come to an acceptable agreement, they could have the charges dropped. That is good for more than just the obvious reason—two less young black males caught up in the penitentiary—but it opens up the opportunity for discourse between two rival gangs that are known to be responsible for drug sales in four middle, two high schools, and a primary school in the city, and accused of two unsolved murders of gang members and a store owner on the upper east side. If these gangs can begin a dialogue without the threat of violence, who knows what might transpire. So, the task at hand is to formulate a plan of proactive attack, as I like to call it. Start with the end in mind and work our way back to the beginning. The question that we are working with today and for the next eighty-nine days is—what's it going to take to make this happen?"

The room was quiet as Simone's words penetrated the space and soaked into their beings. There was a great deal at stake for the future in this room. The actions and decisions made here could affect untold numbers of people both directly and indirectly, Jason thought. *And it will keep you and Simone in the same space for at least eighty-nine days.*

"You were right when you said earlier that this is serious work," Jason said. "I have never considered mediation an option in court or anywhere else for that matter. Since this is new to me and Mike too, I believe, I beg you to go slow with me and be gentle. We are newbies."

Sly chimed in at this point. "Not to worry, man. Simone is good. In fact, she is the best I have seen. For real. She has lectured, trained, and consulted for the Federal courts. She'll never tell you, but she has mediated some serious sh—stuff and the participants have walked out with enforceable agreements that stand up in place of court actions and decisions. She knows what she is doing so if we follow her lead, it's all good."

"My cheerleader," Simone whispered as Sly finished.

"Well yeah. Somebody needs to say it 'cause you won't." Sly turned back to Mike and Jason. "She's got this way of understanding and making you *see* what's real, you know? It's crazy to watch. Just wait. You'll see. Trust me. If we can get these young heads to agree to meet, it's on."

Mike startled in his chair, touching his pants pocket, got up from his chair, and gave the international sign language sign for potty break and left the room.

"Anybody want something to drink? I need to stretch my legs and make a phone call." Sly fiddled with the phone in his hand. "Moni, looks like the Tuesday mediation wants to reschedule again. I'll check to see who is available since we'll be here--for what? At least a couple of weeks?" Simone looked at Jason and at Sly. Jason looked at both of them and said, "At least."

Sly stood up and walked towards the door. "Be right back."

Jason chuckled under his breath and shook his head almost unperceptively.

"Seems as if you are amused by something." Simone said.

His smile broadened to display perfectly even teeth. All without the help of braces that Mim would have never been able to afford.

"No, not amused really. Refreshed is a better word," Jason replied.

"Help me understand what you mean when you say refreshed," Simone said leaning forward ever so slightly.

"Well, let's see. I mean that it is refreshing to sit in this room and hear that there are options for our young black males beyond the confines of a jail cell. It's refreshing to see a group of people so dedicated to making a positive change to the status quo. It's refreshing to feel a part of something that has such potential for good. That's what I mean when I say refreshing."

I also mean that it is refreshing to be in the presence of a stunning woman who has other things on her mind besides whether a Basketball Wife of Atlanta has breasts that sit higher than hers or whether she should de-friend her sister on Facebook because she said that not everything in life needs to be broadcast to everybody. It's good to know that intelligent women, purposeful women do exist. Now that is refreshing.

Sly came back in the room carrying three bottles of Fuji water and one San Pellegrino. He placed the bottles on the table and sat down in the same seat where he had been earlier. He pulled his phone out of his pocket and laid it on the table. No sooner had he put it down than it started to slide across the table buzzing. He picked it up and looked at the message. He mumbled and typed in a response.

"Okay, Tuesday is rescheduled. Amie is going to do it. Need a couple of observers. Just got in three referrals for tort cases and two more court appointed referrals. It's been busy this morning. We need to figure out who is available to handle these while we are here. I might have to split my time between here and there." He talked while he sent message after message. After several minutes, he put the phone back into his pocket. "I'm straight now. Sorry about that but work goes on."

"Work always goes on. It's good to hear that we are busy. Busy means funding. Funding means busy. It works. If you have to split your time, so be it but I would prefer that you find someone to handle those cases. We need you here," Simone said. What she meant was *I* need you here. Don't leave me alone with these guys for three months.

Sly was good at reading Simone's face and her voice. He understood and said, "I will do my best. Shouldn't be too much of a problem. I want to be a part of this. This is going to be huge. And besides, you know I never pass up a chance to work with you, my dear."

"You are too kind," Simone laughed, her voice filled with relief. Just then, Sly's phone vibrated again.

"What now?" He checked the message. "Oh shi—I mean shoot.

Guess what we forgot?" He said looking directly at Simone.

She turned her head slightly, in the way Jason was becoming very fond of, as she ran through the possibilities of things she could have forgotten. After a moment, she shook her head.

"I have no idea. A hint, maybe?"

"ADR conference. Remember? You are presenting. How do we manage this?"

Sly spread his open hands out toward all the files strewn across the table.

"Well, we'll have to, won't we? The trial date is set and if we can't get things together before then we know that it's not going to bode well for either one of them," she said.

"So, what do we do?" Sly asked.

Jason and Mike exchanged glances that said *do you know what's going on?* Sly saw the look and started to explain.

"The national ADR conference is coming up and we are presenters this year. It's a real honor and career booster. It's the middle of next week and it completely slipped my mind 'cause we've been so wrapped up with this and everything else. Simone, you're right, but how can we work on this and be there too?"

"When is it?" Simone asked.

"Eight days from tomorrow," Sly answered.

The room was quiet. No one had a comment or a suggestion for a while. Simone broke the silence. She looked at Mike and Jason. "So, what are you all doing eight days from now?" she asked.

"Excuse me?" Mike asked.

"Let me share what I am thinking. We need to get this worked out and we can't afford to waste a week. Sly and I have to be at the ADR conference, so I was wondering how to kill two birds with one stone. You two could come with us and we could work during the down time which is pretty substantial. We have one presentation on

Thursday, I think?" She looked at Sly who was checking his phone for confirmation. He shook his head in the affirmative.

"So that leaves Wednesday afternoon and all-day Friday, plus the two of you could get a crash course in ADR from a variety of sources. We would get more time together there than we would here, actually," she said.

"So, let me practice my reflective listening. So, what you're saying is you want me and Mike to go to the conference with you and Sly. Am I right?" Jason said.

"Very good. Do you think that is possible? Do you have enough time to make arrangements at work and at home?" she asked glancing in Jason's direction.

"Couple of questions," Mike leaned forward across the table. "How is this going to be paid for? Stuff like that is pricey and our office probably can't justify that kind of expenditure."

"Well," Simone began. "I was thinking about that and since our office is providing the grant for this joint venture including room, board, educational expenses for this, there is definitely funds available because we haven't spent even a fraction of what is allotted. Let me make a few calls to check but I would almost guarantee that this is do-able. What's your next question?"

Mike was still leaning over the table. "Where is the conference being held? Downtown at the conference center?"

"Las Vegas," Sly answered.

"Oh yeah, we can go," answered Mike.

They took some time to work out all the details and then regrouped to get to the work ahead of them. Mike had left again to answer his phone and when he walked in, he seemed more subdued than before he left. Jason noticed how quiet his friend was and wondered what had transpired in the few minutes that he had been out of the room. *I'll ask him during lunch.*

"So back to work," Jason said. "I have a ton of questions so maybe we should list them and as we plan out our strategy some of them will probably get answered. So, who wants to record?"

"I'll do it," Mike said. "Keep my mind off things."

"Are you alright, man?" Jason asked. Something was very wrong here and he couldn't figure out what it was.

"I'm cool. Why you asking?"

"Because your handwriting is illegible," Jason quipped. Mike laughed and the tension in the room ebbed just a bit. Mike stood up and walked over to the computer stand and flipped on the projector.

"Step into the twenty-first century, my brother. Technology rules. You speak, I record. He started typing and everyone looked up at the screen. YOUR WISH IS MY COMMAND popped up in large bold red letters. Tension gone. Mike seemed like his old self, but Jason was still concerned. He made a mental note to ask him anyway.

They opened the numerous files on Tyreek and Shamel, both electronic and paper. Between the two young men there were fifteen counts in the past two years and not one conviction. Everyone sitting at the table looked at each other with questioning stares. How was that possible? Conventional wisdom says that if someone is young, male, and black, he's been to jail whether he did the crime or not. How is it that *two* young black males have eluded conviction on fifteen separate occasions?

No one had to say a word. Something was amiss somewhere. What it was would take some investigation and someone was going to have to do that digging.

"Draw straws?" asked Mike. "They're over on the counter next to the silver bullets, 'cause we're going to have as much luck killing werewolves as figuring out what's going on with this."

"My man, Mike, always seeing the bright side of life. Did you ever think that there might not be a c-o-n-spiracy around every corner?"

Jason asked.

"Yeah, I thought that once. Then I got pulled over driving while black," Mike replied.

"Oh please, you didn't get pulled over for driving while black. I got pulled over for driving while black. You got pulled over for driving with a white woman in the car while black." The men burst out with laughter. High fives and fist pumps all around. Almost. Simone smiled and shook her head, then put her head in her hands.

"I'm sorry Mrs. Dyson, my dear friend, J, has a despicably crude sense of humor. I don't know why I keep trying to save him from himself. Sly, stay away from him. He is dangerous."

Jason glanced at Simone trying to read the expression on her face. It said something like *are you really like that?* He watched her head tilt slightly as though she were processing disturbing thoughts one after the other. *I hope she didn't take me seriously. Shit. She has to know I was playing.*

"I knew when I arrived this morning that it was going to be an eventful day. But I was underestimating the extent. Not to worry, tomorrow I will be ready for you guys. I promise. I thought we were behaving like professionals. Now I know better."

Mike, Jason, and Sly sat in silence. The only sound in the room was the whirring of the heating unit in the ceiling. They looked at Simone while she tried to keep a straight face. She glanced at Jason and cracked a smile. His face was losing color. *Serves him right. He's going to faint. This is too funny.*

She started to laugh. Hard. When they saw her laughing, the rest of the room let out a sigh of relief.

She's okay. The next two weeks should be an interesting to say the least.

Chapter Eight

The plane landed at the airport just as the sun was setting over the Nevada desert. *Beautiful*. Jason thought. Who would have thought just a few weeks ago he met Simone and here he was in Las Vegas with her. *You'd think you were on a vacation or something.* Well, I like to think positively, he said to himself.

And how's that working out for you?

Jason laughed to himself, thinking about how Leela took the news that he would be out of town for the week. She cried, exactly three tears (he counted), said she would miss him, and went upstairs to watch *Housewives of Las Vegas.* How appropriate.

The hotel limousine was waiting as they exited the airport terminal. The ride was a lively one as Mike and Sly set their itinerary for their down time. "Will the grant cover several trips to the poker table?" Mike quipped.

Simone just shook her head as everyone laughed. She realized she would probably be shaking her head a great deal over the next five days.

I hate Las Vegas. So artificial. So phony. Maybe this time it will be different. It has the potential to be.

The last time she was here, she came with Greg and a few of his staff. He seemed to have several late-night meetings while she sat in the hotel room. Thank goodness for good books. Her Kindle was loaded, just in case.

When they arrived at their very exclusive hotel, the doorman escorted them to the front desk. The concierge was behind the reception desk with a look of trepidation and stress on his face.

I didn't think emotions showed through Botox.

Stop it, thought Simone.

What? If that's not Botox, then what is it?

"Good afternoon. Welcome. We are so happy to have you visiting with us. Names, please."

"We have reservations under Dyson, party of four." Simone said softly.

Ethan, that's what the nameplate on his jacket said, repeated Simone's words as he typed into the computer, looking up their rooms. He made an error of some sort and tried again. The phone buzzed quietly, and no one was around to answer it, so Ethan looked up at Simone and said, "Excuse me," and answered the phone, putting them on hold. A bell boy walked up and asked a question. Ethan answered in an exasperated manner with a flurry of hand movements and returned to the computer screen.

"It seems very busy for one person to handle today," Simone said.

"Very, there was a reservation clerk here a minute ago, but she left to take a break. Can you believe that? I guess I should. It's not the first time," Ethan said.

"Sounds like you're overworked and overwhelmed trying to do the job of two people," she said.

"Exactly. They get paid to work just like I do, but this happens all the time."

"Frustrated with the lack of professionalism in your coworkers."

"Oh my gosh, yes. Even the manager doesn't know what to do about it. In fact, I trained the manager. He's been here two months and the place is going to the pocket poodles."

"Sounds like you take pride in your job and want everything to run smoothly and the disregard or inability of the management to run the desk smoothly is irritating to you especially since you can do it so much better."

"That is so absolutely right! I can't believe someone completely understands. Oh my gosh, I feel so much better! I thought I was the one with the problem…Thank you so much for letting me vent. You are the best listener. I guess I really needed to get that off my chest… I apologize for the rant," Ethan said softly.

"No problem, Ethan. Everyone needs an opportunity to voice their thoughts at some time. Today was your time," Simone answered in the same soft tone.

Ethan smiled at Simone as if she was a gift from heaven. "So, you are all together, right? Because the reservations are all over the place."

"Yes, we are here for the ADR conference this week," Simone said.

Ethan put up an index finger. "Wait just one minute." Clickety, clickety, click went Ethan's fingers across the keys.

"How about this, Mrs. Dyson? Since you all would probably benefit by being closer together, I am going to move you all to one of the penthouse suites. It has three bedrooms and a master suite on the upper level. Just for you, Mrs. Dyson." Ethan smiled at Simone. "Don't worry about the cost because…" clickety, clickety, click. "It remains the same as what you were originally billed for. How's that?"

"That's amazing, Ethan. Thank you for your thoughtfulness. It is deeply appreciated. Are you sure it's not going to be a problem?" Simone asked.

"The hotel does this regularly for those on the short list of high rollers. Consider yourselves on the shortest list," he said and smiled again. "In fact," he continued, clickety, clickety, clickety, clickety. "There you are, meal vouchers for any one of the eight restaurants in the hotel, for you all to use during your stay. Five days, three meals a day if you wish and room service. And a little gift from the hotel to encourage you to play in our casinos. Two thousand? How's that? No. that's not quite sufficient… Four, yeah four." Click. Ethan handed Simone, Sly, Mike, and Jason room keys, vouchers, and welcome bags.

"Ethan, you have been overly generous. How can we ever thank you?"

"Just doing my job to the best of my ability."

"Your abilities are outstanding. Seems like you feel a little better than you did a few minutes ago."

"Yes, much. I feel…" Ethan searched for the right word.

"Empowered?"

"Ding ding ding, right again! I like that word—empowered."

The group of four turned around to pick up their luggage and head toward the elevator.

"Mrs. Dyson, the luggage will be delivered to your penthouse along with an hors d'oeuvre tray, champagne and sparkling cider. Remember you all are on the shortest list now. Enjoy your stay."

"You are remarkable, Ethan. Have a good rest of the day."

"Oh, I will Mrs. Dyson. I will see you all tomorrow. If you need anything, just let me know."

"Please call me Simone."

"Miss Simone. It suits you. Enjoy your stay."

"What the hell just happened?" Mike asked as they stepped into the elevator.

"I told you she was good." Sly said.

"That was unbelievable. How did you make him do that?"

"You can't make a person do anything. All anyone wants is to be heard. If you hear them and validate their feelings, they feel—"

"Empowered?" Jason said from the back of the elevator.

"Yes. That's the word of the day."

Chapter Nine

Sheva was in a mood that resembled a can of *caliente* diced tomatoes with habaneros. Things were not going as planned. She had led herself to believe that Greg was going to finalize his divorce with Simone last night. After their conversation yesterday, she came to the conclusion in her own mind that she was important enough to Greg that he would take care of the little annoyance known as Simone. That must have been the reason that he was so abrupt with her in his office. He was trying to find the right words to tell Simone that he was ending their marriage to be with the true love of his life.

She figured that it should take about two or three hours for him to break the news, listen to her cry and beg him not to leave her, calm her down, and walk out with her huddled up in a fetal position beside the door balling her eyes out. What a sight that must have been. Sheva imagined it in slow motion detail over and over again as she calculated the time that Greg would arrive back at the condo and she could make her grand entrance. *He'll leave work around five, hit traffic on the Loop. Get out to the house around six fifteen. She'll let him in and be all excited that he's coming back. Then he springs it on her. How cool is that! She starts to cry and ask why. She doesn't understand. He tells her that he hasn't loved her in a long time, and he wants to be happy--with me. She'll beg him to stay, then cry and cry some more. Yeah, that's what will happen. She'll try to seduce him, but he'll think about me and peel her off him and walk out without looking back. That should take about two, maybe three hours depending upon how hard she cries. He should be back by nine thirty or so. I'll get there around eleven. That gives me time to go to Victoria's Secret and pick up that really hot red and pink negligee I've had my eyes on and then I'll get my nails and toes done...*

She went about the rest of her afternoon and evening planning every little detail. The level of anticipation was so high she slipped into her natural vocal qualities and anyone who didn't know her would swear she just stepped out of the deepest section of Spanish Harlem this morning. *I can't think about two things at once. So, what? I can talk anyway I want pretty soon. I'll be Mrs. Sheva Morales-Dyson before you know it. So there.*

The evening passed so slowly she could barely stand it. After checking her preparations for the hundredth time, she picked up her overnight bag and headed to her car. *No way I'm coming back home tonight. It's time to leave some of my things at the condo since I'll be moving in soon anyway.*

The drive to the condo was easy because the traffic was light at this time of night. She arrived around fifteen minutes before she figured Greg would arrive. *If I had a key, I could be inside getting everything ready. Candles, wine, me in the foyer waiting for him when he opens the door...I need to get a key tonight.* Thirty minutes later she was still waiting. *Wow. She must really be taking it hard. Oh well, so be it. It's like that sometimes.* The future Mrs. Dyson smiled to herself and scooted down in the driver's seat to wait for her future husband. *I'll close my eyes for a few. I'll hear him when he drives up.*

When she opened her eyes to check her watch, she thought it must have stopped or something. The numbers showed 2:15. *Where is he? I hope he hasn't been in an accident trying to get back to me. I couldn't have missed the sound of that engine when he drove up.* She looked around the parking lot for the BMW. She looked over to the condo to see if there was light shining in any of the windows. She squinted as she usually did when she was out in public, and nobody was looking. She thought she saw a dim light in the living room window. The color of the light kept changing. It must have been the plasma TV.

She jumped out of car and tried not to run to the door. She left her overnight bag, but she could always go back for it later. Standing at the door, she took a deep breath and knocked forcefully. No answer. Thinking that she didn't knock hard enough, she rapped again and called Greg's name. Still no answer. "Greg, are you there? I see the light. Are you in there? Greg?" The knocking continued more out of nervousness than anything else. *What could have happened to make him not come to the door?* Knock knock knock.

The door slowly opened about six inches. Greg's face appeared. Sheva took a deep breath of relief. "What do you want?" he asked with a hoarse voice. She tried to peek inside and saw a Hennessey bottle dangling in his hand.

She tried to sound lighthearted as she answered, "You started celebrating without me Papi?" She smiled her most seductive smile complete with lizard like tongue licking of teeth, hoping it would catch his attention like it used to.

"What are you doing here?" Greg looked at her through bloodshot eyes.

"I am here to be with you. We said we would celebrate after you got home. So here I am," she said a little too brightly.

"There's nothing to celebrate. Go home," he mumbled.

"What are you saying?" she asked in a quieter voice.

"Didn't you hear me? There's nothing to celebrate. Go the hell home." He started to shut the door. But Sheva pushed it back open.

"What are you saying?" she repeated. "She won't give you a divorce or what?'

Greg turned around and walked away from the door. She stepped inside and closed the door behind her. The room was dark except for the map of the nation with the weather trends flashing on the seventy-five-inch screen as it hung effortlessly on the wall. Greg walked over to the leather sofa and sat down slowly as if Sheva wasn't even in the room. He stared at the television and turned the half empty Hennessy bottle up to his head. She didn't know whether to speak, sit, stand or leave so she just waited. And waited. What seemed like hours passed until she couldn't take it anymore. She was quickly losing what little composure she had and it could be heard when she opened her mouth to speak.

"So, what happened? Why are you sitting here in the dark? Why didn't you call me to let me know you were home? Where is your car? What …"

"Shut up! Will you just shut up?" Greg yelled. "I don't need to hear your whiny voice, so shut the hell up!"

Sheva was shocked. She had never heard Greg talk like this before. She didn't know what to think but she had to do something to calm him down. She started breathing hard, anger building towards Simone for upsetting her future husband so badly.

"I know it must have been hard watching her reaction to the news but it's okay, we expected it to be that way. She just wasn't going to let you walk away just like that…"

Greg continued to look down at the floor shaking his head from side to side. A low growl or something seemed to be coming from deep in his throat.

"I told you to shut up. Leave why don't you? Get out," he said, not looking up from the floor.

"Papi, you don't need to be alone right now."

"I'm going to say it one last time. Leave."

Sheva didn't know what to think or how to respond. In all of her scenarios, this had never crossed her mind. She didn't know how to handle Greg in this condition. *Better to find out that he has alcohol issues before we get married,* she thought. She walked over to the sofa. The high heels could be heard echoing throughout the room on the hardwood floors.

"Stay away from me,' Greg said as he noticed Sheva coming closer.

"What did you say?"

"I said stay away from me. I asked you three times to leave, and you don't listen. I am not telling you again."

"Why are you talking to me this way? I know that you are upset…"

Greg threw his head back and roared with angry laughter. The bottle dropped out of his hand and rolled across the floor leaving a trail of brown liquor. The aroma of expensive alcohol covering the smell of too much perfume. "Upset? Upset? You think I am upset? No. Why should I be upset?" Greg stood up and walked to the French doors and looked out into the darkness.

"You want answers to your questions? I'll answer your questions and then you can get out. I went home to my wife to tell her that I wanted to come back. She said it was my decision to leave so it was my decision to come back. She didn't cry or scream or whine. She just said it was my decision. Then she walked past me with her suitcase on the way to the airport. Like she didn't care what I did. Right then I realized what a mistake I had made. I left her, for what? You?"

 He didn't turn around, but Sheva felt his disdain and disgust as he continued to speak. "I don't know what I was thinking. I apologized to her and told her I made a huge mistake and that I knew what I wanted for the rest of my life. She just looked at me. Looked right through me. You know what she said to me? 'So, it sounds like you want to come back here. Is that right? I'm sure there is someone that you need to talk to besides me. Why don't you take care of your other business right now? It's getting late. A little too late to be making rash decisions. I have a plane to catch.' What's that supposed to mean? What's she saying? That she knows about you? She didn't ask for a divorce; she didn't say come back. She just took it in stride and left me standing there. What if I've lost her? What if she's found someone else?"

"Who would want her si-ditty ass anyway? She act like her shit don't stink or something." Sheva retorted, trying to make Greg feel her loathing towards Simone.

"You bitch! Don't you ever let another word about Simone come out of your no-good mouth. You aren't good enough to speak her name. You should wish to be as wonderful as she is. That's all you have ever tried to do—be a lady, like her. You'll never make it. She is everything that you wish you knew how to be—quiet, calm, kind, truthful, understanding, and strong. Not to mention beautiful."

"If she is all that, then why did you run into my arms? Huh? Answer me that? Why?"

"Good question. The fuck if I know." Greg took a deep breath and looked at Sheva so long and hard that she felt naked under his gaze. Funny how a few hours ago that's all she had wanted—to be naked under his gaze. *Careful what you ask for, amante.*

"I think I felt that I wasn't good enough for her. She is so special. She put up with all my shit. The moods, the job, the good and the bad, and never complained. I started thinking that nobody could be this good. So, I thought I'd find the complete opposite of her and test her ass. Prove to myself that she is human just like the rest of us. Do my damnedest to hurt her and see how she responds. And you know what? She did what she always does. Rise above it." He stopped talking and sat down again. "I want my life back." She heard him mumble. "I want my wife back."

Sheva was speechless. She suddenly felt cold and gathered her coat around her in an effort to block out the chill that was radiating from Greg. He slowly looked around and she held her breath afraid of what he might say next.

"You need to leave and don't come back. I love my wife and always did. I used you and I am sorry for that, but I'm through. You knew what was what. At least I hoped that you did. I needed—no… wanted a diversion, a change and you were willing. I made a mistake. It was a mistake. So please leave and don't come back."

He walked over to the bar and pulled another bottle of Hennessey off of the shelf. He opened it and took a long swig not even attempting to reach for a glass.

"You need to go now," he said.

"But if she …," she started.

"Are you as stupid as you seem? Which part of leave does not translate for you? Salir? Do you understand that?"

"Oh, don't even try it! My Puerto Rican ass was good enough for you in your office and in your bed and on this sofa, but now you are acting like… like I am not good enough for you and she is some saint or something?"

"No. Your Puerto Rican ass was available and easy. Something to do to make me feel—I don't know—important or something. I don't know. I'm too tired to deal with you. Go home."

Sheva felt tears rolling down her face as her shoulders heaved uncontrollably. She wanted to say something to hurt him as badly as he had hurt her but there was nothing to be said that could do that. So, she squinted up her eyes either to clear them of tears or to see her way to the door. The last sound she heard on the way out wasn't Greg saying goodbye but the sound of a liquor bottle defying gravity again for the umpteenth time tonight.

Chapter 10

Remembering all of past twelve hours caused Sheva to look as bad as she felt as she walked into her office in the morning. She closed the door behind her and hoped that no one needed her any time soon. She opened her desk drawer and pulled out her mirror to see if her makeup was covering the bags and sags that developed over the past day.

There was a knock at the door and Sheva sat up and quickly glanced in the mirror before she slid it back into the drawer. Maybe it was Greg coming to apologize now that the alcohol had worn off. "Come in," she said cheerfully.

"Good morning, Ms. Morales. I have the requisitions for the annexing project that you asked for. I had a really hard time with the invoicing for the construction…"

Sheva wasn't listening and she didn't care what Marisa was saying. Her disappointment was tangible. She couldn't even pretend to be interested in whatever she was saying.

"Thanks Marisa. I'll take a look at it later. Just leave it here and I'll access the rest. Just email the other files to me."

"I did that last week. You said you were going to look at it then so that I could get back to the contractors about their payments that they haven't received."

"If I *said* I would get to it, then I will get to it."

"But you *said* you would get to it last week. These people have been waiting for some information on when they can expect payment for their work. They have employees and bills to pay…"

"I said I would take care of it, didn't I?" Sheva's voice was rising with every word.

"It's just that…" Marisa stuttered.

"Just what?" Sheva leaned forward and hollered.

"It's just that it makes the city and Mr. Dyson look bad. You wouldn't want Mr. Dyson to look bad, would you?" Marisa finished.

"What did you say?"

"I said, you wouldn't want Mr. Dyson to look bad, would you?"

"And what's that supposed to mean?"

"Just what I said, for the third time. You are supposed to be his executive assistant and make sure that everything that needs to be done gets done in a timely and efficient manner. And it's just that we aren't seeing that happening."

"And who is we?"

"Everyone in the office knows--- that some things are-- being missed around here. A lot has been overlooked, Ms. Morales, but you need to make some changes in how you are behaving where Mr. Dyson is concerned." Marisa took a deep breath and stood there with the files folded across her chest as if to protect her from the barrage of heavily accented insults that she expected to come her way in about four, three, two, one…

"If you have something to say to me, Marisa Johnson, then say it. Don't make me come across this desk at chu."

"That shouldn't be too much of a stretch for you since you come *on* the desks so well, coming across one should be no problem," said Marisa under her breath as she turned her back and started towards the door. She was tired of Ms. Native New Yorker, Intercontinental lover. *Ho.*

As Marisa reached her hand towards the doorknob, she felt the full force of gravity bearing down on her back and knocking her to her knees. *Earthquake in Chicago! End of the world! Being dragged to hell for my sins! What the--?* Her vision went dim as fingers covered her eyes and scratched at her face.

Sheva had done what she had threatened to do and in one fell swoop had covered the distance from the desk to the door before Marisa had a chance to take three baby steps. Marisa processed the impending danger and allowed her primordial mind to take control. *Oh no she didn't. She don't know who she's messing with. She may be from New York but I'm from Compton and girlfriend is about to get her ass whupped.*

The police showed up about ten minutes after the office door flew open and Sheva fell out into the hallway. The thong for the day was hot pink, at least that's what the Tweet said that made its way into the Twitter-verse. The video on TikTok wasn't so clear as to whether that really was a thong or something else perhaps. The video had over four thousand hits before the ladies were processed into the holding cells on the first floor of the Municipal Building. That was another Tweet that made the rounds. *Why did it take so long to go 13 floors to break up the best cat fight in Municipal building history?* When the police arrived, Marisa unwrapped Sheva's hair from around her fist and released her head slowly before standing up, brushing off her skirt and straightening her blouse. She smiled at stunned officers and said, "I'll be right back." A minute later she came out of the office with both of her shoes in one hand and a tissue in the other. She wiped the blood off of the heel of one shoe and put one hand on the wall and balanced herself as she put the spiked alligator Kim Kardashian pumps back on her feet. She looked down at the floor at Sheva and then looked at the officers whose faces showed signs of pure delight at what they were witnessing during working hours. *Usually, you had to pay for this kind of entertainment. All we need is some green Jell-O, and a pit.* Smiling at them sweetly, Marisa turned around and put her hands behind her back. She looked over her shoulder at Sheva one last time and said, "You might want to call an ambulance."

Chapter 11

Things were going well recently for Jason. Maia was doing well in school and growing into a beautiful young lady. At ten, she had more common sense than many adults. She was what her grandmother Mim would call an old soul. Able to read between the lines and get to the real heart of the matter.

"Daddy, you have been really happy lately," she said one day when Jason picked her up from soccer practice.

"Is that so?" Jason replied. "I am always happy when I am around you, Pumpkin."

"I know that. But even when I'm not around you are happy."

"How do you know that if you're not around?"

"Because I see the leftover happy when you get home."

"Leftover happy, huh?"

"Yup. Sometimes I see you smiling to yourself, and it looks funny. So, I know that you have happy leftover from earlier and it just pops out. I like that."

Jason thought about it for a minute and laughed a hearty belly laugh that shook the Buick. *That's my girl. She don't miss a trick. Dag! Am*

I that obvious? Maia was right. Since Jason had started working on the ADR project, there was a lot more spring to his step and purpose to his day. He thought back to a conversation that he had with Mike last weekend at Roots, their favorite club for catching a few beers and watching the game uninterrupted by Leela standing in front of the television asking what was happening the way she did every time a game was on. It's like she wants someone to notice her. It's only me and Mike, so what's up with that? *Yeah, what's up with that? They've known each other since college so what's she primping for?*

"The days are flying by, man. Have you noticed?" Mike asked as he nursed his third Coors draft. "We been working on this for what… a month now?"

"Yeah," Jason answered, thinking about all that had happened over the past thirty days, the meetings, the preparation, Las Vegas.

"Doesn't seem like that long," Mike said between sips.

"Time flies when you're having fun," Jason quipped and chuckled at his own attempt at humor.

"Yeah, and you're having fun all right," Mike replied with a snicker.

"What that supposed to mean?"

"It means that I see you eying Miss Simone with her fine self. You like her. Who wouldn't? Shit, I like her too. Hell, Sly likes her. Damn, everybody who sees her likes her."

"Got anymore cuss words in you, man? You just about hit them all didn't you?"

Jason shook his head and signaled the bartender for another Pepsi.

"I'm sure I left one out. Give a minute and I'll use that one too. But for real man, things have been pretty cool working with them, you know? I could get use to working with people who got a clue and care about something besides their paycheck," Mike took another swallow and looked at the glass as if it was supposed to magically refill.

"You don't need no more, man. You getting all profound and shit.

You definitely had enough. Good thing I'm driving you home tonight."

"Thanks for that. You is alright with me, man. You is, you is. No matter what nobody says, you my pardner all the way." Mike reached his glass over to Jason's. Click.

"Ain't nobody gonna say different."

"True that, except for Leela," Mike said.

Jason turned his head toward his friend and stared at him for a minute, waiting for some explanation for what just passed his lips. His first thought was to grab Mike's head and bash it into the top of the bar, but he stopped himself long enough to take a few deep breaths and said, "Help me understand what you mean when you say except for Leela?"

"See that's what I'm talking about, man. She's rubbing off on you and it's cool."

Jason shook his head as if to remove cobwebs because Mike was making no sense. *Maybe it's been more than three beers. I always thought the brother could hold his booze. Now I'm beginning to wonder. It's probably not good to clock him right here when he's stone cold drunk.*

"What are you talking about? What about Leela? What'd she say to you about me?"

"Why'd you marry her, man? I don't mean no disrespect. You my boy and all. I love you like a brother, but I never did get that one. She's pretty and I know you love her. I just think that you would have been happier if you had waited and made another choice." Mike got silent and Jason just sat there for a long time. After what seemed like eternity, Jason signaled the bartender and pointed to the Corona sitting in the cooler. He pushed the Pepsi aside. "Man, it's been on my mind for years and I had to ask you."

"Eleven years? You waited eleven years to ask a question like that? Why'd you think I married her?"

"You loved her. Everybody knew that but she wasn't the marrying kind."

"You're right about that one. She was easy to love. That smile, that laugh of hers. She made a beautiful bride. Took my breath away when I saw her walk down the aisle." Jason thought back to that day so many years ago when he promised her his heart. Even then, he knew deep down inside that Leela wasn't the marrying kind. But what other choice did he have?

Jason looked at his friend and was glad that he hadn't decked him. He was right. Maybe alcohol sharpened people's ability to state the not so obvious.

"No, Leela's got a long way to go to being wife material. She is more like the kind that should always be a bride but never have to be a wife. It doesn't suit her. Requires too much giving, I think. Leela's got to be on the receiving end, you know? Don't get me wrong. She is a wonderful woman. It's just that she wasn't cut out for the day-to-day routine of marriage. You know, changing diapers, paying bills, keeping a house." *Working. Bringing in some green to keep the lights on. Nah, she don't know nothing about that shit.* The bartender brought over the Corona and placed it in front of Jason. He started a tab. It might be a long night. He pointed to Mike's just about empty glass and ordered another for him.

"See on the other hand, you know who makes a damn good wife?" Mike said draining his glass now that he knew another one was on its way.

"Oh Lord, here we go. Halle Berry, Taraji Henson…"

"Yeah, them too. Well, maybe not Halle… Simone."

Jason had to agree in the dark recesses of his mind. He could see her being—a wife. A helper, a partner, a mate.

"You do have it bad tonight, don't you? You start off dissing my wife, then change gears and start talking about somebody else's wife. Maybe I should cancel that beer before you say something you might regret in the morning."

"Hell, I regret it right now. So there," Mike laughed. "But seriously, she is pretty fun to be around and I swear you been downright pleasant the past month after that car shit went down at home. So, I was trying to figure what might have made you feel better and that's the only thing that's changed 'cause Leela is still Leela. Am I right?"

Jason was quiet. "Yeah, Leela is still Leela."

"I'll drink to that," Mike said extending the new frosty glass the bartender had just placed in front of him. *Click.*

Chapter 12

Greg hadn't been to the office since the day before "The Smackdown" as it had come to be known had occurred. Of course, he heard about it vicariously from his brother Karl in an early morning phone call.

"So, hey bro. what's going on up there in high and mighty land? Heard that there was an all out cat fight in your offices yesterday. You didn't have anything to do with that, did you?"

"What are you talking about?" Greg muttered into the phone. He had been asleep, or passed out, hung over from the drinking binge of the night before. His head hurt and he had thrown up twice. His uncle had always told him that the good stuff wouldn't make you vomit. Obviously, he never drank three 750 milliliter bottles of Hennessey in one sitting. "Slow down. What happened?" Greg struggled to sit up in the bed, slowly. Very slowly. "Okay, tell me what's going on."

Karl shared all the details that he had read from the police reports. Of course, that was supplemented by the eyewitness version of the traumatized receptionist and the officers who 'arrived' at the scene. Greg couldn't believe his ears and thought that the hangover was causing him to hallucinate the entire conversation.

"So, you been banging that juicy Puerto Rican assistant of yours? Or should I say Hispanic or Latina? Either way—juicy Sheva with the cleavage. That's what we call her downstairs. She used to work it down here before she moved on up…so to speak. Thanks for keeping your brother in the loop. Can't say I blame you though…I kinda hit that one myself a couple years ago. Although there's a lot more juice than there was then…Keepin' it all in the family huh, bro?" Karl laughed as if that was the best joke. Greg didn't share the humor. Was he saying that he and Sheva had a thing before she latched on to him? Keeping it all in the family?

Greg was speechless. He knew his little brother had a thing about telling him everything that would upset him. From the death of their mother to today's news, Karl always was the bearer of bad news. As if he was subtly trying to make Greg feel guilty for not being around for life changing events.

"The receptionist heard Sheva screaming that she was going to get you to fire the chick before she passed out. Sounds like it was ugly. What have you been doing, man?"

"I haven't been doing anything," Greg answered in a little less groggy voice than before.

"So, you ain't been tapping that spicy ass? That's not what everybody is saying. That explains why you been staying in town. I knew something was up with you and Simone, but I never would have guessed 'Cleava'. Damn, man. How low can you go?" Karl laughed hard into his cell phone as he sat back in his Audi TT. The huge amount of traffic was not a problem today. Give him more time to chat with his big bro.

"What's that supposed to mean? If what you're saying is true, you banged her first. What's that say about you?"

"I'm not married to Simone. You know what I mean? Somebody actually said that yesterday, man. I heard it with my own two ears. They didn't know who I was, and the guy said and I quote, 'Why would anybody in his right mind hit that when he's got that fine wife at home? Have you seen her?' So, I'm asking bro, what's up?

"So, you saw them, Sheva and… who was it anyway?"

"The Procurement Manager, Marisa Johnson. Whupped her ass from what the report said. Put your girl in the hospital. Concussion and multiple contusions and possible broken or fractured ribs. Holes all in her face from spike heels-- Kind of sad actually. Beat down in front of all your co-workers and nobody there to hold her hand on the way to the hospital."

"Where'd they take her? Did you hear if she's all right?"

"Cedar Sinai. I heard she's still there for observation. Did MRI and CT scan to make sure no brain damage was done. I'm sure she's fine, or she will be. Might need some counseling when she gets out. Other than that, she's gonna be just fine," Karl said, enjoying every moment of this conversation. "You want some company when you go to see her? You don't sound so cool. What's wrong? You can't be that surprised, can you?"

"Sheva was my colleague. That's all. Sheva would never say anything about that."

"Oh please. It came out the horse's mouth. Sheva told the whole world yesterday when she jumped across the desk on to Marisa's back. It doesn't take a rocket scientist to figure out why. So how long have the two of you been at it?"

"A little over a year, I guess."

"How'd Simone take that? Well, that's a dumb question, huh, bro? That's why you were never home when I called the house. She put your dumb ass out, huh? Seriously, man, what were you thinking?"

Greg sat up in bed and thought for a moment. His head was getting clearer and clearer the longer he stayed on the phone. The thoughts that were running through his head were tumbling over each other for top spot. *What needs to be done about damage control? Is it too late for that? Should I fire Sheva? Dumb hussy. What was I thinking? Of all the females available, you chose that one? What if Simone finds out?* Do you really think she'd care? She's in Las Vegas. He was so lost in his own thoughts that he hadn't heard his brother rambling on and on.

"...that little number down in Joliet that worked at the university. What was her name? Angela... Angelica, something like that.

Remember? You brought her to the conference in Atlanta that time? She was cute. In a boyish kind of way if you like that type of thing. I kinda wondered about that but she turned out to be all woman from what I saw in the rental car on the way back to the hotel…"

"Hey, I got to go. Got some stuff to take care off. Catch you later."

"Yeah, I bet you do."

"Have you talked to Pops lately?" Greg asked trying to change the subject.

"Nah, it's been a couple of weeks."

"Me neither. Probably should check in sometime soon."

"Yeah, this weekend maybe."

"Sounds good. I'll get back with you," Greg said as he stood up, holding on to the side of the bed.

"Yeah, he and Simone usually have dinner on Saturday, if I remember correctly. Why don't we make it a family thing? What do you say? Planning on bringing a guest?" Karl's take on the irony of the situation wasn't lost on Greg. He loved his younger brother but sometimes he felt that there was some resentment brewing inside of him. Why though? He couldn't answer that but he was sure that it was there.

"I'll see you at Pop's this weekend. Got to go now."

"Yeah, have a good day, bro. Be careful though. The hawk is flying low today. Who knows what might fly in on the breeze," Karl said before he disconnected from his brother. He hadn't even waited for Greg to say goodbye.

Chapter 13

"I would like to keep you another day to make sure that you are healing properly from the concussion and the bruised ribs. The second CAT scan still shows slight swelling and we want to be sure that it subsides before we release you," the doctor said. He had heard about the incident that brought this patient to this particular hospital at this particular time. *Poor thing. So vulnerable and naïve or just foolish. I bet she thought he was going to marry her. Waste of a perfectly good human being. Look at her. Deer in the headlights. Definitely showing signs of shock. Maybe I should increase her dosage of Valium and Haldol. Mental note—write her a prescription when she leaves. Give her the name of a good therapist. Looks like she's going to need one. Gurupriyanka Patel would be a good choice, I think. Takes one to know one.* The doctor unconsciously rubbed his fingers across his wedding band and chewed on his bottom lip.

"I would like to go home now…please. I just want to leave. I feel fine. Honest, I do. I can't stay here. My head is feeling a little sore but that will pass. Nothing more than a slight headache," Sheva said. She was having a hard time processing what had happened to her over the past two days. It was a blur. Which was probably a good thing. The last thing she remembered completely was her conversation with Greg two nights ago. That, she wished she could forget. She could hear her mother's voice in her head, "*Lo que sucede alrededor viene alrededor.*" She was right. It came around all right and when it got behind her, it bit her in the ass. Sheva hadn't seen her mother or spoken to her in seven or eight months. The last time they had been in each other's presence, Sheva had a huge surprise to share with her mother—Greg. They flew to New York for a weekend and stopped in to visit Mrs. Meayla Morales-Diaz and her stepfather Mr. Hernando Diaz. She thought her mother would be happy to find out that her daughter had found a handsome, professional, financially secure man. All Meayla saw was a married man.

"Es casado?" Meayla asked her daughter when Hernando escorted Greg into the living room to watch the World Cup finals.

"Si, Mama. He's married but they are getting a divorce," Sheva answered her mother, trying not to sound like a four-year-old who just got caught smacking her baby brother.

"¿Por qué llevaba un anillo?" her mother asked as she rushed around the kitchen banging pots and pans.

"He just wears it, that's all. It's just habit. He's worn a ring for years and he just hasn't taken it off," Sheva said. It was a good question that she had asked herself on more than one occasion. If he's so through with his wife, why *did* he still wear his wedding ring?

"¿Cree que va a casarse usted?" her mother said as she stood in front of the stove, her back facing her daughter.

"Si, Mama, si! Of course he is going to marry me. We love each other. We're going to start a life together and have a family," Sheva protested too loudly.

"¿Cómo se puede estar seguro?" her mother said in a soft voice that spoke volumes of love and pity.

"I can be sure because we love each other. I told you that already. I am sure because I know. That's all. I know."

"¿Romper su casa?"

"No. I did not, Mama. I did not break up their home. If she had given him what he needed, he wouldn't have turned to me."

Before Sheva could finish her breath, the back of her mother's hand made contact with the side of Sheva's face. Sheva gasped from the shock as much as from the pain. She looked at her mother who had turned several shades of red in the past few seconds.

"Don't you *ever* let something like that come out of your mouth again! Do you hear me? It was someone just like you that took your father away from his home and caused us years of hardship and pain. She was a tramp. A whore. That breaks my heart to think that my only daughter would grow up to be the same thing. You must know that that man doesn't love you. When he comes to his senses, he will go home to his wife and beg her to take him back and look at you like you are good for nothing. I know this to be true. If you don't believe me, ask your padre. Oh, that's right. You can't because you don't know where he is because even after all these years, he is too ashamed to talk to you. Maybe you do this thing because your papa was not here when you were young. The blessed virgin knows I tried to be madre and padre to you. But I failed you somehow. Hernando tried to be a father to you, but I guess it was too late when he came along. My daughter, stop this before you get hurt. This will not go unpunished. I am telling you if you continue to do this thing—don't speak to me anymore. You are not my daughter."

That was the last time Sheva spoke to her mother. As she lay in the hospital bed, it occurred to her that the only person that she wanted to talk to was the one person she had disappointed the most. She leaned over carefully in the bed to avoid adding to the pain she experienced every time she took a breath and reached in the cabinet drawer and took out her cell phone and dialed her mother's number.

Chapter 14

Everything was moving in slow motion for Greg this morning. After talking to Karl and hearing the drama of the past twenty-four hours, he decided that he needed to prioritize his actions today. Hell, he could manage one of the largest cities in the nation, he should be able to manage his own affairs. *Funny choice of words.* He stepped into the shower and was about to turn the water on full blast when he wondered if Simone had heard about 'The Smackdown'. If she had, would she tell him not to worry about moving back into the house? If she hadn't, he still had the opportunity to soften the blow beforehand. He stepped out of the shower and went back to the bedroom. He sat on the bed and dialed Simone's cell phone. It went straight to voicemail. He wasn't expecting that. Didn't wives answer the phone when they saw that their husbands were calling? *Maybe that's only wives whose husbands live in the same house with them and aren't sleeping with other women.* He hung up and sat on the edge of the bed staring at the phone. *She'll see that I called. I should leave a message. And say what? Did you hear the slut I was sleeping with got beat down at work the day after I begged you to let me come back home? Can I still come back?*

"Good morning, lady. It's me. Just calling to say have a great day. I thought that maybe I could take you to lunch when you get back. I thought we could go to that little place you like on the Loop. It'd be just like old times. Get back to me when you get this." *It'd be just like old times. What was that supposed to be? A bad old movie or what? No wonder she doesn't seem to care whether or not you come back.* He stood back up and went back to the shower. He stood under the needles of steaming water. The steam rose along with his blood pressure. How was this day going to turn out? Could this have happened at a worse time? *And whose fault was that?* He got out of the shower when the hot water ran out. Checking his wardrobe, he looked for something that looked casual yet costly. Not for Simone so much as for everyone else. When he walked into the hospital, he wanted to give the impression that he was in charge. That whatever they had heard was just a rumor, couldn't possibly be true of such a well-dressed man.

When he finished dressing, he looked in the mirror and was satisfied with what he saw. He looked around the condo and sighed. *I am glad to be going home. I hate it here. Too quiet. Too much time alone with my thoughts. I will be glad to sleep in my own bed. With my own wife.* Greg took another deep breath and walked out the front door to start his event filled day.

He had talked himself into feeling pretty good in spite of the circumstances of the past few days. Really, he wasn't responsible for any of it. Right? It's not his fault two grown women had a cat fight in the middle of the office while he wasn't there. He wasn't the one whose personal affairs *(there's that word again)* were being aired in public. Well, it was actually but he wasn't the one doing the airing. He was an innocent victim in all this. Right? Sheva just seduced him during a time of weakness while he and his wife were having some incompatibility issues. If what his brother said was true, Sheva was used to seducing people. *At least the people in your family anyway.* Greg put his foot on the accelerator to cover up the growl that was deep in his throat when the cell phone rang. He didn't look at the number because he was sure it was Simone rushing to return his call from earlier in the morning. He pushed the button on the dash and said in his deepest 'glad to hear from you, baby' voice, "Hey, what's up?"

"Good morning, Greg. How's it going?"

"Morning, Vernon. I wasn't expecting to hear from you this morning."

"I bet you weren't. So how are things with you? Gotten any golf in since we last played a round? Seems like you may have been pretty busy lately. I owe you for the beating I took last time we played. It's about time for payback. Don't you think? We have to schedule a day as soon as it warms up. Lots to discuss with an election year in our midst. Speaking of election years and all that surrounds them, I heard a whopper of a tale about your neck of the woods. Tell me, is there any truth to it?" The unexpected voice belonged to the mayor— Vernon Armstrong. His melodious voice was his trademark. It was said that every woman that voted for him did so just to keep him talking. Darth Vader, Barry White, Vernon Armstrong—all brothers of the baritone.

"Depends on what you heard, Vernon."

Vernon's laughter resonated through the earpiece and settled deep in Greg's guilty conscience.

"Depends on what I heard, that's a good one, old pal. We both know that we've got some stories to tell. Remember that convention in Atlanta? So do I. Since that's the case, I had to think twice when I heard about the incident in your offices. Didn't want to come to any false conclusions. So help me out, I have to be ready to do some pro-active damage control over here if the need arises. Fill me in on what's going on."

"Nothing… I was working from home yesterday and didn't hear about anything until this morning. Seems like two employees had words and got into a knockdown, drag out fight. It got pretty raucous and the officers from downstairs were called up and took both parties downstairs. Well, actually, they called the paramedics to take one to the hospital." Greg said with as innocent and dis- interested voice as possible.

"Were any charges pressed?" The mayor was in his official mode now. Greg could hear the change in his voice. It said, "how is this going to affect me?"

"Since it was assault, I'm pretty sure both parties will be charged."

"That isn't going to look too good when that comes out on the court dockets. When the press gets hold of it, they are going to have a field day. So, I was thinking that since you obviously know the parties involved, you might be influential in making this go away quietly."

"So, Vernon, what is it that you are asking me to do?" Greg was so wrapped up in the conversation that he didn't hear the first three or four horn blasts from the cars in the next lane. He swerved back into the correct lane. Thank God for the quick maneuverability found in BMWs. *I could be dead now. Considering this conversation, I might wish I was.*

"Well, City Manager Dyson, it seems that you are responsible for what transpires in your office, it occurs to me that a headline that reads 'City Planner Subpoenaed in Office Brawl' would not be the type of publicity you would be looking for in the near future. Attach that to a front-page picture of a thong smothered by someone that you know that well, I can't see that you would want that. Neither would your wife, I presume. How is the lovely Simone anyhow? I haven't seen her in quite a while. I should do a better job of staying in touch with my constituents." The phone went dead for what seemed like minutes. Greg was sure that he didn't have that kind of luck. His cell phone was fully charged, and he had coverage through the service that guaranteed clean clear service no matter where you were. What luck.

"Mayor Armstrong, I am on my way to the hospital to visit with Ms. Morales as we speak. I am sure that both parties can come to an understanding that meets everyone's needs," Greg finally responded.

"Glad to hear it, Greg. I know you are a man that can get things done. You wouldn't have gotten this far if you weren't. Hell, one day you'll probably have my job… But not this election cycle…. or next, if this doesn't go away quietly. We all have vested interests in what happens with these two ladies. I'm sure you know the right things to say to convince Ms. Morales to see things your way," the smooth voice had returned.

"And what about Marisa? What right words should I use to convince her? She was the one who was attacked, remember?" Greg retorted, trying to stand on ground that wasn't there.

"You will think of something that works for all of us. I have faith in you. Not every man has your skills. That's why you are city manager. There's something up your sleeve. You just need to reach a little farther to find it… Beautiful Chicago morning out there, don't you think? You can feel the chill from in here. Have a great day, Greg."

Greg arrived at the hospital, stopped by the gift shop and purchased a cheesy carnation and bear combo that didn't say too much if anyone would check—not big enough to say I love you or so small to say that I really don't care, I'm just expected to do this bouquet-- and took the elevator up to the fourth floor. When he stepped out, he checked the wall to find out which direction led to Sheva's room. To the left-Psychiatric ward. *Appropriate.* To the right- Rooms 4001-4100. Straight ahead- 4101-4200. Greg looked at the visitor's pass in his hand one more time for the room number. He looked at his smiling face plastered all over the pass with his signature underneath. Anyone who wanted to know could find out that he was here visiting Ms. Morales aka The Dumb Bitch I Let Ruin My Life. Imperceptible to human eye but caught by electronic surveillance, Greg shook his head, drew in the deepest of breaths and proceeded straight ahead. Pictures have been painted on cave walls of men being torn to shreds by savage saber-toothed tigers that seemed happier.

4198 was the number he was trying to avoid, so he walked past it twice. *Avoidance will do you no good at this point. You should have avoided it the first time she sat on your desk with no drawers on.* Since it was easier to face Sheva than his own conscious, Greg walked into the room on his third walk-by. It was empty. The breath he had inhaled so deeply two minutes ago, he exhaled just as deeply. My luck has held out, he thought. Came to check on her and she wasn't here. I did my part. I can leave with a clear conscience. I am the man! Luck be on my side. *Maybe not.* Just as Greg turned to leave the room, Sheva rolled up in a wheelchair pushed by a nursing assistant the size of one of the columns in the parking garage. Sheva looked startled and started to shake. The nurse noticed the change in his patient and put his hand protectively on her shoulder.

"You okay, Ms. Morales?" he asked, the concern apparent in his voice.

"I…I'm fine. I just got a chill that's all. And I wasn't expecting company," she whispered.

"I will get you an extra blanket if you want, once I get you into bed," Mr. Column volunteered.

I bet you would do something once you got her in bed. Greg moved aside and tried to look like this was just a visit from boss to injured employee, so he smiled at Mr. Column and then flashed his cosmetically enhanced pearly whites in Sheva's direction.

"Hey there, lady. Thought I would stop by and check on you personally. Make sure they are treating you good here. Seems like they are. Personal service and all."

Mr. Column helped Sheva out of the wheelchair and positioned her comfortably in the bed. You would have thought she was a nun by the way she covered herself and constantly looked down at the floor.

"Okay Ms. Morales, you alright now?" Mr. C asked with the kind of concern you have in your voice when a small child is afraid of the dark.

Sheva shook her head up and down the way a small child does when they are afraid of the dark and trying to be brave.

"I'm fine," she whispered, more to herself than to either of the two men standing in the room. "I'm fine."

"If you need anything just push the button and someone will be right here. You know that right? I get off in an hour. Carla will here tonight and so will Micki. You take it easy, you hear? It's gonna be alright. Okay?" Greg walked out of the room while Mr. C got the wheelchair's leg flaps folded in.

When he came out, Greg asked him, "So how's she doing?"

Mr. C looked at him like who wants to know.

"She works for me, and I was out of town when I heard that she was in the hospital. Wanted to check on her, let her know that we were thinking of her." Greg said all that with a straight face as if he had rehearsed it for whoever he might have to use it on. Which he had.

Being a college graduate, working on his graduate degree in nursing, Mr. C was quite adept at reading body language and gauging a person's heart rate and blood pressure by just glancing. And at a glance, this man in front of him looked like he was about to hyperventilate in about two minutes. *Better leave the chair handy in case I have to put him in it.*

"Okay," he replied.

"How is she doing?"

"She has experienced a great deal of trauma and her body is recuperating as well as can be expected. Psychologically though… she is suffering a great deal. Her trauma is manifesting itself in bad dreams and aversion to loud noises. Kind of like PTSD. You know, Post Traumatic Stress Disorder."

"Really? That's terrible. Poor kid. Is she getting any help for it? Therapy or something?" *Translation, has she told anyone about me?*

"What did you say your name was?"

Oh shit. "Greg Dyson."

"Greg Dyson. Well, Mr. Dyson, I am sure that if Ms. Morales wants to talk about it to you she will. That's her personal business. I just do my job which is to help all my patients recover as quickly as possible. She looked a little surprised to see you. I think you are the first person from her office to visit," Mr. C said. "Have a good visit. I hope seeing you cheers her up a little. You might want to keep it short." He turned around and pushed the wheelchair down the long corridor. *I doubt she's glad to see you. Bet that's who she was banging and he's here to do damage control. Wedding ring on his finger means he's screwing around and doesn't want the wife to leave him if she finds out. Asshole. And her… she is so naïve and needy. Trying to replace a missing daddy most likely. How dumb can you get? Probably thought he was going to leave his wife and marry her or some dumb shit like that. Stupid.* He parked the chair and walked to the elevator. *Mental note. Send flowers to my wife this afternoon. Tell her I love her and she means the world to me. Stop by the florist and get a dozen roses and maybe a bottle of wine to take to my shorty's. Let her know how much I appreciate her. Yeah, I need to phone home and tell 'em that I'm going to be working late tonight.*

Mr. Column rolled the wheelchair down the hallway as he contemplated his evening plans.

Greg walked back into the room and looked at Sheva lying in the bed. She looked small and helpless. *Damn, Marisa really beat her ass!* Her effervescent overly sensual personality seemed to have deserted her. He placed the flower bouquet and bear on the little ledge under the window. It did very little to fill up the empty space. He stood there a moment trying to figure out how to start this conversation.

"Hey there, lady. How are you doing?" Greg asked trying to keep up the façade should anybody happen to be within listening distance.

"I'm going home soon. Probably later on today so you won't have to come back here to visit me," she said.

Does she actually believe that shit? She looks like death warmed over. A Puerto Rican raccoon or something.

"I'm sure the doctors will release you as soon as you are strong enough," Greg responded in as positive a voice as common sense would allow. "You need to get your strength back. Don't worry about returning to work until you are well. I'm going to transfer someone into your position until you are better. If you find that you need a leave of absence for a while, we can work something out. After all, planning is what I do," Greg said lightheartedly. It didn't go over too well. He could see from Sheva's trembling lower lip that she wanted to say something but was afraid to open her mouth for fear of what might escape from it.

Greg…," she started.

Oh no, here we go.

"Greg…," she started again.

"Yes, Sheva?"

"Did you mean those tings that you said to me the other night?"

Yes. "I said a lot of things because I was drinking and some of them were probably kind of harsh. I am sorry."

"Chu didn't answer my question, Greg," Sheva said quietly through swollen quivering lips.

All that money I spent on speech lessons didn't do a bit of good. Of course, have your head bounced off the floor a half dozen times might affect anybody's speech.

"Sheva…I was drunk. Let's be honest. Where did you think our relationship was going? How could I marry you under the circumstances? Do you know what kind of scandal that would cause? Baby listen, you know when you started this that our being together was just…well, it was just what it was," Greg hemmed and hawed like the true politician he secretly thought himself to be.

Sheva propped herself up in the bed slowly, the pain showing itself in every movement. "So, what was it—our relationship—what was it exactly to chu?"

"It…was…fun. Yeah, that's it. It was fun. We were both adults who knew what we were getting into. No more, no less. And now we need to move on and get past this before it turns into a major scandal for the city and the mayor and for me."

Sheva seemed to have stopped listening after his first three words. All she could hear was *it… was… fun* over and over again in her fevered brain.

"Fun? Is that all it was to you?"

Big fun if that makes you feel any better. Bigger fun than I've had in my office on a desk in years but still…that's all it was. Not worth losing my career or my wife over. Greg took a breath and looked at Sheva as she tried to exhibit some form of composure.

Talk to her like a patient—in the ward down the hall…

"Sheva, we both know that this couldn't continue and if it did, the end result would be that we would always remain friends. As I said earlier, we have to move on and make this all go away before it turns into something ugly."

"It already is ugly. I thought you loved me. I thought we had a future together. I don't understand Greg. I took you home to meet mi mami y papi. Didn't that mean anything to chu?"

No.

"Of course, it did. I felt honored that you thought enough of me to introduce me to your parents. But that doesn't change where we stand at this present moment."

"And where is that, Greg?" By this time tears were streaming down her face and the veins in her neck were starting to pop out. Mr. Column would have said she was on the verge of a major meltdown if he had been in the vicinity.

"Well, Sheva. Judging from what I heard, charges have been filed and this incident will be on the court dockets within a matter of weeks. Do you have any idea what that means? The charges are assault and battery and that carries anywhere between three to five years in this state. And since there are pictures—lots of pictures -- neither you or Marisa can do anything but plead guilty."

"So, you're saying that I'm going to jail? Who told you, Karl?" Her voice was barely audible at this point.

So, Karl did bang her. That no good son of-- "There may be another way…" Greg's voice trailed off for effect.

"Another way?" Sheva's drawn on eyebrows rose even closer to her scalp.

Sucker. "Yes. I've heard that in some cases, the courts would rather the parties go through mediation instead of taking the case to trial."

"Mediation? Like bargaining or something? I don't get it," she said.

I must have been out of my mind. That's what happens when you let the little head do your thinking for you. "I don't know all the details, but I heard that it works and then all the charges would be dropped and none of this need go any further than it already has. Maybe you could check into it when you get out of the hospital later."

Sheva laid there with a blank look on her face for a moment. "I just want my life back," she said blankly.

"This would be the best way to do that, baby."

Sheva rubbed her temples as if the effort she had put forth was taking a major toll on her capacity to process any more information. "My head hurts," she sighed.

Why am I not surprised? Greg said to himself as he leaned over and quickly pecked her on the forehead, keeping one eye trained on the hallway.

"I hate to leave you, but you look a little tired. You need some rest, so you can go home later. I'll check on you tomorrow." Greg slid smoothly out the door and down the hallway before Sheva realized that he never really answered her questions. Did she even ask them? Where did they go from here? Did he still love her, or did he have to say those things to keep his wife from ruining his career?

"That must be it. He's forced to act this way to keep her off his back. I knew it."

She shook her aching head up and down in affirmation of her newest thought.

"That must be it. What else could it be?" she whispered to herself as Greg walked out of the room without looking back.

Chapter 15

Simone was rubbing her eyes, trying to make the soreness that comes from reading the same words over and over again, go away. *What am I missing? There's got to be something here, I just can't find it.* Everyone else in the room was showing similar signs of fatigue and frustration. The small group of colleagues were quickly becoming a small group of friends. Each of them bringing their own specialties and eccentricities to the table. The funny thing was that no one felt uncomfortable showing their true selves. It seemed that the eight or nine hours they spent in each other's presence was the high point of each one's day. It was if their immersion in the lives of Shamel and Tyreek somehow removed their need to think about their own personal lives. They laughed, told jokes, usually instigated by Mike, ate at least two and a half meals together, sometimes three, disagreed, agreed, and listened to each other intently every day for the past six weeks.

The day had started out no differently than any of those other days. Continental breakfast courtesy of whoever's turn it was. Today, it was Simone's. The 'guys' as she fondly called them, had been talking about breakfasts that their mothers used to fix when they were little for the past two weeks. So, she decided that this morning she would surprise them and bring them the healthier version of what they were used to.

Don't want them have heart attacks on my watch. Got to keep them in tip top shape with their pretty behinds.

Don't start first thing in the morning.

What? All I said was their behinds were pretty. True or not true?

True.

All right then. Let's get this party started.

It's not a party.

One person's work with beautiful men is another person's party…

"Ooommph, this is bangin'," said Mike as he gobbled a second biscuit dripping with butter. Sly and Jason were at the counter refilling their own plates while Simone smiled a very satisfied smile as she ate her scrambled eggs and turkey bacon.

"Mrs. Dyson," Mike said between bites, "you got skills, girl. Would you consider taking in a boarder just so I can eat your cookin'?"

Jason and Sly joined Mike in complimenting Simone on her culinary prowess and told her how deeply they appreciated the fact that she worked so hard to start their day off on the right foot.

Leela would have never thought of anything so thoughtful, Jason thought. Then he continued to think.

Wouldn't have made any difference any way, you know she can't cook.

 Ten going on eleven years of marriage and she still burns boiled eggs.

Did you ever think that might be her way to keep from having to cook? Think about it. You get home and she's just starting to fix dinner and then something goes wrong, or she don't feel well, or some other drama and you end up fixing dinner again. Check it out tonight and see if it ain't so.

Jason sat down across from Simone and started to eat.

"Thank you for being so…kind." He wasn't sure that conveyed what he wanted to say, but it was the best he could do and retain his professional composure. Over the past month, he had found himself noticing things about Simone that went far beyond the task of bringing two heavy duty gangbangers to the table to keep them out of jail. She was incredibly good at what she did and maybe that translated into her being an empathetic and reflective listener 24/7. It was true as well that she was easy on the eyes, in a different sort of way. *Mim would have a field day reading her face. Almond eyes so dark and changeable, they peer inside of you. Full lips that white women pay good money for. Smooth eyebrows with natural arch…* Jason smiled to himself. *Maybe I'll take a picture and show it to Moms. What will she say?*

"You are very welcome," she replied. "We've been working so hard and such long hours, I thought it might be nice to relax over home cooked food. Something about eating together makes people closer."

Whoa. I got your closer. Where'd that come from? Next time let me do the talking if you are going to flirt with the man.

"I'm sorry, that didn't come out right, did it?" Simone stumbled over her words as her butterscotch cheeks turned five shades of red.

"It came out just fine. It's true. Eating together crosses a boundary from formal to friendly, distant to more connected…." Jason started.

Go ahead clean this up.

"The four of us have grown a lot more connected over the past month. I think that is only going to help Shamel and Tyreek."

Good save on that one. She'll never notice just how connected you wish you could be.

Jason finished his home fries and got up to clean his place at the table.

Simone exhaled and felt like a fool as he walked away.

You need to stop blushing. I can't believe I said that! He must think

I'm a tramp.

He doesn't think any such thing. How can you be so blind? The man worships the ground you walk on. You are soooooooooo blind. No wonder you still ain't getting none. From nowhere. Hubby will be moving back in this weekend, right? Let's see how that works for you.

Oh, shut up, would you? I swear, you pluck my last nerve.

Likewise.

I wish I could get away from you sometimes.

Oh really?

Yes, really.

Can you say lobotomy?

Mike was washing his hands as Jason entered the men's room before they got started with the day's work.

"Hmmm, hmmm, hmmm…if she were a biscuit, I would sop her up like gravy," said Mike as he dried his hands.

Jason looked at his friend and shook his head. "You and your country ass, I don't believe you sometimes. She's a lady or haven't you noticed?"

"Yes, I have. Yes, I have. I also notice you defending her honor… But I digress… Lady Biscuit is smart, lovely to look at and she can burn. I wonder—"

"Don't even go there," Jason started.

"I ain't say nothing… I was just speculating how such a phenomenal woman ended up married to such a two-timing asshole."

"What are you talking about?" Jason stopped washing his hands and gave Mike his full attention.

"Where have you been? Leela keeping you under a rock again? The City Manager's executive assistant got beat down by a coworker 'cause she was getting down with the boss. Saw it on Facebook and Twitter. Guess who the City Manager is?"

"Nah…That Dyson?" Jason almost choked on the words. He had heard stories over the past couple of weeks but never put much stock in it. He knew enough to know that his peoples love to tear down successful folk. Mexican crab syndrome at its finest. He also knew enough to know that if you hear something from enough places, there's probably at least a hint of truth to it.

"Yup. One in the same. I thought you knew. Can't understand it. She really is a good woman. I know ain't nobody perfect but she's damn near closer than the bimbo whose big ass got beat down and videoed. Here let me show you." Mike reached in his pocket and pulled out his phone. "It's on YouTube too—here look."

Mike held the phone so Jason could see. He wasn't sure he really wanted to. It felt like some sort of betrayal of his and Simone's burgeoning friendship. Like seeing her naked through a slightly open door and staying to watch, then pretending it didn't happen.

And help me understand the problem with that?

The door to the bathroom opened and both men looked up from the exploits of the two lady brawlers to see Sly sticking his head in the door.

"Hey, man. Did you see this mess about the City Manager's assistant?" Mike asked Sly. He walked in and Mike turned the phone around so Sly could see. His eyebrows rose as his nose turned up. It was if he could smell what the pictured probably showed.

"It doesn't surprise me. Sick fuck." Sly mumbled as he turned his head sideways to continue watching the action.

"Whoa, man. Where'd that come from?" Mike asked.

"Nothing. I just know that Greg is no good and this just proves it,"

Sly said.

Jason finished drying his hands and made a three pointer to the trashcan. "I don't need to see anymore. That's between those two. Simone is waiting for us and we're in here disrespecting her marriage."

"We're not disrespecting it. Her husband has a pretty good handle on that, don't you think?" Mike said as he kept looking at his phone. "This is better than WWF," he said to no one in particular.

Sly shook his head and walked toward the door behind Jason.

"All I know is," Sly said as he looked back at Mike, "if he hurts her anymore, I will kill him myself."

Jason did not turn around, but he smiled slightly.

I got your back, bro. Mr. Dyson will be as good as dead.

Chapter 16

Today was Friday. It had to get here at some point, Simone thought. She kept thinking that she should be happy or nervous or something but all she felt was a continued sense of numb. Greg was moving back into the house this weekend and Simone was surprised to find herself not looking forward to it. *Maybe if I fix something special for dinner, that will help a little bit.*

The man is moving back into the house that he shouldn't have moved out of in the first place and you are going to reward him by fixing a special dinner? You really have lost your mind, haven't you?

He is my husband, after all. I should treat him like it.

Since when has he acted like your husband? Not for the past year and ten months. But who's counting? Why do you think he's coming back now, huh? That shit on Twitter?. You think that had anything to do with it? Bring that up in pillow talk tonight. There will be pillow talk tonight if he has anything to say about it. And I'm sure he will.

Be quiet, will you? I can't take any more of your mouth. Just let me handle this.

Oh, like you handled everything else? Like you sat there and let him escort you out of the Christmas party and take you home and leave to spend the night 'elsewhere'? Like you didn't say anything when the joint credit card bill came in with charges for an anniversary bouquet that went somewhere 'cause it wasn't your anniversary? Like you...

 Shut up! Just shut up! I know what I did and didn't do. I had my reasons.

Your reason is you're afraid. Fearful. Why? What's he going to do to you? Huh? Not talk to you? Run up bills you have to pay? Embarrass you? Leave you? Oh gee, he's done all that already. Hmmm. What's left, sister girl?

Simone closed her eyes and rubbed her forehead. The guys were taking longer in the bathroom than teenage girls at the prom. Maybe that was a good thing considering the thoughts running through her head. Was she really up to putting on the 'face' and trying to concentrate and appear professional today? Everything had been going just fine and then she and Jason had a moment to talk and now this. Why was he constantly on her mind? She felt like a little girl with her first schoolboy crush. She didn't want to admit it, but she had an idea that that was the real reason she wasn't thrilled about Greg coming home. It would interfere with her quiet time when she thought about Mr. Copeny.

Her thoughts were interrupted by her three associates entering the room. Everyone settled themselves around the table and prepared to work for the next several hours without a break. Today was the last day of preparation before bringing Shamel and Tyreek together for the first time. The planning that had gone into getting the two of them to agree had taken weeks. Jason and Mike did all the leg work to get the gang members to be willing to participate. Somehow, they seemed to think that they had options. Jason and Mike were convinced that someone was behind the young men's reluctance to go into mediation. They truly believed that they couldn't be tried as adults and if they were they wouldn't be convicted. Who would have the power to keep them out of jail? Why would they be willing to even take that chance? These questions came up over the past few weeks, but no one could find an adequate answer.

So here they sat, making final plans for the big day and all Simone could think about was what was going to happen when she got home this evening.

Get a grip, girl. You got all night to be upset. It's not like it's the first time. Put on your face and get on with your day.

"So, Monday is the big day," Simone started. "What do we need to think about and prepare for that we might have overlooked?"

Jason spoke up. "Me and Mike—Mike and I are going to pick up Tyreek and Shamel. Not together, of course. We'll be here by 8:30. We turn them over to your capable hands and let you do your thing. We will be observers. You say that the sessions last two hours, right? So, we should be done by 11:00, we take them home and come back to debrief and prepare for the next session if they do not resolve their conflict and come up with an agreement. Does that sound about right to you guys?"

"Call me a pessimist but I don't think they will resolve it in two hours," Mike said.

"Well," said Simone, "we will see on Monday. Whatever happens is on them. We just give them the opportunity and direct them through the process. That is all we can do. Most of the time that is enough."

"Okay, that sounds good. Simone and I will get here and set up the mediation room around 8:00. It's on the first floor. We can check it out after lunch, nobody should be using it this afternoon. So, we are spending the rest of the morning in role play. Toss a coin or pick a number, who wants to be Bad Boy One and Bad Boy Two?" Sly asked as he looked at Jason and Mike.

"I've been bad a long time, so I'll be Number One Bad Boy," Jason quipped.

"That is true," said Mike. "I'm just his wingman."

Chapter 17

Greg sat in traffic drumming his fingers on the steering wheel. He was going home. After all this time. His suitcases were in the trunk and the dozen long stem yellow roses were on the back seat. She should like that, he thought.

You think? You hope. You put her through some shit. You know that, don't you? And you expect her to act like you been on a business trip for a year and a half?

She loves me, he thought. She's glad I'm coming home.

Are you sure about that?

Of course, she loves me. Why wouldn't she?

'Cause you lied and cheated and left her. She hasn't sounded real thrilled about you coming back.

You think there could be someone else?

What do you think? It's been over a year. Would you have waited for you?

Hell, no.

Me *neither.*

He pulled out his phone and hit speed dial for Simone. He had reprogrammed her into the number one spot last night. He figured that was his way of erasing the past and protecting himself if she was the type to check his cell phone for phone numbers. He knew Simone wasn't like that but… it's been a long time, people change.

"Hey lady, how was your day?" Greg tried to sound upbeat like he had been calling her every day on his way home. "Was wondering where you wanted to go for dinner tonight. I was thinking Taglioni's. You love their eggplant lasagna and Vinnie loves to make yours with that special sauce…"

Simone was quiet for a moment. "Greg, I had a really long day. I was thinking that we could eat something here."

"Sure, what did you have in mind? I could stop and pick up a bottle of wine, red or white, a blush maybe?"

"Whatever you like is fine. I hadn't planned anything for dinner. I was thinking about ordering from the Dimitrios's. Maybe a hot Reuben? You do still like those?" she asked.

Ouch.

"Sure, that's fine. We can go out any time. I just thought it might be nice to get out and celebrate, that's all," he said.

More quiet. "Celebrate? Did I miss something?" Simone asked.

Greg growled and hoped it didn't travel through the Bluetooth.

Ouch again.

"I just thought it would be nice to celebrate our first night back together."

Oh hell no. He must be out his mind! Tell him he is out his mind!

Celebrate my ass! Like he is doing you a favor. Bull—tell him to kiss your entire—

"Maybe tomorrow. I am really tired. Tomorrow would be much better," she said.

Coward. The Cowardly Lion has nothing on you, that's for sure.

"Okay, then. Call the order in and I'll pick it up. How's that sound?" Greg asked. "Tomorrow would be better, we'll really have something to celebrate by morning, won't we?"

Simone was about to ask what but then she understood. *The mister has big plans and high hopes for this evening, doesn't he? But you knew this, right?*

"Hey, you there?" Greg asked.

"Yes, I think you must have driven through a dead spot or something." *Or something.* "I'll call it in as soon as you hang up." *Hint hint.*

"Would you like me to bring you anything special? Can I do anything for you?"

"No. I am just fine. Thanks for asking. But there's nothing I need from you."

Damn, I knew she could not have meant that the way it sounded. I'm tired and a little nervous. Dealing with shit today was stressful. Then walking into work and having to act like everything was okay was a bit much. Nobody said nothing but you could see it written all over their faces. Laughing behind my back, stopping conversation when I walked into the room. I'm not stupid...well maybe I am, I got myself into this mess and now I need to get out of it. And my own wife is talking to me like that? Nah, it's the stress. Everything is going to be fine at home. She will be so happy to see me. Of course, she will...

Chapter 18

Greg pulled into the drive and up to the garage. He had to leave the car outside of the garage because the code for the door opener didn't seem to be working. He walked around the path to the front door and dug in his pocket for the house key. Should I just unlock the door and go in or should I knock? I live here. Greg thought.

Not for the past eighteen months, you haven't.

As he was thinking through his options, the decision was made for him when Simone opened the door. She stood there, tall and regal even though she was in her bare feet. Her form was apparent even in jeans and a scoop neck sweater. Black was her favorite color and she wore it often. Like tonight. The black sweater allowed the smooth creamy color of her skin to stand out. Greg stood there for a moment admiring what a stunning woman she truly was.

"Hello, Greg," she said as she stepped aside so that he could enter.

No welcome home or nothing? Just 'Hello, Greg.' So much for being happy that I'm back.

"Hey, lady. How was your day?"

Did that sound natural? Something a husband would say to his wife.

Simone had her back to Greg as she proceeded down the hallway into the living room. She found herself trying not to roll her eyes as he tried to sound natural as if this were any other day of him coming home after work.

Is he for real? Honestly, what was I thinking?

He's my husband—for better or worse, and so on and so on.

I get so sick of your do the right thing attitude, you should have shut the door in his cheating face.

"My day was busy and productive. That makes for a good day. How was yours?" she said as cheerfully as she could muster.

Did she know that I went to the hospital today? Who could have told her?

"My day was good. Very productive as well," he answered. "I brought dinner from the deli. And a bottle of Kendall Jackson to celebrate our good day."

Oh yippee. He knows I don't drink. Did he bring anything special for me?

"And for you, I got some pomegranate juice and San Pellegrino."

Yeah, he is really trying tonight, isn't he? Let's see how long this will last. I give it until Sunday.

Saturday morning arrived the same way it always did, early. There was sunshine this particular Saturday and birds singing bird songs. It was all good. For somebody. Somewhere. Else. Simone slid out of the bed and picked up her favorite robe from the floor at the foot of the bed where it had fallen the night before. She walked out of the bedroom into the master bath and closed the door. Greg was lying in the bed with his back turned. She couldn't see whether he was awake or asleep. She really didn't care either way. That surprised her a little, but hey? *What's a girl to do?*

Now that they were 'officially' husband and wife again, sleeping in the same bed and all that that entailed, Simone wondered what that meant in terms of how she spent her time. For the past year, she had been doing as she pleased with her weekends. Now that Greg was back, did that mean that something had to change, and she needed to spend her time with him?

Why should I? New habits die hard. I've got things to do, places to go, shoes to buy.

She turned on the faucet to the shower as hot as she could stand and stepped under the spray as it grew warmer and warmer. Melting into the depths of her. Just like she liked it.

Greg can't do this for you can he? I bet I know someone who can though...

 A small smile curled her lips as she closed her eyes and let the tension flow out of her. She breathed in the steamy moist air and considered her options for the day. It looked lovely outside and a long drive would do her good, she thought. Maybe into the country to a vegetable stand or into the city to an organic grocery. Decisions, decisions.

Give yourself a break today. Don't plan anything and see what the day brings. If you've learned anything at all over the past few months, it should be to let go. You don't control anything anyway so just enjoy the fact that it's a beautiful day and you are alive. What's better than that?

There was a knock on the door to interrupt her thoughts. She heard herself sucking her teeth. She was glad the shower was still running. That way Greg didn't hear anything but the running of water.

"Yes?" She replied to the knocking.

"Hey, need me to wash your back?" Greg asked through the door.

No and hell no.

"I was just getting out. Maybe next time," she said.

She turned off the water and stepped out of the walk-in shower. Donning her thick comfy terry cloth robe, she walked to the door and opened it. A waft of steam and hot air hit Greg in the face.

"Hi," she said.

"Good morning. I thought we could have breakfast," he responded.

"That sounds nice, but I really wanted to get out and run some errands this morning," she said.

"Oh," Greg replied. "Can't they wait?"

"I would prefer that they didn't."

Whoa, that was a good one. High five on that one girlfriend! There might be hope for you after all.

Simone hadn't meant to say it that way, but it was what she had been thinking. Sometime over the course of the past twenty-four hours some sort of selfishness had reared its ugly head. She wanted to do some things that she wanted to do. And right now, she wanted to be alone. The only way that was going to happen now was if she left the house. Her refuge, her safe place.

So be it. If you got to go, you got to go.

She still had a soft spot and a kind heart, so she added, "I'm kind of use to being out and about on the weekend. Sort of hard to break the habit. Sorry. I'll work on it." She smiled at him as best she could.

"Okay then. I'll get showered and we can go ahead and get going," he replied taking the smile as an invitation.

"That's okay. I've got my day all planned out and you wouldn't enjoy it one bit. I'll see you when I get back." She turned back into the bathroom and wiped the double mirror with a towel.

Greg stood in the doorway not knowing whether to enter or leave. After much thought, he decided to go back into the bedroom.

Good choice, Simone thought as she looked into the mirror. *What?* She waited for some smart remark to pass through her head. There wasn't one. "That's what I thought," she whispered to herself.

She got dressed in her favorite jeans and black V-neck tee shirt. Black three inch-heeled leather ankle boots and short red leather jacket with matching gloves. It was the weekend so she wrapped a colorful scarf around her head and donned her Ray-Bans. She approved of what she saw and knew that she must have looked really good when Greg said, "That's the shirt you are wearing?"

"Yes, it is. It's quite comfortable actually. Is there something wrong with it?" she asked innocently. She looked down and ran her hands across the material.

Yeah, it makes you look too damn good.

"No, it's fine. Just thought you might get cold with your chest all open like that," he replied.

"That's what the jacket is for. Besides, I'll be in the car or in the store somewhere. I'm good. In fact…" she walked over to the closet and took out a bright turquoise and burgundy silk pashmina that complimented the red jacket and threw it over her shoulders and around her neck. "How's that?" she asked. Now, not only did she look good, she looked stunning. Model perfect.

"Just don't want my baby to catch a cold," he said walking up to her and planting a kiss on her cheek.

"I'm good. Thanks for the concern." She smiled and scooped up her purse and headed for the door before she bit a hole through her own tongue. "See you later," she called back over her shoulder.

"When will you be back?" Greg called after her as she walked out the front door.

"No clue. I'll see you when I see you. At least you know that I am coming home."

Simone pulled out of the driveway and let the car decide which way it wanted to go. She was so excited and pleased with herself for not asking Greg for permission to leave the house. She felt like she thought an adult should feel. Free. Free to make her own decisions. He hadn't been worried about where she had been going or whether her chest was covered up for the past year, why then, did it seem so important now? One night back in the house and he thought everything was back to the way it was before? He's my husband, not my owner.

I don't think so. That little girl don't live here anymore.

She stopped at the red light and smiled again. This time a real one. A great big one. The man in the car next to her saw her beautiful face and smiled as well. He waved and she waved back. Wow. It felt good to make your own decisions.

No matter the consequences?

No matter.

Okay then. Let's make some more decisions. Country or city?

City.

Shoes or vegetables?

One thing at a time. We'll see when we get there.

Simone thoroughly enjoyed the drive into the city. The Volvo handled so smoothly that she accelerated a little more than necessary, actually, a lot more than necessary, but what the heck. It felt good to be in her own personal space, not feeling invaded. Like she felt last night. It was not a good sign when you spend the night with your own husband, that you feel invaded the next morning and flee the house.

I didn't flee, I left in a determined manner.

Whatever.

At least I'm out for now.

It will get better. I just need to adjust to having someone around again. It has been a while.

It sure has. You'd think you'd feel better than this.

I feel just fine.

You should feel better than just fine. It's been over a year since anyone touched you and all you can come up with is you feel just fine. What is wrong with this picture? Remember the look on his face when you handed him a condom?

He looked so surprised—and hurt, what did he expect?

Especially when your husband has been sleeping with other women.

Hush.

No hush, it's the truth.

Simone knew that what she was thinking was true. Last night had been an odd experience and she had tried to escape this morning as quickly as she could. She remembered times past when she and Greg would linger most of the day in bed just to be close to each other. Last night she turned her back on him and pretended that she was completely spent from the throws of passion so he would leave her alone. How sad was that? The long drought was over obviously but how would a person dying of thirst feel if the first thing someone gave him to drink after being lost in the desert was vinegar and brine?

Now if it had been----

Don't even go there.

What? I was just thinking...

That's why I love you girl, so dramatic.

Simone chuckled to herself as she shook her head. The man in the car next to her smiled at her. Two in one morning.

It must be your lucky day.

She smiled at him the same way she smiled at the other man twenty miles back.

He seemed to sit up a little higher in his seat.

Nothing like seeing a beautiful woman happy first thing on a Saturday morning. Somebody is extremely lucky waking up next to her every day. Last night must have been something.

If he only knew.

Just as Simone was exiting 10B, Etta reminded her that her love had come along. She let it play twice wishing that the words of the song applied to her. She placed her finger on the telephone icon on the dash. Whoever it was wasn't Greg. He had his own tone so that she was never surprised or shocked when he called. Whoever it was wasn't him. So that was good.

"Hello," she said brightly.

"Good morning."

Simone's brow furrowed as she scrunched up her eyes trying to place the voice.

"How are you?" The voice was deep and soothing. *No, it's not possible.*

Anything is possible.

Why would he be calling me on a Saturday morning? *Because he wants to.*

"I'm fine," she responded. Her voice not sounding as sure as her words.

"You don't know who this is, do you?"

"Truthfully no. I am driving and I don't have access to the Caller ID right now. Would you be so kind as to enlighten me?"

The soft laughter on the other end made Simone's heart skip a beat. She had heard that laughter before and her heart had done the skip beat thing then too. Why is he calling me?

'Cause he wants to talk to you. Duh...

"Jason?" The question hung in the air while a whole new set of questions arose in Simone's mind.

"Is something wrong?" she asked.

"No. I just wanted to touch base before Monday. Make sure we were straight on everything."

"I thought we had discussed everything on Friday. You and Mike are picking up Shamel and Tyreek. Sly and I will have the room set up when you all arrive. Time is set. I think we are good." Simone was trying to sound professional and not giggle like a teenybopper with a school-girl crush.

"Yeah, I knew you were on top of everything. Sometimes I just want…"

I just want to hear your voice.

"… I want to double check. No harm, no foul."

"I understand. Better safe than sorry."

"True that. So… what are you up to on this beautiful Saturday morning? I hope I didn't wake you." Jason remembered Sly saying something about Greg running back home with his tail between his legs. Jason couldn't help but feel a little perturbed that Greg would be back in the house and by default back in the bed with Simone.

And why is that, I wonder?

Shut up.

Is that the real reason you drank so much last night?

I said shut up.

"No, you didn't wake me. I've been up for a while and I'm on my way into the city as we speak." Why am I telling him this? It's none of his business.

You want him to know. You're excited that he called. You know good and well he didn't call to 'double check' nothing. He wanted to talk to you. Yeah, he did.

"Really? Where you headed if you don't mind me asking?"

"I'm going to Tally's Market. They've got the best selection of ethnic and organic food in the city and I'm in the mood to do some serious veggie shopping. I'm thinking about having a garden this summer. I want to pick out some seeds and plants. How sad is that? Nothing more exciting to do on a Saturday than shop for vegetables."

Baby, do whatever you like. As long as you aren't in bed with your husband, I am cool.

"Talley's on the west side, right? I grew up three blocks from there. My mom and stepdad still live over there. Would you mind if I dropped by and said hi?" Jason bit the inside of his cheek and held his breath expecting a reasonable excuse as to why that wasn't a good idea. He waited. And waited. The silence kept coming.

"Um," she started, "this is still America and I don't have authority to stop you."

"I was hoping that maybe you might want to say hi to me as well."

You have no idea.

"That would be very pleasant, actually. I just got off the interstate. Probably be there in about fifteen minutes. How come you are out and about so early this morning?"

Had to get out of the house.

"Going to stop in and see my moms for a bit and then catch the guys for some ball and hang out. Everybody needs to get a breather every now and then."

"Amen to that…"

"Excuse me? Couldn't hear you too well."

"Oh, must be the connection. Nothing important."

"So, I'll see you strolling down the aisles in a few then, right?"

"I guess you will."

"Don't think I'm a stalker or anything."

"I know better than that. You're not the type and I don't inspire people to do those kinds of things."

You have no idea what you inspire people to do.

Jason hung up the phone before he said what he was thinking. He couldn't believe he had said the things that already came out of his mouth. No harm, no foul. He just wanted to see her for a few minutes. On the weekend. Just the two of them. Without their spouses around.

What's the harm in that?

Jason felt something he hadn't felt in a very long time—anticipation. He was actually excited about the possibility of seeing Simone. She truly was becoming a special part of his life and he liked the feeling. Anticipation. What a concept. Anticipation of good conversation. Anticipation of being listened to and accepted, no matter what you say. Anticipation of a good laugh or two.

Anticipation of seeing her lovely face and beautiful smile.

Yeah, that too. Let's be honest, I enjoy her company.

Maybe more than you should.

Since when do you act as my conscience?

Since you did what you did last night.

I don't want to think about that.

Well, you should. 'Cause the next time you do it, I'm not going to be your conscience and that guilt you tried to feel isn't going to be there anymore. Think about that.

Jason gripped the wheel a little tighter and signaled to change lanes as he came up to Haverty Street heading towards the west side. As he drove through the familiar streets towards William and Mim's brick rowhouse, he found his mind wandering back to last night.

Jason had parked in front of the house and wondered why he wasn't anxious to get inside after a long day at work.

Maybe because you enjoy work more than you enjoy home lately.

 He took a deep breath and got out of the car. He walked up the front steps and heard Drop It Like It's Hot blaring through the door. He opened the door to find Maia twerking her ten year old behind in the middle of the living room floor. Jason walked over to the TV and switched it off since he couldn't find the remote. Maia stopped dancing like the hootchie on a video and turned around.

"Where'd you learn to do that?' Jason asked his daughter as she ran into his open arms.

"Mommie taught me," answered Maia as she snuggled up to Jason.

"Mommie taught you?"

"Uh-huh. Let me show you some more…"

"No baby, that's alright. What did you learn in school today?" Jason asked, trying to change the subject.

"We learned that everything is made up of particles and stuff like that. So, you know what that makes you Daddy?"

"I don't know baby, what does that make me?"

"A smarticle."

"A smarticle?"

"Yup. You are smart and you are made up of particles."

"Did you figure that out all by yourself?

"Yup."

"Well, I guess that makes you a super smarticle. And Mommie and me are just smarticle."

"No. Mommie is not a smarticle," Maia said losing the smile that was on her face.

"Why would you say that, baby?"

"Mommie forgot to pick me up from school again today. Poppi had to pick me up 'cause Mommie Mim was at the nursing home visiting Auntie today."

Jason didn't want Maia to feel the anger that was building up inside of him, so instead of interrogating her, he used a technique that he learned from working with Simone. "Maia, help me understand what happened when school was over today."

"Well, I went out to wait for Mommie when the bell rang and she wasn't there. I waited and all the buses left and she still wasn't there, so Mrs. Chavez stayed with me and called Mommie. Mommie said she forgot and she would send someone to pick me up. Then I waited in the office until Poppi showed up. Mrs. Chavez gave me a peppermint while I sat in the office. She let me answer the phone. It was fun except I thought that you were coming to get me. We went to Mommie Mim's and Poppi's and waited for Mommie. Then she came and blew the horn and I came outside and got in the car and we stopped at Friendly's and she got me a chocolate milkshake. It was good and now I'm full. So, I was trying to dance off the milkshake."

"Where's Mommie?"

"She was upstairs. I think she was making herself pretty for you 'cause she was painting her toes and curling her hair," Maia giggled. "I think she wants to go on a date and get kissy kissy." She giggled some more.

I got her kissy kissy.

"Go play for a while in the family room until dinner."

"Mommie burned the hamburgers so there is no dinner. Can I watch SpongeBob?"

"Yes, you sure can."

"Yippee!"

Maia kissed Jason on the cheek and ran down the stairs to the family room. Jason rubbed his head, took a deep breath and headed up the stairs to confront his wife.

Yeah, I got your kissy kissy.

He walked upstairs to be greeted by the sound of rushing water. Looking into the master bedroom, he saw that the bathroom door was closed. The shower was running full blast. Steam was curling up under the door. He knocked firmly on the door. No answer. He knocked again, calling out Leela's name. No answer. He stood there for a moment with his hand on the doorknob. Then he realized that the water was just running. The sound of the flow was uninterrupted by the movement of a body in the shower. In other words, the shower is on but nobody is in it.

She's pretending to be in the shower, so I'll go the fuck away. Well pretend all you want. You have to come out sometime.

With that Jason turned around and went downstairs to see what he and Maia could make for dinner.

After the Mercedes fiasco, he and Leela had found a level of civility that was bearable. To the outside world everything looked fine. Loving husband and wife, beautiful daughter. It was all good until the front doors closed on the mini-mansion. Leela would tippy tippy pause up to the bedroom and shut the door and talk on the phone to her friends and family or stay on the computer shopping or social networking until the wee hours of the morning, and then feign sleep when Jason finally forced himself to go upstairs to bed. Maia would keep Jason company as long as he would let her, then he would tell her a story and put her to bed after her bath.

Jason was on his fourth or was it fifth beer of the evening, when he finally decided it was time to call it quits. He thought he could handle his beer, so maybe it was the innumerable shots of Captain

Morgan before the beers that were causing him to feel a little out of sorts. The late basketball game went off two hours ago, so it should be safe to go upstairs. He climbed the stairs and stuck his head into Maia's room like he did every night. That caused him to smile and gave him a pleasant enough feeling so that he could continue down the hallway to the master bedroom. He snickered to himself.

Who was the master here?

Must have been the beer talking. He opened the door and went through to the bathroom and undressed. He walked softly to the bed and climbed in. Leela's back was turned so he moved slowly as not to disturb her. Hopefully she was really asleep tonight and not pretending like she usually did.

Here we go again. I wonder if I'm the only person uncomfortable in my own bed tonight… I wonder what Simone is doing right now.

With that thought, he closed his eyes and let his mind wander as he wondered and drifted off to sleep.

He woke up when he smacked himself in the face trying to clear away the gnat that was flitting around his ear. When the gnat started to giggle, he opened his eyes and swore to himself that three beers was his new limit. Maia was curled up on the bed with a peacock feather that she had gotten on their trip to the zoo last weekend.

"Daddy, you should have seen your face. You look funny when you sleep," she said, waving the feather in the air.

"That's because you took all the beautiful and there's nothing left but funny," he replied as he scooped her up and hugged her.

"You look funny and you talk to yourself," she squealed.

"Oh really?"

"Yes, really."

"And did I say I'm gonna get that feather and tickle you with it?"

"Nope."

"Did I say that you are the bestest little girl in the whole entire world?"

"Nope. And bestest isn't a word."

"Neither is nope."

"Who's your beautiful goddess?"

"Excuse me?"

"That's what you said in your sleep."

"Exactly what did I say?"

"You said 'you're my beautiful goddess'."

"And you heard me say that?"

"Yup. Right here, right before I stuck the feather in your ear last time. Who were you talking to? Mommie's not here. She's downstairs."

"I was talking to you, honey. Even in my sleep you are my beautiful, beautiful girl and I love you."

"I thought so, 'cause you said that too."

Jason was wide awake by now and wanting to change the subject. He was doing that a lot lately.

"What is your mother doing downstairs? How long has she been down there?"

"She was gone when I woke up. That was around eight. I know 'cause I wanted to watch cartoons and you were sleep and Mommie wasn't here so, I watched SpongeBob in the kitchen and had some cereal and then Mommie came home with breakfast from Bob Evans. She was putting it on the plates. I think she wants you to think that she cooked it. So, don't tell her I told you, alright?"

Jason crossed his heart and hooked pinkies with Maia.

"Our secret, just you and me."

"Okay. Let's go. I like the French toast. I get the French toast." Maia sat up and held out her hand to her father who grabbed it. He was about to get out of bed when he noticed that his sweat pants were balled up beside the bed. He frowned and wondered what the heck happened last night.

I'm talking in my sleep. Leela is going out to get breakfast. Sweats on the floor…

What do you think happened last night?

Only one way to find out. Get dressed and go downstairs to the beautiful goddess.

I may have been drunk but I sure as hell know that I wasn't talking about Leela when I said that.

So, you wanna put a name to that thought?

I want to know what happened and what I was dreaming about.

Only way to know is to get up.

"Maia honey, go on down and I'll be right there. I got to brush my teeth."

"Okay daddy, I'll save you a slice of French toast, but you better hurry. Mommie is singing some old love song for the millionth time and she needs to stop. So, hurry up." Maia jumped up and skipped out the door.

Jason bent over and picked up his sweatpants and walked into the bathroom. He looked at himself in the mirror as if searching for clues.

What the fuck did you do?

Jason showered and tried to remember what had happened after his rum and beers binge last night. No matter how much steaming hot water ran on his head, he couldn't clear his mind enough to recall what had taken place. The last thing he remembered was turning off the television and lying back on the sofa.

Thinking about Simone.

He turned off the water and dried off. Standing in front of the foggy mirror, he wondered how bad he would look when he wiped the steam away.

Go ahead. Do it.

He wiped the steam away and carefully scrutinized his reflection.

Not bad for not knowing what the hell happened in your own house last night. Whatever it was, it must have been good if wifey is pretending to cook for you this morning. You musta tore it up.

Jason took a deep breath and put on jeans and a polo shirt. He headed towards the steps and stopped abruptly. He turned around and went back into the bedroom's cavernous walk-in closet and pulled out his gym bag. He checked the contents and changed into gym shorts and sweats, placing an extra pair of jeans and shirt in the bag with a towel and toiletries. He had forgotten that he was supposed to meet Mike and Sly to play some ball this afternoon at the Westside YMCA. Slowly, things began to come back to him. His head was clearing a little bit and he remembered walking up to the bedroom early this morning. He had fallen asleep and stayed on the sofa until around three. Just like most other nights. Something was different last night though and he had gotten himself up and went upstairs to sleep in his own bed that he was still making payments on. Sleep came quickly or maybe it was just the alcohol. Somewhere in the midst of his sleep or drunken stupor, he rolled over and opened his eyes. Leela was sleeping soundly, mouth slightly open, warm breath drifting his way.

You loved her once.

I still do.

Are you sure about that?

Yeah, I'm sure.

But something has changed, bigtime.

That happens when you've been married for a while. It's normal.

Is it? Be honest with yourself for once. If she hadn't been pregnant, would you have married her?

Whoa. Stop, right there. I am not having this conversation. Leela and I have been together for eleven years. We've made a life.

And how is that working out for ya, huh? You are not happy and you can be honest about it...when has she ever been happy? Nothing you have done has made her happy, satisfied her, made her love you. All you wanted was to be a good husband and father. Something that you had no experience with growing up. Promised yourself you would never do that to a child....

I ain't up for this shit right now. All I want is to go to sleep.

Is that all you want? You want something else whether you admit it or not. Or should I say someone?

Jason laid on his back staring at the ceiling in the dark room. The only light coming in through the window from the silvery moon. His mind wandered to what it might be like if Leela was happy. What it would be like if she could agree with him about anything, if she could connect with him the way married people were supposed to, if she were supportive of him.

...if she were Simone.

That's all he could remember as he walked down the stairs, his thinking interrupted as his nostrils opened wider as he smelled something he usually didn't smell in his home unless he had prepared it himself.

"Hey baby. Good morning." Leela stopped piddling around the table to tippy tippy over to Jason. She leaned into him and stood on her toes to plant a slow, passionate kiss on his lips. He tried not to look surprised and closed his eyes to receive the kiss that he had so longed for such a long time. He felt himself responding to Leela's kiss in a way that he hadn't felt in years. The moment was interrupted by the giggles issuing from Maia who was sitting at the table.

"Mommie and Daddy sitting in a tree, K-I-S-S-I-N-G," she sang happily.

Leela stopped abruptly and stepped back from Jason. He let her go and looked at her for a moment. What was that about?

That was a response to something you did last night. I figured as much. *True that. But let's be honest, at least with yourself, who were you doing it to or with? Your wife? I don't think so. Who were you kissing just now?*

Let's not do this right now. Whatever happened last night made Leela happy this morning. And a happy Leela makes for a happy house. I was here with my wife. Right where I was supposed to be. Let it go. I'm doing what I'm supposed to do—being a husband and father. *Being everything---except happy.*

The three of them sat down at the table and had breakfast together, laughing and listening to Maia tell funny stories about school and soccer practice. Leela was even letting Maia have center stage—not stopping her in mid-sentence trying for one-upmanship of a ten year old. It was all too surreal. You would have thought Leela had morphed into a twice baked June Cleaver and the Beave was waiting just outside the door.

After they finished breakfast and spent a bit more quality time, Jason rose from the table. Maia pounced up as well and ran to get her soccer bag.

"Mommie come on. I don't want to be the last one to show up for practice again. The coach makes us do extra suicides and I hate those. Last time I was the only one who was late. I don't want to be late for the third time. The coach says it makes me look like a weak link. I don't want to be a weak link."

"Okay baby. Mommie's coming. Let me just say goodbye to Daddy first."

Since when does she want to say goodbye? She usually just jiggles out the door. Leela sashayed up to Jason and put her hand on his chest, making small circles with her tiny fingers.

"So, what are your plans for today? I thought we might spend some time together today while Maia is at practice. They always go to Chucky Cheese's afterward so she'll be gone for most of the day. We could go to the outlets and pick up something pretty for me. And then stop at Diamond Row and look around," Leela cooed.

"Why would we do that, baby?" Jason got that feeling in his gut that told him that he was on the verge of being hoodwinked and bamboozled. Malcolm knew what he was talking about even if he had been referring to white people.

"Well, after all that you said to me last night about being your goddess and all, I thought that I should be representing during the day too," she giggled.

Now I know where Maia gets it from.

"You are my goddess, baby," Jason said a little less than enthusiastically. "But I promised to meet the guys for some ball this afternoon in town, so I gots to go. We can schedule the shopping thing for next week maybe."

Yea, that's it buy yourself some time to figure out what the fuck is going on. Oh shit, here it comes.

Leela's lip was starting to twitch. A sure sign of what Mim would call 'tuning up to cry'.

"You and 'the guys', all the time. You and the guys. First it was Mike, since college, always Mike… Mike this, Mike that, and now it's this Sly person. I bet he is too. Who names their child Sly anyway? Since you started working with him and whoever else you work with, you don't pay any attention to me. How come they're so special? Huh? I just wanted us to spend some time together, like husband and wife. I should have known better. What? You were just saying those things last night 'cause you wanted to get some? Well, you got it, didn't you? I gave it to you real good too, didn't I? I should have known better. You didn't mean a word of it did you? That I was beautiful? That the first time you saw me I took your breath away? That being with me makes you whole? What was that all about, huh?"

She turned around and stomped towards the garage door. "Come on Maia, you're daddy has to go play with his friends now," she said as she slammed the door behind her.

Jason stood there stunned while he tried to digest what had just taken place over the last hour. Loving, ecstatic wife turns into purveyor of death and destruction. How'd we get here? Mental note--- lock up the rum and beer until you get a grip on your emotions. You pay too much money each month to sleep out in the garage.

Count your blessings. At least you didn't call her by the wrong name.

Chapter 19

The parking lot of Tally's was packed as it usually was on a Saturday morning. All of the suburbanites making their pilgrimage to the city for the day. Organic vegetables for their tables, overpriced handbags for their arms, sophisticated haircuts designed to look unsophisticated, and on and on. And here sat Simone in her pearly Ice White Volvo S80. She felt a little conspicuous waiting in the row for the black BMW 750i to pull out of the parking space. Guilty was a better word. The car looked exactly like Greg's. The poor defenseless unsuspecting husband that she had left at home this beautiful Saturday morning to meet a man. *Not just any man. If you are choosing to feel guilty for buying vegetables, go ahead. You were planning to come here long before you found out that he grew up right down the street.* So did Greg and his brother, actually. Not right down the street but somewhere not too far away. He never talked about it. Small world when you get out in it, isn't it?

She pulled into the parking space and got out of the car. The brisk air felt really clean and refreshing this morning. It had the feel of snow, without the snow. The thought of a good hard snow made Simone smile again. This was a good day for that it seemed. She snagged a cart that was left in the middle of the parking lot, knowing that there would be very few left inside the store. She loved to come here. It was like Christmas, Kwanzaa, and the Fourth of July. Everything and everything at your fingertips. She started at the produce and was completely lost in the jicama and pomegranates when she heard a familiar voice.

"My mother says that you need to be really careful when purchasing those. If you don't use them quickly, they get pithy on you."

"Really? Pithy? Your mother said that?"

"Yeah, she is really into the weirdest things. You should meet her. She would love to read your face."

Simone looked at Jason and started to laugh until she saw that he wasn't joking.

"Seriously. She reads faces. The ancient Chinese art of Meng Shieng. Face reading."

"And what do you think she could possibly read in my face?"

"Why don't we find out?" Jason had put his hand on her elbow and she had tried not to flinch. "I was going over there after I left here. Need to talk to my Pops about something that happened yesterday. You could talk to my mom and keep her out of my conversation for a minute." He did smile that time.

"Aaah. Run interference for you?" She nodded just like a conspirator should. She also noticed that Jason hadn't removed his hand from her elbow. "What?" she asked.

"You look really lovely today," he said.

Ole Greg musta put it on her last night. Hit it like he owned it or something.

Shut the hell up.

What? She looks beautiful. What does that to a woman? A good stiff—

I told you to shut the hell up.

Nah, seriously, women look like that when they're in love.

Simone scrutinized Jason's face, wondering what was really going on behind those clear, dark eyes. She watched them change from being filled with sheer pleasure to something resembling sadness in just an instant. She half expected him to crack a joke or something, but he just stood there, waiting for her to do or say something. She swallowed and looked at the floor, then back at him.

"After I get my veggies, I'm willing to run interference for you. But you owe me big time, you hear me?" She poked her finger in his chest in a manner she hoped he took as playful. She smiled at him. Not like she had smiled earlier in the day but a tender, warmhearted smile. Like a connection of some sort existed between them and they had yet to acknowledge it.

"Cool. I'll let you get your veggies and I'll pick up some munchies for after the game. You might want to join me and the guys for that too. Make it a working weekend. Mike and Sly would love to see you. That would make the teams even."

"Don't push your luck. I played guard in college. It's been a while, but I still got game," she replied as she went back to inspecting the jicama.

Jason finally removed his hand from her elbow and stepped back.

"So, I'll meet you at the registers in about twenty minutes? Is that enough time to get your groove on? You seem to got it real bad this morning," he said.

You have no idea how bad I got it this morning.

"That sounds great. Keep me from doing but so much damage. See you in a few," she replied. What am I doing, she wondered. I can't believe I'm going to this man's parents' house. I must be out of my mind. What is wrong with me?

Oh Lord, here we go! Let me step back so I don't get in the way of you beating yourself up. It's not like he's taking you home to introduce you 'cause he's gonna marry you. Get over it girl. The man likes you and enjoys your company. Although right now, I don't understand why. I can't believe you said yes with your scared ass. Good job. Acting like a grown up. It's about time.

Don't make tell you to –

I know, shut up.

The two of them met at the registers with their purchases. Simone put hers on the belt behind Jason's, who told the clerk that they were all one order. She nodded at the couple and started to ring the groceries.

"Hey, wait. These are two separate orders," Simone interjected when she saw what had happened.

Jason looked at the clerk and waved his hand. "It's okay the way it is. You can go ahead."

The clerk went back to swiping the Doritos and PowerAde. Simone looked Jason in the eyes. She saw a look there that said, 'just let me do this' and she decided not to argue. She looked straight ahead wondering what to say. He leaned over to her and whispered in her ear.

"You said I owed you big time for running interference with my Moms. I'm a man of my word," he said. He moved away and swiped his debit card and paid the bill. He tried not to smile on the outside as much as he was on the inside.

This shit ain't even funny. You're paying for her groceries like she's gonna fix them for you. You done lost your damn mind.

Yeah, but it makes me feel good this morning. My wife wants me to spend hundreds of dollars in payment for services received last night. This woman has never asked me for anything and would never think about it. The way I see it, I've saved over five hundred bucks this morning. Besides, I get to spend some more time with her.

Priceless.

They walked out to the parking lot carrying several bags. They laughed when they got to the Volvo because they had to search the bags to find whose items were whose.

After sorting and resorting, Simone followed Jason out of the parking lot and through his old stomping ground to Mim's house.

Since it was still relatively early, there were parking places on the street in front of the house. The neighborhood was quiet and you could tell that it had been part of the revitalization project that one of the former mayors had kept from his campaign promises. When Simone was about to open the car door, she closed her eyes and wondered again what she was doing.

When she finished her breath, Jason was standing there with his hand on the car door ready to help her out. She grabbed his hand in her gloved one and he squeezed it as if offering moral support. When they turned around, a tall, dark, muscular Ving Rhames look alike, and a Lela Rochon clone stood in the doorway. Jason's parents, Simone thought.

No wonder he's so damn fine.

She could immediately see where he got his dark chocolate color, beautiful eyes, and his strong chin and full lips.

"You favor your parents," she said to him as they walked up the sidewalk, still holding hands. He just smiled at her.

"Hey Moms, Pops. Ya'll don't miss a beat, do you? One day I'll sneak up on you."

"Not today, boy," William said. "Your momma had a feeling you would be here this morning , although you are a little later than she expected." William glanced at Simone.

"Got sidetracked at Tally's," Jason replied looking at Simone. "This is Simone Dyson, my colleague and friend. We're working on the mediation project I told you about."

Mim smiled at Simone like a long-lost friend and stepped aside to welcome her into her home. William gave her a hearty handshake and pat on the back.

"We have heard a lot about you and the project, so it's really nice to be able to put a face with the name now," Mim said softly. "Have a seat. Would ya'll like something warm to drink? It's chilly out there this morning. Hot chocolate, tea, hot lemonade?"

"I'll have my usual. Thanks," Jason said to his mother. "No such thing as caffeine in this house. I have to settle for chicory when I'm here. Not too bad actually. Once you get used to it."

"Good. Maybe it counteracts all that coffee you drink at work," Simone replied. She felt unusually comfortable in this house. Everything was placed as if it served the purpose of causing peace and tranquility. A real feng shui thing going on.

Kind of like my house.

"Simone," Mim asked, "what would you like?"

"I'd like tea, please."

"Well, how about we take a look at your choices and let your body choose the one best suited for you today," Mim said as she rose from the sofa. She gently touched William's arm as she rose. It was an unconscious gesture that moved Simone to her core. It was so natural. Something existed between the two of them that was deep and profound. It went beyond just being together for many years. Simone could understand why Jason thought it perfectly natural to reach out to her in the store this morning. She cast a glance at Jason who was leaning forward in the armchair across the room. He smiled at her.

"Good luck making a choice. There are too many to mention. Have fun," he said.

She followed Mim into the airy and spacious kitchen. You could tell it belonged to a woman who was at ease there. The open shelves on the far wall were filled with labeled apothecary jars filled with loose leaves of different teas, raspberry, elderberry, chamomile, kava kava. Simone stopped reading after several moments. There were also little brown bottles with droppers in them lined up on the shelf under the tea jars.

"Well, let's see… how are you doing this morning?" Mim asked as she looked closely at Simone. Her complete attention was focused on Simone. The funny thing was that Simone did not feel uncomfortable at all. It actually felt good to have her undivided attention, like she was the most important person in the world. How wonderful it must have been to grow up with a mother who could make you feel like that with just a glance.

"I'm feeling…pretty good actually," Simone surprised herself and giggled a little, not wanting this woman to see the blush that was slowly creeping up her neck.

"You sound surprised that you feel good."

"Honestly, I am. I don't usually show up uninvited at someone's house first thing on Saturday morning. This isn't like me at all."

"Well, you were invited, and I am glad that you chose to take him up on the invitation. He wouldn't have asked you if he didn't think very highly of you, believe me. I like it that Jason wants us to meet you. We didn't even meet his wife until the day of wedding. So, this is a real step for him."

"Me too, I guess. I tend to be more—" Simone searched for the right words to explain her thoughts.

"You seem like you are a very careful person who thinks through the consequences of every action."

Simone nodded and smiled timidly. "Yes, that's definitely me. I'm always asking myself what if, what if this, what if that, how is this going to look to somebody else, what could happen, stuff like that." She couldn't believe that she was sharing those private thoughts with a woman that she just met.

"Sounds as if you are fearful and timid and that those emotions are a burden to you."

Simone threw her head back and laughed out loud. Mim tilted her head to the side and searched Simone's face patiently waiting for an explanation. "I'm sorry, but you sound like me in mediation. Wow. I've never experienced someone reflecting my feelings back to me."

"So, judging from your response, you are fearful at times?"

"Most of the times, truthfully. Sad but true."

"It must take a lot of energy to show confidence to the world while you feel fearful inside."

Shaking her head again, Simone took a deep breath and pinned her eyes on the fascinating woman sitting across from her. "You are very perceptive. I try really hard to keep that under wraps. You figured it out in less than ten minutes. I've got to work on that," she said quietly.

"No honey, you hide it really well. Nobody else would ever see it."

"You did."

Mim smiled at her. She reached across the table and touched Simone's hand lightly. "Simone, it's written all over your face. Let's make you some tea. I've got something that will fix you right up."

Jason and William went downstairs to the family room to have a little privacy. It was evident from the conversation and laughter coming from the kitchen that supervision of Mim and Simone was not necessary. Jason picked up his cup of chicory and headed off behind his stepfather. As the two men walked down the stairs William looked back and said, "She's real nice. Don't meet those kind of people very often."

"Yeah, she is good people," Jason said in as casual a voice as possible.

"So now it seems we got two things to talk about. First things first though. You wanna know about what happened yesterday with Maia. Let me ask you something first. How'd you find out? Who told you?" William asked as he took a bottle of water out of the refrigerator behind the bar.

"I see some Heineken in that fridge. Moms know you got those?" Jason quipped, trying to ease the tension he felt building inside of him.

"She don't bother my stuff, I don't bother hers. Lord knows being with your momma has changed me for the better. Don't drink half as much as I used to. Don't need to. I'm a better man. But I ain't perfect. It's awful early but you can have one if you want."

"No thanks, I'm good. I've sworn off for a while," Jason said.

William was quiet for a minute while he sipped his water.

"So, who told you?"

"Maia mentioned it yesterday when I got home from work. She was upset about it. Leela ain't got shit to do all day. She should at least be able to remember to pick up my daughter from school. Damn. I don't ask much from her, you know?"

"Maybe that's the problem."

Now it was Jason's turn to sip for a moment. "Help me understand what you mean by that?"

"She gives you what you expect. Nothing. You work all day and all she does is whatever makes her feel good. You've been husband, provider, father, and probably housekeeper, cook, maid, and babysitter to hear Maia tell it."

"What's my daughter been saying to you all, old man?"

"Nothing but the truth. Out of the mouths of babes and all that. Maia talks about her day and her day is filled with adventure and details of her life. Which includes you and her mother."

"I swear I try. I do everything that I think I'm supposed to do to keep a family together and it's never good enough. I don't know what she wants from me. House ain't big enough, car isn't expensive enough, jewelry didn't cost enough." Jason took a breath, then continued. "You remember when we got married? I swear on my grandmother's grave, a week after we were married she wanted me to get her another ring because the one I got for her 'wasn't making the statement' that she wanted it to make." He shook his head.

"You sure you don't want a beer?"

"I'm good. Things ain't what they ought to be. I know I'm a grown ass man and I'm smart enough to know that life ain't perfect but it don't have to be a constant struggle in my own house. I guess I understand now why Moms stayed by herself all those years. Smart woman."

"Better to be by your damn self than with the wrong person. That's for sure. Which brings us to the second thing to talk about. The lovely lady upstairs."

"What?"

"What do you mean what? You bring this woman to our house who is not your wife and all you can say is what? You know your momma is plying her with flowers and unraveling all the mysteries the woman has, don't you? You better be careful. I could tell when she got out of the car that Mim liked her."

"She's my colleague and— how could you tell?"

"She said one word after she looked at her… Water."

"Oh Lord…We're working together right now, that's all—"

"You're talking to me, remember? What's going on? I know you ain't hitting it. She ain't the type. I can tell this is more than just wanting some ass. And that's dangerous. You can get that anywhere. You don't bring that home to meet your family. So--what?"

In an effort to prolong the inevitable answer he would have to give his uncle, he said, " Oh, and I am the type to cheat on my wife?"

"You a man, ain't you? Therefore, you're the type. And no, I ain't never looked at another woman after I was with your momma. The only reason I looked before was 'cause I couldn't have her. Those kind of women do something to you and you don't want nobody else after that. But there ain't that many of them around. If you run across one though, look out. That's why men cheat. They looking for the women like the two upstairs. Start sniffing up the wrong trees at a young age, ruin a man for life. Remember boy, I knew you from way back when…Back when you was a young buck smelling yourself and everything in a skirt. Oh, what was that child's name? The one you used to sneak in your momma's house? Something like your wife's name … Laila, Lila—"

"Alayah, her name was Alayah," Jason answered quietly. The only sound was the refrigerator humming. Both men were remembering things but not the same things.

"Real shame about her. They never did find out who killed her. Another black child dead for no reason. One good thing is that you got away from here before it ate you up too. You know, despite how your wife's lack of appreciation makes you feel, you've done good for yourself and your family. You may not hear it at home, but you done real good, boy. I bet that lady upstairs has told you that."

"You know, old man, I am a thirty something year old man and you still calling me boy. I'm about tired of it now." Jason smiled at William.

"And you will always be 'boy' to me. Keeps you humble. Now tell me all about this lovely Miss Simone."

An hour later, Jason and Simone walked down the steps to their cars. The temperature hadn't risen much outside. Mim and William stood on the steps and watched as Jason helped Simone into her car.

"Thanks for coming with me today," he said. "They really like you."

"They are wonderful. Mim—your mom asked me to come back next weekend. She's going to show me how to make pasta from scratch. You know she is the first person I've ever met that doesn't think I'm a little odd when it comes to food. I'm glad I came too. She also gave me some flowers she says will balance my emotions. I took the one she's named after a little while ago. We'll see if it works." Simone realized she was jabbering away like a schoolgirl on crack. Jason let her.

"You will be fearless within the hour. Sure, you don't want to come ballin' with me and the guys?"

"No thanks. I think I'll go shopping. There's something that I've wanted to do for a long time. I think today is a good day to do it. Thanks Jason." She closed the door and drove off. Jason waved back to his parents and got into his car.

Mim shook her head and laid it on William's shoulder.

"What?" is all he said.

"I knew he married the wrong person. I told him that on his wedding day. Don't do it, I said. I think you should wait, I said. He's wood.

Leela is fire, quick tempered, fickle, hot one minute, smoldering the next. Look how that's working out for him. Simone is water, deep, goes with the flow, flexible, willing to give. What does water do for wood?"

"Nourishes it, makes it grow. It's life giving."

"Exactly, look at us. Maybe the universe is giving him a second chance."

"Maybe you should let the man live his own life and make his own decisions."

"Looks like he's made his decision already. He just doesn't know it yet."

"Should be interesting. Now bring your watery self back in this house before you turn into a block of ice."

Chapter 20

Simone hadn't been to the condominium since Greg moved there for the Sheva Chapters of their marriage. She often wondered why not. Her name was on the deed, not his. She was responsible for the mortgage when he didn't feel like paying it or didn't have enough money because he spent it on impressing whatever shorty was smiling at him at the time. As she drove up to the gate of the development, she took a deep breath. It didn't seem so scary today.

Maybe Mim's flowers work.

She smiled to herself and rolled down the window to be buzzed in.

The guard looked up from the scores from last night's Bulls' game and reached down to push the entry button. When he saw Simone, he broke into a grin that stretched far across his face.

"Hey, Ms. Dyson! How you been? It's been ages since I seen you here. How's it going?" He leaned so far out of the booth, Simone thought he might fall out.

"Hey, Harvey. It has been a while, hasn't it? It's good to see you. How's Alisa and little JamJam?"

"Lissy's good. We're expecting our second now. Doctor says it's another boy. Jam ain't so little anymore. He's going on four."

"Has it been that long?"

"Sure has. Um, Mr. Dyson ain't here. I haven't seen him since Thursday. Maybe he's out of town."

"He's moved back to our house, so you shouldn't see him here anymore. I'm here to do some early spring cleaning, I guess. So, I'll be in and out all afternoon. Good to see you, Harvey."

"You too, Mrs. D." *With your fine self. So, your dumb ass husband finally got a clue and went back home where he belongs. Got sick of his grinning ass every night acting like he's got a stick up it. And that sleazy slut he was hanging out with. Why he'd want to eat chicken franks when he got filet mignon at home I don't know. No accounting for taste.*

Harvey buzzed the gate and Simone drove through to her condo. She parked in her parking space and found the key in the glove compartment of the car. She made a mental note to have the locks changed since Greg hadn't given her the other key back yet.

Since he was home now, what did he need it for?

She walked to the door and unlocked it. Sticking her head in slowly, she looked around before entering. *What did you expect?* She entered and walked through each room wondering what had happened in them over the past two years.

If the walls could talk.

I'd probably sell it.

I know that's right.

She pulled up the shades and opened the windows in the living room and the bedrooms to let the sunshine and cold fresh air in. She turned on the heat full blast and sat on the leather sofa.

I pay the electric bill in this mug so I can turn on the heat and open the windows if I want.

She ran her fingers over the Italian leather of the sofa and looked around.

I hate this sofa. Greg wanted leather furniture. Said it was manly. He was probably thinking about turning it into his little bordello then.

She stood up and walked into each bedroom again. She opened the closets and dumped the towels and linen into the hallway. She took the curtains and window treatments down from the windows. Then she went back into the living room and opened her purse and took out her cell phone. She 411'd for the number she needed and dialed.

" Hi, I would like to donate furniture to the Salvation Army closest to Brooklawn Heights.

Yes, I am the owner of the furniture… a whole house full. Yes, two queen size beds, dining room set, leather living room set, end tables, lamps, dishes…the reason? Oh, early spring cleaning…Yes. Can you come by this afternoon? This is the only day I have to do this and I would prefer to donate to you than to have the waste company take it away….Sure I can hold….Thanks so much. I'll see you in three hours then. Bye."

Three hours, that gives me time to go the furniture store and see what I would like to have in my house. Maybe they do same day delivery.

PART TWO

Chapter 21

Langston Morantz, better known as Harlem Morantz to the guards and fellow inmates at the Illinois State Correctional Facility, sat in the day room watching the regional news on the cable news channel that was permitted to be broadcast in his permanent residence. Langston earned the name because most of the people he knew had no idea of who his namesake was. Langston Hughes. His momma loved that poetry shit that Hughes wrote. Life ain't been no crystal stair. You got that shit right. It touched her New York soul. Funny thing was, Langston, the younger, had a way with words as well. Seemed that nobody could appreciate his talent the way they should. His mother would tell him that he could talk the panties off of a nun. So, he tried it one time—she was right. When he mentioned his connection to the great Harlem Renaissance poet, to the people he met, all they could seem to grasp was Harlem. And that stuck.

Peoples today were so uneducated about their own.

He liked the news because it usually gave him something to write about and the CNN broadcast babes were hot. He loved the way Frederica and the white chick crossed their legs when they interviewed people on that sofa. Hot. Bare legs. Miles and miles of bare legs and high heels and ankle straps. Just the right blend of class and sleaze. Made your blood boil. Works every time. The show should be on in about twenty minutes so he could patiently wait for his favorite part of the day. Might even learn something about what is going on outside in the real world in the meantime. *Them folks out there is buck wild crazy.* Harlem felt safer among the convicted criminals in ICSF than those who were out there running loose on the streets-- politicians, preachers, bankers, and the rest.

He looked up at the screen and caught the sight of someone who looked slightly familiar. He asked the guard in the cage if he would turn up the sound.

"…has just received commendation from the Mayor of Chicago for his unprecedented dedication and will replace the retiring Police Commissioner, Howard Strassman, as Acting Commissioner until permanent placement proceedings are concluded. The former police detective has been singlehandedly praised as the catalyst that calmed the rioting during the gang warfare that crippled the eastside…."

"Oh, hell no. Tell me this shit ain't true. That son of a bitch is going to be running the police force now? And he fuckin' bashed somebody's head in twenty years ago for the fun of it and now he's holier than thou and a good public servant, what the fuck? Nah, this shit ain't gonna fly," Harlem mumbled to himself. He looked around to find the guard staring at him.

"You alright Harlem?" the guard asked.

"Nah, I need to talk to somebody. The Mayor of Chicago 'cause they about to put a murderer in as Chief of *Po-lice*. Me, locked up in here for life, and he gonna be running shit? Hell no. Call somebody for me to talk to! I got some information 'bout to blow the roof off this shit. Call somebody, *please.*"

Chapter 22

Simone was sitting at her desk staring at the computer screen and not seeing anything. The weeks since she and the guys, as she had come to call them, had returned from Las Vegas had been a blur. Now with this mess that had happened with Jason the other day, she wasn't sure how the mediation with Tyreek and Shamel would progress. Jason was just a 'person of interest' in a cold case from twenty years ago. But the way that the Officers of the Court had come into mediation room and handcuffed him was disturbing to say the least. The way that he accepted it like he knew it was coming was even worse. Mike had the same look on his face. Like he expected it and wondered why it had taken so long. He left with Jason and she hadn't heard from either one of them for the past two days. That was highly unusual. It had become a habit between Simone and Jason to 'check on each other' every day to make sure that they were keeping their head to the sky. She had come to look forward to the talks. Now nothing.

It did leave her time to focus on work at the office. So much to do trying to coordinate the schedules of the participants for the mediations in addition to keeping up with the day to day goings on in the office. Since she and Sly had been working with the Courts and the State's Attorney's Office, lots of mediations at the Center had been moving slower than expected. Two mediators left the Center, one moved, the other was fraternizing with a participant, sleeping with, actually. It made it difficult to maintain neutrality when you just finished pulling up your pants. New mediations were backing up because there were two less mediators to get the job done. With all that going on at work, there was little time to think about her personal life. Maybe that was a blessing because there was no personal life to speak of. Yes, Greg was home every night. Simone couldn't tell if that was a good thing or not. Two years ago, she would have jumped for joy to have him with her. *That was then. This is--*

The phone on the corner of her desk softly buzzed. She reached for it without looking up, glad that it had prevented her next thought.

"Good morning. May I help you?" she asked as she answered the phone. She had been taught that you should always state your name when answering the phone because it was a positive affirmation of who you were. A kind of mental masturbation. Simone could understand that might work for some people but she was pretty clear on who she was and therefore didn't feel the need to affirm herself to others.

"Good morning. This is Claudio Veracruz, Deputy Assistant to the Mayor," the voice on the other end of the line masturbated in an affirming way.

"Good morning, Mr. Veracruz, how may I help you?" Simone asked again.

"I am calling for Simone Dyson, Director of ADR Services. I was connected to this line when I called the Center," Claudio replied.

"You have been connected correctly, Mr. Veracruz."

There was a moment of silence on the other end, as if Claudio was thinking that this woman doesn't act right. He was the Deputy Assistant to the Mayor after all, and she didn't seem the least bit impressed. He was on his way to not liking her, but he had to admit, he was intrigued. That smooth, silky voice...*I wonder what she looks like?*

"Ms. Dyson, is that the correct title to use to address you or is it Missus or Miss?" he asked in a less than professional manner. *Tennis ball boobs, for sure--*

"That works perfectly well, Mr. Veracruz. How might I be able to assist you this morning?" she responded.

"Well, Ms. Dyson, the Mayor would like for you to interview a subject who wishes to make a statement concerning actions being taken under the city's jurisdiction."

What the heck does that mean? Simone thought.

"Help me understand, Mr. Veracruz, why the Mayor is requesting that an interview be done by this office?"

Shit. She's got questions. Nobody told me she'd have questions. Everybody else just does what they're told. She's got questions. Long legs too, I bet.

"Well, Ms. Dyson, the understanding that I have is that the Mayor requested that you personally interview the subject." *Bam. Take that.*

"So, what I'm hearing is that the Mayor has selected me to interview this individual and that you have been given the task of informing me or asking me?"

There was a moment of silence while Simone gave Veracruz think time. Then she continued.

"This seems highly unusual since interviewing is done either by lawyers or Court representatives or the Police department."

Silence.

"Yes, Ms. Dyson. The Mayor asked for you specifically. It seems that the subject will not speak to anyone related to the Mayor's office or any of the other agencies which you mentioned. He is looking to speak to a neutral party so that he feels that, in his words, 'his statement won't be misconstrued or swept under the rug'."

More silence.

 Then in a pleading tone, "Ms. Dyson, the Mayor is very concerned about what this subject has to say. This may be something that could affect the higher echelons of power and cause major turmoil in city government if not handled carefully. The subject has said that he will talk to someone, if not through the proper channels, then through the media. And he says, and I quote, 'CNN will have a field day with this one.'"

"Mr. Veracruz, my schedule is rather crowded for the next several days, weeks actually. Do you know the name of the person to be interviewed? Where does this person reside and when did the Mayor envision having this interview?" Simone was pulling up her planner on the computer screen.

"The gentleman's name is Langston Morantz and he resides at the Big Muddy River Correctional Facility."

"That is a three-hour drive from Chicago," Simone responded. Her voice never changing even though she was in shock.

"That is why the Mayor is sending a car for you. It should be there in about twenty minutes. Please bring whatever you would need to record the information that you receive. Thank you, Ms. Dyson. Nice talking to you." Claudio hung up quickly before Simone had a chance to say anything. *Full lips too, he thought.*

As the Mayor's official car, one of them anyway, glided along the interstate towards the rural, empty, and sparsely populated part of Illinois, the only spot that the voters would allow a secure medium security prison to be built, Simone surveyed the country side as she read a novel on her IPad. No sense in thinking too hard about this situation since there was absolutely nothing that she could do about it. She had tons of questions and she had to admit that she was just a little bit curious about all the cloak and dagger paranoia attached to Langston's request for a neutral party to tell his story to.

Should make for an interesting day and now you won't get home until late, and you know Greg is out of town 'on business'.

Stop it. Lord, please, save me from myself.

She focused on her book; it was really quite good. Since she was an avid reader, she had already figured out that the protagonist's family would probably end up dead, but she still wanted to see how the sociopath would get away with it. She liked her books with a bit of a sick twist to them. *Kind of like real life.* This one was very sickly twisted. And the protagonist was fine. Even if he was just words written on paper. A well-turned phrase was sometimes more pleasurable than—well, a lot of things.

The facility was coming into sight. Big Muddy River was nowhere near a big muddy river. There was nothing anywhere around for miles, just flat open space. And dirt. Simone looked at her simple yet elegant titanium Movado watch. It was approaching 1:00. *Leave it in your purse, along with those wedding rings of yours. So bright. make a blind man see. Somebody would chew your finger off to get at those. Leave it to Greg to go for overkill. Pride in ownership and all that.*

First sensible thing you said all day.

As she placed the watch and rings in her purse, the car turned into the prison's entrance road.

And why are you here again? What exactly did you do to deserve this? Be outstanding at what you do maybe? And they send you to prison for that?

 Not now. I don't need this now. I got to be on my game. No fear in here. It smells.

That's right girl, only thing they need to smell in here is your No. 19.

If she had known that she would be spending the major portion of her day in a medium security prison, she would have dressed a little differently. Her suit was dark and conservative—pencil skirt slightly above her knees, silk blouse, fitted jacket ending at her waist, and a pair of Jimmy Choo's to die for. But nothing she could do about that either. Simone took a deep breath and looked in the rearview mirror at the driver. He was smiling at her. She reciprocated. He spoke in a deep African accent that she tried to place. Ethiopia, maybe? "We are here, Ma'am. Are you ready to go inside?"

"Yes, thank you," she answered as calmly as possible.

He stepped out and opened the door for her.

"My name is Ishua. I will be waiting for you. Please call for me if should need me for anything," he said.

"Thank you, Ishua. I will be fine. All in a day's work, correct? You need to rest from the drive. You have to do it again in a few hours," she answered as he held her hand and helped her out of the car. A true gentleman. Most men don't do that anymore.

Jason does.

"No problem, Ma'am. It was my pleasure. Not often do I get to drive someone such as you. I enjoyed being of service. I will be waiting here when you are through with your task." Ishua stood by the car and watched as Simone walked toward the entrance of the prison. She looked around and saw acres and acres of space surrounded by fence. As far as the eye could see. She took a deep breath and walked up to the guard stationed at the entrance door.

"Name please and may I see two forms of ID?"

"My name is Simone Dyson. Here is my ID," she said in a clear, professional voice. Like she did this every day.

"Ms. Dyson, your name is not here," said the guard, not looking at her but running his finger down his clipboard searching for her name.

Wouldn't you think someone would have TOLD somebody you were coming?

Simone took another deep breath and focused on it coming in and going out. Coming in and going out. Coming in and going out.

"Who are you here to see today? You need twenty-four-hour approval and your name is not on the list," said the guard looking up for the first time ready to dismiss her. He looked out to the official looking black vehicle with the large official looking seal on the side and the large black official looking driver still standing beside it.

"I am here to see Mr. Langston Morantz," she replied.

The guard's expression changed in mid-breath. He typed something into the computer and waited only a split second before the look on his face changed again. He looked at her ID again, then at the screen and then back at her. He handed the IDs back to her and handed her a VIP Visitors badge. Simone didn't know there was such a thing.

Who would want to be a VIP visitor in a maximum-security prison?

"I'm sorry, Ms. Dyson. Didn't mean to make you wait. What with Mayor Armstrong sending you and all. The warden would like to see you as soon as you clear processing. There will be an escort coming for you shortly. We'll be calling for Mr. Morantz to be sent to an interrogation room. He will be waiting for you when you arrive," said the guard who suddenly seemed to have diarrhea of the mouth. He picked up the phone and requested an escort, then typed something else into the computer, then smiled at Simone like he didn't get out too often.

Clear processing? What exactly might that mean for VIP visitors? Simone thought.

A large manly woman came through the gates and approached Simone. Simone swore that she saw the woman lick her lips as she walked in her direction.

Can you say strip search?

The female guard, she had to be female because the ID badge she wore had the name Amelia Lockhorn on it, escorted Simone to the Warden Darmunth's office and left Simone at the door after she knocked on it and heard the warden say, "Enter."

 Simone opened the door and walked inside. The office looked just like the man standing behind the desk—pretentious. She recognized pretention when she saw it. Reminded her of someone she was married to. Everything about the room looked like he Google-imaged 'authority figure's office décor' and purchase ordered it with State of Illinois tax dollars. Even the suit, shirt, and tie ensemble looked like he scanned the Brooks Brothers catalog. Simone guessed that his socks cost more than Amelia's daily wage.

He stood up and reached a well-manicured hand across to her in an effort to shake her hand or display the expanse and the richness of the mahogany desk. "Thank you for coming all this way, Mrs.

Dyson. I am Warden Wendell Darmunth, pleased to make your acquaintance," he said, his voice sounding as pretentious as his office looked.

Does he sit in here and practice or what?

Simone sat down in the chair at the side of the desk instead of the one that Warden Darmunth so elegantly pointed to with his outstretched hand. His plastered smile seemed to crack for a nanosecond, but he regained his composure quickly. "Please have a seat, wherever you are comfortable." He sat down behind his desk and folded his hands in his lap. Leisurely pose, in charge, yet relaxed. Straight out of that lawyer show on USA network.

"Mrs. Dyson, I will be totally honest with you. I am not enthralled with your presence here, but when the Mayor of Chicago speaks, humble warden that I am—listen." Display of teeth, Lumineers actually. "Please take a look at Langston Morantz file and you'll see that it would be hard to believe anything that comes out of his mouth. He is a lifer with no hope of parole, so I don't see what he hopes to gain from making up some story after being here for the past fifteen years." Darmunth slowly pushed a thick file across the mahogany desk in Simone's direction.

"There's no need for me to see his file, Warden. I prefer to remain neutral, which is what I have been sent here to do. All I am doing today is listening and recording the words of a man who has something to share that he believes is important enough to speak about at this time," she replied.

"Well, in that case," said the warden as he straightened his already straight tie, and stood up. "Let me inform you of the visiting rules of our facility. You will be in an interrogation room with Mr. Morantz. He will be secured to the table and the floor. An armed guard will be stationed outside the door. This is highly unusual and completely against regulations but because of the nature of the situation – whatever that might be—you and Mr. Morantz will be alone— unsupervised, the room is soundproof but does have a two-way mirror to allow for third party viewing to ensure that you remain safe. At no time are you to touch Mr. Morantz or allow him near your person," Darmunth smiled the Lumineers again as he looked over her person. "It's not often that Mr. Morantz or any of our inmates see a woman such as yourself. Please do not be surprised by any outburst of vulgarity that he may dispense," said Darmunth waiting for a sign of shock from Simone.

"Sounds like he doesn't get out much," said Simone. "In my line of work, I doubt that there is much that I haven't heard."

Warden Darmunth stood up and escorted Simone to the door where the guard was waiting on the other side.

"We will soon see, Mrs. Dyson. We will see."

Chapter 23

Amelia walked in front of Simone, night stick, walkie-talkie, Smith and Wesson, pepper spray, Taser, and a couple other things Simone did not recognize, dangling from her belt.

Now, why does she have a walkie talkie when she has that thing attached to her epaulet on her shoulder? Isn't that a bit of overkill? If she hollers in one and nobody's listening, they might hear her on the other? What?

  Simone's mind was racing as she followed the guard to the interrogation room. How should she handle this? She was a mediator, not an interviewer, or somebody trained to do depositions.

Do what you do, girlfriend. Like the movie says, 'nobody does it better.' Just do what you do and let the pieces fall where they may. They aren't your pieces anyway.

Then whose are they? Simone had been wondering that the entire drive up here. She was about to find out. Amelia stopped at the door and gave her the once over, again, one more time. The look in the guard's eyes made Simone think that a strip search was not out of the question if she could somehow create a reason for one. The guard licked her lip once too often and took a deep breath into her barrel shaped chest as if inhaling the Chanel No. 19 for future dreams this evening. She opened the door and stood in the entryway so that Simone had to brush past her to enter the room. Simone smiled and thanked her as if she expected everyone to breathe in her air.

Good going. Never let them see you sweat. You can fall apart when you get home.

She immediately surveyed the room just like she did for premeditation set-up with Sly. Thinking about something familiar eased the tension that was building inside of her. She smiled to herself, took a deep breath and sat down on the side of the rectangular table closest to the door. Safety first, was one of the first things she learned as a mediator. Know the exits and be close to them—just in case things go south. Since she was in a medium security prison about to spend a great deal of time with a convicted man serving a life term for murder—it was good to sit by the door. She laughed out loud at that one. There was a second bolted door at the opposite end of the room with no knob and no Exit sign above it. Odd, she thought. *You watch too many movies.* The knobbed door opened, and it sounded like Marley from <u>A Christmas Carol</u> rattled into the room, chains dangling behind him.

Lord, they done locked up Cornel West.

But it was Langston "Harlem" Morantz. Simone imagined that in an alternate universe, it was possible that Dr. West could have ended up just like this man—black, intelligent, opinionated, imprisoned—it's possible. Look what happened to Skip Gates, after all.

She was glad that she had requested to be in the room before Langston arrived. That way her physique would not be a matter of distraction for him or of intimidation for her if he was the type to want to try. The guard led him to the table and sat him at the end where the hooks protruded out of the floor to attach the chains. It was time for Simone to take charge of this situation, if at all possible. She shook her head and quietly pointed to the chair across the table from her saying to the guard, "If that's alright with you."

Langston looked at the guard and then looked at Simone, then back at the guard who hadn't made a decision on his own for at least a lifetime. "Not 'sposed to do it this way. For interrogation, they 'sposed to be sittin' where the chains 'sposed to be hooked," he said with worry and confusion in his voice.

"For protection during interrogation from dangerous individuals. Is that right?" Simone asked quietly looking at the guard with an easy smile.

"That's right. For *protection*," emphasis on the word protection.

"Well, this isn't an interrogation. It is a meeting that Mr. Morantz requested, so there is no need to be concerned about dangerous individuals," Simone said.

Please God, let that be true.

She glanced at Alternate Cornel as if waiting for his agreement. In an instant, Langston furrowed his brow and nodded in agreement to what Simone proposed. The guard shuffled slightly and wiped the sweat from his brow.

"Um, a'ight. Um, yeah, a'ight. This ain't usual, so, um, since it ain't a interrogation, I'ma let you sit 'cross here and talk to this here lady. But I'ma be right outside the door, and nobody can get in or out without going through me," said the guard trying to take back control of the situation that he never had.

I feel so much safer now.

"Thank you for making this decision to allow this and for staying close by in the event that either of us needs you for anything. We appreciate it, Officer—"Her voice trailed off.

"Marvus. JaQuan Marvus."

"Thank you, Officer Marvus. Both Mr. Morantz and I appreciate your help," she said in her most soothing and appreciative voice.

Work it girl, mental massage these men.

Officer Marvus smiled and took a deep breath.

Lot of that going on around here.

"No problem, ma'am. Just doing my j-o-b. I be right outside if you need anything."

JaQuan looked at Langston and then at Simone like he was wondering who he'd have to kill to spend time in a room with a woman like that. He walked out and locked the door behind him, leaving Langston and Simone sitting across the table from each other. Neither spoke for a moment, Langston just sat there staring at Simone as if he was trying to read her—determine whether she was afraid. Try his jailhouse psychology on this one. The one they sent to hear him out. Why her? What was it that made her the one they chose?

She don't look like she the kind that fucked her way here. Eyes too bright, too sharp. If she can get that dumbass Marvus to leave me in here unchained, she got skills and she ain't afraid of me. Well let's see how 'fraid she gonna be when she hear this shit I got to say.

"Good afternoon, Mr. Morantz. My name is Simone. I am here at your request for a neutral and objective party to listen to you and record your statement concerning an incident that happened a number of years ago. Is that right?"

No response. Just a continued stare, then a hint of a smile.

"It looks like you are smiling, Mr. Morantz, is that right?"

"Yeah. You can call me Langston if you want. You heard that name before?"

"Langston Hughes, the great poet of the Harlem Renaissance, is the only Langston with which I am familiar," Simone replied.

"That's the one. I knew you'd know. You just look smart like that. Which poem do you like the best?"

Simone thought for a moment.

Jailhouse psychology going on here? I don't have anything to lose and I'm just building a foundation for trust here.

"'Friends'. I like that poem very much. It touches a cord, I guess."

"I like that one too. Short and to the point. You have good taste. I thought you would."

"Sounds like you have an idea about your expectation of me? Is that right?"

"Well, you ain't—aren't what I was expecting, that's for damn sure. I'm sorry, 'scuse my language. Not a lot of necessity of talking correct up in this place. Gimme a couple of minutes to adjust. I'm just surprised, that's all."

"Sounds like you are satisfied with the choice of listener that was sent here today? And that it was important to you that someone is here that meets your approval and takes you seriously?"

"Yeah, and looks good. This is better than CNN. You give Frederica a run for her money. Not as high on the yellow totem pole but not far down. I think that it's the lights though that make her so pale, you know? You're pretty damn—I mean darn close. Nice butterscotch. Real nice to look at. I could talk to you all day."

"Feeling comfortable and willing to share. Appreciative of my appearance and equating my ability with the way I look?"

"I…guess so. Now that you mention it. Yeah, that's right. You know… you're good. I'm glad they sent you. I wish I had something better to tell you. You seem like a nice lady and this shi—stuff ain't nice. I apologize for what you gonna hear but people need to know before it's too late. I shoulda said this years ago. Maybe shi—stuff would be different now. People still be alive."

"Well, Mr. Morantz, whatever you wish to share, I am here to record for you so that the proper agencies and entities will be able to address it."

"Langston, call me Langston."

"Langston."

"I like it when you say my name."

"I am ready to record whatever you wish to share, Langston."

"Okay, but don't say I didn't warn you. I remember it like it was yesterday, even though it was twenty years ago. A secret kept for that long is bound to come out sometime. And now's the time. What's done in the dark always comes to light. So, sit back Miss Simone, you gonna be here a while."

Chapter 24

Harlem, CK, and Jax were on their third bottle of Mad Dog, a piece, in the alley behind the dilapidated rundown strip of stores looking for a way to get more money to get more booze and weed. It was early still, maybe 10:30 or so and the moon was high in the sky and there was dirt to be done and pussy to be had...

Speaking of pussy, CK was telling stories about his latest pieces of ass. There was always more than one and Harlem wasn't stupid enough to believe any of it. He had known CK since they were snotty little kids in preschool and nothing the boy ever said was true. If he said the sky was blue, it made sense to go out and check for yourself. So, when he went on and on about girls, Harlem just shook his head and pulled another drag on the joint between his fingers. Sometimes, Harlem wondered if CK even liked girls. But Harlem wondered lots of things, most of the time. Jax was leaned up against the dumpster to keep from falling. He couldn't hold his liquor or his weed. Put the two of them together, like they usually did, and Jax was pretty much good for nothing, which was pretty normal. After deciding how they could get some more weed on credit from T-Mac, the local dealer on the corner a few blocks over, Harlem saw movement down the street. It was too dark to see who it was, but he could tell it was female. Very much so. Hell yeah. Or hell no, since they had no money, how were they gonna get some ass tonight? That's the only kind of female that would be walking down these streets at this time of night. Couple more tricks before the night was over. Maybe they could get a deal. Three for the price of a couple of drags on a joint? Street walkers were usually high anyway, so for a hit of something, it just might work. Have to be high to do the shit that these chicks did. Like my moms, Harlem thought. He took another swig of Mad Dog. He kept looking in the direction of the figure as it got closer to the streetlight. Nobody else had noticed at this point, CK was too busy lying out both sides of his mouth, wishing that he had done the things that he was talking about. The female staggered forward, looking at nothing as she walked. She seemed numb to everything around her. Dazed. Every now and then, her hand would rise to her eyes to wipe them. Then she would stagger forward some more. CK and Jax had their backs to the street counting what little money they had left between them. Harlem recognized who the female was. Fine ass Alayah Brittingham. She never had time for nobody except that football playing son of a bitch Jason. Why wasn't she at the championship game tonight? Harlem knew J was starting tonight. So why wasn't she there? The bus left at least four or five hours ago. He had often wondered what it would be like to have a honey like that paying attention to him. Everybody knew that she was giving it up to J every chance she got. Surprised that she ain't had no kids by now. The way she looked at J in the hallways at school made Harlem's poetic heart skip a beat. He'd never tell anyone that she was the inspiration for some of his best work that was hidden between his mattress and bedspring. So, as she walked closer to the street light, he watched her closely, analyzing every move she made, every breath she took, so that he could remember it for later. Even though he was high as a kite, he would remember this night. Her skirt fit her form so nicely. Tight enough to see that no lines appeared across her backside, so no drawers. Although her demeanor was one of sadness and dejection, her breasts bounced with every step she took. Harlem could tell she was without a bra. Nature had endowed this sweet young thing with everything a woman needed but tonight it didn't seem to be enough.

CK and Jax were laughing and drinking and counting the money when fate sealed each of their futures. A car rumbled by at just the same moment that Alayah was directly across the street from them. CK looked up to check the car—in case it was Five-0.

194

"Well, look at what we got over here! It's Miss Thing. Fine ass 'Laylay. Hey girl, come on over here and speak to a brotha," CK hollered across the street now that she was the focus of his attention. Alayah kept walking, her dazed expression not changing as CK addressed her.

"Come on girl. Give a brotha some time. Shit. Lover boy ain't here. But I am. Hell, we all here," he said as he waved his hand out toward Jax and Harlem. Alayah kept walking, not even looking in their direction. Harlem noticed that her hands went to her eyes more frequently now that CK mentioned J. CK noticed it as well. "Whoa, I see Laylay got tears. What'd he do? Hit it and quit it? That's all he wanted you for anyway. Didn't you know that, girl? Come here, girl. I got somethin' for ya," CK started walking across the street. Alayah seemed to snap out of her daze. She walked a little faster. Breasts bouncing and skirt rubbing. Just what CK needed to see. He grabbed her arm and started to direct her towards the alley. She didn't resist, which surprised Harlem. She had always been fiery and seemed to look down her nose at every male that wasn't J. Tonight, she didn't fight. She just kind of –gave up, like the life had been drained out of her. Even with her large gold hoops in her ears and gold necklace that resembled a playing card with the Queen of Hearts on it dangling between her upturned breasts, she looked beaten, broken.

CK put his hand on her lower back and offered her a drag of his joint. She sucked it in as if it would relieve her pain. As she sucked in the smoke, CK's hand wandered some more until it was up under her skirt. She flinched as Harlem understood what CK was doing to her. He continued as Jax walked closer and started to gawk at what was going on in front of him. With one hand under her skirt, he took the other hand and cupped a breast. Alayah squirmed a bit but still didn't fight as much as Harlem expected her to. Before he knew it, CK had pulled her skirt down and bent her over the lower of the two dumpsters. He pulled down his zipper and stepped behind her. She groaned and he put his hand over her mouth and started using her as a receptacle. She just laid there, not fighting or trying to stop him. Harlem saw CK shudder and knew he was done. For now. Jax had watched the entire thing from close up and was more than ready for his turn. He traded places with CK and did his best to make her forget that CK had just been in there. Harlem watched him shudder as well. He stepped away and left her laying across the dumpster. Both of his friends turned to him and looked at him in a way that said it all. Your turn. Harlem knew that he couldn't walk away. These were his pardners, his running buddies. He didn't have any choice if he expected to continue to live in the neighborhood. He walked up to her thinking that if he moved slowly enough, she might get up and run away. But she stayed put. Maybe it was the alcohol or the weed or both but his body was ready to do just what his friends had done. He unzipped his pants and instead of walking up behind her, he rolled her over on her back and pulled her toward him. As he did the same thing to her as CK and Jax, he looked in her eyes and saw the despair as the tears rolled down her lovely cheeks.

Jax and CK cheered him on while they waited to start round two. Harlem continued to look down at Alayah and felt something that he couldn't explain. He leaned close to her in a way that resembled affection which actually was exactly what it was. "I'm sorry. I'm sorry. I'm sorry," he kept whispering with each thrust. She just laid there and let the tears continue to flow. She moved her lips, saying something that Harlem heard between his own litany of apologies.

"J, what did I do? I loved you. I still do. I love you," she whimpered, eyes staring off into nothing.

Harlem couldn't take it. Alayah's voice whispering words of love was more than he could bear, even if they weren't for him. For a moment he pretended that they were and emptied himself in a way he hadn't before or since. Except for the two more turns he took with CK and Jax.

When the three were completely drained, they stumbled away from Alayah and the dumpster. They laughed and recounted the activities over the past hour and a half while Alayah rolled herself off of the dumpster. She collapsed on the ground beside the dumpster and curled up in a ball. CK turned and looked at her like she had done something wrong by being there.

"Thanks Laylay," he laughed. "I'll be sure to tell J all about it on Monday. I hope the game was as good as your ass was," he continued. She tried to unroll herself but was unsuccessful. What remained of her clothes was piled up beside her. She tried to reach for them but couldn't stretch that far. Her chest heaved, breasts

rising up and down, smooth flat stomach going in and out. "Get up and get the fuck out of here. Nobody wants your cheap ass around. Go'n ya fuckin' ho." CK turned the Mad Dog bottle up to his lips to drain it dry. He had turned his back on Alayah to give a hi-five to Harlem and Jax. Maybe the alcohol and drugs were wearing off or maybe there hadn't been enough but the Harlem and Jax were starting to see the horror of what they had done. They looked at each other, then at Alayah as she struggled to stand up. Jax took off his jersey and was about to hand it to her when CK said, "Oh hell no, let the bitch walk home butt nekkid. Maybe pick up some more action on the way."

He laughed some more, waiting for a response from his boys. Alayah crawled towards Jax and Harlem sensing that they were feeling some remorse for what they had done. Jax leaned towards her and Alayah reached her hand out to him. CK turned around at that moment and swung the empty Mad Dog bottle as hard as he could, hitting Alayah at the base of her nose splaying her all over the pavement. A beautiful body attached to a devastated face. She lay there, not moving for a moment. Harlem and Jax ran over to her checking to see if she was breathing. CK stood over them staring at the huddle on the ground. "What? She fine. Ain't nothing wrong with that bitch. Get out the way, let me see." He pushed Jax and Harlem aside kneeling over the unconscious body. She groaned when he started to grope her body. "See, I told you ain't nothing wrong with her... Ho. I told you."

"Ah man. Leave her alone. Shit," Harlem said. "We need to take her to the hospital or something. You broke her face, man. What you thinkin?"

"I'm thinkin' you need to shut the fuck up. Bitch is fine," CK said as he continued to grope. Alayah groaned again and slowly moved her head in an effort to gain full consciousness. He looked down at her as her lips moved. He leaned his head closer to her. Her lips moved and it looked like she was saying something in CK's ear. Then she spat right in his face. Blood and saliva dripped from his face and hair. He stiffened and grabbed her by her hair and started banging her head on the pavement, hollering the whole time, "Bitch, I'll kill you! Ya hear me... kill your ass!" He grabbed the gold necklace from around her neck and attempted to shove it completely in his pocket.

Harlem and Jax grabbed him by both arms and pulled him off of her. He struggled, punched the air, and foamed at the mouth like a rabid dog. He was struggling to get away from them when they saw movement farther down the alley. Everyone stopped. Maybe it was just a shadow. But from what? Whatever it was, was bigger than a rat. They looked at each other.

"Let's get out of here," CK said, snatching his arms away from Harlem and Jax.

"We can't leave her here. We gotta get her to a hospital," Jax said.

"We ain't got to do nothin' but get out of here. Get in the car. Fuck her," CK answered.

They trotted to the classic Dodge Challenger that CK inherited from his uncle. They got in the car and drove out into the street leaving their victim lying motionless under the streetlight beside the dumpster. CK drove down the street with the lights off, breathing hard and looking around as if he were hunting for something or someone. About a block down the street, he saw it--someone was running. A young girl, maybe twelve or so. She was fast too. Running like she was trying to get away from something evil. CK sped up. She darted across the street and into the closest alley. He drove faster trying to figure out where she might come out on to the street again, mumbling to himself the entire time.

"There she go, there's the little bitch." He swerved around the corner and came up behind the little girl who was running for dear life. Harlem recognized her from around the way. Pretty little girl with a twin sister. Pretty little girl with a brother named Jason. Who played football. Who had a girlfriend named Alayah. Who was bleeding to death beside a dumpster six blocks back. Small fucking world, Harlem was thinking, when the car lurched forward, and he saw the pretty little girl fly over the hood and hit the ground and roll into the gutter. He looked out the rear window and watched her roll and roll as the Challenger sped off.

Chapter 25

Harlem had been talking for the better part of two hours. Once he got started, he had needed very little prompting to tell his story. Simone was beyond words, trying to process what she was hearing. She had asked him at the beginning if it was alright with him if she took notes. That's what she always did during mediations. Trying to identify feelings, values, and topics that were important to the participants. But this was something else. A few times she had to put down her pen and remind herself to breathe. Could this be true? Was it possible? Nobody could make up anything as horrible as this. And why would he? After all these years? Simone thought it would be a good time to ask that question since he was so quiet right now. He had his head in his hands as he leaned over the table across from her.

She got up and walked to the door and knocked on it. JaQuan immediately opened it as if he might need to address a dire situation that was going on inside.

"Officer Marvus, would it be possible for us to have something to drink? Maybe a couple of bottles of water?" she asked as pleasantly as she could. She didn't want her voice or face to betray what was happening in the room. She turned to Harlem and asked, "Langston, is that okay with you? Would you like a snack or something?"

He shook his head up and down. Looked up and tried to smile, somehow picking up from Simone that a happy display was in order right now.

"Sure, Ms. Dyson. I'll bring some ice and cups too. You want anything else?" he asked ever so willing to give Simone whatever she asked for.

"No thank you, JaQuan. That's really thoughtful of you to bring the ice and cups. I hadn't even thought of that," she smiled at him.

"No problem. Give me five minutes, okay?"

"Sure, take your time, we're in no rush," she replied.

JaQuan closed and relocked the door. Simone returned to her seat and tried to sort out all that she had heard.

My God, is there more?

She was afraid to ask. So, she tried another approach.

"Are you alright, Langston? You talked for a long time. Is there anything I can do for you?"

No response. Just head in the hands. When he finally looked up his eyes were red. He had lost the color in his face. He was a shell. Prison does that to a person, but this was something deeper than that. This prison had been of his own design. He built the walls in his own mind to house the horror of that night and all the ripples that it caused. Today, the walls started to crumble and the horror was oozing out. He knew that it was going to get worse before it got better. How do you prepare another human being for that?

"You probably wondering why I kept it to myself all these years. I wanted to forget 'cause I ain't get caught, you know? It was some terrible shit and it wasn't even over. Hell, it ain't over now."

"So, you're saying that the police never found out who attacked Alayah?"

"Or ran over the little girl. Her name was T—something. I can't remember but I do remember that I heard she was brain damaged 'cause of it and they had to put her in a nursing home somewhere.

Last I heard she was still there. You know she died—Alayah, I mean. They found her in the morning when the trash truck rolled up. She was still alive then too. Can you imagine laying out all night, butt naked, rats all around, bleeding, torn up--" he stopped talking and put his head back in his hands. "Shit, that's some terrible shit."

Keys could be heard in the door and Langston and Simone watched JaQuan enter the room carrying a cafeteria tray with bottled water, glasses filled with ice and a plate of cheese and crackers. Simone had to smile to herself.

How sweet is that? In a prison no less?

"Wow. Thanks so much, JaQuan. We didn't expect all this," she said.

"Yeah, thanks man. That's real nice of you," Langston chimed in.

"Yeah, no problem. Ya'll must be kinda hongry or something'. Ya'll need anything else, I'm right here." He closed and relocked the door. He was taking his job very seriously.

Langston looked relieved that JaQuan had left. He looked like he had more to say as he reached for a bottle of water. "Don't drink out of the glasses," he started. "You know, after it was all over, CK wanted to go somewhere and get something else to drink. Me and Jax had had enough. We just wanted to go home. Told CK to drop us off at the projects and he could go on 'bout his business. He got madder and madder as he drove. Kept mumblin' shit 'bout nobody snitching 'cause we all guilty as hell and that's what homeboys do— got each other's back. Jax told CK to kiss his black ass and he ain't the one who bashed 'Layah's head in. CK was in that shit all by hisself."

Langston drank some more water and reached for the cheese cubes. He chewed for a minute like it was a real treat. It probably was.

"How did Jax hold up through all of this? It seemed like he regretted what had happened that night."

"He did, we both did. He didn't have to regret it for long though. Two weeks later he got shot in a drive-by. Strangest thing. He ain't had no enemies. No gang shit going on. He was walking home from Tally's market with groceries for his momma. They ain't never figured out who did that shit either. That's when I left town. I wasn't gonna stick around and let that crazy nigga shoot me too."

"So, you're saying that CK killed Jax?" Simone asked.

"Yeah, who else would have a reason to? He bashed Alayah's head in and ran down that little girl. Yeah, that's what I'm saying and now the mayor of Chicago want to make that motherf—excuse me—make him Police Commissioner."

"Langston, why did you call him CK? That's a nickname or something?"

"Hell yeah. He thought he was real smooth, you know. Everybody always knew he had a short fuse and acted like a nut. So, we called him CK. He thought we meant smooth like Calvin Klein, we meant Crazy Karl. Crazy Karl Dyson."

"Karl?" Simone repeated.

"Yeah, Karl Dyson? You know him?"

Chapter 26

Simone's head was reeling as Ishua drove back to the city. Nobody could make up a story that elaborate. Even the sickest, twisted imagination wouldn't be able to invent the things that Harlem told her this afternoon. Just when she thought she had heard enough, he had more to tell. She watched him ever so closely for signs that what he was saying were lies. There were no telltale signs. She was pretty good on spotting a liar. In her line of work and after being married to Greg, she knew a liar when she saw one.

Maybe it ran in the family.

If what Harlem says *is* true, then her brother-in-law is a rapist, hit and run driver, and a murderer.

Poor Horace. What will he do if when finds out? Can he handle that truth about his son?

The ride was a blur. Every now and then, Ishua would look into the rearview mirror and see Simone staring into the darkness. It was approaching 10:00 by the time the car approached the bright lights of the Windy City. Not even the wind could shock Simone right now. The driver pulled the car up in front of her building and opened the door for her.

"Mrs. Dyson, we are here. Would you want me to wait until you come back down to your car?" he asked as he looked in the mirror.

"No thank you, Ishua. I'll be fine," she replied seeing the concern in his face, she continued. "I don't have to get anything inside. If it's in there tonight, it can wait until morning. I'm going home. So should you," she smiled a tired smile.

"After I know that you are safe Missus, I will. Nothing would disturb me more than to know that you had difficulty on my watch."

"Sounds like you are getting paid extra," she said trying to make a joke.

"Self-appointed. Done for free. I watched you today Missus and you handled yourself well. Very well under the circumstances."

"The circumstances?" she asked.

Ishua turned around and looked at her. "Missus, nobody knows what was said to you today except you and that man but everybody *wants* to know. Something is going to happen because of what he told you today, whatever it was. Please be careful. No one over there is happy," he said as he nodded in the direction of the City Hall. "I will pick you up in the morning to drive you to the Mayor. I am sure that he will have trouble sleeping tonight. Him and some others." He turned off the engine and stepped out to open the door for Simone.

"Rest well tonight, Missus. Tomorrow has the gift to be a lion's heart day."

"A lion's heart day?"

"Yes. A day that will belong to the strongest. Either the lion or the one strong enough to eat his heart," Ishua said with a somber look on his face.

And I think I know who that will be.

"Gee, I thought it was Wednesday," she responded quietly trying to lighten the mood.

"I will see you in the morning Missus. Be safe and alert on your drive home. I can follow if you like."

"No, thank you, I am fine. See you in the morning."

Simone walked to the parking garage and found her Volvo. She took a deep breath and pulled out on the street. Traffic was light this time of night and her mind was going over the events of the day. She didn't notice the black official limo pull out a few cars behind her. Ishua lowered his window a bit to get some cold, fresh air as he trailed Simone home. No way he was leaving her before morning.

Chapter 27

Jason sat in the Jeep Cherokee staring out the window as his stepfather drove away from the city jail. He was eager to get to William and Mim's house so that he could wash off the stench of the jail cell that he had occupied for two days. That's what happens to a 'person of interest' when there is no evidence linking a person to a crime. Fortunately, because of Jason's size and disposition, no one felt the need to challenge him for control of the very small territory of the holding area. When he was transferred to a regular cell, he knew that his past was finally introducing itself to his present and he wondered why it had taken so long. He thought of Maia. He knew she was safe with Mim. Leela was too devastated by the shock of Jason being in jail to take care of her own daughter.

So, what was new?

He wanted to hold his daughter and protect her from the type of people that were out there waiting to do to her what he had done to someone else's little girl so many years ago.

Alayah, I am so sorry. I may not have killed you, but I am responsible. I may not have killed you, but I killed someone. And if given the chance, I'd do it again.

When they arrived at the house, Mim and Maia were out. William had called ahead and made sure that the two of them would be busy for a few hours. Time enough for Jason to regroup. Time enough for Jason and William to talk. After Jason had showered, shaved, and eaten some of Mim's delicious fried eggplant and polenta, he sat downstairs with William, who was nursing a Coors. Neither man spoke for a long time. There was nothing to be said. They both had an idea of what happened that night twenty years ago but neither knew everything. They didn't need to or so they had thought all these years. Time has a way of making things seem less traumatic maybe even bearable. Or just numb. Maybe that was it. Bringing all of it to the surface was hard. Like digging open an old wound that had healed over and had been forgotten.

"How long's it been now, twenty years? Your sister's been in that place twenty years now. I'm surprised she has made it that long to be honest. Thought your momma would die when the police showed up at the door. First, she thought it was about you. Thought the bus had turned over after the game or something. When she heard it was Tisha, she almost died. Didn't even know she was out the house. Went out the window. Wonder where she learned that. She had put the kids to bed around ten and here it was after one and the police show up saying Tish was laying up in the hospital on life support," William took a long pull on the beer in his hand before he continued. "That was a bad night all around."

"Alayah," whispered Jason.

"Yeah, *that* poor girl. She made some poor choices but ain't no way in hell she deserved what happened to her. Whoever done that needs to be locked up for life. Never did find them and now they want to figure it out. What the fuck is that all about?"

"Don't know. Doesn't make no sense after all this time. Something has happened for them to reopen it after all these years. They didn't seem to care too much back then. Another black-on-black crime most likely, so who gives a fuck?" Jason said through clenched teeth.

"Whole bunch of black-on-black crime that fall. Alayah, Tish, that Jam, Joe—"

"Jax, his name was Jax," Jason said.

"Yeah, him. Somebody took care of that piece of trash real quick. What goes around comes around, your grandmama always said."

Ain't that the truth.

Jason lifted his head long enough to take a deep swig. "Drive-by is what I heard."

"Yeah, craziest thing. I swear I was losing my mind for a week or two there. Couldn't remember where I put my gun. I remember thinking that, and then when I checked again, it was right where I left it. Cleaned it real good after that and put it up. I was so glad I hadn't misplaced it or something. Locked it away so I wouldn't lose it again. Lots of shit can happen when a gun is just laying around."

"Good idea, Pops. Real good idea."

A few hours later, Jason was lying in bed staring at the ceiling. He had checked in on Maia who was sleeping peacefully in her 'away from home room' down the hall from him. Mim and William's home was spacious enough for everyone to have their own space. He and Leela had never stayed the night, they barely visited as a couple. Only on alternating holidays did Leela grace their home with her presence. Jason smiled because he knew that Mim preferred it that way. It would take her hours to dispel all that negative energy after she left.

He wondered what would happen next. The shit was definitely hitting the fan and he had a feeling that the speed was about to be turned up. He hadn't talked to Mike at all today. He was out of town for a workshop with Sly. Life went on even with him behind bars. When the court appointed representatives showed up at the Municipal Building to take him in for questioning, he and Mike exchanged glances. Mike was leaning forward, about to say something when Jason shook his head ever so slightly. The look in his eyes said it all. *No need, brotha. The gig is up.* The only regret that he had was that it had happened in front of Simone, and he hadn't had a chance to explain anything to her. *What did she think? What could she think? How in the hell could he explain it to her? Why the hell did he think he needed to?*

He reached over to the night stand and picked up his Droid. He smiled again realizing that he was intending to call Simone instead of Leela. He wasn't too concerned about what his wife thought. She didn't think too much of their daughter, dropping her off the way she did, so he was pretty much through with her for the moment.

Besides, who the hell cares what she thinks?

He scrolled to Simone's number even though he knew it by heart. He just wanted to look at her name in front of him.

How pitiful was that?

Actually, it felt pretty good right about now. The problem was, it was 10:45 at night and what would she think of him calling her after being taken to jail for God knows what.

You won't know until you do it.

Putting his finger to the screen, he touched her name and took a deep breath.

I can't make it. It's too far and I'm too tired. Condo, here I come. Nobody is at the house, and I don't need to deal with a long drive for no reason. Greg won't be back until tomorrow so, no harm, no foul. Besides, I'm grown.

Mim's flowers were definitely having an effect on Simone's thinking lately. She thought about her and realized how lucky Maia was to have such a strong and wonderful role model in her life.

Wonder what her mother is like? She must be something else, having such a beautiful little girl and such a...

Simone stopped herself before she finished that thought.

I'm really tired. Get a grip and focus on the highway before you wrap yourself around a guard rail.

Ishua kept a respectful distance as he followed Simone to her development. He couldn't get through the security entrance so he parked down the street and walked to an area where he could see her building through the hedges. She unlocked the door and went inside. The lights came on in several rooms and the blinds and the shades closed.

Good girl. Sleep tight, Missus. I will meet you first thing in the morning. Keep the doors locked.

Chapter 28

Jason and his boy Mike were chilling out before they went back to the school to catch the bus to go to Decatur for the State Championship game. No one had expected a team from the Southside of Chicago to advance to the Championship game, but no one except a high school from Southside Chicago had Jason Copeny as its star running back. Jason's head wasn't the only thing that was swelling as he thought about how many new honeys he would have after tonight's game. Sure, he had Alayah, the girl loved him to death, but it was time for some new, virgin territory, so to speak. He had told Alayah he wanted to hook up before he left for the game, so she should get herself to his house by two o'clock. That would give them some time and he could get himself together before his little brother and nosey ass sisters got home from school. Of course, she said she would be there. "Don't wear no drawers, let them titties bounce too," he said, knowing that whatever he told her to do—it was as good as done.

Mike had brought a couple of joints with him for celebration after the game but Jason figured that one or two before wouldn't hurt. After all, tonight was going to be the bomb. No way nothing could interfere with the magic that was going to take place tonight. The doorbell rang at ten minutes to two. The earlier she got there, the earlier she could leave. He let her in and led her upstairs. She was looking good in her denim mini skirt and scooped neck tee shirt and gladiator sandals. They were having Indian summer in Chicago, and nobody knew how to dress. Her shirt barely covered her belly button, and her skirt barely covered her butt. Just the way a seventeen-year-old boy would like it. She stopped smiling when she saw Mike sitting in the chair by the window. Confusion and annoyance replaced her smile. In an effort to remain positive, she said, "Look baby, see what I got with the money you gave me? Ain't they cute? The earrings got little hearts on 'em. Just like the necklace. It's a Queen of Hearts playing card. 'Cause you said I'm the queen of your heart, right?"

Jason put his hand on her butt and answered, "Yup, you sure are. And tonight I'm gonna be king. So gimme a kiss, girl." Alayah started to protest because Mike was still sitting there, a little too high to figure out it was time for him to go. Jason looked over at Mike and said, "Don't worry about him. He won't remember anything anyhow." He kissed her hard on the mouth and after a moment's protest, she responded and seemed to do just what Jason said—forget Mike was there. After a minute or two, when she opened her eyes, she realized he was still there and looked at Jason expecting him to tell Mike to leave. He didn't. Instead he said, "Don't worry about it, Laylay. Let's show him something he ain't never gonna get to do. Take off your clothes."

Alayah's head turned slightly as if she had heard a dog whistle. Her brow scrunched up showing that she could not understand what she had just been instructed to do. "What?"

"You heard me. Take off your clothes. That's what you usually do when you get here ain't it? Today ain't no different."

"But he's here."

"And?"

"Baby, I thought it was gonna be just you and me and we could spend some time…" her voice trailed off.

"We are spending time. I just want my boy to see how lucky I am. And how fine you are. Here let me help you." Jason slowly pulled up the tee shirt, fully expecting Alayah to stop him or slap him or something. She didn't. That fueled his excitement and he proceeded to fondle her breasts and whisper softly in her ear that she was

giving him just what he wanted and showing him how much she loved him. He noticed the tears as they fell in his fingertips but the joint made it easier for him to ignore them. Now that the shirt was off, he started on the zipper of the skirt. She resisted only for a moment as he continued to whisper and fondle.

Mike tried to get up to leave but by now he was hooked on what he was watching in real life from a front row seat. Nobody seemed to mind, so why should he? A moment later, Alayah was standing there completely undressed except for her sandals. She was beautiful and frightened but excited at the same time. Excitement won out and she responded to Jason's every move and command. She didn't come out of her trance until she looked up from all fours and saw Mike handling his business in front of her while Jason handled his from behind. That seemed to break the spell and both boys finished at the same time. Jason moved away and Mike slumped back in the chair. Alayah fell on the floor and balled up in the fetal position as if she had been kicked in the stomach. "Get up Laylay. You got to go. We got to get cleaned up for the game." She didn't move. Tears flowed freely now and they were becoming annoying. "Girl, get up," he said. He walked over to his bed and reached under and pulled out the shoebox filled with cash. He counted out ten twenties and tossed them over to her. The money seemed to rain down in slow motion landing all around her, with one twenty landing directly on her behind. "Come on now, get up. Get you a king of hearts this time. That's what I am to you, right baby?" He laughed. Mike snickered. Alayah did just that. Lay there. "Girl, I ain't tellin' you again. Get your ass up. My nosey ass sisters will be home any minute and your nasty ass needs to be gone." He didn't mean to say harsh words to her but he needed her out of the house. If what Mr. William had told him was true, then everybody knew about these visits and someday, somebody would tell Mim.

At that, Alayah rose from the floor and gathered her shirt and skirt and walked to the corner and turned her back and put on her clothes. She smoothed her hair and wiped the tears away from her beautiful caramel face. Jason breathed a sigh of relief knowing that she would be out of the house in a few more minutes. He smiled his most winning smile and grabbed her necklace and pulled her toward him." Thanks baby girl, you knew just what I needed. Don't forget to get you a little something something," he said pointing to the money that still lay on the floor.

"Bye J. I love you, you know that? I still do." She looked over at Mike, who put his head down and stared at the floor. She turned and walked out of the room.

"You know your way out, right?" he called after her. He turned and looked at Mike who was staring at him. "What?"

He hoped that she would answer but then hoped that she wouldn't. Simone had no idea of who he really was—or at least who he had been when he was younger. At that time Jason thought the world revolved around him and treating a woman like dirt was what a man was supposed to do. They weren't put on this earth for any other purpose. Right? He had thought that all of his life, up until he had that run-in with William. It was then that he began to have any idea of what it truly meant to be a man and how a man was to treat a woman. He began spending time with William and watching him as he interacted with Mim and every other woman he met. Never once did he speak to her the way he saw some other men talk to their women or any woman in general. In fact, he noticed that men talked and treated some women the way he treated Alayah. And then, those same men were courteous, respectful, and mannerly when Mim was around.

Jason started noticing lots of things around that time. The more he noticed, the angrier he got that his uncle, not his father was the one to open his eyes to it all. That was one of the reasons he abused Alayah that afternoon. He was 'smelling himself' as William called it. Wanting to prove that his version of manhood was the right one, not the one that his uncle was exposing him to. If he accepted this new version, his young mind processed, then he would be rejecting what he thought his father was. He had nothing else of his father to cling to but this twisted version of manhood. And for him, that was better than nothing at all.

Jason was snapped out of his wonderings by the sound of Simone's soft, warm voice easing his current state of distress as the uninvited past was weighing on his mind.

"Hello, Jason. Are you alright?" The words floated through the phone and into his being.

I am now, he wanted to say but held his tongue. "Hey there. I wanted to apologize for the interruption the other day." Like he just had to leave for a doctor's appointment or something.

"We managed. Shamel and Tyreek agreed to meet on Thursday, so everything is cool. Sly and Mike are out of town 'til tomorrow and I was really busy today on… other cases," she replied carefully, trying to keep her voice steady even though she was so happy to hear his.

So, which one of ya'll is going to say it first?

"I really called just to hear your voice," Jason said quietly.

Ding ding ding. Collect 200 bucks. Go girl, go!

"I hope you don't take that the wrong way. It's just been a rough couple of days and talking to you always makes things make sense…I can't explain it real clearly right now. I know I shouldn't have called this late. I'm sorry. I hope I didn't disturb you too much. Tell your husband I'm a drunk mediation participant or something," he said.

Coast is clear now. You can say whatever you want. Go ahead.

"I'm glad you called Jason. It's good to hear your voice. You can tell how a person is through their voice," she said quietly moderating hers.

"How am I?"

"You are better than I would be. And you are not bothering me. I just got in a few minutes ago, so it's no problem."

"Kind of late on a work night. So, you go clubbing after hours or what?" he tried to make a joke. He was better than even he expected.

"Ha ha. You got jokes in the middle of the night. No. I worked late and was too tired to drive home, so I stayed at the townhouse. Close and comfortable. What more could I ask for?" she said.

Company?

No response for a minute. "So, this is not a problem for you right now? My calling for no apparent reason?"

"I thought you called to hear my voice. I'm like… audio-therapy or something. Is that right, Jason?"

"Yes, you are, Simone. I feel more focused already."

"Is this a problem for you—being on the phone so late? You're not keeping your wife up are you?"

Smooth.

"I'm at William and Mim's. Maia is here too. Sound asleep down the hall."

"Oh. So, it looks like we're not bothering anybody."

"That's what it looks like."

"Wouldn't it be easier to talk face to face?"

That's it, girl, say what you're thinking.

"I would like that very much," Jason sat up on the bed.

"So, would I. Do you have something to write down the address?"

Mim, did you know this would happen when you gave me the flowers?

Simone sipped some more water and flowers from her glass.

Yes, she probably did. Why do you think she gave them to you?

The knock on the door came about forty minutes later. It was a firm confident knock. No hesitation. No conflicted thinking behind the rap rap on the townhouse door.

For the past forty minutes Simone wondered what the hell she had done and why she had done it.

All I did was invite a colleague, and friend, to my house after a harrowing experience. After all, he did call me looking for solace, right?

Do you really believe that? You know exactly why you invited him here.

And why is that? Say it out loud and shame the Devil, my grandmother always said.

I like him.

I like Sly too, but you don't see me inviting him over here in the middle of the night for – conversation.

Hush.

Well, girl, be honest with yourself for once. What do you want from this man? He's fine.

He's married.

He likes you, that's obvious.

He's married.

If that's your only complaint, then no biggie. It's not like anybody you know seems to think that being married is too important.

Well, I thought Jason did. I thought I did too.

Well, I guess you were wrong then, huh?

It's possible that we just want each other's company. Someone to talk to.

Who actually listens.

Exactly.

Someone who cares.

Jason stood on the other side of the door, waiting for Simone to answer. Part of him hoped that she wouldn't. Maybe she had come to her senses and realized that this probably wasn't the best idea. The part that thought that was very small. The larger part that got him out of the bed and into the car at William and Mim's was the part that had been controlling his thinking since the first day he saw her at the courthouse.

"Boy, where you think you're going in the middle of the night?" William had asked when Jason picked up his keys from the stand next to the front door.

"Need some air. Maia is sleep. Just checked on her. She's out for the night," he replied as he put on his leather jacket.

"Some air, huh? It's twenty some degrees outside and you need some air. You couldn't just open the window?" William studied Jason for a minute more.

Jason finished zipping up his jacket and put on his gloves and Kangol. "Yeah, just need to get out."

"Well, you be careful out there. Black man driving while black at night. I just picked your ass up from jail. Don't want to have to do it again."

"I'm good, Pops. No problem."

"So, you be back?"

" 'Course, be back in a little bit."

"Well, like I said, be careful," William mumbled as he leaned against the staircase rail.

"Always," was the reply as Jason shut the door behind him.

William turned around and looked up the steps as his beautiful wife came downstairs in her silk gown and robe.

"Where's he off to?" Mim asked in her sultry low voice. The sound of it still made William's knees weak after all these years.

"Where you think he's going?" he responded as he put his arm around her waist. She laid her head on her husband's chest and wrapped herself into him.

"Took him long enough," she whispered. They stood there for a moment before smiling that smile that only two people who love each other can smile. They both wished the same thing at the same time, that one day Jason would be able to smile that way too. Mim took William's hand and led him up the stairs. He followed, hands gently caressing the smooth silk as it flowed gently behind the love he had waited all his life for.

Simone opened the door and welcomed Jason into her humble abode. It was truly anything but humble. Everything seemed so new. So tasteful and understated, like its owner. Jason took off his jacket and held it, not knowing where to put it. Simone took it from him and hung it in the hall closet, as if she had done it a thousand times before. The corners of Jason's mouth curled slightly. A warm sense of déjà vu enveloping him. Like he had done this before. Like he was home.

She waited for him to step up into the living room and find a comfortable spot. He hesitated for a moment and then chose the white-on-white sofa. It looked too elegant to sit on but then again so did everything in the room. Like it had just been photographed for one of those bougie magazines that Leela left around the house, trying to convince people that she actually read them. Since Simone didn't seem to have any problem with where he sat, he settled into the very comfortable and cozy furniture. She sat at the other end and pulled her legs up under her. She was barefooted, and he found himself wishing that he had caught a glimpse of her toes before they had disappeared from sight.

There was a moment of silence as they sat at opposite ends of the sofa. Simone waited patiently for Jason to relax and compose himself. She could tell that the experience of the past two days had taken its toll on him and that he must really be having a hard time processing it all to actually reach out to her in the middle of the night. You only do that with a person that you trust. Completely. Totally.

So why didn't he go home to his wife?

"Thanks for letting me come over here so late. I—"

Didn't want to go home—had no place else to go—wanted to be with you.

"I needed to clear my head before I went home, and it was a little too late to start explaining things and Maia was asleep at Mim's…" he stammered.

"Sounds like you needed to refocus before you could address everything else that's waiting for you. Needed some down time, space to breathe a little. No expectations, no questions. Is that right?" She smiled as she spoke, hoping that he would get her mediation humor.

He smiled in return. "That's why I like talking to you. You got skills," he quipped. "You hear me. Actually, hear me and I don't have to explain myself. Yeah, I just needed some space." The room fell silent again and Simone waited for him to open up. She knew it was bubbling right under the surface and if she was patient, it would push its way out. It always did. Even if it took years. And she knew enough to know that Jason had been holding on to this one for a long, long time. Just like Harlem.

"Would you like something to drink? I have teas, courtesy of your mom, ice water, seltzer…" Simone said as she sensed that he needed more time to ease into what was on his mind. She got up and walked into the kitchen. He got up and followed her, sneaking a peek at her toes as she went by.

Pretty.

"Tea would be good right about now? Did Mim give you anything to calm a nig—person down?" He caught himself as he sat on the barstool in the breakfast nook.

"Kava, currently unavailable in these United States. Valerian, chamomile, and her special blend of all of them. I don't know what she puts in it but I was relaxed and at peace with the world for days," she said.

"Yeah, I'll have that. Thanks."

Simone turned on the tea kettle. Jason watched her as she moved easily around the kitchen. Watching her reminded him of watching Mim when he was a little boy. So graceful and beautiful. "She really likes you, you know? Birds of a feather, I guess. She says you are watery."

"What's that mean exactly?"

"Hell, if I know."

"She's great. I like her too. We're supposed to get together sometime soon and check out the bookstores in town. That should be fun," she said as she leaned against the counter waiting for the water to boil.

"Beware. Make sure you've got all day. She is a monster when it comes to books. She owns iBooks and they know her by name in most of the bookstores in the tri-state area."

"Seems like you and your mom are very close," Simone said, speaking honestly.

Jason silently thanked her for the segue into what was on his mind. "We are. When I was little, she was my everything. Then I turned into a hardheaded, know it all teenager and lost sight of who she was and all that she had done for me and my sisters and brother. I thought I knew it all. That sure came back and bit my ass. Took it twenty years, but here I sit telling you my troubles instead of being at home or at least with my daughter. Mim might call it Karma. William would say what goes around, comes around."

"What would you call it?" Simone asked, still not sure what 'it' was.

The kettle was steaming, she never let it whistle, she hated the shrill, high-pitched sound of it. She poured the water into the waiting cups and dipped the tea balls in, just like Mim had taught her. Another moment of silence while Simone covered the cups to let them steep.

She brought them to the table and sat across from Jason. He took a deep breath and looked down at the cup.

Here we go, she thought.

Will she throw me out after I tell her this? he thought.

Chapter 29

Karl was making the most of his paid leave of absence on the river boat casino, Ole Miss, when his cell phone rang. He reached into his pocket to check the number before pushing the Bluetooth attached to his ear. If they want to fuckin' get rid of him over some shit that happened twenty years ago that they can't prove, then he didn't have to answer the phone when they called. He told himself that with much bravado, but somewhere close to the core of his being, he wasn't as brash as he pretended to be. What had happened that night was supposed to be as dead as Alayah. How had it managed to show up now? He had made sure that there was nothing that could be traced back to him. They didn't do reliable DNA testing back then. Any other evidence was safe and sound… The others involved had either disappeared or died. Things had a way of working themselves out, it seemed. Would the evidence still be good after all this time? What caused them to reopen the case in the first place?

When the Mayor had called him to his office for the 'meeting', he had no clue as to what was about to happen. Karl walked in feeling on top of the world. He was sure that the mayor was going to invite him to a gala event celebrating his pending promotion. The cool smile he had on his face was practiced and plastered so that he looked self-deprecating enough to appear meek and appreciative.

"What the fuck have you done? Do you know what this shit is going to do to me? You are already ruined whether you did it or not!" Vernon Armstrong bellowed across his mahogany desk. His jaw clenched in that way that means a man is so pissed he's fighting to control himself or he's about to have a heart attack, or some combination of the two. He sat back and swung his chair around to face the window.

Karl thought for a moment. He had seen someone else do that same dismissive power move. His brother. *Maybe that's where he got it from. Wannabe mayor one day? Practicing the moves?* Karl stood there waiting for Vernon to turn back around. Running through his mind what he could possibly be talking about. Slowly Vernon did just that. Turned around and faced him. He pushed a file across the desk toward Karl. It was old and worn. *They don't even use files like that anymore,* Karl thought.

"Open it up. Take a good look. Anything or anyone look familiar to you?" Vernon asked in a quieter tone.

Karl's brow scrunched up, still not grasping what could be inside the file that got Vernon so riled up. He opened it innocently enough and looked at the first picture. That was enough. He knew now. He kept his head down for a minute trying to decide how to play it. The look on his face in the next few seconds would tell all. He knew that Vernon was waiting to read his reaction. Everything lay in the balance. His career, his future, his freedom.

"Oh man, that's horrible. Looks like she was a pretty girl. What happened and what's it got to do with me?" Karl looked the mayor straight in the eyes.

"Well, I'll be damned. You are a real piece of work. You know that? Anybody else would have cringed or something. You just look and say, 'that's horrible, what's it got to do with me?'"

That's 'cause I saw it first hand and it was much worse in living color. Karl opened the file again and flipped through the murder book. Snapshots from so many angles. Police reports, forensics, such as they were. Eyewitnesses. Karl tried not to bunch up his eyebrows, but he never heard anything about eyewitnesses. He was about to read further when Armstrong snatched the file out of his hands.

"Give me that. I shouldn't have shown it to you in the first place, but I needed to get some background real quick before the media gets hold of this. And they will. They always do. Talk to me, Karl. Between you and your brother, ya'll are gonna end my career." Armstrong sat back and took a deep breath like he hadn't been breathing at all for the past ten minutes.

"I remember hearing about this when I was in high school. Happened over on the west side of town, I think. I didn't live over there so it was all hearsay, you know? Some girl got herself raped and killed one night. They said that the dude who did her got shot in a drive-by a week or two later," Karl paused for effect. "So, like I asked earlier, what's this got to do with me?"

"What it's got to do with you is that it seems like your story via hearsay doesn't match up with a confession from someone who says that he was there—along with you."

Chapter 30

The sky was in the process of leaving midnight black and entering predawn blue when Jason stopped talking. He didn't know that he had so much pent up inside of him about that time in his life. It wasn't just the tragedy with Alayah and his sister. It was everything that had brought him to that point. His lack of a father, his misguided idea of what a man should be, his encounter with William. It all came running out of him in a way that he hadn't known possible. At the end of it all, he was drained. Empty. Vulnerable in a way that he had never experienced before. This was worse than being naked. His nerves were bare, stripped, raw. He felt undone. He sat there waiting for some reaction from Simone. No woman could possibly stomach being in a room with a man who had treated a young girl in the manner that he had treated Alayah. He waited. How could he look her in the eye after all that he had said and done. Even if it was so long ago. To him, it felt like yesterday.

Simone got up and walked to the closet. Jason hadn't expected her to be that abrupt. Maybe a little lecture before she threw him out into the darkest part of an early morning. He shook his head and heard her footsteps coming toward him on the hardwood floor. She stood in front of him and he got a really good look at her lovely toes. Only covered with clear polish, they seemed to twinkle in the light from the kitchen's chandelier. He drank them in knowing that after he lifted his head he would probably never have the opportunity to see any of her ever again. She couldn't continue to work with him, let alone continue on as his friend. How could his past so mess up his present? Had he just made her an accomplice by sharing the truth with her? He had had enough sense not to mention what happened to Jax. He took a breath and lifted his head. He frowned for a second, not processing what she was giving him. It surely wasn't what he expected. Instead of his jacket, she was giving him a comforter.

"I thought you might want to cover up for a little while. You look really drained and I think you are too exhausted to be on the road right now. The guest room is down the hall. You saw it on the grand tour," she said with a slight smile. "I'll turn the water back on. You could use something to help you relax."

He looked in her eyes, trying to read what was behind the soft, dark orbs. He saw what he always saw—warmth, compassion, even understanding of pain. She smiled again as she held out the comforter.

"I like to wrap myself up sometimes and cover my head," she said sounding a little like Maia when she explained something important to him. "It helps sometimes, believe me. Blocks out the world. Gives you a feeling of safety and that everything is okay. At least for now."

Jason stood up and grasped the down-filled blanket. He looked at her and didn't know what to say. *I'd like to wrap you up in my arms for the rest of my life.* She looked back at him, and he knew that he didn't have to say anything. He followed her to the bedroom where she stopped at the door and turned on the light.

"Towels and stuff are in the bathroom. Hope the bed is comfortable. No one has slept in it yet, so thanks for christening it for me. What time would you like me to wake you?" she said in her best Hilton concierge voice.

"I just need a few hours. I can wake myself up. Maia is fine. William knows that I was coming over here to talk to you, so it's all good. Leela – well she probably expects me to be at Mim's so—no problem," he replied. "Thanks Simone," he continued. "I didn't think… you would understand. I just want you to know the truth." *And what is true homeboy, huh? You are here with this woman instead of home with your wife. At least tell yourself the truth. You never even told Leela this shit and still don't plan to. Tell the truth—you love her. You love this woman. Just tell the truth.*

"You don't need to say anything Jason. That's what friends are for." She smiled at him, took a deep breath and walked down the hall back toward the kitchen, leaving Jason listening to the soft sound of her feet on the floor.

Chapter 31

Simone sat at her computer staring at the calendar for the day. *So much to do, so little time* .... The funny thing was that she didn't really care. She was thinking about the morning. It was so easy, her and Jason waking up, getting ready for work, rushing around like a – *like a what? A happy couple?* She thought about putting the thought out of her head, but considering what her day looked like, she decided to hold on to it just a little while longer. She might need it later. She had to be at the courthouse in an hour for the first session between Tyreek and Shamel. Everyone had worked so hard to set this up. It had taken so long that she had to petition the court not to charge Tyreek as an adult if the mediation fell through. She wasn't planning to inform the young men of that fact. If they continued to think that they might end up charged and probably convicted as adults, they might be more agreeable to the benefits of mediation. She logged off of her laptop, packed it and her files into her case and headed for the door. As she closed it, she realized that there was a spring in her step and the slightest smile on her lips. Why not? She was going to see Jason for the second time in one morning.

Tyreek arrived with Sly, Shamel got out of Mike's car right around the same time. The men gave each other dap and waited to see if the young brothers would do the same. No acknowledgement of any kind took place between them. Sly and Mike exchanged a glance and lead the way into the bowels of the courthouse. Jason met them at the door of the mediation room. He had gone back to Mim and William's to change his clothes and say goodbye to Maia before Mim took her to school. Mim smiled her all knowing smile at him when she came downstairs and saw him guzzling orange juice from the carton.

"That's why I got two. That one is yours now. Make sure you put it in a spot, so you know which one to guzzle from next time. Replacing depleted energy this morning?" she asked.

"I was up late. I need something to get me through the morning," Jason replied.

"I'm sure you do," she said.

"It was good to have someone to talk to. You know what I mean. I always talk to you and Pops. That's a given. I mean … I don't know what I mean," he said as he cleared a spot on the refrigerator door for the carton of orange juice. "We talked for a long time. Well actually, I talked, she listened. Then I slept in her guest room. Slept good too. Got up this morning and fixed something to eat, talked some more and left. She eats like you do only not so …well, you know…*you*." He stood there facing his mother and lowered his head like he did when he was six. " It was good. I needed that. But you knew that didn't you?"

"It doesn't matter what I know. It is written all over your face. It's what *you* needed to know. She is a good influence on you. It would have been nice if you met sooner in life. But all things work for your benefit. You needed to experience—some things so that you could truly appreciate what you now have in your life. Make the most of what has been presented to you. Give her time, she'll eat according to what she needs. She's a baby—just learning."

Jason looked at his mother for what seemed like a long time. What was she saying to him? He hated when she said something that had a double meaning. Just learning what?

"Morning Daddy, morning Mommie Mim," Maia pounced into

his arms interrupting his thought and the conversation. He had to remember where they left off because he really wanted to continue this train of thought with Mim as soon as he returned tonight from work. *Returned here tonight? What about going home?* What about it? He answered himself, kissed Maia and headed towards the door on his way to see Simone… Oh, to go to work.

Chapter 32

Sly and Simone sat across the table from Shamel and Tyreek. Mike and Jason sat at the far end of the room as observers. Sly welcomed the two young men, introduced everyone in the room and started to explain the mediation process. He and Simone had run through this what seemed like a thousand times, trying every scenario. Trying to figure out who the young men might respond best to. No matter how they played it, the possibilities seemed uncertain. So they decided-just go for it, let the chips fall. They'd picked them up before.

Sly was finishing his part of the process and Simone started hers.

"Everything said here is confidential unless it is a credible threat of violence, child abuse or elder abuse," she began.

"Hold up," said Shamel. "You saying that no matter what I say you can't do nothing about it?"

"Unless it is a credible threat of violence or abuse of a child or an elder, the information shared during mediation is confidential." Simone said.

"So you saying that if we was to tell you about selling drugs on the street corner, you can't rat us out?" Tyreek asked, now as interested in what was being said as Shamel.

"What is said in mediation is confidential," she said.

"So if I said you is fine and I'd like to---"Tyreek , said with a smirk. Jason immediately felt himself tense up and Mike placed his finger up slightly to settle him down.

Simone looked directly at Tyreek and said, "So it sounds like you find me attractive, is that right?"

"Hell, yeah. I'll be Thundercat to your cougar," he laughed and looked for dap from Shamel, who gave it to him.

"Help me understand what you mean when you say Thundercat to my cougar. It seems like you're saying that even though I am much older than you, you think I am fine? Is that right?"

"Damn, straight. You is sweet, with your high yella ass. All long, tall, and shit."

Jason was about to spring, but it was Sly who gave him an almost imperceptible glance that made him sit back just a little. His jaw tightening even more.

"So, let's see if I am hearing you correctly, what you are saying is that even though I am old enough to be considered a cougar, you think that I am high yella and fine. And that you would be my 'boy toy' or Thundercat if I wanted you to be because I am all long, tall, and shit. Is that right?"

Tyreek sat for a minute. He hadn't expected Simone to remain so calm and neutral. He had expected the men to jump to her rescue and the whole mediation be called off. "Yeah," he answered since he couldn't think of anything else to say.

"So, it sounds like you are pleased with my appearance, surprised maybe, and that expressing your desire to do something with or to an attractive woman old enough to be your mother is important to you. Is that right?"

"Whoa, wait I ain't say all that. You fine and all, but don't say I want to fuck my mom!" Tyreek stammered across the table. Shamel cracked up laughing.

"Then I'm not clear. Help me understand what you did say, then. Sounds like maybe you were trying to say something to see if we meant what we said about confidentiality and remaining neutral. And if you said something that you thought would upset me, would we end the mediation. Is that right?"

Tyreek looked around the room. Everybody was staring at him.

"Yeah, I guess so," he answered.

"So, feeling unsure of the situation, testing the process and our neutrality? And that trust and honesty is important to you, is that right?"

"Yeah, you can't trust po-po. So why should I trust ya'll?" he said, trying to be defensive.

"Sounds like you've met po-po that you didn't trust, is that right?"

Both young men snickered. "You can say that again. I could tell you some shit," Shamel said.

"Why don't you. That's what we're here for," Simone said quietly with her fine ass.

Mike wrote on his legal pad and put his pen down. Jason glanced over and deciphered the sloppy handwriting. NOW AIN'T THAT SOME SHIT?

The next two hours were spent with each young man blaming the other's gang for the crime, violence, and drugs that decimated their neighborhoods. Neither would take responsibility for anything other than they did would they did as a response to something the other did first or to hold on to their territory. To an outsider, it would look like nothing had been accomplished. Simone and Sly were ecstatic because at least the boys were talking and shouting and cussing and blaming. *All in a day's work.* Simone thought.

When the two hours were up, Mike and Jason took the boys home or at least back to their respective neighborhoods. They would return to debrief about what had happened in this room today.

By the time that they returned, it was past one o'clock and everybody was starving. They decided to celebrate the small victory of surviving the first session and the young men scheduling a second. All in all it had been a good day. Mike suggested some place where they could get several beers because he was exhausted from all that observing. They drove to a casual restaurant off of Lakeshore Drive and got a table with a great view of the skyline.

"That's some crazy shi—stuff ya'll do, you know that?" Mike said over his second beer and buffalo wing basket. "I thought my man was gonna come out of his skin when youngblood started going at you like that Simone," he kept talking and eating at the same time. He turned his head towards Jason who was quietly eating a Reuben and fries.

Sly spoke up at that moment. "I told ya'll before but you didn't believe me. Miss Thing over here can hold her own. And probably yours too." He looked at Simone with pride. "We've worked together what? Six, seven years and I've never seen anyone mess with her and live to tell about it," he said and laughed.

Simone smiled a little and ate another zucchini stick. *God, she loved these things--- the zucchini sticks.* The men looked at her for a comment, but she just raised an eyebrow and cocked her head to the side.

"These are really good," she said.

"So, what's next? They really had a lot to say once they got started. Seems like there's something else going on that they don't want to talk about though," Jason said, changing the subject.

It worked because Mike continued, "I know. Did you see how they both would glance at each other? Even when they was cussing and blaming each other, they'd get to a point and back off. What's up with that?"

"I noticed that too. Thought it was just me," Sly said.

"Maybe they know something that needs to be kept on the down low. No matter what we said about confidentiality," Jason continued.

"Or someone," Simone said as she reached for her San Pellegrino.

"How can you drink that stuff? All fizz and no flavor," Mike asked.

They heard a quiet remark slip from Jason's lips, "Yeah, I heard the same thing about your love life."

Mike kept right on talking as if he hadn't heard. "We're gonna have to take you out and get you drunk. If you're gonna hang with us, you gonna have to keep up."

"Somebody needs to drive your drunk behinds home," she laughed.

"Yea, well, you right about that. So, we got 'til next Wednesday to poke around and see what they ain't tell us."

"Or at least get some clue so that we'll be listening for it when they start in on each other again," Sly said finishing his beer and taking out his wallet.

"So, we'll check in tomorrow with ya'll and plan a good time early next week to get together. Sound good to everybody?" Mike asked looking around for the server.

They each put in their portion of the bill plus a healthy tip, enough to dispel the rumor that black folks don't tip well and said their goodbyes with hugs all around. Jason glanced at Simone and walked over to her as she headed towards her car.

"Hey, I wanted to say thanks again for last night."

"My pleasure, if you need space again, you've got the code for the door. Feel free to use it," she said.

"Will you be there?" he asked trying to sound like he wasn't serious.

"Not tonight. Going home after I finish up at the office. Greg is back from Dallas, or so the message says." She pointed to the phone in her hand.

Jason felt his good mood wasting away. *She is married, you know. What exactly did you expect?* He smiled a weak smile, trying to hide his disappointment. "I suppose that I should check in at home too. Maia is staying at Mim's til the weekend so that she isn't bouncing back and forth. Give her some stability, you know? She doesn't know what happened and I want to talk with her mother about it without her around in case—" He wanted to say, in case it doesn't go well. "Well, you know what I mean," he continued.

Simone nodded and tried to get him back to a better place. "It was nice talking to you. I hope we can do that again sometime."

He smiled and said, "Under better circumstances next time."

Under any circumstances, she thought.

Chapter 33

When she got back to the office, she was back in her little daze, reliving the events and conversation from the night before. Her desk phone buzzed softly. Inside line. Sly. "Hey, what's up?" she asked. No need to be formal with Sly.

"Problem, Sela went home sick. Everybody else has left. There's a mediation scheduled for this evening and no observers and now, no mediator. Too short notice to start calling people at home. "

"Can it be rescheduled?"

"Doesn't look like it. State's Attorney case. Seems to have been stuck in here at the last minute. Don't know what's up with that. Court date is next week unless they can mediate this thing before then."

"Who did the intake?" she asked, her brow starting to furrow.

"Don't know. Stuff is missing. Says it's an assault and battery case. Two women at work. That's it," Sly answered. Simone could hear him fumbling through the papers in the file. "So what you want to do? Do this ourselves or let these two ladies be at the mercy of the court and face five to ten in women's correctional and a five thousand dollar fine?"

Hmmm. Mediate or go home to Greg…

"I've got time if you do," she replied.

Chapter 34

Sheva wasn't feeling too happy about this situation. She felt that now was her moment to spring. To lash out at this woman who was keeping her from her destiny. Being 'Mrs. Greg Dyson'. Now that it clicked who she was, it seemed like fate had dropped this last chance to be with Greg into her lap. She had the opportunity in the palm of her hands. He would thank her for being strong enough to do what needed to be done for them to be together. Her brain was feverish with jealousy. Her breath came quicker and her eyes narrowed as her face started to resemble a bull about to charge. The only problem with what her emotions were telling her to do was that some small, small part of her otherwise fevered brain was trying to tell her to slow her roll. She couldn't put words to it but something in her told her that this woman, this current Mrs. Dyson wasn't the one to play with. *But wouldn't she do what married women do when they find out that there's another woman? Cry? Fall apart? Leave? Of course, she would.* Sheva sat up straighter in her chair, unconsciously trying to make herself leaner and taller, mirroring her rival across the table. She took a deep breath, hoping that the extra Zoloft and Paxil she took would kick in soon, she started to play her part.

"So, what I'm hearing is that you were upset that morning over what Marisa said to you. And that after the bad night that you had had, you exploded and took your frustration out by leaping across the desk and jumping on her back as she headed towards the door, is that right?"

"That's exactly right."

"So, feeling frustrated and angry about the night before, you needed to vent your frustration since you couldn't do it with the person responsible, your lover?"

"No, he's not responsible."

"Help me understand who is."

"You are."

The air in the room exited with a whoosh. Sly's jaw tightened as he cast his glance over to Simone. He held the urge to jump out of his seat and grab Sheva by the neck. Marisa's neck almost broke as she shifted her gaze to the love-crazed female sitting beside her. Simone sat perfectly still processing the vibrations that had just assaulted her eardrums.

You Puerto Rican two-bit bitch. You come into my job and throw this shit up in my face in front of my coworker. Oh Greg, you do know how to pick them. I'm done with you and about to be done with her too.

Simone took a deep breath and thought about how she was feeling. In less than a few seconds, she had reflected back her own feelings and knew how she should proceed. She was at work after all and needed to practice her skills.

"So, what I'm hearing is that the man you are having an affair with is my husband. Is that right?"

What the fuck is she doing? Sly thought to himself. He looked at Simone and then back at Sheva. He had known Simone for the last seven years and loved her for the past six. He would do anything to keep her from being hurt and now that good for nothing husband had brought his shit here and dumped it right into his wife's lap. Now it all made sense. That's why the intake information was missing.

"No. It's not an affair. Greg and I are in love. He just hasn't left you yet because he's concerned about you falling apart when he leaves you for me."

"He's being thoughtful because I'm so delicate and might not be able to handle it?"

"That's right. He's caring like that."

"I might be overcome with grief and try to commit suicide and end up in the hospital, medicated and having to meet with psychiatric doctors for several days? Is that what you are saying?"

Sheva swallowed so loudly it was audible to everyone in the room. Marisa bowed her head and looked at the table while suppressing a grin the size of Illinois. Sly leaned forward in his chair.

"He loves me, chu know? If it hadn't been for chu whining and sniveling that night, he would have come home to me and none of this would have ever happened." Sheva sat up in her seat in a last-ditch effort to appear as if she were in control of herself. She hadn't expected the response that she got from this woman sitting across the table from her. How did she look so cool and calm when some woman just told her she was sleeping with her husband? She sat there looking at her like she had just said that the sky is blue. *Duh.*

"When you say come home to you, help me understand what you mean." Simone asked in the most detached and neutral voice she had. Then she looked at this pitiful excuse for a woman sitting across from her and waited, like a panther about to spring on its prey after watching it run out of energy from the long chase.

"His condo in the city. Our love nest," she said with a hint of bravado in her voice.

"You mean the three-bedroom townhouse with my name on the mortgage that I let him live in since the last time he had an affair? The townhouse that he can't afford to purchase on his own because of his bankruptcies, plural, due to his excessive lifestyle? That townhouse?"

What is she doing? This has crossed the line of ethics. I should have done something. It would have been better if she had jumped across the table and whupped her ass. Sly noticed that his leg was twitching. Sure sign of nervous energy. He'd been doing that since he was a kid. Most of the time now though, he had it under control, but this was different. The woman he loved had been attacked by a bitch and he was seeing a side of Simone that was new to him. He always knew she was dangerous, in a quiet, secret kind of way, but tonight he felt he was about to see something new under the sun.

"He said he owned it! That we needed our own place until the divorce was final and we could buy our dream house," Sheva shouted, leaning forward in her chair, fat little fists pounding the table. Simone thought of that little pig in the insurance commercials. Sheva looked back and forth between Marisa and Sly as if she were trying to convince them as much as she was trying to convince herself.

"Feeling lied to? Trying to make yourself believe him because you wanted what he told you to be true? And that truthfulness is important to you?"

"It was true--is true. He loves me and you know it. You sitting up there all tall and shit, thinking that you're like some kind of a model in your expensive clothes and shiny wedding rings, hair all perfect with your fancy ass job. You're just jealous because I'm young and Latina and I got what he likes!"

 "What I'm hearing is that you are comparing yourself with the wife of your lover, is that right? And that you need to convince me that you are what my husband likes whereas he is still married to me, do I understand that correctly?" Simone stopped talking hoping that shorty was able to process what she was hearing.

No response. The heat came on and filled the room with the only sound.

Dumb bitch. Simone pursed her lips the way she did when she was trying really hard to deal with participants who were too stupid to come in from a shower of shit. Sly took a deep breath and concentrated on his twitching leg, anxious to see what was about to transpire.

"Feeling like you have no self-worth? I'm all tall and wear expensive clothes and have diamond wedding rings, that you're not as good as me because I'm the wife and you're the wannabe and that after two years of spreading your legs for my husband and letting him use you like a whore, he still won't divorce me. And that looking beautiful and classy is important to you and it makes you feel angry and cheap, that even though you are young, Latina, and do whatever he wants you to do it hasn't helped much? He still came home to me? Did I understand what you were saying?"

Sheva twitched once. Sly leaned forward a little more in case he had to thrust a pen in her mouth to keep her from swallowing her tongue. He watched as she started to rock back and forth slowly. Tears began to well up at the corners of her eyes.

This should be on reality TV. Mediation Meltdowns. Girlfriend is good! Tore the bitch a new ass and didn't lay a finger on her. I wouldn't have missed this shit for the world. It was worth getting arrested. I can't wait to get back to work tomorrow. And Mr. Thing over there is about to jump out his skin. Could it be that he got a thing for Mrs. Dyson. Look how he look at her. Damn. I want someone that fine to look at me like that. Mr. Mayor, you might have to get to stepping. Mr. Mediator can observe me anytime…There's something to be said for this mediation shit. Marisa turned her body slightly in Sly's direction and took a deep breath that caused her breasts to push against her Donna Karan silk blouse.

The rocking back and forth had turned into a roll back and forth, with a moan attached. Sheva held herself and moved her lips as the tears escaped and raced each other down her flushed cheeks. Her forehead was damp by now and tiny tendrils of limp wet hair hung in her eyes. White people aren't the only ones who smell like wet dogs when their hair is wet. Sheva looked up from the daze that was creeping up on her as she glanced at Simone with the look of a lost toddler written all over her face.

Part of Simone wanted to feel sorry for her-- but just a small part. Some part of her wanted to tell her that Greg was an ass, that she wasn't the first and she probably wouldn't be the last. And that she used to hurt just like she was hurting now but you get over it, if you choose to. But not now. This was too therapeutic to mess it all up with sympathy. Besides it was good practice. She proceeded with no fear. *God bless you, Mim.*

"I'm sorry, Sheva, did I hear you say something? I didn't want to miss it with the heat on and all. We've taken up a large part of the session with only you having had a chance to speak. Marisa still has to share as well."

More rolling and moaning. "Why?" Sheva asked.

"Help me understand what you mean by why?"

"Why doesn't he love me? I do whatever he wants. I try to be …to be…"

Simone leaned forward slowly and said quietly, "To be me?"

Sheva let out a choking wail. The tears gushed as she covered her face with her hands.

Simone stayed close to Sheva's ear and said, "You can't." She sat back and looked at Marisa and Sheva. "We have run out of time for this session. We'll have to schedule another that is convenient for all parties. I'll check the calendar." She pushed back her chair and stood to her full 6'1" with heels, smoothed her skirt and pushed the tissue box in Sheva's direction before she walked toward the door. She stopped, turned around and said, "It will have to take place this week as your trial is scheduled for next week."

Sly escorted Marisa from the room and left her in the waiting room while he went to find Simone.

Chapter 35

"Are you okay?" he asked as he entered Simone's office. She had her back to him scrolling through the digital calendar in search of dates and times. She turned around slowly.

"Why wouldn't I be? Just another mediation, right?"

"Simone, I had no idea."

She smiled, "I know that."

He stepped closer. "So, are you okay?"

She took a deep breath and replied, "How is she?"

"Still rocking when I left. I've got to give it to you though, you handled your business."

"Just practicing my skills," Simone said softly.

Just then, Marisa ran through the door. "I think you better come quick. Sheva's on the floor and she's not moving."

Chapter 36

Simone rose from her chair and ran into the mediation room not stopping to put her shoes back on. Sly and Marisa followed close behind. Sheva was sprawled beside her chair as if she had spilled out of it, which was probably the case.

"I came back into the room to get my pocketbook 'cause I wanted to check my text messages and she was—she was—she was—like that," Marisa stammered.

Simone was already kneeling beside her checking for a pulse and respiration.

"Call 911," Simone said to Sly, but he had already gone to the office to do just that. Simone took a deep breath and stared at the pitiful heap on the floor.

Let her miserable nasty ass die. Serves her chili pepper eating ass right.

Marisa was huddled in a corner, wide eyed, and wondering what could possibly happen next. Then she found out. Simone grabbed a pair of scissors from a drawer of the nearby desk and slashed the front of the polyester sweater that was housing the fat tissues that Sheva called breasts that Greg had manhandled for the past two years.

"Not on my watch you won't. You will not die here. You're going to have to do that on your own time," Simone whispered. The words were so soft that Marisa barely heard them. She started pulmonary thrusts trying to get Sheva's chest to rise and fall on its own. One two three four five six…

Sly re-entered the room and watched as Simone continued to work on Sheva. She worked for five minutes or more with no apparent results. The more she pounded, the more her face contorted to the point that Sly wanted to pull her away.

"No! She won't die! You hear me? She won't die! Not today, she won't. Come on, Sheva. You dumb bitch! That good for nothing son of a bitch is not worth dying over. I gave up part of my life for him and I will not let you do the same. Breathe bitch! Breathe!"

Simone pounded again. Sheva's body convulsed one time. Simone hit her again not knowing if it was to save her or to punish her for sleeping with her no-good husband. She felt hands pull her away. The paramedics had arrived and took over where she had left off. They loaded Sheva onto a stretcher and headed her towards the ambulance. Sly was answering questions for the driver when another paramedic asked who was riding to the hospital with the victim.

"I will," answered Simone.

Dammmmmmnn, thought Marisa. In all the commotion, Marisa had a thought that it might serve her purposes to start working on Sly. He was standing with Simone, arms encircling her, rubbing her back and talking softly to her. The paramedic walked over to them and said, "If you hadn't done what you did, she would have died. You did real good, you know?"

Simone closed her eyes and tried to find a quiet place in her mind to get away from the horror that had taken place tonight. Had she pushed her too far?

You're good girl, but you're not that good. They said it was an overdose of prescription drugs. Pocketbook full of them. She took them before she walked in here. If it's anybody's fault, it's that no good husband of yours. Can't blame yourself for anything other than staying married to him. And that's going to be corrected real soon.

Simone smiled a weak smile at Sly and he tenderly kissed her on the cheek. She was too preoccupied to notice just how tender it really was.

"I'll be right behind you. Meet you there in a few," he said.

"No, I'll be fine. Could you send out an email that the Center is closed tomorrow? I'm sure the police will have questions or something. Thank you, Sly. What would I do without you?"

"Hey, we're partners, right?"

"Right. Is Marisa alright?"

Sly looked over at the wide-eyed woman as she wrapped her arms around herself. Looked like she was in shock. Maybe she needed to go in the ambulance too. Sly walked over to her and asked if she was okay.

"I think I'm too upset to drive home," she offered. "Maybe you can give me a ride?"

"That would be inappropriate even under these circumstances. I'll call an Uber, okay? I have to get to the hospital," he replied looking back over his shoulder at Simone as she walked toward the back of the ambulance. He opened his Uber app and gave the address of the Center. She snuggled up against him and leaned her head against his chest. He absentmindedly put his hand on her shoulder, but she noticed that his attention was on the ambulance as it drove away.

Chapter 37

Harlem had acquired rock star status in the prison since Simone's visit. Officer Marvus had told another guard that this fine-ass Beyonce-built woman from Chicago had come up in here to talk shit with Harlem. That guard told someone else who told someone else who told someone else who repeated it to a parole officer who told a City Councilman who told someone else who repeated it to Karl Dyson.

By the time Karl heard it, it sounded like this—some bitch from the city's news station had been up to see a murderer who raped some young girl twenty years ago and was blaming the next Police Commissioner so he could get off death row. *That sounds pretty good to me. I thought the ole boy was dead. He sure went to a lot of trouble getting away. Got sent to prison for life just to hide from me.* Karl laughed to himself as he lay in his bed rubbing his nostrils, making sure that he didn't miss any of the fine white powder he had just inhaled a few moments ago.

He looked over at the pretty young thing on the other side of the bed. She reminded him of someone from a long time ago. They could have been sisters…

250

Being locked up don't mean shit. He got messages to send, then so do I.

He slapped the Alayah clone on the behind causing her to whimper in her sleep.

"Get up girl, you got to go," he said as he uncovered her and made comparisons to her long-deceased look alike. Only difference was that this one didn't have the slim, trim waistline of the original. *She used to, didn't she?*

"But Karl, it's late. There is no bus at this time of night. My grandmomma will have a fit if she finds out I'm out. I shouldn't have come here in the first place," sweet young thing replied; her voice not as mature as it had sounded a few hours ago. She knew she should make better choices. *What would--*

"You're right, but you did. Lesson learned. Get dressed and I'll give you Uber fare. Can't take you home. Not too interested in looking at your brother right now. He ain't' been acting right lately. Tell him I asked what's up. And my supply is drying up. He needs to handle his business quick, fast, and in a hurry. Or I'll handle it for him. "

Karl picked up his cell phone and started punching numbers. No speed dial for whoever it was. He sat up and turned away, wiping his nose and mumbling as Ronjai absentmindedly rubbed her stomach as she slipped out of bed and into the bathroom.

Chapter **38**

Just like with credit cards, seniority had its privileges. Harlem had been in prison so long, he had his own room that he didn't have to share with anyone. He had it all fixed up just the way he liked it. Bookcase filled with his personal selections of bestsellers and classics. Framed drawings and sketches. Table, chair, and notepads and other materials set up specifically for writing … If he didn't pay attention to the wire running through the unbreakable bullet proof glass that housed his 'home' he could almost imagine he was someplace else far far away from here and the murderous sons of bitches waiting like ravenous hyenas to slit your throat for a pack of smokes—and tonight was proving to be no different than any other around there. In the distance, he could hear someone being 'welcomed' to the floor by his new best friends. Closer to him though, he could hear the sound of someone walking softly towards his neighborhood. Funny, he thought. He hadn't been expecting company.

The visitor strolled by. Just admiring the sites, like he was touring gay Paris or some vacation spot like that. The strolling lasted off and on until lights out. The guard was obviously new to the wing because Harlem knew everyone since he had been around longer than most. About an hour after lights out, the visitor made his way into Harlem's home and inched over to his bed, making sure not to wake the sleeping figure. The visitor took a thin wire from his back pocket and stretched it between the fingers of both hands and slowing lowered it around the neck of the still figure in the bed.

Must be dead to the world. If he ain't, he soon will be.

Harlem had an 'end unit' on the wing. Kind of like the end unit on a section of townhomes. Bigger, better, quieter, and farther away from the action. Except tonight, all the action was coming from there.

A Signal 85 was called summoning "ERT" to the affected wing as the facility was immediately placed on "MSC" (Maximum Security Conditions). "ERT" (Emergency Response Team) arrived to find a smoldering body twitching in the middle of the floor. The "team" rushed in with fire extinguishers dowsing the figure with foam. Radios squawked a mile a minute trying to contact the infirmary to come pick up the toasty individual on the floor. It would require a medevac to take him to the nearest burn center in Chicago. If he lasted that long. Between the smell and the moaning, everyone in the room hoped he didn't last much longer.

"What the fuck happened in here? I ain't never seen no shit like this before. It's like the movies or something," a skinny, young guard said.

"Looks like what happened was, an inmate was attacked by a guard with a piece of razor wire and a fight ensued during which a fire was ignited, and someone got burned on ninety percent of their black ass."

The team turned and stared at the figure in the corner. Harlem unwrapped the wire that was twisted around the scarf he always wore around his neck and tossed it on the smoldering body. He then took off the scarf to reveal four little notepads taped around his neck. He slowly removed each one and tossed them back on the writing table.

"What? And ya'll thought I was just being fashionable? I'm gonna need a new place to sleep. Oh yeah, and witness protection would be good. Can somebody call the governor and CNN? I got something to say. Frederica is gonna hear about this." He walked over to the smoking figure on the floor and spit on him. The guards looked at Harlem in disbelief.

"What? I was trying to help, that's all. Maybe it would have been better if I had peed on him. Every little bit helps my grandmomma used to say."

That's alright, CK. I got your message delivered loud and clear. Now you gonna get mine. Your crazy ass ain't seen nothing yet. I'll be here when you get here along with a whole bunch of folks who you put in here. You'll get the message then, won't you? Actually, I'll be on CNN sitting across the couch from Frederica with her long yella legs crossed in them high heel sandals with the pink toenail polish and the straps around the ankles and I'll be peeking up the side of her dress—

"Harlem, you alright, man? You been through some shit tonight. You look funny in the face," said the skinny guard.

"No. I'm fine. You just interrupted my train of thought, that's all. I'm fine... I'm just fine. Kind of hungry though, all this smoke in the air—I got a taste for some barbecue?" Harlem smiled at the guard as he headed out of the cell.

Chapter 39

Jason was sipping his second cup of chicory in Mim's living room as he read the morning paper. Even after all these years, some young, entrepreneurial boy was trying to make a few legal bucks by delivering newspapers before sunrise. Jason remembered doing just that after he recovered from the beatdown he had received from William and his sister all those years ago. In the age of digital everything, it was amazing that newspapers still existed in Chicago. *Maybe just a little while longer.* He smiled. *Getting old there, son.* He could hear William laughing at him as he sat on the sofa drinking orange juice and reading the news from his iPhone.

"Seems like some real shit is brewing downtown. Wouldn't want to be trying to get reelected right now," William said between sips. "That whole Alayah tragedy is getting more attention now than it did when it happened. Wonder what Dyson got to do with it?" William took a larger gulp of his juice, then looked up from the device. "Hey, ain't your friend's last name Dyson? Tell me she ain't married to him?" William waited.

Jason looked up from his paper. He took a deep breath before he spoke, "No, she's not married to him."

"That's a relief," William mumbled. "That's a common name around here. There was a family cross the way, back in the day. Had two sons. The father used to work on cars. I remember 'cause me and your dad used to sweep up in the shop at the end of the day and he would pay us a dollar or two. Added up after a while. Real nice man, Mr. Dyson."

"Simone is married to the other brother, City Manager Dyson. That Mr. Dyson you're talking about must have been his grandfather," Jason said.

"Damn small world ain't it?" William replied.

"You know, you hardly ever mention your brother. Still, after all these years. Why is that?" Jason had put the paper down by now and leaned forward in his chair the way he did when he wanted to understand something that only William could make clear.

"I don't talk about my brother because I fell in love with your mother. That wasn't supposed to happen and I guess somewhere inside of me I feel some—"

"Guilt?" Jason asked. Not in an effort to be cruel, just trying to gain understanding. He truly had learned a lot from being around Simone.

"No. No guilt at all. How could you feel guilty to love and be loved by such a beautiful woman as your mama? I think it's regret mostly. Regret that he made such bad choices. Four beautiful children, a phenomenal good woman, a future… and he gave it all up. And for what?"

"You talked to him lately?" Jason asked as he picked up his cup, mostly to keep his hands busy. He still found himself getting nervous when the subject of his father came up.

William pretended to read as he watched Jason fiddle with his cup and try to keep his jaw from clenching up the way it did whenever his father came up in conversation. "He only touches base when he needs something. He knows where to find me, which is more than I can say about him. He could be anywhere. It's been what—three years? Maybe four."

Jason laughed, a dry sounding gruffness to his voice. He wondered what his father felt to know that Mim was married to his brother. Through all the years, Jason had never had the nerve to bring up the subject.

"So how did he take the news of you and mom being married?" Jason asked.

"Who the hell knows? When he wants something, that's all he wants. He calls, makes an excuse of why he needs money and that's it. Never asks about any of you all, so I see no need to bring it up." William answered.

"Has Mom seen him?"

"You know how your mama is. She's *watery*. *Like water under a bridge.* Once she's through with you, she's through with you. Puts you out of her mind—she flows right on. That's the end of it. She don't flow upstream," William said. He looked at Jason with a quizzical look on his face. *Why after all these years was Jason asking these questions?* "What's wrong with you, boy? What are you thinking about? He had more chances than most to get it right, and he chose to keep on keeping on."

"Papa was a rolling stone has special meaning in this house, huh?" He sat back, leaning his head back on the cushion. "What a waste, four kids with no father. What a fucking waste."

"Whoa, what am I, chopped liver?" William retorted in a playful manner. He understood what Jason didn't have the heart to say. Why would any man create children and leave them like they were nothing? How might things have been different if he had stayed around and been a father to his sons and daughters. Might Alayah still be alive? Might Tisha be married and raising children of her own instead of being spoon-fed every day by her mother? Would things be different?

Would you have ever met Simone?

What's she got to do with this conversation? *Since we're just supposing...*

Your father don't know how to be a man. You had someone who did to train your black ass. And he did a hell of a job with your hard head. Whatever is wrong with your life, don't take it out on your child. Remember that if you don't remember nothing else. Don't make your child pay for your stupid choices.

Neither man spoke for a while. When they looked up, Mim was standing in the middle of the room.

"Damn, woman, you just materialize, don't you?" William laughed. His eyes filled with that look he always got when she was around. Jason looked at William closely.

Do I look like that when Leela walks into a room? Or is it only when it's Simone?

Mim just smiled at the two men in her life. Each of them looking so strong and handsome. How she loved them both. She glanced at Jason again.

What did I do to be rewarded this way? You can tell they're related. If only his father could see him now.

"Yeah, she does that. I remember when I was real little, it seemed like she would just appear out of nowhere. I used to ask her how she did that, and she always said that she could 'minimize her force field, draw in her antenna, and disappear'. I believed her too, for years." Jason said, grateful for the change of conversation that Mim's presence sparked.

She looked at the two magnificent men in front of her and smiled again. "Seems like the conversation was serious. Whatever it was, be careful. The universe has a way of bringing things into being. It doesn't tolerate a void," she said.

"What's that supposed to mean?" William asked as he finished the last swig of orange juice.

"Don't be surprised if whatever you all were so serious about doesn't pop up again in a few days. Haven't you ever noticed that when you mention a song or a book, within a few days, you hear it or see it somewhere? It's just the way the world works," she said as she sat down next to William and curled her feet up under her.

Mom's got really pretty feet. Like Simone. I never really noticed that before.

"Well, I need to talk up some extra money, then," William laughed.

Jason stood up and left the two of them. They've earned some together time for all the shit his father put everyone through. He knew when Mim said things like that, they would probably happen just the way she said it would. The last thing Jason needed right now was anything having to do with his father.

Jason gathered up Maia and they leisurely drove off for a wonderful lunch at the mouse play place. Lousy pizza and great bonding time made for a perfect Saturday afternoon. Then on to the mortgage he paid and the bed he hadn't slept in…

How many days has it been since he and Maia have been to their own home in the suburbs for more than the time it took to pack more clothes? Maia's closet at Mim's and William's was more complete than the one in her real bedroom. *What's real anymore?*

Leela was never there when they arrived. Jason would look at Maia to gauge her reaction.

"Mommie Mim said that we were having Moroccan food tonight and I could fix the vegetables in the tagine, so we better hurry. Last one back downstairs has to dry the silverware." With that, she was gone.

Jason shook his head and dashed up the stairs behind her; he hated to dry the silver.

Chapter 40

Simone was staying in the townhouse a few days a week since she told Greg that she was divorcing him. It really was more convenient on the nights she had to work late or check on her new friend at the hospital. It was comfortable here in the townhouse. Peaceful, calm, relaxing, after a long day of watching people climb the arc of anger and either tumble down the other side or stay at the top and refuse to go any farther. She could understand their wariness. It's scary on the other side. What do you do after the truth comes out? After the most horrible and hurtful words are spoken? It's easier to stay angry than to work to resolve the problem that caused them to be in this place.

That's why you should have left girlfriend on the floor. But noooooo. You have to go and save her life and hold her little fat sweaty hand and listen to her on the way to the hospital. When are you going to learn? Stop listening to people. They get confused and think that you actually care.

Jason listens to me.

That's different.

How is that different?

It's different because you listened to him first. Now he thinks you care.

I do.

Oooooh, honesty. You are really making progress. Being honest with yourself. Mim will be so proud of you when she finds out you spoke your mind to your spouse. Since you can speak your mind, be honest and admit that Jason cares for you. Go' head with your grownup self! Just stop listening to everybody else. People get too attached and then you've got—pets.

Sheva.

Shevardnadze. Good name for a pet.

Stop it.

No seriously, one of those little fat pocket poodle dogs with the flat face and red bow over its ear and glass chips on the collar—

Simone had to stop herself before she started to get images in her head that she couldn't control. She wanted to take a hot shower and head over to see Dad. She had made a surprise for him—rice pudding with raisins. Mim had told her how to make it—had volunteered to show her actually but Jason and Maia were there, and she didn't want to intrude or confuse his beautiful little girl, even though her face lit up on both occasions that they had seen each other. It was touching for Simone to see the bond Jason and his daughter had between them. Maia had looked at Simone, then at her father and said, "Smarticle." Then she ran into the kitchen to help Mim. Jason smiled and nodded.

After her delicious shower, Simone wrapped a scarf around her hair in Moroccan turban style, threw on a pair of jeans, a black scoop neck and boots. *You might want to look in a mirror.* Why? It's not going to change anything. I'm still me and if someone doesn't like it--well, I like it.

Yeah buddy, all grown up. Scared of you.

As you should be. She laughed at herself as she put on her leather jacket and sunglasses and walked out the door. She didn't see the black car pull out behind her as she drove out of the complex.

Thirty-five minutes later, she pulled up in front of Horace Dyson's house like she always did. She was a little surprised that Dad hadn't turned on the lights in the front of the house. It was approaching sunset and he always had them on for her whether she needed them or not. She knocked on the door and waited with her offering of rice pudding, just like a little girl waiting to show off her newest accomplishment to her daddy.

Like Maia does.

 She knocked and waited a little longer. No response. Simone wasn't one for drama or jumping to conclusions, but with everything that was being broadcast on the television, on-line, and on the radio lately about Karl's involvement in a cold case from twenty years ago, she was concerned about the effect it could have on Horace. Putting down the rice pudding, she ran to the side of the house to look in the patio windows. She could see clearly into the kitchen and down the hallway. She squinted and cupped her hands against the glass panes. She heard the TV playing in the family room and thought she saw what looked like stockinged feet sticking out into the hallway on the hardwood floors. She banged on the glass and hollered out Horace's name. No response. She did it again. Same response. She stepped off the deck and looked around. *This will do just fine.* She picked up the terra cotta flowerpot holding the Elephant Ears' bulbs she had planted last year and hurled it at the panes of the patio door.

"Hey, baby girl. Right on time. Can set my watch by you. I knew you would come, it's Tuesday," Horace smiled into Simone's worried face. "No need to get all upset. I'm fine."

"How can you be fine if you're sprawled all over the floor?" she asked as she knelt beside him and checked to see if he was severely injured.

"I slipped on these waxy floors," he said, wagging his feet back and forth. "See, think I might have twisted my ankle is all. Paying more attention to the news about my damn fool son than paying attention to what I was doing. Damn idiot. My son, I mean." Frederica was reporting her heart out about the breaking news in Chicago. Simone glanced at the screen. She was beautiful. No wonder Harlem was in awe.

"I know, Dad. It's awful. I just want to know that you're okay. I should call 911 so they can take you to the hospital to check you out."

"I'm fine."

"I believe you. It would just be nice to have a doctor check too, that's all."

Horace peeked around the corner toward the patio doors. He looked up at Simone.

"I'll pay for that. I'm sorry but I had to get in the house. I'll call Greg," she said as she started to get up and walk to the phone on the kitchen wall.

Horace called out after her, "Listen, honey. All that happened here was that I slipped. I may be getting up in years, but I am healthy in mind and body. I've seen young people slip and fall too. If you call that other no-good son of mine, he'll be looking for the most convenient nursing home he can find and appoint himself master over everything I worked fifty years for. So, this is on a need-to-know basis and—he don't need to know. This is what you'll do. Call the ambulance. Then call my lawyer."

Chapter 41

Simone checked her understated titanium Longines watch as she sat in the emergency room waiting area. The watch had caused a passive furor in her husband when she had returned the diamond encrusted Rolex that he had purchased for her as an 'I'm sorry. All forgiven?' gift. He obviously didn't take her seriously when she said she was divorcing him. She told him that she appreciated the thoughtfulness of selecting a watch for her but something more practical was more appropriate for her job. After all, she didn't want someone to be overwhelmed and pass out on the floor during mediation and need CPR or anything…she lowered her eyes as her thoughts took over.

A watch was a perfect gift, though. Constant reminder that it's time for you to get to stepping.

The doctor walked through the double doors with Horace in a wheelchair being pushed by a mountain of a man who looked like one of the columns holding up the front of the Parthenon.

Majestic men, this city is full of them.

She stood up and walked toward the trio.

"Thank you for making sure that Mr. Dyson came in to be checked over. He was right, he is fine, but we want him to stay over tonight for observation. No signs that he hit his head but to be sure there is no concussive symptoms…" the doctor said as he thought of the goddesses of ancient Greece.

This lady carries herself like one.

 Not every older patient he saw had someone who cared enough to sit and wait for hours to see if they were in one piece.

"We will get Mr. Dyson settled in and then you can come up to see him if you like."

Simone smiled and touched Horace's shoulder. "I would like," she said.

The majestic man wheeled Horace toward the elevator. "Bring Franklin up with you when he gets here, please. I told him to look for the woman who stands out the most in the hospital and he would know he found you." Mr. Majestic looked back at Simone whose color was changing as she stood there.

"You're lucky to have such a loving daughter," he said.

"You're right. Daughter-in-law. Can you believe it? Treats me better than my own flesh and blood. She's a good woman. Too bad her husband is such a fool," Horace complained as the door to the elevator opened.

Mr. Majestic looked at the name on the folder attached to the wheelchair. "Well, Mr. Dyson. Sometimes sons don't turn out the way we had hoped."

Horace looked back over his shoulder. "You must know my sons, then."

Yeah, met one of them a few weeks ago. Saw the other one on TV tonight. You're right, man. They are no good.

The elevator door closed and headed toward the fourth floor.

Chapter 42

Greg called Simone's cell phone for the fifth time in two hours. She might have said that she wanted a divorce, but she couldn't have meant it. She was just in shock over what had happened at the Center. He had never anticipated that that crazy Sheva would actually do something like she did. The mediation was supposed to be the answer to all his worries. Two women would argue and cuss at each other for a while. The mediator would do whatever it is that they do, and everybody would go home. No harm no foul. He had never imagined that Simone would end up in the room with that dumb bitch. She is the director, for God's sake, she shouldn't have to work…

He couldn't get the scene to stop replaying in his head of Simone when she finally came home. He was sitting on the sofa in the formal living room with a glass of Chivas Regal in his hand, thinking of all the snide remarks and innuendos that he had in store for her. He heard her key in the front door and he took a hearty swallow and stood up and proceeded towards the door.

"Here, let me get that for you. Thought maybe your key might not work anymore. How've you been?"

She walked past him, not looking in his direction and headed towards the stairs.

"I'm fine, Greg. How are you?" she asked with only the slightest exasperation in her voice.

Liar. Just go in the kitchen and get the butcher knife and cut him! Do a Bonquiqui on him! I'll take the blame. Say you were insane at the time. Too much stress! People would believe you.

"Thought you forgot where your house was," Greg said as he swirled the liquor around in his crystal glass. "Work been keeping you too busy to come home lately?"

Simone stopped dead in her tracks. She felt as if the air she was breathing had been sucked out of the house and she had been left in a vacuum filled with nothing but the ugliness building inside of her. She closed her eyes and tried to pray for strength to endure. She tried to breathe in, breathe out. She tried to bite her tongue but realized that she had hurt herself enough. She continued to walk to the bedroom. Her eyes narrowing to slits.

Maybe I should go to the kitchen.

Greg followed in close pursuit. He put the glass up to his lips again to hide the smirk that was building there.

Got ya that time, didn't I? Think you're slick staying away from home. Trying to punish me, huh?

"Well, Greg. Let me tell you why you haven't seen me for a while," she started quietly. "I had a mediation the other night because there was nobody else to do it, except for Sly. Two women, fighting at work. Seems like one of them is having an affair and she thinks that the man is going to leave his wife for her. Typical, right? What's not so typical is that she is having an affair with you. And she blurts that right out in the middle of the session. In front of my co-worker, then she proceeds to overdose on prescription meds and go into cardiac arrest on the floor of my job! And I have to decide whether to watch her dumb ass die or try to save her life. I rode to the hospital with her and stayed with her for two days listening to her confessions until her mother got here from New York. That's right, you know her mother, don't you? Visited her in the Big Apple last year, right? I've been listening to all kinds of shit, and now I'm tired. Really, really tired. I'm especially tired of you and your bullshit. Get away from me." The space between her brow had darkened to a deep dark red. Mim would say that it was intense anger bordering on hatred. *She would be right.*

"Simone, I—I…"

"Shut up! Don't you Simone, me! You need to pack your bags and get out! Now!"

She entered the bedroom and walked into the closet, throwing Greg's clothes out into the room.

"You don't understand…"

She stopped and turned towards him. "What don't I understand? You're the one who doesn't understand. I said get out and you're still standing there."

"We need to talk about this."

"No, you need to leave. Now."

"So, I'm to go back to the condo until you're clear headed?"

"Oh, I'm quite clear. My name is on the deed at that condo. The locks have been changed and you will never step foot in there again. Are you clear?"

"So where am I to go?"

"Greg, I really don't care where you go but you're going out of here."

Chapter 43

Horace and his lawyer, Franklin, had been talking for the past hour and Simone could tell that they were nowhere near being finished. So, to make the best use of her time, she thought she would walk back down the hall to the psychiatric ward to see her new friend. *Pet.* Pet's mother was planning to head back to New York the day after tomorrow and she wanted desperately for her daughter to return with her.

As do I. She's gotten very attached over the past few days and it's not healthy. I feel sorry for her, but she's got a mother and I don't need—a pet.

Simone showed her approved visitor's badge and was buzzed in through the double doors. The colors of the hallways were soft and inviting. Noticeably different than the rest of the hospital.

The paint at the Center was subtle too and the dumb bitch still liked to have died on my floor.

Simone was about to check herself but the more she thought about it, she had to agree. She walked to the solarium trying not to step too heavily fearing that the sound of her heels on the tile floors might be upsetting to people who were probably already hearing noises in their heads.

Soft colors to keep people calm. With tile floors? Wouldn't soft, quiet carpet have made more sense?

She couldn't argue with that either. She had noticed that she wasn't arguing with herself as often. And that felt really good. She was smiling as she walked over to the window seats where Sheva and her mother sat in the evenings watching the colors of the fading sun decorate the sky.

Maybe that's where they got the idea for the shades of paint!

They can't compare with the way God paints, but we do our best, I suppose.

I know that's right.

Sheva looked around and saw the smile on Simone's face and misinterpreted its meaning and smiled back at her as if they were BFFs.

Best Friends Forever, Both Fucking Idiots would be more like it.

Her mother looked at her daughter, then at the woman who had saved her life, and felt her eyes fill again as they had every day for the past week.

"Hi," Sheva said sweetly.

Is it the medication or is she really that stupid? What's that ancient Chinese saying about saving someone's life—now they are your responsibility? Truer words were never spoken.

"Hi Sheva. Hello Mrs. Diaz. How are you both today?" Simone sat down next to the tall ferns. She was starting to feel the effects of the day's experiences. She hoped that she could hold it together for a little while longer.

Sheva's mother looked at Simone and said in heavily accented English, "I was just telling Shevardnadze that she should come home with me when I go. I can get another bus ticket for her. No problem. It would be good for her to be at home with people who love her and start over in new surroundings. Don't chu think?" She looked at Simone with a pleading gaze etched on to her face.

I agree wholeheartedly. Girlfriend's got to go.

As Simone opened her mouth to echo her agreement, Sheva spoke up in a determined yet assured tone. *Meds.* "I know I can't go back to work—where I was—but this is my home now. I don't want to go back to New York—like this…" she turned to face Simone. "Did you know I used to clean houses and sit with the seniors at the Adult Day Center before I moved here? I don't want to go back and have them ask me why I came back from Chicago to scrub floors again. I'd rather do that here, if I had to. I can't get better by running away." She put her head down and sniffled. Fat little fists wiping at her eyes.

Simone looked at the two lost women in front of her.

Mama don't let your daughters grow up to be pitiful homewreckers…

That version of the Willie Nelson tune played through her brain.

What else is there to say? I can't even be mad at her. Wasted energy that I can use for something productive. Mim… you have rubbed off on me. Maybe I can use my skills for good—this time.

"Sounds like you have been thinking about this a lot over the past few days."

Sheva shook her head up and down.

"Wanting to start fresh but wanting to hold on to the good things that you have here? Not have to start over or take what seems to be a step backward?"

"Exactly. You do understand! I called Marisa today and apologized for what I did. I was wrong about so many things. But I can start fresh! I can find a job here. I can! I'll scrub floors, whatever is available is fine. I'm beginning to understand that what I wanted all the time wasn't—a husband—it was to be someone that somebody could love. I've always thought that if I had been more lovable Papi wouldn't have left us when I was little. I thought if I could get your husband, I would be finally be lovable enough. I would be good enough. Then finally I would be happy. I really wasn't. He didn't want me. All he really wanted was you and I was so angry and jealous of you. I wanted to be someone like you, so that a man like that might want me. I am so sorry. I didn't understand what you really were like. You could have let me die. I heard what you said to me before the ambulance came. I'm sorry—I'm so sorry. Please forgive me," she hung her head and cried.

Ah, therapy. Isn't it wonderful? My work here is done.

I agree.

Simone headed in the opposite direction to see if the powwow between Horace and Franklin was finished. When she walked in, she could see that it had grown. The doctor had joined the pair. The three men looked up with conspiratorial grins on their faces. The furrow started between Simone's brow.

"Nothing is wrong. Everything is just hunky dory, so take a breath. I saw you starting to get upset. I can go home in the morning. My ankle is sprained, and I just have to stay off of it for a few days. Told you, I'm good." Horace was propped up in the bed looking quite pleased with himself.

"Actually, Ms. Dyson," the doctor began, "he is correct about the sprain to his ankle but he's overly optimistic about leaving in the morning. Maybe the following day, if he can find a caregiver or companion to be with him until he is officially able to be back on his feet."

"What kind of care will be required?" Simone asked. She was careful with the way she spoke as not to make Horace feel as if he was not in the room or unable to participate in the conversation. She always hated to see older people relegated to bystanders in their own lives.

"Nothing much, really. Someone to fix meals for a few days, handle household chores but mostly keep an eye on Mr. Dyson so that he can recuperate and rest," the doctor seemed pretty satisfied with his prescription.

"So, I'm stuck in here until we find one of those agency places that supply people I don't know to come into my house?" Horace had a furrow spot too. Simone had never noticed that before.

"It doesn't have to be a person from an agency, Mr. Dyson. You are not in need of skilled care, just custodial. A relative or family friend is fine, just as long as we know that someone will be there if you need them," the doctor said.

"How long will they need to be there?" Simone asked.

"Maybe a week…until the follow-up appointment," answered the doctor.

Horace looked over at Franklin, who looked at the doctor, who looked at Simone.

"I think I know just the person. I'll be right back."

Chapter 44

Three U.S. Marshals guarded the entrance to the safe house that was to be Cornelius Hughes-Easterly's new abode until permanent digs were in place. Two more sat across the street in a Mr. Mop-It Maid Service van. The location of Cornelius's permanent home, his occupation, and such were supposedly, still up in the air, at least to the government. Cornelius had always known that his true calling was that of an owner of a quiet but profitable bookstore in an eastern Goldilocks city, because this Midwestern shit just wasn't working out. New York was too big, Meridian, was too small, *besides they hang your ass in Mississippi,* someplace like Hoboken would be just right. The prosecutors had told him that 'dependent upon the legitimacy of the information provided and on whether it leads to a conviction,' would determine whether he would be allowed to stay in Witness Protection or return to Big Muddy River.

It sure as hell will lead to a conviction and a life sentence for premeditated murder, attempted murder, manslaughter, rape, and who knows what other shit that dirty bastard's been up to all these years...

"Mr. Easterly, sir, what would you like to order for dinner tonight?

You don't have to be at the studio until 6pm, so there's plenty of time before your interview on CNN to have a good meal delivered," the female federal marshal asked cordially.

Harlem—Cornelius, thought for a moment.

They're asking me what I want to eat? I ain't been able to decide what I want to eat in seventeen years. I don't even know what I can have. Moosh, mashed moosh, and stewed moosh is all I can remember. Not sure my stomach can handle real food.

The marshal must have been psychic because she presented Cornelius with only two of the seven or eight menus, she had available for restaurants in the area. "When I'm in Atlanta, I like to eat at La Dolce. They have great Italian food and juicy steaks and prime rib, if you like that kind of thing. You get plenty of food and the best homemade Italian bread in the city."

That was the clincher. The bread. Harlem always felt safest eating the bread at mealtime because he felt there was very little that could be done to poison or drug it. Just take it out of the bag and slap it on the tray. So, Italian it was. Probably cost a fortune…But cheaper than the $85.89 that it cost the State of Illinois to keep him locked up each day. Since this was his first meal of his brand-new life, he decided he would dine like the man he was beginning to be. "I'll have what you just said and a nice Chianti." He had heard that in a movie somewhere and it sounded really smooth. The cannibal had planned to eat the snooty doctor's brain for dinner. Cornelius just planned to serve up Karl Dyson's ass on a platter.

Chapter 45

Time often has a way of rushing forward without anyone's permission. Before you know it, days, weeks, and months pass and you are left wondering how that happened. Simone and the guys were feeling like that because the trial date for Tyreek and Shamel was two weeks away. In the midst of the 'Dyson scandal' as it had come to be known, and the 'Sheva drama', a great deal of time had been spent focusing on damage control and clean-up. Jason had not been interrupted at work since that fateful day a month ago and the state investigators from ADR had completed their review of the mediation incident and determined that there was no fault on the part of the Center or the mediators. The most interesting occurrence was that no one who was interviewed, Marisa, Sly, even Sheva, mentioned the circumstances leading up to the situation. Truly everyone held fast to the statement that everything said in mediation was confidential.

Tyreek and Shamel had made significant progress over the past two months. It seemed as if they really liked each other. If they had been born three blocks closer together, they would have been dead up pardners instead of mortal enemies. But in the safety of the mediation room, they could be themselves, honest, open, and working toward the same thing. When it was time to leave, they still left in separate cars, from different entrances, just in case. It was important to keep up appearances. For who, Simone hadn't figured out.

Pre-mediation usually lasted an hour but Simone and Sly had been giving this case a lot more time than that. This morning was no different. The boys wouldn't arrive with Mike and Jason until 10:00. It was 7:53 and Sly was on his second cup of coffee.

"Look back at your notes from last Thursday. Remember what you wrote down about Shamel saying that neither gang could move drugs the way they do without help?" Sly said.

"Yeah, I see it," Simone answered.

"Then you asked him what he meant by help."

"And he said, 'that's gonna stop since he got his own problems.' Then Tyreek mumbled something that I didn't get. When I said that I missed what he said, would he repeat it, he just shook his head and shut up. Both of them did."

Sly ran his finger down the yellow legal paper filled with handwritten notes searching for –

"Here it is. I thought I heard him say, 'like my sister…' What's that mean? Who are they talking about?"

Oh my God. Oh my God. Please Lord, no.

Simone immediately flipped through the folders looking for the intake papers. Sly noticed the urgency with which she searched and said, "What's wrong?"

Now Simone was muttering to herself. *Please God, please God…* she found it. Tyreek's address, two blocks from where a woman was strangled to death in a fast food restaurant three years ago. The same restaurant that Simone would take Ronjai on special occasions because she loved the fruit and yogurt parfaits.

Suddenly, she knew why Tyreek seemed familiar to her. She had seen him once before, about four years ago. He had been cussing and calling women bitches. She had asked him for an address. Ronjai's address. The same address she was now staring at in his file.

His sister.

"You okay? You look like you saw a ghost," Sly leaned forward, ever aware of any change in Simone.

She put her hand over her mouth. "We've got a problem," she whispered. Her hand proceeded from her mouth to her eyes. The silence was interrupted by the vibration of her phone on the desk. She looked at her ever useful watch. 8:18. She picked up the phone and read the text.

can u come by 2day? need 2 c u. please.

The name on the text said Ronjai.

Chapter 46

Sly couldn't believe what Simone had just told him. They were too far along to stop due to this new information. It was new information even though it had been sitting in front of her face, literally and figuratively, for three months.

That explained the whole conversation on the first day of mediation. Tyreek was testing the waters to see if I remembered him. All this time and he hasn't said a word. Baby boy really does know how to keep a secret. That explains why we still don't know who is pulling the strings. But I'm beginning to figure that out too.

Simone really wanted to cancel the mediation today but there wasn't much time left to reschedule sessions. The boys were meeting twice a week as it was and even though they had two hours each time, they still hadn't addressed the major issue of stopping the sale of drugs in their respective neighborhoods or the retaliatory drive-by shootings. Had she really believed that something like that could be solved through mediation? Maybe Greg had been right about one thing, she had her head in the clouds most of the time.

Screw him and the thought he rode in on.

She and Sly discussed whether to tell Mike and Jason when they arrived or wait until after the session. It might be better to wait. The fewer people who knew, the more normal things would be. If Tyreek was this tight lipped now, what would happen if he realized that Simone had figured out who he was. What else might she figure out? Were they being unethical at this point? The aspect of neutrality was completely gone out the window. Should she mention it to Tyreek or try to get him to open up? They didn't have many opportunities left and if he was hiding what she thought he was hiding…She looked at her watch. 9:42. Jason and Mike didn't travel on CP time so she knew they would be arriving soon. She and Sly agreed to keep the morning's findings on the down low until the debriefing this afternoon.

Do you and ask for forgiveness later.

She had learned that from Jason. She smiled in spite of herself. Sly took a deep breath. Simone looked a little more relaxed. They stood up and did final prep. Sly opened up his arms for a brief hug. Simone very naturally walked into them. He needed to feel that she was going to be okay. She needed strength to deal with whatever would happen in the next two hours and with whatever Ronjai wanted to tell her later on today.

They both got what they were looking for. They stepped back from each other but not before Sly said, "You do what you think's best. I have complete faith in you. You'll know what to do. You always do…"

He kissed her gently on the forehead. "You know, as always, I got your back." He held his hand out and opened the door for her. She walked past him, and they exchanged a look that each of them understood.

"Let's do this," she said. She took a quick internal survey, not enough fear to cripple or paralyze. She nodded to herself and walked through the door.

Mike and Shamel had just entered the mediation room and were settling into their usual seats. Everyone was waiting for Jason and Tyreek. Simone thought it unusual for them to be late. She glanced at her watch and then at the digital display on the wall monitor. She looked at Mike who just shook his head.

"I talked to him about a half hour ago. He was turning on to Tyreek's street then. Don't know what's up. Traffic maybe. Give him a few. If something's wrong, he'll call," he said.

It sounded good but the feeling the entire morning had been one of some impending dread. Nothing specific though. That's what made it so dreadful. Simone was sure that being around Mim had put her more in touch with her watery nature and because of that she was more aware of emotions, feelings, and situations than she used to be. She wasn't becoming 'otherworldly', just more aware of the world around her and what was happening in it.

"It probably is traffic. If he's not here in five, will you give him a call please?" she asked in her professional voice. No sense in Shamel seeing a personal side to her.

The three adults proceeded to the pre-mediation room, leaving Shamel to get juice or coffee and plug in to his IPhone or text for a few.

"It's cool. He'll get here. Nothing seemed wrong when we talked," Mike said again.

Simone was about to speak when the door opened, and Jason walked in. She immediately felt her shoulders drop and her breathing slow down. Even though her sense of relief was a comfort, she could tell something wasn't the way it should be.

"We've got a problem. Tyreek has disappeared."

Chapter 47

Mortimeous Randolph Quick sat at his desk at the 12th Precinct examining his 401K and its ever-increasing shrinkage due to the fall of the economy over the past thirty-two months. How was he supposed to keep up his standard of living, pay undercover child support, finance a daughter in college, save for another on the way, keep a roof over everybody's head and keep gas in the car? Eighteen months until retirement. That really sucked. Being a greeter at WalMart wasn't going to supplement his pension quite enough. Sure, he had a little something something set aside from his 'consulting' services, but he needed to be careful with 'consulting' now that the department was under Federal scrutiny because of the Dyson mess. Morty knew that something had to give. He was still treading water, but his nose was staying under a little while longer every time.

His thoughts were interrupted by the vibration of his cell phone. He turned his gaze from the computer screen to see who it was. Very few people called him at work because he was… at work.

He pressed the speaker button and wondered who was on the other end of the unknown number. "Yeah, Quick here, what can I do for you?"

"Yes, you are. Got it on the first ring. I like that, Mighty. How's it going?"

Morty could feel the few hairs left on the top of his head start to prickle when he recognized the voice. He jumped up and walked around his desk to shut the door and lock it.

"So Mighty, you still there?"

"I'm here," Morty grunted, not wanting to continue. He hated to be called that. He acquired the name when he worked the streets on Vice. The ladies on the corners near Cabrini-Green would offer him services in return for him not hauling them downtown. It got around that it didn't take much time for the officer to get his and you could be back to work 'mighty quick'.

"So, how's it hanging? It's been a little while, hasn't it? Just wanted to touch base and see how the family is doing. How's that lovely wife of yours? Yolanda, right? And the girls? One in college, the other on the way?"

"Yeah, next year."

"Wow, that must put a strain on your finances."

"It's more than a notion."

"Maybe I can help you out with that. Just like old times…I need a messenger to make a delivery for me. I was thinking, who better than Mighty. He knows the streets and could find just the right messenger to deliver a large order of …flowers for me."

Morty sat back down at his desk and dabbed at the droplets of sweat forming on his upper lip.

"I don't think that's possible right now. Messengers for a delivery like that are hard to come by," he muttered.

"Exactly why I came to you. A young one who wants to make more deliveries in the future would be perfect. All those baby bangers out there on the street. Besides, you and I go way back. Oh yeah, how's the other family? I know they had to move when Cabrini-Greens got torn down. Brand new Target's there now. Time flies. Hopefully you haven't had to get someone else to help you make your domestic violence situations disappear. Have you been seeing someone about that? Counseling for anger management maybe? Oh, and how is what is sweet young thing's name, Keeta, Peeta…"

"Rakeetah."

"How is Rajeetah?"

"Rakeetah."

"How is Rakeetah? And the kids?"

"They're fine."

"How old are they now?'

"Three and five." *One on the way…*

"Wow, time does fly. How does Yolanda feel about that? Or haven't you mentioned that to her yet?"

"Okay, I'll get a messenger to deliver your… flowers. But this is the last time!"

"I'll say when it's the last time Mighty. Now live up to your name and take care of this mighty quick. Write down this address."

Morty picked up a pencil and with shaky hands and sweaty palms scribbled the address that Karl dictated over the phone.

Chapter 48

"What do you mean, disappeared?" Mike asked.

"He's gone," Jason said. "I didn't want to call to you. This is too important to talk about over the phone."

"How do you know that he's disappeared and just not feeling it this morning? You know, not want to come here?" Sly asked.

Jason walked over to the door and opened it, checking on Shamel. He was focused on texting. Earbuds in place, not paying attention to what was going on around him. Jason closed the door and continued to speak, "I got there at same time I usually do. We meet at the Micki D's down the street. He doesn't want me to come to the house. Says you never know who's watching. So, I get there and he's a no show. I wait. Nothing. After a half hour, I call him. No answer. Send a message. Nothing. So, I go to his house and knock on the door and his grandmother answers, real quick. She sees me and gets upset. I tell her who I am and that I'm looking for Tyreek. She starts crying and saying that she and his sister haven't seen him for two days. That it's not like him to not come home. I try to calm her down and tell her I'll check the neighborhood and see what I can find out and get back to her. I tried to see if I could talk to the sister, her name is…"

"Ronjai, her name is Ronjai," Simone said from across the room. "She's my mentee. She sent me a text this morning saying that she needs to see me as soon as I can get there."

"Whoa, wait a minute. His sister is your what? I thought this mediation stuff was supposed to remain neutral. Where's the neutrality in that?" Jason barked.

Sly spoke up, "She didn't find out until this morning. We were talking about it right before you got here."

Simone took a breath and said, "I only saw Tyreek once and that was three or four years ago. I didn't know he was related to Ronjai. I thought he was just another kid on the street. Ronjai never mentioned him. I didn't check the address on the files. It didn't occur to me that where he lived would become an issue."

"Well, now that we can't find him, it's an issue," Jason said.

"What's wrong with you man? Simone didn't lose him. He just took off. We need to focus on why. He's been doing his thing with us and Shamel, now poof, he's gone. We need to figure out why and where he went," Mike interrupted.

"You're right. I'm sorry. This doesn't make sense and I'm feeling like he split on my watch. Trial's coming up soon and people don't just disappear like this unless something big is going down. I don't like this…don't like it at all." Jason walked to the window and looked down upon the city, wondering if Tyreek was even still in it. He thought about how he had snapped at Simone a few moments ago. She hadn't done anything wrong. He wasn't angry at her as much as he was angry at his younger self. The one who had caused tragedy so many years ago and got away scot free. Now another young black boy who has made some bad choices is out there somewhere. If he doesn't show up and finish what they've started, he'll be going to jail, for a long, long time.

Like you should have.

"Sorry...I don't know what got into me," he said again.

"What about Shamel in there?" Sly pointed to the other room. "Think he knows anything?"

"You all ask him, I'm going to meet Ronjai," Simone said, trying to remain calm.

"Where is she?" Jason asked as he checked Simone's face, trying to read it.

"I sent her a text to find out. She hasn't answered yet. So, wherever she is, that's where she'll be when I get there, right?" She picked up her briefcase and pocketbook. She looked at Sly and gave him that 'you got this' smile and walked out.

Jason punched the back of one of the leather chairs knocking it to the floor.

"Now what?" he asked.

"We have a little coming to Jesus talk with Shamel," Sly said. The three men walked toward the other room.

Chapter 49

I m at skul. Can u come?

Simone saw the message as she walked to the elevator. Today wasn't the day to navigate the winding staircase. She tried to take a deep breath, but it wasn't happening right now. No amount of mindfulness could change the tension that had built up in that room. The heaviness of the day was trying to pounce on her as she moved a little faster.

Honey, you haven't seen heavy.

She swallowed, listening very carefully to her inner self. She was getting really good at it. It usually was right. Today wasn't the day to second guess it. The elevator seemed slower than the steps today. When the doors opened and she emerged in the lobby she was able to take a deep breath. It worked this time and she felt a little more at ease.

Focus, stay focused. That's all you can do right now. Focus on the facts. You are going to meet Ronjai at school. She sent you a text this morning. Her brother is missing…no, her brother did not come to mediation…

Simone was so focused on the facts that she didn't focus on the black car that pulled out behind her when she left the parking garage.

She arrived at the school and found Ronjai standing on the sidewalk in front of the main building. She unlocked the car door and Ronjai jumped in. As frightened as she looked, she still was utterly beautiful. Her smooth skin seemed to glow and her hair had grown over the last few months.

"Hey, are you alright?" Simone started.

"Can we go somewhere?" Ronjai asked.

"Tell me where," Simone said.

"Ice cream would be good," she said with the smile of a little girl. "Micki's works, I guess."

"You're sure? We can go anywhere you want."

"No, that's good. It's a safe place."

They drove in silence. Simone didn't want to push Ronjai to say whatever it was that was bothering her so badly today. Once they arrived at the McDonald's and ordered, Ronjai seemed a little more relaxed. Familiarity and good memories perhaps.

Neurons that fire together, wire together. Thanks,, Mim.

Simone thought it funny that she had chosen a table toward the back of the restaurant. Usually, they sat in the main dining area. After a few spoonfuls of her second parfait and yogurt, Ronjai looked Simone in the eye.

"I'm pregnant. That's why I haven't called you lately. You would be able to tell by my voice that something was wrong. Sorry, I guess this messes up college, huh?"

"Just adjusts the course, that's all," Simone said. "Have you talked to the father about it?"

Tears started flowing down Ronjai's face. She put down her spoon and covered her eyes. "It was an accident. I was afraid to tell him because I thought he'd be mad. But not like this…he's…older, you know? And … I know I shouldn't have. We talked about this; you told me about making good choices but I…" her voice drifted off.

"That's in the past, honey. We can't change any of that. We will figure this out, though. Together. Have you told your grandmother yet?"

"No! She's so upset about Tyreek. I can't tell her now."

"What about Tyreek? What's going on with him, Ronjai?"

"You know he's in a gang and dealing drugs and all that. He's really in deep. He knows names and he's done things that can get him locked up—or killed. He thinks that …someone is after him. So, he's hiding."

"Who does he think is after him?"

"His supplier. The guy he's been working for since he was little."

"We can contact the police. We can get them to protect him if he comes home," Simone said.

"No, we can't. His supplier is going to be the Chief of Police," Ronjai said.

"What!" Simone replied.

Ronjai continued through her tears, "He's also my baby's daddy."

Oh my God. I should put this in a book. Nobody would believe this shit. Her thoughts were interrupted by Ronjai.

"When Tyreek found out about the baby, he wanted to kill Karl. He said something about there was no way he was going to let him destroy anybody else in the family, he'd done enough already. So, he went out after him. I tried to stop him and begged him not to do anything. He got really mad with me and left. I haven't seen him since. That was a couple of days ago. He texts me every day to check on me and see if Karl has said anything to me."

"So, Tyreek thinks Karl is dangerous?"

"He knows he is. Ty says he's crazy and that I should stay away from him. What am I supposed to do?"

"Where is Tyreek?"

"I don't know. He won't tell me. I told him I would call you, that you would know what to do. He trusts you…he said you were cool people. You and the guys you work with."

"Let him know I'm with you now. That everything is going to be alright."

Ronjai took out her phone and texted her brother. Simone watched her and wondered at how close the two of them must be. Tyreek was the younger of the two and here he was protecting his sister as if she were his daughter.

Somebody has to step up and be daddy when there isn't one around.

"He says he's on his way. He wanted to know if the other guys were with you. He wants to know if you can call them."

"Tell him I'm doing it now." Simone pulled out her phone and started sending messages. She knew they would be waiting to hear from her so one mass text should do. Barely any time passed before she got multiple responses.

"They're on their way. Everything is going to be fine."

Ronjai looked behind Simone and smiled. Tyreek had walked in the door and was headed to their table. Ronjai stood up and he grabbed her and held on for dear life.

"You alright, Jayjay?"

Ronjai shook her head and the two of them sat down across from Simone. She couldn't see the door or the street from where she was seated, so she did not see the black car that had parked across the street from the restaurant. It had been parked there for the past twenty minutes. An unmarked patrol car had driven by twice. Tyreek thought it odd to see so much activity in the neighborhood today. It confirmed his suspicions that something was going on. He forced himself to be even more vigilant than usual. A self-taught student of Sun Tzu, he understood the art of war and knew that he was in one. *The enemy of my enemy is my friend. So, what does that make the family of my enemy? Maybe he's her enemy too.*

"So, Dyson is your last name, isn't it?" Tyreek asked.

"Yes, but you know that don't you?" Simone answered.

"So why are you still here, if he's family?"

"He's the brother of my husband. Your sister is like a daughter to me."

 Tyreek looked at Ronjai and saw her nod her head. She and Simone were holding hands across the table. *According as circumstances are favorable, one should modify one's plans.*

"Okay, so you will take care of Jayjay? She can't do this by herself, and our grandmother is too old. Jayjay is gonna need some help," he said.

"Where are you gonna be?" Ronjai asked.

"Look, I got to get out of here. When I get situated, I'll send for you. But right now, I need to get gone. He's out there. Looking for me. I can smell him. He thinks he can do whatever he wants…"

Tyreek looked directly at Simone. His eyes had been darting around the restaurant, noticing everyone who entered and left, everyone who went into or out of the bathroom. *If he is secure at all points, be prepared for him. If he is in superior strength, evade him.*

"Promise me you'll take care of her? I trust you. I've listened to Jayjay talk about you for the past four years. Miss Simone this, Miss Simone that. Then I got to see for myself. I've watched you for the past three months. I tried to piss you off, just to see you go off. But you never did. And the next time I saw you, it was like it never happened. You are for real. When I'm out of here, I'll get her and then I'm gonna bring his ass to his—"

Tyreek never finished his thought because his eyes spotted a little kid that he had seen several other times during the past week. The kid couldn't have been more than twelve and he should have been in school—at least some of the time. The boy was small for his age but had that look that eleven and twelve-year olds get—like they know something even when they don't know much more than their name. His dreads hung to his shoulders, and he reminded Tyreek of a baby predator from those movies. Maybe they grew them here in Chicago. Tyreek remembered being one himself. *Attack him where he is unprepared, appear where you are not expected.*

The baby predator reached behind him into the band of his jeans and pulled out a .22 caliber instrument of impending death. Guns don't kill people…baby predators kill people.

"Down!" Tyreek jumped across the table to knock Ronjai out of the way. Bullets flew left and right. People dove for cover. Simone hit the floor when the table was overturned. She reached for Ronjai and covered her as much as she possibly could. She couldn't see everything that was happening, but she saw someone run up behind the shooter and knock him down. The gun slid across the floor and landed about three feet in front of her. The lack of gunfire was now apparent, and she started to get up when the door to the restaurant flew open and a balding man came in with his gun drawn.

"Freeze, police!" the man shouted.

The man who had tackled the boy was holding on to him, trying to keep him from squirming away. The blood on the floor was making that close to impossible.

"It's his fault! It's his fault!" the baby predator screamed. The man holding him knew that one more good squirm from the shooter would set him free. He was right. The boy slipped across the floor until he fell forward, eyes open and staring at Simone. The bald man had aimed and fired, hitting the boy in the back.

The boy stared at Simone. He no longer had that know it all look on his face. He just stared as if he was surprised that real bullets actually hurt.

"Quick," he sputtered, "it's his fault." Then his eyes closed.

Simone wanted to reach out to him, but she remained huddled over Ronjai. Simone's hands and face were covered with blood. She could process that in her brain, so she decided that it must not be hers. Anyone who had lost that much blood must be close to death. That narrowed it down to Ronjai or Tyreek, who was lying very still on the floor in front of her.

Chapter 50

After the events of the past fifteen hours, there was no way that anyone was going to leave Simone by herself. Jason, Mike, and Sly had set up camp in her condo. They had no reason to stay but couldn't bring themselves to leave. Mim, William, and Maia had stopped by briefly as well. Mostly because Mim wanted Jason to know that Maia was doing just fine and wasn't in need of him. He didn't have to feel guilty about wanting to be in two places at the same time. Mim brought Star of Bethlehem to help everyone with the shock and grief of the day's tragedies. After a pot of tea and pleasant conversation—for Maia's sake, the three said their farewells with hugs and kisses all around.

"Night night Daddy. I'll call you in the morning when I get up," Maia said as she squeezed Jason as tightly as she could.

"Hey little lady, you're so strong I can't breathe. Why are you hugging me so tight? I'll see you in the morning, just like always," he replied.

Maia leaned her head up towards his ear. "So, you can pass it on to Miss Simone. You need to stay right here. Miss Simone shouldn't be alone, and you can make her feel safe," she whispered.

He bent down and whispered back, "And how do you know that?"

"Because you always make me feel safe, that's how I know." She let go and reached for her coat. She kissed him one more time and said, "And you'll feel better too."

The men had decided to keep around the clock watch on Simone in addition to whatever the police were doing. Jason took first shift. Mike and Sly left about three hours later. They had talked Simone into going to bed around ten, swearing that they wouldn't tear up her house or eat her out of house and home while she slept. She thanked them and gave each one a hug and kiss and headed off toward the bedroom without any argument.

Jason was sitting in one of the wingback chairs to keep himself from falling asleep. He heard a noise in the hallway and tried to focus his gaze in the darkened room. He heard the soft sound of bare feet walking in his direction.

"I couldn't sleep. I kept waking up thinking that I was dreaming. Sorry if I wakened you," Simone said. She stood there in her sweatpants and hoodie holding an oversized afghan. "May I join you?"

"Please do. That way I don't seem like a stalker by peeking in your room to check on you," he said.

Neither spoke for several minutes. What was there to be said? Four people were in critical condition. One was in a coma. There were no words.

"It was really nice for your parents to bring Maia tonight. She is really a lucky little girl to have so much love in her life," she said. Jason wasn't sure whether she was talking to him or to some unseen ghost from the past.

 "She deserves that. Every child does," he said. "You know, I've never heard you talk about your family. You're a mystery."

"You know me. Probably better than most people. *Definitely better than my soon to be ex-husband.* There's not much to say. You don't want to hear it. *And I'm not sure I'm strong enough to tell you.* It's a long story," she said as she pulled the afghan over her feet.

"Maia says I've got all night, so I can't go anywhere. Besides, I remember you listened to me once." Jason stood up and went into the kitchen. "Want some tea or something?"

She shook her head and watched him as he moved around her kitchen, opening her cabinets, starting the teapot, filling the tea balls. He finished and sat down on the other end of the sofa.

Simone took a deep breath and tried to figure out where to start. There were no flowers to help her through this, she thought. The fact that she felt strong enough to tell anyone about her family was hard for her to comprehend. The truth was that during her entire marriage to Greg, she had never even considered telling him the truth about her family. Deep down inside, she had always had a feeling that he would somehow use that information against her.

Then why did you marry him? It's taken all these years to realize that you made a mistake. It's taken almost losing my life again…

"I was born in Guam. My father was in the Air Force so we traveled a lot. There were three of us girls. I was the youngest. My sister, Lexine was two years older than me and Tara was the oldest by four years. My mother was so beautiful. She had such big pretty eyes. I remember that. Daddy always said that I looked just like her except I got his frown. He was stationed in Hawaii but had been deployed for the past year and was home on leave for thirty days. I was ten at the time. He took us camping on Moloka'i for three days. It was so much fun. We rented a camper and attached it to the back of the car and pulled it up to the campsite. On the way back down, Daddy let me ride in the car with him; Mommie and my sisters were in the camper. I remember coming around the curve when I heard this really loud noise. Daddy started cussing because the camper started to swerve off the road. The back end of the camper went off the road and started to pull the car down with it. Daddy hollered at me to unlock my seatbelt, but I couldn't do it because I was so scared. The camper and the car fell into the ravine and started to sink. Daddy got out and swam over to pull me out, but I was stuck. He finally was able to get me out through the window," she stopped and pointed to the scar on her neck. "That's where I got this," she continued.

"He pulled me to shore and went back in for my sisters and my mom, but he couldn't get to them because the camper landed upside down on the door. I can remember him going back down over and over but he couldn't save them. I sat on the edge watching him, praying that he wouldn't go down and not come back up. It seemed like hours before the rescue crew got there. Daddy and I were taken to the hospital. Lexi, Tara, and Mommie…"

She stopped talking. The sound of the teapot on the stove broke the silence. Jason got up and poured the water into the cups and dipped the tea balls. He brought them over to the coffee table.

"Daddy and I moved to California after that. Four years later, we went back to the spot on what would have been my parent's twentieth anniversary. We sat there for hours. Then we went home. Daddy died three months later. I'm still afraid of the water. That's really funny because I love to be near it. I'll sit by the edge of a lake or on the beach all day I but can't bring myself to get any closer." Simone sipped her tea.

Jason moved closer to Simone, and she put her tea down. She put her head on his chest and he wrapped the afghan around her. She closed her eyes, and they stayed that way until morning.

Chapter 51

Sly showed up at 7:00 sharp. He didn't seem to mind that Jason had been there all night and was busy setting out four plates for breakfast. He took it as a good sign that Simone must be up to eating. She looked exhausted when she opened the door but considering what she had been through, she was still beautiful in his eyes. He stepped inside and hugged her tight and gave her a kiss on the forehead. Jason saw it out of the corner of his eye. He smiled to himself.

I can't blame you dawg... How could you not? I ain't mad at ya... one thousand one, one thousand two...get to steppin'.

"Mike is on his way, I'm sure," Jason said. "He called this morning, and I made the mistake of mentioning food." No sooner than he finished speaking, the doorbell rang, and everybody laughed.

Simone went to the door and it was déjà vu all over again. Hug, forehead kiss. *Girl, you should get shot at more often...all this attention. All this love. You could get use to this, men coming out the woodwork. Hmmm hmmm hmmm.*

They ate and talked about other things for a while. Then Simone's cell phone started to serenade the group from the bedroom. Her love had come along, and he was sitting at the dining room table with her and their friends. *How embarrassing.* Maybe no one noticed or attached meaning to it. Jason looked toward the bedroom and silently agreed with Etta.

When she came back into the dining room, her brow spoke for her. "That was the hospital. Mrs. Henderson has to make some decision about Ronjai. She isn't expected to make it and she asked that I be there," Simone hesitated. She couldn't lose her composure in front of them. They would understand but that would show her emotions and that would make her feel vulnerable.

Is that so bad? You are human. If you haven't learned that over the past twenty-four hours, then what have you learned?

She sat down, then stood back up. Not sure of what to do next.

"We'll drive over with you. Take your time getting ready and we'll clean up."

Jason spoke mildly trying to give direction through the fog that seemed to encompass his beloved friend.

"Yeah, no need for you to drive. When it's time to come home, you got your choice of chauffeurs," Mike joked.

"Yeah, me or J. She don't have to ride in that hooptie you got," Sly added.

That broke the tension and gave Simone a moment to regroup.

"I'll be ready in a few. Thanks guys."

She went back toward the bedroom.

Jason stood up and gathered up his plate. "I'll wash and ya'll can fight over who dries the silverware."

Simone and her self-appointed bodyguards arrived at the hospital to a flurry of activity. It almost seemed as frantic as it had been when the ambulances started arriving last night. The sight of the building alone brought a knot into Simone's chest and caused her breathing to become irregular. Sly noticed the nervousness in her and put his arm around her. She mustered a smile and continued on. The four of them entered the elevator that led to the ICU. No one spoke during the ride up to the 6th floor. The doors opened, and it seemed as if Simone's feet were leaden, preventing her from moving out of the spot where she stood.

Maybe its fear. I can't bear seeing them this way. I can't do this.

She felt strong hands reaching from behind her to place themselves tenderly on her shoulders. "You're not alone, baby. We are right here with you. Nobody will ever hurt you. I promise," Jason spoke softly in her ear. Mike and Sly reached out, each taking one of her hands. Jason stayed behind the group. They escorted her out of the elevator and down the long hallways leading to Ronjai and Tyreek.

It was apparent as much from the signs as the police stationed outside of the ICU, that this was a very special place. Four officers were posted outside of the double doors. Three men and a woman. *Oooooh, affirmative action at the CMPD.* When they saw the group approaching, they immediately stood and assessed the risk. Surmising that it might be somewhere between moderate and minimal, they did not draw their weapons, but Jason noticed that two of them had placed their hands on their holsters.

"Identification is required to enter. Who are you here to see?" one of the officers with two free hands inquired.

"This is Simone Dyson. She received a call this morning to come here ASAP concerning Miss Ronjai Henderson," Jason answered.

The officer checked the approved list and found her name. "Who are they?" the officer pointed to her entourage.

"They are with me. They have been taking care of me for the past twenty-four hours," she replied.

The female officer glanced at Simone and then back at the three men who had been taking care of her for the past twenty-four hours and saw the intensity on each one of their faces. She looked to her colleagues and said, "Call the front desk and inform them that four will be arriving at the desk shortly. We have checked IDs and checked for weapons. They're cleared for entrance."

Honey, you're using up other women's men, you need to share. Shit.

The officer directed the other three to do as she had said and when they had patted everybody down, they buzzed them in. "I'm sorry, Mrs. Dyson about what has happened. CMPD offers its apologies," she said.

Simone smiled weakly. She felt as if she had no strength in her to proceed but she had no right to stay put. Someone beyond those doors was suffering more than she. When the group arrived at the front desk, a company of doctors was gathered there.

"Good morning, Mrs. Dyson. I am Dr. Gupta and these are my colleagues." Introductions were made between all of the people standing at the desk. It was like a small convention.

"Mrs. Henderson is in the conference room. We will be meeting in there to update you both on the condition of Tyreek and Ronjai."

Jason, Sly and Mike took that as a clue that they would be excluded from the conference, which suited each of them just fine. They knew that Simone would be alright even if she hadn't figured that out yet. That's just the way she was. Besides, they knew she was safe. They would see to that. She hugged them all and thanked them again. Mike said that they would be in the waiting area and that they could see the door from there. "We got you, baby girl," he said.

When the assembly entered the conference room, Simone's first thought was that she was to be part of a medical convention. The massive oak table was set up with laptop stations, folders, notepads and booklets. Multiple projector screens were on the walls with the names of the victims from yesterday's shootings. Simone read the names: Tyreek Henderson, Ronjai Henderson, Ky'Rell Ballard, Ishua Sekou N'Diaye, Alyetta Cosmey.

Simone didn't recognize the last name on the list. *That must have been the girl cleaning tables. Thank God that it wasn't later in the day. The list would have been much longer.*

She continued to look at the list and saw a name that sounded familiar. *Ishua? Is that you? What were you doing there?*

Then she remembered something. The man who tackled the shooter…*tall, dark, athletic, accent…*

Ky'Rell…that must be the boy.

You are blessed that your name isn't up there. You could be laying up in here with tubes down your throat just like…

Stop. Please, just stop.

Just want you to stop feeling sorry for yourself. You're a lot better off than any of those people on that list. So, like Churchill said, stay calm and carry on.

She walked over to Mrs. Henderson, who looked like she should have her name up there on the wall with the others. Seventy-four years old and still raising children. Ronjai had told Simone about her family's history. How her mother ended up in prison for life for murder. How her aunt had died when she was young. Nothing but heartache it seemed. *And now this? Will it ever end?* Mrs. Henderson's eyes were practically swollen shut from grief, lack of sleep, and shock. A lace handkerchief, the kind you don't see much anymore, lay balled up in front of her. Simone bent down and held her as tightly as she could, hoping that some of her reserve energy would flow into this tired, defeated woman who had been through so much.

"For those of you who are been brought in for consultation, let's begin this evaluative session with a recap of the event that brings us together today. Mrs. Henderson is the grandmother of two of the victims, Mrs. Dyson was present at the shooting and fortunately not seriously injured. Mr. Crafts, from Chicago Metropolitan Police Department is here to share what has been determined as of this morning," Dr. Gupta said and sat down, waiting for Mr. Crafts to start the projector.

"At approximately 11:02 yesterday morning, twelve-year-old, Ky'Rell Ballard walked into the McDonald's on Ashcroft Avenue and opened fire. The fire seemed intended for Tyreek Henderson, who was seated at a table with his sister Ronjai and Mrs. Dyson. Tyreek is a known gang member and drug dealer who is scheduled for trial on a variety of charges the end of next week. The shooter is the son of Curiel Ballard, who is incarcerated at the Women's Detention Center and whose father, Pious Waters, a guard at Big Muddy River Prison in upstate Illinois, was tragically killed in a fire at the facility two weeks ago…"

At the mention of Big Muddy River, Simone immediately wondered about Harlem. *Did that incident have anything to do with what happened yesterday? Was Harlem okay? What was going on? Karl's grasp on the world couldn't cause ripples like this. Could it?*

By the time Simone went back to listening to the voice outside of her head, the speaker had changed. One of the doctors was stating the condition of each patient.

"…since the report on patients was received this morning, eighteen year old, Alyetta Cosmey, employee of the restaurant, has died from her injuries. Ishua Sekou N'Diaye, a patron, has been upgraded to stable condition and is expected to make a full recovery from a gunshot wound to the leg. Tyreek Henderson underwent a six-hour surgery last night to remove two bullets from the thoracic cavity and the spleen. Prognosis for at least partial recovery is good. Ky'Rell Ballard was shot in the lower spine, vertebrae L4 and L5 specifically, by an off- duty detective, Mortimeous Quick, who happened to be in the area. Surgery lasted nine hours and the prognosis is very unlikely that he will walk or ever have sensation in the lower half of his body. Ronjai Henderson was shot in the right temporal lobe with the bullet lodging itself in an inoperable area. At this time, she is in a drug induced coma to sustain her vital functions until a decision can be made about what to do considering her condition. Miss Henderson is fifteen weeks pregnant, and the fetus sustained no trauma during the shooting," the physician took a deep breath and closed his laptop as if he had seen enough.

Mrs. Henderson let out a wail that shook the souls of everyone in the room. It was so loud and deep that the guys were startled in the waiting room. Jason jumped but Sly grabbed his arm.

"We expected some shit like this. Nobody's being wheeled out," Mike said.

Jason sat back down.

Not yet anyway.

Chapter 52

The doctors explained the situation to Mrs. Henderson and Simone translated it into layman's terms. After the moments of intense anguish were released, the Henderson matriarch was composed and accepting, giving it over to the Lord.

The explanation by the doctors had lasted longer than the incident that caused it. The charts, graphs, research, and data for what they were proposing as the viable options for Ronjai were overwhelming. The end result, however, was always the same.

She's going to die. She might as well be dead now. If they remove the bullet, she'll die. If they wake her up, she'll die. The only reason they are continuing to let her 'live' is so the baby won't die. Was it even humane to consider letting the baby live? No mother, father most likely going to prison for life. Was the great grandmother going to be expected to raise this child too?

The meeting ended two hours after it started. Mrs. Henderson's only words were that she had to pray about it. She held on to her walker and inched slowly to whichever grandchild's room came first. Simone could hear her singing, "Precious Lord, take my hand, lead me on, let me stand, I'm tired, weak, I'm so worn…."

The nurses were beginning to gather together, talking in more hushed voices than usual and pointing to Simone and the TV monitors mounted in the waiting areas. The breaking news on CNN was scrolled across the screen in bright red and orange.

Kind of like emergency and danger signs. I wonder if they did that on purpose.

Simone walked closer to the screen as if that would make it make more sense. Jason, Mike, and Sly rose and stood beside her.

Shooting in Chicago's East side tied to indicted Interim Police Commissioner. Full report at 12:00pm.

Frederica and Don looked like the conversation between them was quite serious. Simone wondered how Harlem was taking Frederica sharing the sofa with an attractive black man. Maybe it was okay since she had on closed toed shoes today. After all, it was a little chilly recently. Even in Atlanta.

"So, when did an indictment come down? I didn't hear anything about that anywhere," Mike said. He and Sly started their own conversation about what type of information the court would have to have to indict Karl Dyson.

They looked back up at the screen to see the list of charges scrolling by.

Attempted murder, drug trafficking, manslaughter, rape…

It seemed as if the entire floor was standing there in a daze. A new level of shock to add to the past twenty-eight hours.

Can it get any worse?

Jason put his arm around Simone, and she leaned into him for support. Everyone was so engrossed in the news that no one heard the footsteps entering the waiting area.

Surrounded by men. I recognize one of them but who are these other two? And why does that one have his arm around my wife? So, this is why she wants a divorce.

Greg stood there like a statue, taking it all in. Behind him, the footsteps continued. A group of blue and black jacketed individuals with big letters of the alphabet plastered across their backs, DEA, ATF, FBI, proceeded towards the main desk attracting the attention of everyone in the room. While the spokesperson for the group was placing documents in front of the duty nurse, Greg stepped toward Simone and the three men who surrounded her.

"Hello, Simone. It's good to see that you are alright," Greg said.

Simone turned around to see Greg and hear a sound rising in the back of his throat.

"Greg," she said acknowledging his presence.

He stood there as if his presence would cause the men standing with his wife to shake, quiver, or at least move. It didn't work.

"Jason Copeny," the man standing closest to his wife said as he offered his hand.

Mike followed J's lead and extended his hand as he introduced himself. Sly just grunted, "Greg."

Asshole.

Greg stood there wondering what was happening. He was kicking himself for waiting to see Simone after he had heard about the shooting. He had fully expected her to call him, crying and begging him to protect her and keep her safe. Then, he could be magnanimous and allow her to come running to him. The call never came. He was beginning to understand why.

She don't need you anymore...maybe she never did. But who are these niggers with her? I know that damn Slick, Sly, whatever the fuck his name is. But these other two?

Greg wracked his brain trying to remember whether Simone had ever mentioned somebody named—*what did he say his name was? How long has she known him? How well did she know him?*

"Do you always hug your co-workers?" he sputtered.

"Actually, I do. At least I don't sleep with them. Why are you here, Greg?" she asked.

"I came to see if you were okay. I am still your husband. I guess someone else beat me to it," he said.

No reaction came from Simone. She replied. "Like I asked earlier, why are you here?"

Greg answered, "Can we talk somewhere?" He looked directly at Jason as if that statement was enough to make him step away from Simone. It didn't work.

"Greg, I really don't have anything to say to you and I'm not interested in hearing what you have to say," she said.

"If we could have some privacy—I…"

"Mrs. Simone Dyson?" A deep voice wafted through the air in the direction of the small group. They turned toward the voice. A tall, official looking man walked their way. He had the look of Idris Elba, confident and secure with himself. Just the kind of man that Greg couldn't stand. The same kind as the three still surrounding his wife.

"Mrs. Dyson, I am Special Agent Adamian Hyland. My colleagues and I have some questions for you about the shooting that took place yesterday. Could you come with us, please?" Special Agent Hyland looked at the group and wondered what he had interrupted.

Jason gave Simone a supportive hug as did Sly and Mike. She looked at Greg and turned and walked away with the Special Agent in the jacket labeled FBI. The three hugged men looked at the unhugged man and walked away too.

"Damn, this shit keeps getting worse and worse. What do you think they are here for? This shit is bigger than just a shooting of a local gang banger," Mike surmised.

"That no good Dyson," Jason said.

"Which one?" Sly asked. They tried to laugh at the joke but by the time the elevator arrived, another person was entering with them. The doors opened and the music in the elevator reminded Jason of an episode of the show, Miami Vice, that he loved to watch, back in the day. Phil Collins was letting everybody know what was in the air tonight.

"I suppose I should thank you for staying close to my wife yesterday. She and I aren't seeing eye to eye right now," Greg started. There was no response from anyone in the elevator. So, after a small growl, he continued. "Yea, you know how wives are, right? I don't have a problem stepping aside, you know? It was good while it was good. Now—it might be time to move on. Kind of cold now days, you know what I mean? Whoever gets with that is going to need a crow bar to pry those legs open."

Jason knew exactly what was coming in the air tonight—IT was his fist smashing into Greg's jaw. The music reached a crescendo as Greg crashed into the wall of the elevator and crumbled to the floor. Sly and Mike looked at each other and simultaneously said, "Dammnnnn."

They pulled out their phones and snapped photos of the City Manager sprawled all over the floor as the doors of the elevator opened. "At least he's already at the hospital," Mike said.

Sly took another photo at a different angle. "I can see the title on YouTube, "City Manager floored by brother's indictment'." He and Mike laughed heartily as they stepped over Greg. Jason stayed behind and bent down toward Greg, "And you're going to need a shovel to pick up your teeth."

Chapter 53

Shevardnadze was placing the placemats on the dining room table, hoping that Mr. Horace would enjoy the meal that she had prepared. She had worked so hard that first week to be a good companion. This was the start of week three and for the first time in her adult life she felt satisfaction and fulfillment. She felt that she had a purpose and was truly appreciated. It was funny when she thought about it, her mother had been correct, she needed a father figure, a man who could help her learn what it felt like to be special and important. If she had learned that earlier in life, she would have made better choices.

 The days passed quickly, and she was always sorry to have to leave at five o'clock. During the day, the two of them would talk, laugh, cook, read, and listen to each other. Mr. Horace had great stories about his childhood and the thirty-two years of marriage to his wife. In addition to being a wonderful storyteller, he was a wonderful listener. When Shevardnadze spoke about her life, he was never judgmental. She made sure never to tell him about her relationship with his son—either one of them. There were plenty of other things in her life that haunted her.

She always liked to make sure Mr. Horace had his dinner before she left so that he wouldn't have to be fiddling around in the kitchen when no one was there. She knew that Simone would be there on Tuesday afternoons and for some reason, she really wanted Simone to be assured that she had made the right choice when she gave her this job.

"Hmmm mmmm... Something smells like corned beef brisket and cabbage. My favorite food! How did you know? My Becki used to fix that for special occasions. Smelled just like this!" Horace stood in the entryway to dining room leaning on his cane. His ankle was healing nicely, the doctor said, but he still had to use the cane until the next appointment. He watched Chevy—as he called her, rush to and fro.

That name of hers was a mouthful. Besides, she reminds me of a Chevy. Basic, hardworking and dependable. Always wanting to be something special, never realizing that basic, hardworking and dependable was something special. Poor chile. Wonder what happened to her. If I let her stick around long enough, I'm sure I'll ind out. Simone wouldn't have recommended her without a good reason...she has done a good job. I've got no complaints and it's kind of nice to have a woman's touch around here again. Wonder why she was in the hospital...

She escorted him to the table and sat down across from him. She would have served him, but he told her on the first day that his ankle was hurt not his hands—he didn't need a nurse and he could do that for himself. She looked reprimanded, so he smiled at her and proceeded to ladle food on to her plate. "See, I told you my hands work just fine," he had said. No one had ever served her except her mother and that only lasted until she was big enough to do it for herself. Shevardnadze wrote about it in her journal when she got home that evening under the heading of Things That Made Me Feel Special.

The first five minutes of the meal were eaten in silence. After the food was blessed, the two ate. Horace put down his fork and looked across the table at the cook. "This is just about as good as my wife's. How'd you do that? She used to do something to the cabbage that made it real tasty. You know, cabbage can be bland if you don't cook it right."

"Yesterday, I was cleaning out the closet in the back room upstairs and I found a box of cookbooks. There were notepads and recipe cards. I figured that they belonged to your wife. I saw this recipe and it had five stars next to it, so I thought it must be special. I wanted to surprise you," Chevy said.

"Well, you sure did that. This is really good. Thank you very much, Chevy," Horace noticed that he felt like something was caught in his throat. He swallowed hard. He thought about his wife every day, but this meal made it even more real today. The memory of her filled the room like the aroma of the food. He took a deep breath and tried to change the subject. He would spend more time with it after Chevy had gone home. "What else did you find up there in that closet?" he asked.

"There were photo albums and loose pictures, a little wooden box with keys and jewelry in it—well, an earring. Some receipts were there too. I put the receipts in an envelope," she said.

Horace thought for a moment. "Those must be from one of the storage facilities. I own a couple of storage buildings in town and in Joliet. When I used to do the books, I'd keep the receipts from the rent before I hired a management group to do it for me. Maybe that's what the keys are from too. I stored some of Becki's things away after she passed. All that stuff in the closet might need to go over there too. I'll have to remember to ask Simone if she wouldn't mind going over there and seeing what's in them. It's been a long, long time. Could be anything, I betcha."

They went back to eating and discussing how to properly cook cabbage.

As the dishes were being cleared from the table, Horace asked half in jest, "So what's for dessert?"

"Homemade bread pudding," was the reply.

"And it's not even Tuesday," Horace grinned as he carried the placemats to the kitchen.

Chapter 54

Basketball Wives wouldn't be on for another half hour, which gave Leela enough time to log on and update her status, upload the newest photos of her pedicure and manicure, showcasing the emptiness of the third finger of her left hand. Would everybody get it?

It had been well over six weeks since the traumatizing day when she had been interrupted by a phone call from that root woman, Mim, informing her that her husband was being questioned by the police for something that happened before she met him. Since she didn't know him then, she felt it nothing more than an inconvenience to inform her. What was she supposed to do?

Drive all the way to the city to pick up Maia? Why couldn't witchy woman do it? Maia liked her better anyway…Maybe she was hexed. That must be it. Mim had to be a witch or something. No ordinary fifty some year-old woman could look that good and be that attractive. No wrinkles, small waist, upturned breasts…It's not fair. So… she must be a witch. All those flowers and grass and weeds she had…

Leela stopped thinking, long enough to finish her upload. She commented on forty-three friends posts and friended fifteen people that she had never met. When she finished, she felt superbly important and well loved. Now if her sister and family would stay out of their house for another couple of hours, all would be right with the world. She looked at the calendar on the wall in her new room, aka the guest room of her sister's house. It was Thursday. She should reach out to Maia today.

Of course, if she missed me, she could call me or text me more than she does. Truthfully, it's nice not to have to try to answer all those questions she asks. Always wanting to read books and play with dolls and run around outside. I don't get it, she's as boring as her father. He must be her father, then. The root doctor definitely would have said something if she thought otherwise. That's why I hate being around that woman. She can read you or something.

Still not thinking, Leela went downstairs to the kitchen for a snacky before her show came on. The house was still quiet. *Thank God.* No teenagers—the kids had after school track and band practice this afternoon, her sister worked the swing shift and that mountain she called a husband kept really weird hours at the hospital. So, all in all, she could be pretty sure that the plasma TV and snacky snacks were hers until much later. It occurred to her that she might start dinner and surprise the family but that thought quickly faded as it was replaced with *Ooooooh...Double Stuffed Oreos.*

After eating in the hospital cafeteria, everyone felt much better. Jason had kept his back to the wall and eye on the door, waiting to see which government agency would come looking for him concerning the 'fall' that Mr. Dyson had in the elevator about forty-five minutes ago. No one came.

Maybe that was out of the jurisdiction of the Feds. He is only local government. Wish HE understood his own importance—or lack thereof.

Mike had returned from the bathroom and sat back down, looking sour in the face. He chewed the inside of his jaw as he tried to figure out how to say what was on his mind. Sly saw the look on Mike's face and decided it would be a good time to take a walk to help his shepherd's pie digest. He said his see you laters and left the cafeteria saying he'd keep a look out for any black-eyed Dyson he saw coming their way.

"So, what's up, man? You look like you saw a ghost or something. If they come for somebody about what just happened, it will be me. I hit him."

"As you should have. He's lucky, we didn't take turns. This is really serious, though," Mike said quietly.

"What?" Jason asked.

"When's the last time you talked to your wife?"

Jason stopped and thought about it. With so much happening recently, the thought of dealing with Leela hadn't been a priority. Maia was fine, his parents were fine, Simone was fine and if Leela was not complaining, she must be fine too.

"Couple of days, I guess. Why?"

Mike didn't speak. How could he?

"Why?" the question came again. More forcefully.

"Man, she's leaving you," Mike said.

Jason sat there, not in shock. Just surprised at how he was hearing the news.

"So, let me get this straight. My wife is leaving me, and I hear it from you? Why did she tell you and not me?"

"She didn't tell me specifically. She put it on Facebook."

Chapter 55

Cornelius had become quite the familiar with the studios of CNN. He was introduced as an integral part of a federal investigation spanning several years. Little was known by his new BFF (Beautiful Footed Frederica) or her counterparts as to his real identity, although he was sure they were investigating as much as the budget would allow, to find out whatever they could about his past. Since the budget was huge, he figured they'd figure it out sooner or later. Although he was never photographed or appeared on camera, he sat with Frederica and Don regularly, sharing what the Feds told him he could share, which wasn't much, but when he heard it broadcast on national TV, it sounded impressive.

He was feeling pretty good about his newly birthed life. He had been flown to Jersey City Regional Airport and given his birth certificate, driver's license, checkbook—with money in it—and credit cards.

Wasn't America wonderful? Who wouldn't love this country?

His task for the next few days was to get settled in his new hometown of Hoboken, New Jersey. His research and that of his handlers, had located two bookstores that were for sale in the area. The proprietor of one had had a stroke and the greedy children wanted to get out while the getting was good. No one else in the family had the desire, drive, or brains to run a bookstore. From what Cornelius gathered during his conversations with two of aforementioned greedy children, they might not be intelligent enough to read. Poor Papa, his future did not look too bright.

The other bookstore was called AMIATTTaW. When Cornelius saw the name of the bookstore, he thought it was a misprint. The typist had been freebasing and typing at the same time or something. What the hell was that? As he continued down the webpage, he saw it. *A Mind Is A Terrible Thing To Waste. Hell, if that ain't the truth.* It made sense now and he liked it. He liked it a lot.

After renting his first car ever with his first credit card ever, he programmed the address into his Frederica. He changed the name; TomTom was somebody's dumb-ass bitch he remembered from Big Muddy.

He followed the road signs and the female voice on to the NJ Turnpike and headed toward his new endeavor. He might have to shorten the name. Had too many letters- AMIATT. That would be perfect. *'Cause it's even more true than the original.*

After two hours on the Turnpike, Cornelius turned around and headed back in the direction he had come. The feeling of freedom was making him giddy. This was the first time in over twenty years that he was completely unescorted and not accountable to anyone for anything.

At least for a few days. Fuck, that's like a lifetime. These peoples out here don't know how good they got it. Jobs to go to. Houses to live in. TVs that they can change when they want to. Restaurants to eat at. Different clothes to wear. People to fuck—well I had that to if I really wanted somebody like TomTom…you know what I mean. Life is good out here. I get to drive up and down this road as many times as I'm willing to pay for it! Now that's freedom! I can be as damn stupid as I want!

He pulled into the rest area and surveyed the wonders all around him. A restaurant just for hotdogs. Another for pizza. And his personal favorite—Starbucks. He had never been to one, but he had seen them in the TV shows at Big Muddy and he really wanted to order a venti sweety mocha creamy thingy-chini. *Yeah boy, life is good.* He sauntered into the bathroom first, though. He was going to take his time. After all, he was a free man.

Chapter 56

Simone had taken a week away from work after the shooting. She really didn't want to; thinking that staying busy might be the best way to work through what had happened. After all, she wasn't a weak-minded individual who couldn't handle tragedy. She had seen tragedy at an early age and she survived so what was so different about this? This wasn't even her family. She would be fine.

She had gotten even more comfortable staying at the condo. She could have company if she wanted, stay close to what was happening at work and know that Greg probably wouldn't be anywhere in the vicinity. He hadn't tried to contact her since that day at the hospital. Perfect. She called Mim two days into her self-imposed rest. She couldn't understand at the time why she felt a need to talk to her, but she had begun to trust her feelings and follow through on what they were telling her.

"I'm so glad you called, sweetheart. You have been on my mind," Mim said when she answered the phone.

"I was hoping that I wouldn't disturb you," Simone said quietly.

"Never. It is always good to hear your voice."

Simone laughed a little. "Can you read my voice too?"

"What would it tell me?"

Simone thought for a minute. She balled herself up on her sofa, pulling her comforter closer around her. She felt so much like a child in need of her mother but there wasn't one to turn to. The closest person she had was the woman on the other end of the phone. That thought struck her at her core and she couldn't speak.

Why am I still alive again? Why? I don't understand why I'm still here. Ronjai didn't hurt anyone. She didn't do anything to deserve this. Neither did my mother or sisters. And here I am again. Alone.

She sat there, thinking. After a minute, she realized that Mim was still on the phone.

"I'm so sorry. I was thinking about—everything."

"Hard to find words it seems," Mim said.

"Extremely," Simone replied.

"Maybe they're not necessary right now," Mim said.

"I don't know what I'm supposed to do."

"Wanting to help?"

"Yes, but I can't."

"Feeling like you have no control?"

"I don't. I can't control what happens. I always thought I could, but I know better now."

"It is a blessing to be able to learn that lesson. You can't control what anyone else chooses to do. You are right about that, but you have never had control over anyone else. You are the only one over which you have power. You can do so much, if you allow it. You can pray. You can let go of the guilt you feel because you weren't injured. You can look at your life and be assured that you were spared for a purpose. The best thing that you can do right now is give yourself permission to live," Mim said.

Tears flowed down Simone's cheeks. Mim couldn't see them or hear them, but she could feel them. She could sense Simone's pain and anguish. She had known that it was there and had been there for a long time. The way her brow knitted up, the smoothness of the rest of her forehead. Something had happened as a child, and she never worked through it. Maybe this will cause her to deal with that too. Whatever it was.

"I think you should rest for a while. Find a quiet space where you feel safe and allow yourself to feel what you have bottled up inside. Is there anything that I can do for you?"

Simone spoke before she realized it. "I want to go home. Would you mind driving me? I don't think I can do it myself. I want to be in my house. I didn't realize it until right now."

"I'll be there within the hour. When you are ready, Jason and I will bring your car. We will keep an eye on it until then. Is that alright?"

Simone shook her head up and down as if Mim could see her.

"I'll be there shortly. Stay covered up until I get there."

"Is there a tea for this too?"

"There will be by the time I see you. Think of this day forward as a new chapter. What happens next is completely up to you."

PART THREE

Chapter 57

Florian Andros held his fiancé's hand as they sat across from each other at the restaurant. It had been too long since the two of them had enjoyed the fruits of their labor. This was the third anniversary of *Tanja's*, The Faerie Queen. The name so suited the love of his life that he wanted to share it with the world or at least with this portion of it. The candlelight danced on the crystal glassware and the twinkling lights that lit the walls and the ceiling gave the impression of a far distant world where faeries would dance and play. It was a beautiful scene. The patrons dined quietly, enjoying the delectable fare served to them by friendly well-trained waitstaff. Amidst so much loveliness, Florian was worried. His love hadn't spoken a word in the past several minutes. She was deep in thought. He knew when she was like this that something was weighing on her heart and mind. There would be no peace within her until it was resolved. Florian had never truly known her to have peace. Even after splendid sessions of lovemaking that took his breath away, he could tell that the deep well within her was still flowing at full strength. What was it that tormented her so? And why had it risen to the surface so strong as of late? He knew better than to ask. That had never worked. When she was ready, she would tell him. Wouldn't she?

"I have to go back for a while. There is something that I need to do. Something that I should have done a long time ago. I was—afraid," she grasped his hand tighter and gave him a sad smile. "I want to be your wife and I have to be free of my past to do that and to feel at peace with myself. I want you to meet my parents and my…family but I have to do this first. I hope you understand," she said quietly.

Florian didn't know how to respond other than to squeeze her hand and ask, "As long as you return to me."

"This is home. Wherever you are is where I will always be."

"When are you leaving?"

"As soon as I can schedule a flight from Cointrin," she answered.

"How about in the morning? I need you here with me tonight. I will miss you too badly if you leave me before daylight," Florian replied trying to sound strong and supportive only sounding empty and afraid.

What if IT is stronger than she is? What will I do then?

He reached in his pocket and pulled out his cell phone and searched for the number of the airport and scheduled a flight from Geneva to Chicago. He put the phone back in his pocket and fiddled with the small box that contained the engagement ring he had planned to give her tonight after the dessert course.

Chapter 58

Special Agent Adamian Hyland had spent every day of the past week debriefing Special Agent Ishua Hyland in his hospital bed. Today, Agent Ishua Hyland had been permitted to leave his room, under heavy guard, to start therapy on his leg. He had been shot so close to the femoral artery, that a half inch to the left would have meant certain death from blood loss. *The ancestors were with me.* He chuckled to himself. *Not ready to deal with me yet.*

"So, when can I leave this place?" Special Agent Hyland asked his brother.

"If it were up to me, I'd send you home on the first plane. You always have been hardheaded and look what happened," his brother responded.

"Things work out. It's been three years of undercover work sniffing behind this gutter snipe. Look how close we are now," Ishua replied.

"It almost got you killed. All that time and effort and it breaks wide open because the mayor's driver was sick one day," Adamian said.

Adamian pushed his brother into the therapy room and watched as Ishua pulled himself into a standing position between the parallel bars. It upset him to see his brother in so much pain but better to see him in pain then to never see him again. Ishua winced and grimaced but made no sound. As the younger brother, he never wanted to show signs of weakness and now was not the time to start.

"So, tell me about the lady you drove to the prison," big brother asked.

"Aaaah. Miss Simone. Is this official questioning or personal interest?"

"Why do you ask? From what you said the other day, you've been following her for weeks now," Adamian said.

"Just doing my job, bro. Just doing my job."

"Well, I'm just doing mine. Tell me about her before I shoot you in the other leg."

After a torturous hour of rehabilitation, Ishua was in tremendous pain. He wanted to rub his leg but knew that touching it would only make it worse. The nurse had offered powerful pharmaceuticals but that went against his moral code. *If pain means that you are alive, then I am going to live forever.* The older Hyland brother waited patiently for his sibling to adjust in the hospital bed. Even though they were only two years apart, Adamian had always taken care of his baby brother. As children back on the continent, they had no one but each other after their parents had died of AIDS. It was three weeks before the missionaries found the boys in the small hut with the body of their mother. Five-year-old Adamian had seen enough by that age to know that Mammam would not wake up. He walked to the watering hole twice a day with the biggest pan that he could carry. There were very few supplies left in the hut, but Adamian always made sure that his baby brother had something to eat each day, even if he did not. At night he would sing the lullaby that Mammam sang before she became too sick. Now, as he watched the man that Ishua had become, he felt overcome with immense pride.

Mammam would be proud too. I did my best, Mammam. I promised you I would take care of him. And I'm promising you now, I will find out who's responsible for this, if it's the last thing I do.

Mighty Quick was in the hospital elevator on his way down from ICU. Still too many armed official alphabet jackets in the area for him to feel comfortable. He had an IA inquiry in the morning, and he would feel so much better if he knew the condition of the baby predator. When he had called for information, the system would not permit access without an authorization code. Without the code the call was automatically switched to one of those alphabet agencies that had set up residency in several of the conferences room throughout the hospital.

Mighty had been feeling less than his nickname recently. His home life was in shambles as his youngest daughter was receiving death threats over Instagram because of her father's police brutality toward another innocent young black male. Had this poor child been wearing a hoodie when he was gunned down? His wife was traumatized over what could have happened to her husband.

Maybe you should retire now instead of trying to reach sixty-five. We could use the money, but it doesn't matter if you're dead. You're not as young as you used to be and you need to watch out for your heart. Remember what the doctor said?

He could hear every word she had said playing over and over again like an old scratched vinyl record. It hurt him to think that she thought of him as old and sick. It hurt him more that she was right. He made an excuse to leave that night and went to his other family, where he was appreciated. Or at least properly flattered.

The morning was not going to be pretty. He was fairly sure that no one knew about the search for a messenger or the delivery that had been made. Word on the street was that Ty had pissed off his supplier and the hit was payback for some shit that gone down over the last few months. Decrease in sales is bad for business. *So is leaving witnesses.* Mighty rubbed his chest and tried to lose himself for the moment in the excitement of his negligee'd babies' mama, Rakeetah.

"Ooooh, daddy, don't you wanna come and get it? Come on, big daddy," she moaned.

Mighty rubbed his chest some more and looked at Rakeetah. Young, needy, clueless. What did she see in his old, tired, balding ass? Then it hit him.

"Don't call me daddy."

Chapter 59

Jason was sitting in the family room of his home staring at the screen of the sixty inch plasma TV. The Bulls were playing like goats and that left him lots of time to think about what Mike had told him. Corona in one hand, Droid in the other, he opened his Facebook account and realized that he had never visited his wife's site because he knew there was nothing there that he wanted to see. He noticed her status-Free and Fabulous! The next thing he noticed were the pudgy fingers showing off a manicure of the most artificial nails he had seen outside of a horror movie.

So, what did she do with the ring I worked my ass off to buy? She better get a good price at the pawn shop.

He read some of the posts from her friends and noticed that she had barely stopped short of calling him a convicted felon and how she couldn't live in fear for her life any longer. She was a victim because he had misrepresented himself all those years ago. She felt blessed that she had escaped with her life. Her only recourse was an annulment.

It was so bad that even the third beer couldn't make it any less ridiculous. He had read back through months of posts and noticed something that he couldn't understand.

Who can't handle two at the same time? Been there, done that. I did learn something in college! I know how to handle my business.

What the fuck is she talking about?

Jason went over to the bar and said hello to the Jamaican captain he had locked up several months ago. He wasn't happy to see the captain smiling at him with a smirk that implied that he should put him back before something bad happened. The bottle seemed to open itself and to pour without much help. Jason remembered what had happened the last time he imbibed at this level. The dreams of a beautiful woman whom he loved to the center of his being. This time didn't have the potential to be as pleasurable.

There were days on campus that reminded Jason of the Spike Lee movie, School Daze. Everybody knew it was satire, but it hit awfully close to home. Jason had been so happy to get a football scholarship and get out of the city after the death and damage that occurred two summers before. It was really cool to be going to the same college as his boy Mike. It would be good—a new start. Jason could put that summer behind him. Alayah, his sister--both of them. Tasha was never the same after the accident. She seemed distant. Jason understood the connection between twins, but he always felt there was something more to it than just that. It was good to leave all of that behind.

Mike and Jason had tried to be assigned together in the dorms as freshmen, but it didn't work out. Mike was in with the party dudes and Jason was assigned to a nerd named Kyle. It was exactly what he needed at the time because Kyle was as skilled in explaining things as he was at being a nerd. Jason had in-house tutoring for his first two years of college. By the time he was ready to pledge with the fraternity of his dream, he felt incredibly confident that his godlike physique, athletic prowess, model worthy smile and 3.6GPA would be more than enough to get him laid and pledged. He was successful at both.

After he and Mike were inducted into the fraternity, they moved into the house on Greek Row. Parties, sorority sisters crawling through, and a sense of brotherhood that he hadn't experienced beyond the time he had spent with Mr. William and Mike gave him a new lease on life. Then there was that really cute chick that he saw at several of the frat parties. He introduced himself twice, but she barely acknowledged his existence. He asked Mike what he knew about her and got nowhere. Seems that Mike knew just as little as Jason and that was saying something. The more Jason couldn't get with her, the more he wanted to. Leela. He finally found out her name. He liked it. He shared his goal of hooking up with her with his new roomie, and Mike just grunted and laughed.

He set his goal and proceeded to accomplish it even though it was a slow and arduous journey. He was giving up a great deal of his time and she wasn't giving up anything. He would walk her to classes, take her to shows on campus, help her with her studies and wonder where she was while he waited for her at the library. One afternoon, after waiting for her at the library for over an hour, he walked back to the frat house. The room to the door was closed but Jason didn't think anything of it at the time. He opened the door and saw Mike's ass facing him. Jason stood there for a moment and wondered where Mike was burrowing to---when he saw the two feet sticking out from other side of Mike's behind. Jason understood and backed back out of the door and closed it quietly. He snickered and made a mental note to hi-five his boy for hitting it like he owned it. He strolled over to the dining hall for an early dinner to make sure he gave his friend enough time to handle his business. He wondered who was the owner of the little fat feet.

He awoke to the sound of footsteps in the bedroom. Since he was in his own home and Maia was at a sleepover with one of her BFFs, there should be only one other possibility of who the footsteps belonged to. He sat up in the bed to see Leela tipping toward the closet.

"I'm awake, so you don't have to tiptoe," he said.

"Jason, we need to talk," she replied without looking at him.

"Yes, we do," he said as he got out of the bed and pulled on a t-shirt.

Leela pretended not to look at him, but she couldn't help admiring his muscular physique. She watched his chest ripple as he pulled the shirt down over his head. His tight abdomen descended into his sweatpants just like those male models in the fashion magazines she so loved. And he was her husband of more than a decade. He worked really hard, took good care of her daughter and didn't cheat on her the way most of her friends' men did, so why wasn't she satisfied?

He let me down! He was supposed to get rich and famous and that didn't happen. I was supposed to have a real mansion in California and drive a Mercedes and shop on Rodeo Drive. But no, here we are in Chicago twenty minutes from where he grew up. He's working to save people from jail. Where's the glamour in that? It's not fair. He tricked me. All smooth and nice… I thought he was the right one…

"Leela, are you listening to me?" Her thoughts were interrupted by Jason's voice. She looked at his face. Even in her self-absorbed stupor, she could see the tiredness on his handsome countenance. She expected to see anger or confusion on his face. She saw neither, in fact if she were honest with herself, he looked relieved and not the least bit upset. Her eyes scrunched up and she frowned.

What's wrong with him? He should want to hit me or holler or something. I saw it on Las Vegas Housewives…

"I want a divorce," she stammered, taking a deep breath.

"I heard," Jason answered. She gave her usual 'I'm confused look'. So, he continued, "You put it on Facebook. Remember? So, everybody knows." He turned around and started to make up the bed. "You could have told me yourself."

"Who told you? You don't go on Facebook. Who was it, Mike?"

Funny that's her first choice. BINGO! I should have fuckin' known. Damn.

Jason kept working on the bed while millions of circuits fired, wired, and reconnected in his brain. *Unfuckin' believable.* He took a deep breath and stood up looking at his wife as she stared at him, like she was waiting for something.

"So, what do you want? Just tell me and it's done," he said.

"Don't you want to know why? Why aren't you saying something? Trying to stop me or something? Don't you love me?" she sputtered.

No, actually. Not the way I should.

That must have come from the rewired part of Jason's brain. If this had happened a year or two ago, he knew his response would have been different. What had changed?

Everything. My thinking. My dreams, my mind. And it had to do with one person. And it isn't the one standing in front of me.

"Leela, we both know that things aren't the way they should be, and I apologize for not being what you needed. I did try. I should have told you about that stuff when I was young, but I didn't think it was important. I thought I could just move on. Marry you, have a family. I was wrong. So, let's do this the right way, for Maia. Tell me what you want and that's fine with me."

"I don't understand how you can be so relaxed. There's someone else isn't there? That's why you haven't come home. You don't love me! I'm the mother of your daughter. How dare you!"

You're the mother of somebody's daughter.

Jason couldn't believe that thought ran through his head. He couldn't keep the onslaught of images and memories from hitting him like a ton of bricks. It was unbearable—like being at an endless concert of heavy metal artists on crack.

"Leela, I don't have anything to say. I'm not going to argue with you or holler. It's not worth it. I told you, whatever you want. It's done," he turned toward the bedroom door. He had to get her out of his sight. Go someplace to let his overstimulated brain calm down.

"I don't want anything from you! You never gave me anything worthwhile anyway. I doubt that you can start now," she hissed.

Jason stopped in his tracks. He reached for the door handle to keep from being knocked over by the harshness of her words. The way he just stood there, so still, made Leela think that she had truly crossed the line and that she could actually feel his negative energy building toward her. She unconsciously took two steps back.

"So, let me understand what I hear you saying to me. You're saying that nothing I have giving you over the past eleven years has meant a thing to you. Is that right? Help me understand, does that include Maia or did someone else *give* her to you?" Jason finally turned around and looked directly into Leela's eyes.

She swallowed and opened her mouth to speak but no sound came out. Not even a breath. She tried again with the same results. Then two more times—before she passed out.

Good thing the floor is carpeted.

Jason checked into the Hilton after the episode at home. He checked to make sure Leela had still been breathing. When she opened her eyes and started grabbing on to the bottom of his pant leg, he knew she was fine. He packed a bag and told her he was leaving. If she wanted to stay in the house, she could. If not, leave the key. She screamed and cried, and 'tried to explain'. But what was there to explain? He understood completely—Maia was definitely Leela's daughter. His—maybe not.

Usually when shit went south Jason could talk to William or Mim or both. But not this time. He couldn't turn to Simone. She was suffering through her own trauma and he couldn't help her. There was only one person left and that was the one person he couldn't bring himself to talk to right now. He didn't know what to do.

I am a grown ass man and all I want is for my mama to tell me what I should do. I don't need my mama, I need what she taught me over the years. Look at the facts. See the facts because that's all that's real.

Fact: Leela said she wants a divorce.

Fact: Mike fucked Leela in college.

Fact: I fucked Leela in college.

Fact: Leela got pregnant.

Fact: I married Leela.

Fact: I've known Mike since we were 6 years old.

Fact: Mike is my best friend.

Fact: Maia is Leela's daughter.

Fact: I've loved Maia since before she was born.

Jason's head was swimming with facts. He tried to block out all the opinions, what ifs, and supposes that kept fighting for position in his cerebrum. He tried to drown them out by running steaming water over his head in the shower. All that did was hide the tears that were running down his face. The thing about the tears was that they were not for him losing a wife or eleven years of his life. They were for the little girl who was his life. What would she do if things got any worse than they were right now? She deserved a father. He had to make sure she had one. He had tried so hard. Had done all he could and look where it had got him. He heard the sound of his phone over the shower. He stuck his hand out and reached toward the sound. It was the only other person he could talk to right now.

"Hey bro, haven't heard from you in a minute. What's up?"

"Hey man, I'm at the downtown Hilton, room 8064. Can you come by?"

"Sure, you all right? What's up?"

"I need some help. It's about Maia."

"I'll be right there, man. Is she all right? What's wrong?"

"She's okay. She's fine."

"Man, you got me worried. I'll be right there."

Just like any good father would.

Mike called when he arrived at the Hilton and Jason suggested that they meet in the lounge. They were lucky to find an empty table near the back since it was Saturday night and the best jazz quartet in the city was booked for the night.

"What's going on man, you talk to Leela?" Mike started right in. He could tell it was bad, so no use pussy footing around.

"You were right. She wants a divorce. Seems like you been right a lot where she is concerned. What was going on with you two in college?" Jason asked as calmly as he could. "I'm pretty good at math so I need to know when you slept with her."

Mike sat quietly for a long time as if he were trying to translate hieroglyphics. Then it hit him what Jason was trying to say.

"Ah, hell no man! As soon as you said that you were seeing Leela, that shit between us stopped. I didn't know and she sure didn't say anything about you. She'd show up when you weren't around, stay for a minute and bam—gone. I figured what the hell, I was getting mine, so I figured it was all good. No way, man. You're my brother…I would never do that to you."

"So, when did you stop seeing her?"

"It was right before Thanksgiving break. Remember, we were coming home, and we missed the last bus and had to hitch rides until we got to the Atlanta and then wait five hours for the next bus north. You remember that?" Mike asked.

"Yeah, I remember. We missed the bus 'cause your ass was late," Jason grinned a little at the memory.

"Yeah, well she was why I was late. One for the road, you know. You told me about the two of you on the way home, so that was it for me."

Jason really was good at math. Maia was born in September…It was New Year's Eve the first time he and Leela got together….

"What happened today, man?" Mike continued.

"Leela happened, that's all," Jason said. "Why didn't you tell me? You're supposed to be my boy and all that? Why didn't you let me know?"

"I tried. Often. Besides, I thought you knew how she was, and it just didn't matter to you. You loved her, so you weren't listening to me. Hell, I even tried on your wedding day, so did your moms. Too little too late, I guess. I'm really sorry dawg. I swear, I'd never do anything to hurt you," Mike said.

Jason finished his drink. Seems the Captain followed him into the city. "Do me a favor—next time you think I need to know something, make sure you say it, whether I want to hear it or not."

"Sure man. I promise. So, what are you gonna do about Leela?"

"Divorce her, that's what she wants and Leela always gets what she wants."

He held up his empty glass for a toast. The emptiness was appropriate, he thought. The very attractive waitress rushed over and took his glass, gently touching his hand as she did.

The two men talked freely about those days for another few hours. The potential for heated words ebbed and flowed throughout the night the way it always did between the two. When they parted, the consensus was that Leela won the battles but she sure as hell wouldn't cause Mike and Jason to lose each other.

"So, we're straight right?" Mike asked looking at Jason.

"Yeah, we're straight. We've been through worse than this. We're good. From now on though, no secrets. So, I'll see you at work on Monday, right?"

"First thing. We got to figure out this ADR mess. The trial has been postponed and Tyreek will be in the hospital for a while. Who knows what's gonna happen now."

"Dyson's going to jail. That's what's gonna happen. It will be good to do something that makes sense again," Jason said.

"How's Simone? You talked to her recently?" Mike asked.

"No. I don't want to bother her, you know? Give her some time to regroup," Jason replied, realizing what a void he had been feeling over the past two weeks.

Maybe I'll check on her when I go back upstairs.

"So, no secrets from now on. Right?" Mike asked.

"Right," Jason replied.

"So, if I get a fine for double parking in front of the hotel 'cause I rushed in here to save your black ass, I'll let you know right away." Mike hugged his friend who was closer than a brother and stepped out into what was left of the night.

Jason watched him go and wondered how much the ticket was going to cost him.

Chapter 60

Karl looked down from his seventeenth-floor luxury apartment to the street below. The view looking straight ahead was magnificent, but it couldn't hold Karl's attention today. Down there, somewhere, were FBI, ATF, and DEA agents lurking behind ATM machines and pretending to be street cleaners and shoppers and business people on their way to work. Everywhere he went, he knew someone was following him, recording his every action, his every word. So, he stopped talking to people, which wasn't too hard since he didn't like most people anyway. His father and his brother weren't exactly the ones he wanted to have a conversation with right now, either. Especially not his brother since he was slightly responsible for his wife's near-death experience. He hoped bro would understand.

She shouldn't have had her ass there anyway. Although, it would have been worth it to get rid of her since she was fucking up my business on the street. Tyreek had been a good boy until her ass started fucking up shit.

He sniffed and rubbed his nose. Since the indictment, he hadn't been able to re-up his supply of recreational pharmaceuticals. He was lucky to have been able to be released on bail. Twenty-five million.

Nice to know he had such value. The bail was set to be astronomical since the federal prosecution believed him to be a flight risk. His lawyer, Arcadius Werman, was the top criminal defense lawyer in the country and regularly dealt with the Feds. When the bail hearing was completed, ole Cady opened up the sleek titanium briefcase he had at his side and removed several stacks of bills and placed them in another smaller case. He gave the original case to the court officer who carried it to the judge, who counted the money. Two point five million dollars. Karl looked at Cady and then at the small suitcase on the table.

"I was a Boy Scout as a child. Always be prepared," he said with a heavy Brooklyn accent.

Karl watched the action transpire as the judge and prosecutors tried to figure out what to do next.

Now, they'll be looking for off-shore bank accounts. Too bad they won't find any. Not in my name anyway.

Karl shook his lawyer's hand and said, "That suitcase looks almost as full as the first."

"We in the business call that fluff. Nothing to be concerned about. Good doing business with you, Karl. Now go home and be a good boy, will ya?"

So, Karl was at home being a good boy. How boring was that? He had to figure out what was going on with his good buddy, Mighty. He seemed to have dropped off the face of the earth. Dumb ass couldn't even kill a kid or accidently shoot three more people in the mayhem. There was no good reason why all three of those troublemakers shouldn't be dead right now and he could be moving on with his life. No witnesses, no crime. It had worked twenty years ago. What's so different today?

Can't get good help these days.

Karl walked back over to his living room that looked out over Lakeshore Drive. The only thing that separated him from the sky and clouds were three immense walls of glass. As he sat there, he wondered about his old friend Langston. Last he had heard, the feds scooped him up after the pig roast at Big Muddy. Where was he and how could Karl get to him? Would anybody really believe what he had to say?

He's the only witness. It's his word against mine. No worries about that. The only other people there are dead or might as well be. No witnesses, no crime.

Karl sat back in his handmade Corinthian leather chair and played the same game that Greg played—Master of All I Survey. If Karl had known Greg played too, he would have wished he was at the restaurant that day with Simone. He had heard that being an only child was really rather nice.

Chapter 61

High up in the offices of Mayor Vernon Armstrong, the sound of Marisa's voicemail message was playing for the fourth time today. It was Wednesday afternoon and the two of them always spent time together on Wednesday. He knew that he didn't have time to wonder what was going on between them. Or maybe he should say not going on. When he took the time to think about it, things had changed right after the mediation with Greg's bimbo. Vernon had enough on his mind without wondering why Marisa was ducking him. He knew she was ducking him because he had ducked enough women over the years to know what it looked like when he saw it.

Does she think I'm too old? I thought she liked a mature man. Most young girls do. Sugar daddies and all that. Maybe she found someone more her age.

He looked in his desk drawer to check the bottle of ProMale that he kept on hand for when he needed a little extra assistance in getting the job done.

Maybe she found someone who works harder—so to speak.

Getting older was no joke. Thinking about it was no joke either.

There was a knock on the door. The mayor was grateful for the distraction. "Come in," he said, trying to find his official Barry voice.

"Good morning, Mayor Armstrong," said Agent Hyland as he entered the room. Adamian walked over to the mayor's desk, extending his hand as Vernon stood up and closed the desk drawer.

"It's good of you to see me today. I understand how busy you must be running the city, so I won't take any more of your time than absolutely necessary."

Adamian sat down in the chair facing Vernon before Vernon offered it to him. He was on a mission—two missions actually. One for the FBI and other agencies interested in Karl Dyson and one for his brother who had been moved to a rehabilitative facility on the west side of the city. It was a long-term care facility, but Ishua was determined that his stay would definitely be for a short period of time. After talking to Ishua's doctor, Adamian wasn't as confident as his brother concerning his complete recovery. The doctor's diagnosis was skeptical at best that Ishua would ever regain full use of his leg. The thought of that made his brother's jaw clench as he stared at the Mayor who had sent Ishua off to Muddy River and started this entire chain of events. As a professional—a Special Agent of the FBI, Adamian knew how to control his emotions and to read them in others. Today, though, he was struggling with mastery of his own.

Stay in the moment. Stay focused. Now is all there is. Everything else is not now.

"Tell me how the Mayor's office became involved in this situation," Agent Hyland said.

Vernon was prepared for this question, but he still felt uneasy as he glanced across the desk at the FBI agent. Vernon knew there was more at stake than just his political career.

Can you say prison?

"I received a call from the warden at the correctional facility in upstate Illinois. Big Muddy River, you've probably heard of it. Maybe sent some folks there yourself," Vernon tried to snicker at his own funny. There was no response from across the desk. "Anyway, I got a call that a lifer had some information about the Interim Police Commissioner."

"Is that what the warden said—lifer or is that your expression?"

"Does it matter? That's what he is after all," Vernon said.

"It matters, Mayor Armstrong, because I am here to gather facts, not inferences and innuendo. The more facts that you share with me now, the easier it will be for you later, when you are on the witness stand during cross-examination. If you are in the habit of labeling individuals, that slants a person's opinion of that individual. For instance," Adamian reached into his pocket and pulled out his IPad Mini and scrolled through for a moment, then continued, "for instance, if someone were to look at your activities, it might be misconstrued that the early morning and late night phone calls to one single number might have special significance. The credit card charges for hotel rooms charged to the city for non-city business might cause you to be labeled in ways that diminish your credibility and—fidelity. As mayor, of course."

Vernon wondered how the thermostat in the office got turned up so high and he hadn't left his chair. He'd have to talk to maintenance about that. His heart raised behind the Italian handmade shirt he wore, and no amount of Degree could keep him dry right now.

"The warden and I are on friendly terms and sometimes things are said between friends that wouldn't be said under other circumstances," Vernon sputtered. Barry and Darth had left the room.

"I'm happy to hear you have friends in high places, Mayor. It's good to know people on all sides of the law. You never know when those friends will come in handy. Let me make this plain for you Mayor Armstrong, these are other circumstances. Now, I would like to ask you two questions."

"Go ahead. Ask away," Vernon replied.

"First, I'd like to see the Murder Book on Alayah Brittingham. I was informed that you had it in your possession, which strikes me as odd."

Vernon had no response because it was odd.

How the hell did he find out about that? What else did he know? I didn't kill the girl...

He got up and walked across the expanse of the office to the wall safe behind the photo of him and the President. Chicago boys through and through. He returned with the thick yellowed file. He handed it to Agent Hyland and sat back down before his quivering knees could give out.

"Thank you. I'm going to take a few minutes to look through this if you don't mind. Then I'll have some questions for you," Special Agent Hyland continued, not looking up at the mayor.

"Take you time, my time is your time," Vernon said.

"Yes, it is. Oh, and by the way, the second question---please think about it first—exactly what was said when you received the call from your friend the warden? I will be recording the information shared today for a determination as to whether you will need to be deposed. Make yourself comfortable, Mayor. There's nowhere else you need to be on this Wednesday afternoon, is there?"

Chapter 62

Cornelius was on his way back to Illinois for the event of a lifetime. Hell, everything now was the event of a lifetime. His trip to his new home of Hoboken, the purchase of AMIATT, the introduction to the bookstore's former owner, Celestial Abernathy—it was turning out to be a wonderful life.

Celestial Abernathy, what hell kinda name was that? But it suits her. She is a heavenly body. Her parents must have been doing hard drugs or some shit. Listening to Richard Pryor or something. But they sure as hell made a beautiful baby! And smart too, likes poetry--Langston, Phyllis, Countee, all of 'em. Yea, me and Miss Celestial gonna be seeing stars! I could be a good husband to her I bet. I could tell her my story…she must like stories, she owned a bookstore. We could work in the store together. It could be good, real good. Frederica, you're my girl and all, you kept me strong for all them years and I love you for it, but Celestial—she's gonna be my wife. But first things first. Got to get all this old shit behind me.

He sat next to the window and gazed at the tops of the clouds. *God made some beautiful sh—stuff. People ought to look up a little more, they're missing a lot.* The flight attendant was coming his way pushing the lunch cart filled with tasty airplane victuals, all for a small fee. The attendant caught Cornelius's eye and asked, "Would you be interested in a Turkey Club Luncheon or Roasted Reuben Meal? The cost is twelve dollars each."

Cornelius still had problems making decisions when it came to food choices. He thought back to the dinner he had had with Celestial the night before. Pasta, seafood, steak, lamb, veal. It was all overkill. But it was exciting overkill.

"Twelve dollars each you said?"

"Yes sir. That includes chips, a non-alcoholic beverage and a slice of kosher dill pickle," the attendant said with a smile.

Please God, don't let this one cuss me out too. I don't set the prices, I just push the cart.

"I'm kind of hungry, I'll take one of each."

What the hell? This is America and I'm a respectable businessman with a beautiful friend named Celestial.

He smiled a huge smile and handed the attendant two twenties. "Keep the change," he said. For the first time in his life, either the old one or the new one, Langston/Cornelius had a thought—*God is good.*

O'Hare Airport was as busy as usual when Flight 4795 arrived from Geneva. It had been a quiet flight giving Tasha hours upon hours to think. She had wanted to leave first thing in the morning but neither she nor Florian could let go of each other, so she stayed another two days. She wondered what Florian saw in her that caused him to love her so deeply. He was the poster child for the Swiss Alps. She teased him that he was her Triple B. Blond, blue-eyed and beautiful.

She said that together they made a perfect Oreo cookie. It took him a while to grasp the humor in that statement. When he finally understood, he painted an Oreo cookie on the wall of their living room. Constant reminder, he said, that they were better together than apart.

She had always been suspicious of men's intentions as she was growing up but as she watched her uncle William in the presence of her mother, she learned what love looked like. When she saw it in Florian—that attentiveness, that gleam in his eyes, that smile that happened only when she was around, the tears that he wouldn't allow to fall when he was overcome with passion for her.

This could be my life forever. This step I take coming back here leads me one step closer to truly living my life.

She passed through customs, gathered her bags, and headed toward the exits. She hadn't called Mim to let her know that she was coming.

She probably already knows. She hasn't changed a bit.

Tasha smiled at that thought and remembered that she had thought the same thing the night of the accident, twenty years ago.

She probably already knows that I was there too.

"Get up, will you? Come on, I want to show you something?" Tisha squealed as she yanked and pulled at her sister.

"Show me in the morning. It's late and be quiet, Byron and Mama are asleep."

"God, you're boring. Come on. I want to get some Krispy Kremes. Get up."

"Stop it! It's after eleven o'clock. There's no donuts anywhere at eleven o'clock at night." Tisha knew she had her sister now because she was talking to her about it. Once Tasha was engaged, it was a

done deal.

"Yes, there is. That's the really cool part. At the bakery, they start making the fresh donuts for the morning deliveries in the middle of the night. So that means all the leftover donuts get sold for a nickel. Can you believe it? Even we have a nickel. We could go get a dollar's worth and have them here for breakfast in the morning."

"We can just get up early and get them then," Tasha rolled back over and covered her head.

"It won't be as much fun or as special. J will be home with his Championship Trophy and that stupid Mike that you love so much will be here and Mama and Byron and..."

"I don't like stupid Mike either," Tasha jumped up at the name and threw her pillow at her sister.

"Yes, you do, and I'm going to tell him next time I see him if you don't come with me," Tisha stood there with her arms crossed. Where had Tasha seen that before? It must run in the family. Works every time.

Tasha got up and walked over to the closet.

"Wear something dark and your black sneakers. That way nosey people won't notice us," Tisha said as the sisters got dressed.

"Nosey people are the only ones up at this time of night. We shouldn't be doing this. You know we're not supposed to go out at night," Tasha said.

"J does it all the time," her sister replied.

"So, do you," Tasha responded.

"And nothing ever happened, so why should tonight be any different? Hurry up and come on."

The sisters looked like mirror images of each other as they climbed down the fire escape and out into the street toward the bakery. Tasha had to admit it was exciting being out so late. They raced each other through the streets. Each pretending to be her own personal heroine—FloJo and Jackie Joyner Kersey. They were almost that fast. The speed made their hearts race and Tasha soon forgot that they were breaking every rule of their mother's house.

After three sprints and two jogs, they had made it to the bakery. It was exactly like Tisha had said, which led Tasha to believe that she had done this before. They purchased one dollar's worth of donuts and the owner's son threw in four more to make a perfect two dozen for two perfect girls. They headed home promising to eat only the free donuts. Vanilla angel filled. How perfect was that?

"Let's go this way," Tisha said between bites.

"That's not the right way. That's where the 'you know what' are," Tasha said.

"Exactly. Have you ever seen them? They hardly have any clothes on and it's cold outside. Standing there waiting for someone to drive by and pay for…"

"Shhhhh. Did you hear that?" Tasha whispered, pulling her sister away from the street lamp.

"I didn't hear anything."

"Shhhhh, somebody is crying or something…Look, over there!" Tasha pointed across the street toward a pair of dumpsters behind some old stores. They saw three teenage boys and a naked girl. They couldn't believe their eyes. Did the boys pay her so they could do those things to her? Tisha dropped her donut when Tasha said, "That's J's girlfriend, Alayah!"

"Well, she's not J's girlfriend tonight," Tisha said, not fully comprehending what was happening across the street.

"We need to get out of here, now," Tasha said as she checked to see that they had a way to escape without being seen. Just as she was about to grab her sister, the bag of donuts and run, one of the boys hit Alayah across the face with a forty. The glass and beer splattered all over the naked girl making her glisten and shine in the glare of the overhead streetlamp. Tisha screamed.

The boy with the bottle looked around to see where the sound came from. The other two were still as statues staring at the body of the once beautiful girl on the ground. The boy dropped the neck of the bottle—all that was left and hollered to the other two to get in the car. Tasha recognized the type of car it was because she liked to look at Mr. William's muscle car magazines. She always imagined herself owning one that she could drive off to college in a few years. Black 1976 Dodge Challenger.

Tisha was hysterical at this point. Tasha knew that she had to be the one that figured out what they needed to do because the engine of the Challenger had roared to life and would be prowling for the source of the sound at any moment.

"Go," Tasha said. "I'll draw them away. You go down Gilroy, then cross over to Harding. Hurry up!"

"What about you? Come with me," Tisha said, tears in her eyes.

"I'll meet you at home. Probably beat you there. I'm faster than you anyway," she smiled weakly. "Besides, they can't chase both of us. Go!" The sisters hugged and kissed each other.

"I'll see you when you get home," Tisha said and ran off into the darkness.

The Challenger sped off in the direction that Tasha led it. She was fast, and the Challenger lost her after a short chase. She breathed a sigh of relief and headed back toward home. She saw the Challenger back up and turn down a side street. Harding. That's where Tisha was headed! Tasha turned and ran like a panther toward the sound of the car engine. She heard it rev up as it approached the running figure in the street. Then she heard the thud before it sped off into the darkness. People ran out from their houses at the sound of the commotion. Someone screamed, another yelled to call the ambulance and the police. Tasha stood down the street and watched it all. She dropped the donut bag and ran home, climbed the fire escape, and crawled into her bed and waited for her sister, who never came home.

Chapter 63

"When was the last time you visited your sister?" Mim asked Jason as he folded up Maia's laundry.

"It's been about two weeks ago. It's a lot easier now that I can come and go a little more easily," he said as he placed the Hello Kitty pajamas in the suitcase. "Maia loves to visit her auntie and do her hair and sing for her. She amazes me," he said.

"How so?" Mim asked.

"You know how kids can be. Maia sees only her lovely auntie," he stopped talking and continued folding.

"Children mirror what they see at home. If they feel loved and accepted, they will be loving and accepting. You know that. You did well." Mim said as she watched her son. She would never offer to help him because she knew he would take it the wrong way. After all, Maia was his child, his responsibility.

"Thank you, oh masterful teacher," he laughed and then got very serious. He hadn't mentioned the drama with Leela at all but now felt like as good of a time as any.

"I saw Leela at the house the other day," he started.

"So how did that work out?"

"Maybe you should tell me. I just didn't get it," he said.

"The moon was full last week so I imagine it was drama filled. Tears probably and it's all your fault," Mim said.

"Exactly. She wants a divorce," he continued.

"That was to be expected. I am surprised though that it took this long," she said.

"You too. I guess I was the only one who thought this marriage would work," Jason said.

"Pretty much. I have learned that you should marry for love," his mother said.

"I did," Jason replied.

"Are you sure?" Mim asked quietly. She had a way of saying things that just seeped into Jason's soul. Once it was in there, he had no choice but to deal with it. Jason thought back to when Leela had told him she was pregnant. He was so torn. He was happy about the new life, but he was only partially glad about the person he had created it with. He had been noticing how much the two of them didn't have in common and that moving forward knowing that was difficult for him. Then, Leela's announcement. What was he supposed to do? Leave her like his father left Mim? Repeatedly. Or take care of his responsibility and be a father to his child.

"Maybe you're right," he said after a few minutes. "I had good intentions, what else could I do?"

"Even though you didn't think so, you had choices. You made a choice. The right choice for your daughter. You've done exceptionally well by her. She is remarkable. She'll be just fine no matter what her mother decides to do. The question now is, what are you going to do?"

"I agreed to whatever she wants," Jason said.

"Was this before or after the tears?"

"Before," he said. He waited for his mother to say something. "What?" he asked.

"Did she ask if there was someone else?"

"She did actually. Why?"

"You agreed too quickly. You made her feel unwanted. She's going to try to make you pay for that."

"What? That I agreed with her? That I'm giving her what she wants?"

"No, that you didn't fight to keep her. That she isn't important enough to you to fight for her."

She isn't actually. Maybe that's why it's been so easy. Maia and I are on our way home tonight and it's cool. With both of us.

"Be careful, though," Mim continued.

"What evil this way comes, oh great seer that you are," Jason joked and kissed his mother on her cheek.

"Leela isn't the kind to go quietly. Her need for drama isn't being met. She's addicted to it. She'd rather stay married to you and watch you be miserable than free herself and see you happy. Just be careful, that's all." Mim stood up and walked toward the kitchen.

"How's Mike? How's he taking all of this?" Mim asked over her shoulder.

Oh, great seer that you are....

The ringing of the doorbell prevented Jason from having to respond to Mim's query. He looked at his watch and wondered who it might be at this time of day. Maia didn't get out of school for another hour, William was at the shop, and his beloved wife would never come over here of her own free will. The only other person he could think of was Simone. He felt his heart jump in his chest at the thought of it. He and Mim had delivered her car to her house last week although he didn't make any effort to see her. She had been through so much, he didn't want to crowd her, especially after the elevator incident.

Had she heard about that? There was that picture on YouTube...

He went to the door and saw the image through the gold embossed glass. The image of Tisha stood straight and erect on the other side of the glass. It startled him so badly that he forgot to breathe. He opened the door and stared.

"Hey big brother. This isn't the Swiss Alps, it's Chicago and its cold out here. Could you move so I can come in?"

Chapter 64

Not only seeing his little sister but hearing the reason that she had returned had been a shock to everyone's system. He had watched his mother very carefully as she listened to Tasha share what had happened that night. He wasn't skilled in reading faces like his mother, but he knew enough to read the anguish that was housed behind her tear-filled eyes. There was something else too, but he wasn't sure what it was exactly. Verification, maybe?

He thought about all of that as he sat in his office. What an overwhelming period of time. Had she been there, Mim would have said that the universe was bringing itself back into balance. It might take a while, but it will always balance itself.

So, what does the universe have in store for me? He chuckled to himself; some of the things that his mother said sounded a little too esoteric for his tastes but when he thought about it, it didn't matter how she said it, she was right. *What goes around, comes around. What's done in the dark... it's all the same.* And once again, he realized she was right. She had also said that he had an opportunity to make his life the way it was intended.

Divorcing Leela may be the start of that since I probably wasn't supposed to marry her in the first place.

He rubbed his forehead like he usually did when he started going down the rabbit hole this way.

If I hadn't married Leela, then I wouldn't be here, and I wouldn't be working on this—then it hit him like a ton of bricks—*if I hadn't treated Alayah that way that afternoon, I wouldn't have met Leela...*

He drank the rest of his cup of tea, picked up the apothecary jar of leaves and whatever else was in there and placed it in his briefcase. He had twenty minutes to get to the courthouse. He, Mike, Sly, and Simone would be together for the first time since the shooting. He felt himself getting nervous, afraid that something may have changed over the past few weeks. He realized that would be more than he could bear right now. It was hard to fathom how much this one woman meant to him.

She's like family—she could be family if I'm lucky...the universe is balancing itself.

He straightened his tie and made sure his shirt was neatly tucked in his pants. As the thoughts of the morning raced around in his head, he wasn't sure even Mim's tea could help him through the day.

Sly and Mike were already at the courthouse, making up for lost time. They both thought it odd that Simone hadn't arrived yet but it was her first day back so they cut her some slack. When the door opened, and Jason walked in without her, the concern started to show on their faces.

"Where's Simone?" were the first words out of Jason's mouth.

"Haven't heard from her," Sly replied. "Thought you might have talked to her."

"Not since the hospital. Maybe we should call," Jason said.

"Give her a few. You know how women are. Takes them forever to put on their faces. As good as Simone looks, it probably takes her twice as long," Mike joked.

"We're talking Simone, not regular women," Sly said as he pulled out his phone. They stood frozen like the clay soldiers in that three-thousand-year-old Chinese emperor's tomb. On guard for whatever might happen in the next few moments. Chopin's Nocturne played softly while they waited for her to answer. Jason hadn't realized it was such a beautiful piece of music—which meant that it had played too long. She wasn't answering. Sly looked at the phone as if it was malfunctioning moved closer to the window and redialed, hoping for a better outcome this time.

Jason swallowed the knot that had developed in his throat. He knew that she could take care of herself. She was strong like his mother, but every human being had a limit. Had she reached hers? Surviving a shooting, the impending loss of Ronjai, even the separation from Greg was a lot for any person to bear.

Where are you, baby? Are you alright? Just let me know you're alright. Please God....

Simone stood on the opposite side of the door with her hand outstretched toward the knob. The vibration of her phone sent tiny ripples through her body. She knew that her three protectors were on the other side of the door, wondering where she was. Knowing them as well as she did, she knew they were probably in the process of preparing to track her down like a runaway slave. She smiled a little at that thought. At least she still had a sense of humor. The guys would appreciate that when she told them. If she could just open the door.

Why am I so afraid? They won't hurt me. They're my friends and they'll understand, won't they?

She thought about it a little longer while people walked past her on their way to and from justice. Remembering some of the conversations that she had with Mim, it occurred to her that her fear of her own emotions was causing her to be frozen in this spot— unable to open the door, yet unable to walk away. What's on the other side of that door that is so frightening?

My future maybe? What if I'm feeling this all by myself? I couldn't take that. I'm not that strong. What if he's feeling it too? I can't look at him and wonder. Everyone will see this written all over my face... I can't work with him now. I'm not that strong.

She took a deep breath and touched the doorknob. She immediately let go as if she had been burned. She took a deep breath and turned back toward the stairs. The tiny ripples plagued her until she stepped under the thick walls of the parking garage, where the universe mercifully ended her pain.

She drove the thirty-five minutes to the hospital to visit Ronjai. Seeing her dear young mentee caused her heart to ache. The tubes running in and out, the sound of the machines beating and recording every breath that was forced in and out of her lungs. Simone sat beside the bed and talked to the lifeless form. She told her what had happened to her, the condition of her brother, and how her grandmother was holding up. She even talked to her about the baby. As Simone held her hand, she prayed for some sign that Ronjai had at least heard something that she had said.

After an hour, Simone said her goodbyes. As she walked out of the hospital, she felt the ripples again. She took her phone out of her purse and stared at the name flashing on the screen. It wasn't one of the three names she had expected to see, so as it flashed, she felt herself relax a bit.

"Hello," Simone said finally.

"I was thinking about you this morning and wanted to see how you were feeling," Mim said.

"Having a really hard time today. Maybe it's too soon to go back to work. I couldn't do it. I tried but…" Simone said.

"Maybe it's not your time. You'll know when you're ready. My daughter is here from Geneva. I would love for you two to meet. I think you all would get along well."

"I think I'd like that," Simone said.

"Well, Tasha and I are going to the nursing home in an hour or so. Please feel free to join us. Maybe we could have lunch with Tisha while we're there," Mim said.

Simone felt a sense of peace coming over her. Maybe it was just relief at having somewhere to go and something to take her mind off of her fear for a while. She thought about meeting Jason's sisters.

Why do I feel so close to these people? Why do I want to be?

She disconnected from the calming voice and sat there breathing more deeply than she had all morning. The messages on her phone showed that she had six calls and eight texts. She must be important to someone.

The nursing home wasn't far from Tally's grocery store. Simone was beginning to feel quite comfortable in this section of the city. It was a very residential looking building that blended in well with the surrounding neighborhood. Its brick and shrubbed exterior gave a comforting and welcoming effect. Mim was the Director of Nursing and had been for twenty-two years. She had been offered numerous positions across the city for her ability to motivate staff and improve the quality of care provided but she chose to stay close to her beloved daughter. Every day with her child was better than any promotion that took her away.

Simone parked and followed the walkway around to the front of the building. When she entered the nursing home, the bright, open foyer immediately reminded her of a five-star hotel. She walked up to the receptionist's desk and was greeted by a warm smile.

"Good morning, I'm here to meet Mrs. Anderson," she said.

"I'm sorry. I don't know a Mrs. Anderson," answered the receptionist.

"Mimulus?"

"Ms. Copeny? Yes! You must be Mrs. Dyson. Welcome!" The receptionist picked up the phone and pressed three numbers. "She will be here in just a few minutes. Please feel free to have a seat in the solarium. There is coffee, tea, refreshments."

Simone entered the peaceful space and perused the assortment of teas while listening to the soft meditative music that filled the space.

"Hello, Mrs. Dyson. It's good to see you again. Safe and sound," a deep voice said from behind her. Simone turned around to see Agent Hyland leaning on his walker.

"Ishua, it is so good to see you," Simone said excitedly. Without thinking, she reached out to hug him. Even with the walker between them, the hug was sincere and heartfelt. Ishua held her close, forgetting for a moment the never-ending pain that was now his constant companion.

"I didn't know you were recovering here," she said. She looked at him for a moment. "I don't know if I should call you Ishua or not, is that your name?"

"Yes, my given name is Ishua Sekou N'Diaye. My brother and I have taken the name of the missionaries that adopted us when we were very young. I prefer to use my given name whenever possible; it's all I have left of my parents. It helps me feel connected to them. Silly, isn't it?"

"Of course not. Whatever you can do to remember your family is a good thing. I wish that I had done more over the years to remember mine. It helps you to remember who you are," she said. They slowly walked to a table and sat down. "I want to thank you again for what you did. I don't know what to say. It's hard to believe that you were there that day. You were assigned to follow me after the trip to the prison?" she asked.

"Self-assigned. I felt obliged to keep you safe, I suppose. I really don't have words for it. It was a feeling, I guess. I believe in following my instincts," Ishua said. He looked at Simone closely and noticed that the mass of diamonds that had encircled her finger was no longer there. "I am just glad that you are safe, and I am so sorry that I could not have done more."

"I am forever in your debt," she said. The two sat quietly for a long while.

Ishua broke the silence, "You are visiting someone today?"

"Yes. I will definitely come back to visit you as well. If you don't mind," she said.

Ishua smiled in spite of himself. "I would like that very much," he said, meaning every word of it. The sound of footsteps approaching them made Ishua turn and glance behind them. He felt as though he shouldn't have had his back to the entrance. His brother would have something to say about that, he was sure.

Two beautiful women approached the table. Ishua recognized one of them as Miss Mimulus. The other woman was new to him although she looked like a slightly younger version of Miss Mimulus. *Younger sister?*

Ishua slowly forced himself to his feet. He may be recuperating but he was still a man in the presence of beautiful women. Mim gave him a hug as she did every time they had met. She made introductions all around. Hugs were exchanged as well. The group had grown as had the comfort level. Simone was feeling much more relaxed than she had earlier in the day. Her thoughts were occupied with how similar Tasha was to her mother. She had the same dark penetrating eyes and soft full lips. *Just like her brother.* After a few more minutes, Ishua excused himself. His leg was throbbing in a way that demanded attention. He hugged Simone again and she promised to come back to visit again.

"I am so glad that you came, Simone," Mim said as she reached out her hand.

"Me too. Thank you for inviting me," Simone answered.

"I told Tisha about you a while ago. She is excited to meet you. Shall we?"

So, what does the universe have in store for me?

Chapter 65

Greg was tired of the hotel. It might be five-stars but it was still a hotel. A person can take but so many mints on the pillow at night. He had a king suite but after eleven days and ten nights the space was growing increasingly small. He remembered that his mother used to say that some places were 'too small to cuss a cat'. He was beginning to understand what she meant by that. It surprised him that he thought of his mother. He wasn't one for sentimentality. *Maybe that's why Simone doesn't want you.* He tried to change his thoughts to something less distressing and turned on the television in the 'living area' of his new home. As he remotely searched for some sound to cover up the sound of the happy couple in the room next door, he saw his brother's name scrolling across the bottom of the screen.

How embarrassing...that dumb fool disgracing the family name. Humph—there's been a lot of that lately.

Greg continued to read the scrolling embarrassment. The trial was set for two weeks from now. Seems as if the Mayor was very interested in seeing that justice was served in a timely fashion in the City of Chicago.

Election year coming up. Get the justice system doing its job. Or maybe it's the FBI. Or maybe it's the DEA or ATF. Damn you, Karl.

Greg got up and walked to the mini bar and took out four of the mini bottles.

Damn you, Sheva.

He opened them and poured them into a glass. He turned it up to his head and swallowed heartily.

Damn you, Simone.

He had put himself on Family Leave to care for his wife after the shooting because he was a good and loving husband.

And I needed time for the swelling to go down. Damn you, whatever your name is.

He went back to the mini bar and took out three more mini bottles. *Damn you*—he was about to damn anyone he could think of but the only person who came to mind was himself. Standing in front of the bar and looking into the large, gilded mirror on the opposite wall was more than he could handle. The swelling around his eye and unshaven jaw had finally disappeared but his skin had a grayish tint to it and his usually well-trimmed hairline was overdue for a shape up.

Maybe, if you want to damn somebody, you should start with the man in the mirror. Sheva didn't do any more than you let her, and Simone didn't do any more than you made her. And what's his name—that shit really hurt—and I deserved it. Saying something so ugly about your own wife. She never did anything but love you and put up with your shit. Now somebody else has noticed how wonderful she is, and you try to dog her… So damn you is right.

Greg picked up the glass of brown liquid and hurled it at the mirror.

The distorted and splintered face in the mirror looked back at him with no sympathy. He thought he saw emptiness and loneliness instead. Must be the broken glass…

Damn you.

While Greg was licking his wounds, Simone was licking her finger. What a day it had turned out to be. She had started out fearing that she couldn't face the one man in the world who made her feel safe and ended up spending the afternoon with the women in his family.

You can't get away from them. And you don't want to. So, stop trying.

She remembered how kind they were to her, accepting her like one of their own. Tasha was as beautiful as Mim, in attitude as well as appearance. Simone hadn't known what to expect when she met Tisha, but she was surprised that twenty years of disability didn't do the damage that she had pictured in her mind. Mim explained that she worked with Tisha every day and that her friend, Aisha, an acupuncturist, visited weekly to make sure that her chi continued to flow freely. Tisha's doctors couldn't explain why she was doing as well as was she was either, so they stopped trying to interfere and started trying to understand.

Simone's heart was lighter when she left the rehab center. She had promised to come back in a few days to see both Ishua and Tisha. Mim had invited her to her home for dinner so that Tasha would have someone to spend time with. Living in Geneva didn't make it easy to stay in touch with the people she had grown up with. No mention of Jason, for which Simone was grateful. She knew Mim well enough to know that she could read her thoughts and understand that speaking of him would be too much right now.

After saying her goodbyes for the third time, she decided to stop by Dad's since she was so close. He would be surprised and Sheva should be gone. Simone smiled a little. Sheva really wasn't so bad at all. She was just vulnerable and needy.

Been there, done that. You can't blame a girl for that.

Simone had come to terms with a lot of things since the shooting. In the scheme of things, some things really didn't matter. Wasting energy on regret and anger will kill you.

Since God allowed me to still be here in one piece, I choose to use my time and energy on more positive things.

She knocked on the door of Horace's house. Technically it was her house, since Horace gave her power of attorney over all his affairs and business dealings. She had been shocked at the holdings of Dyson Enterprises. Horace was quite the businessman. With the real estate ventures, subsidiary businesses—storage, and automotive—he was set for—well—life and then some. Simone wondered whether Greg and Karl knew how well off their father actually was.

If they did, they would have pushed him down a flight of stairs years ago.

She wanted to smack herself, but she somehow knew that she wasn't too far off. The whole idea of Horace signing everything over to her was unbelievable at first and she had protested that night in the hospital. But after he and his lawyer discussed it with her and she saw the pleading in his eyes, she agreed, much to Horace's relief.

The front door opened and there stood the man himself. Straight, tall, and grinning from ear to ear. He scooped her up into one of his famous bear hugs and she thoroughly enjoyed it.

"See, no cane. I am back to stepping! What a surprise. Come on in. Good to see you. Chevy was just talking about you today," the big man said.

"Oh really? What exactly did she have to say?" Simone asked.

"Now don't be that way. What could she say other than you're wonderful?" he said in return. "I think she wants to make up to you for something. Don't know exactly what but I bet it's got something to do with my no-good son. So that narrows it down some."

Simone looked at the floor and walked into the living room.

"It looks really nice in here. She does a good job," she said trying to change the subject.

Horace took the hint and responded, "Yes, she does. I don't need her anymore as a caregiver, but I think I'll keep her on as my housekeeper. She does good work, and the girl can cook. Not as good as you or my Becky but she does real good."

"What does she think about that?"

"It was her idea actually. When I had my last checkup and the doctor said I was fine, she pulled out this proposal she had written explaining how she could keep the house, cook, run errands, whatever I needed done. Even came up with hours, days, and wages," he said.

"Really? Very industrious, isn't she. Wages too, huh?"

"Yeah, they were a little low, so I adjusted them a bit," he said with a smile.

"I bet you did, Dad."

They sat in the living room and enjoyed each other's company for a long while. Horace didn't ask about Greg, he didn't have to. Simone seemed happy and that meant that Greg was out of the picture for the moment. Greg had called his father about two weeks ago and had sounded artificially happy the way he usually did. Even Becky had noticed when Greg was a child that he always seemed to be putting on a show of how wonderfully well he was doing. Horace remembered that, and it made his heart ache. Not only for the wife he had lost but for the son he still had.

Poor boy, you done messed up bad. Hurt at least two women that I know of and neither one of them seem to care a hill of beans about you now. Just like your uncle. Just like him.

Simone had been talking and Horace hadn't heard a word she had said.

"Did you say something, honey? I was lost in my thoughts. Been doing that a lot recently. Since Chevy got here actually. She cleaned out the closet in of the bedrooms upstairs. Used to be Karl's room. Found all kinds of stuff and it brought back a lot of memories," he said as he reached over to the end table beside the overstuffed chair.

Simone noticed that the television wasn't on. She remembered when she was here a few days ago it wasn't on then either. *Too much painful information about his son, maybe*? She wondered how he was taking it all. But she didn't want to ask. Horace had dealt with a lot in his life, she figured he would deal with this too. He picked up a carved wooden box and opened it.

"I was wondering if I could ask you a favor?" he said.

"Of course, you know that."

"Would you mind driving over to Joliet one day and checking out these storage units for me? The keys have been here who knows how many years and I have no idea what's in there. Probably need to throw it all away and free up that space for somebody who needs it. Could have made a small fortune if I had charged myself rent. Karl's probably got his college stuff in one of them. After all this time, I'm sure he won't care if I get rid of it. Not like he needs it for anything." Horace rummaged through the little wooden box. "Keys, earring, receipts…" he held up the dangling gold earring shaped like a playing card. This is real gold. Hasn't turned green in all these years. Wonder what happened to the other one," he said.

"I will do it after I leave here," Simone said.

"Thank you, honey. Got to let go of the past to get on with the present, I always say," Horace said.

Simone thought about that coming from her father-in-law. She really wanted to let go of the past.

Will he still be my father-in-law after Greg and I are divorced?

Horace must have heard her thoughts because he said, "Come on, daughter of mine, let's go try out some of Chevy's bread pudding. You have to teach her to make that caramel sauce…."

Chapter 66

Simone joined the flow of traffic heading out of the city. She really didn't mind though. The drive gave her time to think and prepare for her day tomorrow. She had to go back to work. The guys were capable of managing without her, but she felt that she was the glue that held them together and kept them focused. She giggled at the picture that brought to mind. Sure, they were grown men but maybe that was part of the problem.

That was just too much manliness to have in one place. Somebody has to turn it down a notch. Dirty job but somebody has to do it.

She smiled again. She really was feeling better. Spending time with so many people that cared for her was therapeutic. The next person that she wanted to spend time with was the one she was afraid to see this morning. She made up her mind that tomorrow she would face her fear and let the universe have its way. If she never said anything to Jason about how she felt, she could at least admit it to herself and be satisfied with the friendship that they had created over the past several months. It would all work out as it should.

After following Horace's old school directions—*make a left at the church with the brick steeple, then go down to the firehouse and turn left again...* she arrived at Joliet Storage- a subsidiary of Dyson

Enterprises. A huge billboard pointed out a huge warehouse. Behind the warehouse were several more warehouses numbered one through ten. On each building were letters of the alphabet, all the letters repeated on each building. Simone calculated how many units that must be, times three storage facilities that were part of Horace's 'holdings', as he called them.

 She drove to the unit that had the same number and letter as the receipt she had in the little wooden box that sat on the seat next to her. Fourth building, units D and R. Why they were so far apart when you own the building she couldn't say. But that wasn't her concern. Parking in front of 4-D, she tried the keys from the box until she found the right one. The lock was old and rusted from disuse. After a few attempts, it finally opened. Simone pulled open the door and peeked inside letting her eyes adjust to the total darkness enveloping the space. The unit was small, about the size of a bathroom and the light switch was close to the door. The walls were lined with labeled boxes--Becky's books. Becky's jewelry. Becky's shoes. Becky's clothes.

He didn't get rid of anything. Poor man. To lose someone that you love that much, I can't imagine it. Maybe that's because you never loved anyone that much—until now.

Simone shook off the thought and kept checking the boxes to see if there was anything that Horace might want her to bring back to him. She searched throughout the unit and decided to report back to him the contents and see what he would like her to do next. She took pictures of the boxes and some of the contents so that she could show him when she returned. She knew that he wouldn't have his cell phone near him at this time of day. He'd be busy enjoying one of Chevy's attempts at a favorite dish from one of Becky's cookbooks.

She locked up the unit and thought about calling it a day.

What could be any different at the other unit?

 The only problem with that thinking was a nagging voice in the back of her head that said she should check that unit as well. Since she was practicing listening to the universe, she got back in the car and drove around to the other side of the building until she found 4-R. It was a much larger unit, about the size of a two-car garage.

This one had a double padlock on it. She tried the remaining keys until she found the right ones. The door was extremely difficult to raise due to the lack of use over the years. Simone could tell that this unit had been sealed for a long, long time.

It was filled with boxes toward the front, just like the other unit. But behind the wall of boxes was furniture. It looked as if a house had been emptied and the contents forgotten in this dreary location. Simone walked around and touched the furniture. It reminded her of the period pieces that you would see at estate sales. The story of someone's life to be sold to the highest bidder.

The unit was bigger than she originally had guessed because there was something even larger in the back. She walked over to the object that was covered with a dark tarp. She stared at the tarp that was cracked with age and covered with dust. She gingerly touched it as if it might bite her. Then she lifted the corner and peeked under it like a little girl looking for hidden Christmas presents. Feeling bolder, she rolled the tarp back to reveal an automobile.

Wow! A muscle car. Daddy used to love these kinds of cars.

The thought of her father was bittersweet, but she was learning to accept the pain so that she could experience the pleasure of thinking about her family. She pulled the tarp off completely and walked around the car. She wanted to touch it but thought better of it. A black Dodge Challenger. It was in excellent condition except for the front fender. It looked as if it might have hit a something fairly large.

A deer maybe? In Chicago?

She'd make sure that she mentioned it to Horace tomorrow.

Chapter 67

Simone was at her desk early the next morning, reading endless emails. Sly had addressed the important ones and forwarded the urgent ones to her over the past couple of weeks. She wasn't really worried about them or anything else for that matter. Things really did take care of themselves one way or another. People were still having disputes and they were still settling them—one way or another. Through mediation or through the courts. The thing that was looming in her mind was seeing Jason today. After ditching work yesterday, she felt a little guilty and sent a text to Sly last night to let him know that she would be in tomorrow and would he please let the guys know so they could figure out where the ADR program would go from here. She thought that sounded casual yet businesslike to cover her nervousness at what the day might bring.

While she was thinking about all of that, there was a knock on the door. She looked up to check the time. 7:38. She looked back at her computer screen.

Sly is as bad as I am.

"Come in," she said as she continued to hit the delete key.

The door opened and Jason stepped through it. Simone looked up and drew in her breath at the sight of him. He stood there for a moment and thought how beautiful she looked when she saw him. The rise of her chest as she took a breath, and the slight parting of her full lips made him reach out his arms to her and walk toward her desk. Simone stood up without her own permission and walked around the desk and into his arms.

Jason enfolded her in his arms, and she wrapped her arms around his neck. They stood there holding on for what seemed like dear life. She closed her eyes and tried to hold on to her senses. She didn't know what to say. What was there to say? He kissed her scar, slowly and gently as if the right touch might heal all of her pain.

"Baby, don't ever scare me like that again. I thought something had happened to you. I thought I had lost you," he whispered the words into her hair.

"I'm right here," she replied.

"So am I. So am I, and I always will be. As long as you want me. You understand what I'm saying to you?"

A small part of Simone wasn't sure, so she just shook her head. Jason saw the uncertainty in her eyes.

"You know I love you, don't you? I don't throw words around. I only say what I mean… I love you, girl." He ran his fingers through her hair and closed his eyes feeling something close to ecstasy.

Sly stood in the open door and watched the couple. That's what they were. He could tell even if he couldn't hear the words exchanged between them, he could read the emotion that poured out of both of them.

I ain't mad at you, dawg. How could you not love her? You're a hell of a lot better than what she's married to. I would be feeling the same way if it were me. I wish it were me...

He turned around and went out for coffee, for three, and a green tea with lemon and fresh ginger, just the way Simone liked it.

Chapter **68**

Jason felt as if his knees were about to give way. He thought that he was stronger than this. He had been in the presence of this phenomenal woman for a long time now and it had never affected him like this before. Maybe it was smell of her hair or the scent of her perfume enhanced by the warmth of her body that was sending him into a state of no return. All he could do was close his eyes and hold on to her. He placed his hand on her cheek and stroked it gently. It felt like the richest velvet under his touch. Simone leaned into his touch as if to draw him into her.

I was just kidding when I said she was a goddess…but she's got power over me…

He knew he needed to step away from her for a variety of reasons. His body was about to betray him. He had been near her far too long and she was so warm…there was no way that he wanted her to think that all he was feeling was physical. Being married to that ass for so long might have made her believe that all any man wanted was another notch in his belt. Jason had had plenty of notches in his belts, but this was far beyond that. If he was honest with himself, this was the first time in his life that he had experienced this type of emotion and he wasn't sure how to deal with it. The only love he had ever felt that was this pure and complete was toward Maia and his family. All he knew was that he wanted it to continue for as long as breath was in him.

He was brought back to reality when he thought he heard someone in the room. He looked behind him and guessed that it had been his heightened imagination. He was grateful for the distraction, because the spell Simone had cast over him this morning was too powerful for him to break. He stepped back and looked at Simone. Her cheeks were flushed, her hair was slightly out of place and her eyes were smoldering.

I wonder what she looks like after…

The phone rang on the desk and the spell was broken when Simone turned around to answer it. Jason was relieved that she hadn't seemed to notice how his body reacted to her closeness. He watched her as she smoothed her hair back into place and ran her fingers over her cheek where his hand had been.

"Hello, Sly," Simone said into the phone. "Thanks for doing that. We'll meet you in the conference room." She hung up the phone and looked at Jason.

"Sly bought breakfast for everybody. He said Mike just pulled up," she said. They were back in the same positions that they had been in twenty minutes ago, but nothing would ever be the same from this point forward.

"I love you, Simone Dyson. And if I have my way, that last part of your name will change. I promise you that." Jason excused himself to find an exit so that he could find some cold air to relieve his fevered mind and body before entering the conference room.

What the fuck done happened here? Dammmnn. Somebody done put it on Miss Moni real good. No wonder she didn't come to work yesterday. That must be some good leftover lovin'. Afterglow still burning hot! Mike looked Simone as she walked into the conference room and gave him a hug. She was so warm that he could smell her Chanel as it drifted on the air. He really needed to find out the number. Who needed fifty shades of a color when you only needed nineteen or twenty some sniffs of perfume?

Jason walked in a few moments later and greeted his best friend. Everyone exchanged hugs and handshakes and thanked Sly for breakfast. Simone looked at Sly to thank him and their eyes met.

"He loves you, doesn't he?"

"Yes, he does."

"Good for you. Your husband is an ass."

"Yes, he is."

"I love you too."

"I know that now. I'll always love you too. You are so special to me, and nothing will ever change that."

"Likewise."

Simone stood up and walked around the table to Sly who hugged her long and hard. He kissed her on the opposite cheek. She held his hand to her heart for a moment. Mike looked confused for a second and then looked at Jason hoping to get some clarification. Jason just smiled at Simone as if no one else was there. Mike frowned for a second as if the effort of figuring out what he was missing was causing him physical distress. His eyebrows scrunched together. He looked at Simone and Sly, then back to his best friend. He'd known Jason more than half of his life and he had never seen this look on his face before.

Oh, hell no, she done turned him out! He ain't even tapped it and he's drowning in it. Nose open so wide the Titanic could fit inside. If she looks this good now, wonder what she looks like after...

Mike patted Jason on the back, but he didn't seem to notice. Mike sat back, took a sip of his coffee and a chunk out of the vanilla angel donut. It was going to be an interesting day.

So, I get to be best man again...I can live with that. Wonder what Miss Piggy Feet will say about this?

Chapter 69

The subpoenas had been delivered weeks ago, the depositions were almost completed, and the witnesses were more than willing to share their knowledge of the defendant at the upcoming trial that was becoming known as the Chicago Sensation. Only Michael Jordan and the Bulls Three-Peat back in the day had garnered this much attention.

Tyreek Henderson was out of Intensive Care and was able to sit up in a wheelchair. The doctors did not feel comfortable stating the prognosis for his recovery, but they were amazed that he was doing as well as he was. Several of them surmised that their skills as surgeons were the reason for his survival. They did not know that the desire for revenge was a strong motivator.

Agent Adamian Hyland thought about all of these things as he drove to the last deposition. It was a strange one, he thought. The email that he received said something about meeting a possible victim of the alleged crime that had started this snowball rolling. Adamian had read the report from the mayor's office on the Brittingham murder and there was no mention of any other victims besides the Brittingham girl. Adamian was truly curious not only about the so-called victim but also that he had to go to the rehab facility where his brother was recuperating for the meeting. Bizarre circumstances. After it was over, he and Ishua would go out to dinner.

A twenty-two ounce steak for me and a plate of grass for my tree hugging brother.

That thought made him smile, he had a feeling he might need that shortly.

When he entered the rehab, he once again felt immediately at ease. He was surprised because that same feeling overcame him every time that he had come to visit his brother. Nursing homes and rehab facilities were not the place that caused most people to feel comfortable. He thanked the ancestors, especially Mamman for bringing his brother to such a special place.

After he had signed in, the very friendly receptionist offered to accompany him to his destination. He thanked her but said that he wanted to say hello to his brother first and walked down the plushly carpeted corridor toward the elevator. As he waited for it to arrive, he thought he heard a melodious voice singing a familiar tune. The bell for the elevator's upcoming arrival chimed but Adamian turned toward the sound of the rich tenor voice. He walked past several doors until he found the source of the sound. It struck him that the tune was the lullaby that his mother had serenaded her baby boys to sleep with every night. The source of the lullaby was his brother as he sat with his back toward the door holding the hand of a young woman in a wheelchair. She was intently listening to Ishua, Adamian could tell, but he could also tell that despite her lovely face and long, thick beautifully braided hair, she had experienced some sort of trauma. Her eyes looked past Ishua to his brother. Adamian immediately put his finger to his lips, hoping that she understood the universal sign for quiet. She tilted her head slightly and smiled. When she smiled all traces of her trauma temporarily disappeared. Ishua missed the entire exchange, as his eyes were closed, and his heart was filled with love for the mother that he could barely remember.

When he finished the last note, Tisha looked into Ishua's eyes and smiled the best she could to convey her thanks. He squeezed her hand and held it for a moment before kissing it gently and placing it back in her lap. Her eyes looked past him again and he caught it this time. He turned to see his brother standing in the doorway.

"What'd I tell you about your back being towards the door? Didn't you learn anything in the academy?"

"I'm in rehab, for God's sake. I've already been shot," Ishua slowly stood to hug his brother.

Adamian watched as Ishua rose to his feet, but he didn't offer to help. Ishua was a proud man, he would never take that away from him. He did notice though that the struggle was less intense than it had been the last time he was here.

"This lovely lady is my friend, Miss Tisha Copeny. She allows me to spend time with her and sing a little," Ishua said as he introduced the two.

"I only sing a little because that's all I know. But it is pleasant for both of us. Miss Mimulus says it's therapeutic and restorative, whatever that means," Ishua continued.

Adamian looked at his brother and saw something new. He was standing straighter and taller and had a look of a man—restored— or was it in love? Whatever it was, it looked good on him—really good. Adamian noticed that Tisha could not move her own hands very well, so he placed both of his over hers and greeted her.

When he stood up, he addressed his brother, "You said Mimulus, that's the name of one of the people I am here to see today." He quickly checked his notes and continued, "Mimulus and Tasha Copeny…" His voice trailed off as it hit him that Ishua had said that Tisha's last name was Copeny. His head snapped toward Ishua.

"That's right, Tisha's mother and twin sister."

"What the…," Adamian started.

Mim and Tasha were entering the room right about the time that Adamian was beginning to wonder what was going on. Ishua introduced Adamian to the two ladies who had entered the room and he noticed the strong resemblance between them all. It wasn't just the thick dark hair or the deep, penetrating eyes, or the smooth butterscotch complexions, it was a presence… *An aura.* Adamian caught himself. Mumbo jumbo was something he had left behind when the missionaries flew him to England, years and years ago. *But there was something.*

Mim hugged Adamian and said how glad she was to meet him, and he could tell that she meant it. She looked at him very intently. *There's something about her.* The group headed towards the conference room so that there was adequate space to be seated comfortably. Adamian watched his brother push Tisha's wheelchair with barely a limp in his stride. He set up his laptop and video recorder to begin the deposition. He was still unsure how all of this was connected to a crime that happened over twenty years ago.

Tasha held Mim's hand and looked at her sister whose hand was being held by her new friend. Tasha took a deep breath and released it slowly. It was time to unload the burden that she had been carrying for so many years. Not only the burden on her shoulders, but the guilt attached to not telling her sister's story since she was unable to tell it for herself.

Adamian looked to Tasha and asked her to state her name and explain her connection to Karl Dyson.

"Tisha and I watched him kill my brother's girlfriend before he ran down my sister and left her for dead."

Chapter 70

The trial would start in an hour and forty-five minutes and the court room was already packed. The prosecutors and judge were discussing whether they should consider the possibility of this being a closed trial. The potential for it becoming a media circus was astronomical since reporters from every station in the city and cable news networks from around the nation had been sitting outside the courthouse since 7 a.m. FOX NEWS had sent their token darker reporter since he might be able to get a better 'slant' on the story.

Simone had always loved coming into the courthouse for its architectural beauty and for what it represented. The justice that had been meted out here had never affected her directly, but today was different. Ronjai lay in the hospital on life support. Horace was here looking tense and worried over what his son had become and of what might become of his son. Mrs. Henderson sat beside Tyreek's wheelchair. Shamel sat beside her. Simone had noticed that Shamel had pushed Tyreek into the courtroom and helped him and Mrs. Henderson get settled on the padded wooden benches. The entire Copeny-Anderson family was present except for Maia. *They are all so beautiful. Even the men.* Sly and Mike were sitting with Jason, who seemed to be in deep conversation with William. Ishua was seated next to Tisha's wheelchair, holding her hand. Simone noticed how attentive he was to her. Could it be that he was caught up in the spell cast by the Family Copeny? *Like I am…* She smiled and he smiled back when he saw her, proudly displaying a beautifully carved walking stick. Ky'Rell Ballard sat in his wheelchair next to his Caseworker and his aunt, Rakeetah, and three small children. Ky'Rell looked very small and timid in his navy polo shirt and khaki pants. The baby predator seemed to have died on the floor of the restaurant that day when the bullet entered its spine, leaving Ky'Rell to live out his life suffering the consequences. The contingents that represented the federal government were in full force and Special Agent Hyland was directing the hustle and flow of the group.

So many people affected by one man's actions. *Butterfly Effect in real life. Ripples that go on and on and on.* Simone remembered hearing that there was some really long scientific term for it, but it could be summed up as Chaos Theory. *Chaos is right. All of this is hard to believe. If I wasn't part of it, I wouldn't believe it.*

There was one person that she didn't see as she looked over the myriad of faces in the courtroom.

Where was Harlem? I would think that he should be here.

She wondered where she should sit. She ached to sit with Jason but felt it wouldn't be appropriate with Horace there. Deciding to take a bathroom break before she got settled, Simone left the courtroom and proceeded down the busy hall. As she walked past the crowds that were milling in the hallway, hoping for some glimpse of the defendant when he entered the court, she felt a hand grab on to her arm.

"Hello Simone," said the familiar voice. The voice seemed to have lost some of the bravado that had usually accompanied it.

Simone knew who it was before she turned around. She didn't know what to expect but she was somewhat surprised and shocked by his appearance. He had lost weight and even though he was well groomed, something wasn't right.

His eyes. They are so…empty.

"Greg," she said as she looked at him.

She looks beautiful. Absolutely beautiful. Like she's happy, like she's in love.

Greg looked at her and felt a stab of anguish like he had never experienced. He suddenly was at a loss for words. He had spent the previous evening preparing his speech. He was sure it would have won him an award for Best Actor. Strong yet sincere. Candid yet remorseful.

"I've lost you forever, haven't I?" he stammered.

"You didn't want me, if I remember correctly," she responded.

"Simone, I was wrong. I made a mistake," he said still grasping her arm.

"Yes, you did," she said.

"Baby, don't be that way. Sure, I messed up, but I'm human. Haven't you ever done anything that you're sorry for?"

Married you. Really sorry about that one.

Simone took a deep breath and could see where this was headed.

"So, it sounds like you are remorseful, maybe? Thinking that some of the choices that you made weren't the best? And now you want to talk to me and apologize, is that right?"

Greg's grip immediately tightened on Simone's arm.

"Don't talk to me like I'm one of your mediations," he snapped.

"I'm not. When I'm talking to them I'm concerned about maintaining the relationship that they have with another individual. That's not the case here. Please let go of my arm. I have to go inside," she answered.

"What? And sit with that black nigger in there?"

"That's no way to talk about your father. I'm sitting with Dad, which is where you should be," she said as she pulled her arm out of his grasp. She turned around and walked toward the restroom. She realized she was trembling but still on her feet.

Go 'head girl! You may be scared to death, but you told him. Just keep your head up and keep right on walking. You can faint when you get in the bathroom.

Greg looked down at his Rolex and watched the seconds pass away. He hoped that if he stared hard enough the second hand would reverse itself and he could start that conversation all over again. He had a feeling that he wouldn't have too many more of those with his wife. He looked at the courtroom door as if the devil himself were on the other side. *Karl hasn't even shown up yet.* He took a deep breath and composed himself and headed toward the stairs. He didn't feel comfortable taking elevators lately.

Outside of the courthouse, the piranhas were feeding on whoever was unfortunate enough to be snagged by a reporter.

"Excuse me, are you a part of the Dyson trial that begins here in about an hour?" asked the long-haired blond from HLN.

"Yes, I am," responded the well-dressed gentleman.

"My name is Lyndsey Ellerbe from HLN. Are you acquainted with the defendant Karl Dyson?" she asked. Headline News was hoping to scoop CNN this time. It always seemed that Frederica had a jump on her. Maybe it was her gorgeous creamy complexion.

I wonder where a good tanning salon is around here?

"Why, yes I am," the man replied as he straightened his tie.

"Have you been a business or government associate of the accused?" she asked.

"I have known Mr. Dyson for a number of years, and I am a very strong advocate in the pursuit of truth and justice," the man stated in an adamant voice.

"So, you are here as a character witness for Karl Dyson?" she asked.

"No. I am here to make sure the motherfucker goes to jail for the rest of his life," he replied.

He pushed his glasses up on his nose and proceeded into the courthouse. Lyndsey Long-hair just stood there staring at Harlem's back as he channeled his inner Cornelius and hoped that his alter ego surfaced before he said anything else this morning.

The awaited hour had arrived and Alphonse Cordano, an officer of the court, escorted Cady Werman and his client, Karl Dyson, into the packed courtroom. The suits that they were wearing would pay the officer's salary for at least two months. The shoes and shirts would pay his mortgage for a similar amount of time, and the briefcase Cady carried might be a down payment on the new Dodge Durango that Alphonse drooled over every time he saw the commercial on Spike TV.

Their entrance caused a stir throughout the court. Mim quietly watched the man who was responsible for so much pain and suffering in so many lives, including her own. She noticed the air in the room seemed to stand still and become stale. This wasn't a figment of her imagination, many of the people in the courtroom had started fidgeting and clearing their throats. *His energy is bad. Tainted some way...* She looked closely at his face as he sat at the defendant's table. *The eyes...definitely fire. The nose. Really strong... metal— maybe too much metal. Calculating to the point of cunning, High forehead... four fingers. Bright, very very bright. Indention of the temples. Addictive behaviors.* She put all of that together and didn't like what she saw. An incredibly intelligent man capable of being calculating and analytical, who could explode at a moment's notice. She hoped that she was wrong, but in her heart, she knew she had read him correctly.

Everyone stood as the judge entered and took her seat. The bailiff stood straight and tall and announced that court was called into session. The Federal District Judge, Honorable Elayna Burkiss, presiding. The formalities were spoken with an air of authority that caught everyone's attention, except Karl, who seemed to be in a parallel reality. He slumped slightly in his chair and looked disinterested and distracted. He sniffed once and patted his tie as if he was complimenting it for being a good tie.

He's high as a damn kite. I know a crackhead when I see one. All these years. You been walking around free, causing nothing but pain. You no good...

Cornelius still hadn't shown up and Harlem was okay with that. There were some things that only he could make right. This was one of them. Cornelius had the rest of his life to live but Harlem had only a short time left. And he wanted to enjoy every second of it.

...sonofabitch.

The attorneys were given their instructions, as were the spectators in the court. Everyone seemed to understand but Simone wondered how long that would last. She couldn't put her finger on it but the mood in the courtroom seemed to have changed. She sat next to Horace and squeezed his hand gently. She could feel the energy that it took for this strong, proud man to look at his son sitting at that table, accused of so many hideous crimes.

Lord, please give him strength.

She glanced around at all of the people who had been affected by this one man.

Give us all strength.

Chapter 71

The first day of the trial was excruciating. The prosecution made its opening remarks and was nowhere near completion when the day ended. So many charges to address. The defense might have an opportunity to start tomorrow sometime after lunch. It seemed that even the judge was exhausted from trying to comprehend it all.

Jason had checked on his sisters from time to time to make sure that they were doing as well as could be expected. He had been shocked this morning when he saw Tisha sitting in the court. She smiled her soft sweet smile at him. Her eyes saying everything that her voice was unable to.

I'm fine, big brother. For the first time in a long, long time, I am fine.

 She turned her head towards Ishua who was talking to his brother. Jason couldn't believe it, but he knew in his heart that the universe was doing just what Mim said it would do. With that thought, he found himself searching the courtroom for the someone that would make his universe right. He couldn't find her.

He knew that she would be there, they had talked about it last night over the phone. The two of them were very aware of the intensity between them but they were also very aware that now was not the time to give into it. The commitment that they made that day in

Simone's office was real and neither one of them was going to back out of it, so what was the rush?

We've got the rest of our lives.

The thought brought a smile to Jason's face.

I can wait. If I had learned that a long time ago, things might be different this morning.

He continued to look for Simone, but she was nowhere in sight. That disturbed him a great deal. He went out in the hall and surveyed the sea of people. She had to be somewhere. That's when he saw Greg headed towards the stairs. The look on his face was that of a defeated opponent. His jaw was clenched yet the eyes said that it was all over.

Hope he can see to get down the stairs. Looks like he healed pretty good. Gotta keep that in mind, should I have to shut the other eye…

As Jason turned around, he saw who he had been searching for and smiled in spite of himself. Simone was walking out of the restroom, statuesque and lovely. All was now right with the world. He didn't want her to think that he was stalking her or that he was worried about her—but he was.

He ducked back into the courtroom and sat down, able to focus on whatever the day would bring. It was all good right now. His family and loved ones were all safe and secure. Time to sit back and watch the show.

By two o'clock that afternoon, everyone knew that this trial would be a long, complicated ordeal. The judge was ready to adjourn for the day so that everyone would have a chance to regroup and start fresh in the morning. The jury seemed in shock from what they had heard during the prosecution's opening statement. One of the jurors had to be helped from the jury box and escorted by Officer Cardone to the rest area before dismissal.

Jason watched it all. *What a day, what a day. What else could possibly happen?*

Maia had finished her math test before most of the others and was reading her favorite poetry book again. She was trying very hard to capture the style of poets in the book so that she could write a perfect poem for her daddy on his birthday. She still had two weeks, but she wanted to frame it the way Mommie Mim had taught her. She was lost in her thoughts when she heard her name announced over the intercom to come to the front office for dismissal. She looked at the old-fashioned clock on the wall. The big hand was on the three and the little hand was on the two. She was one of the few students in the class that could tell time on a clock. School wasn't out for another forty-five minutes. She gathered up her books and backpack from her cubby and rushed towards the office.

Why would Daddy or Mommie Mim pick me up early today? We didn't talk about it this morning.

She ran down the steps and felt guilty for running. She was a safety patrol captain, and she knew better than to run in the halls.

I'll give myself a demerit tomorrow.

She got to the office and opened the door looking for the reason that she had been called out of class.

"Hey baby, I'm here to pick you up today!"

"Mommie?"

"That's right, honey, I thought we could start our evening a little early today. What's another forty-five minutes of school? Let's go sweetie. I've got big plans for us." Leela signed the school's sign out log and grasped Maia's hand. Maia looked up at her mother and back at the school secretary who waved goodbye to the beautiful little girl.

"See you tomorrow, Maia," the secretary said. She could have sworn that Maia shook her head side to side as she walked out with her mother. Maybe she just needed to clean her glasses.

Chapter 72

Day Two and Three of the trial were carbon copies of Day One. Unending opening statements from the prosecution and the defense. The list of charges against Karl was long enough to keep two Chinese laundries in business for the next several years.

Not one witness had been called yet and three jurors had asked to be removed from their duty because they felt they could no longer be impartial towards the defendant and give him the due process that he deserved as an American citizen. After the crime scene photos of the shooting were displayed, a juror had to be removed because she lost her breakfast on the shoulder of the juror in front of her.

A spectator who had been sitting in the back of the courtroom each day stood up and hollered at the top of his lungs, "Murderer! Murderer! That's what you are! Pushing that shit on the streets. Gunning down our young people! You're gonna pay! You hear me? You're gonna pay! The Lord don't like ugly!" The bailiff, Officer Cardone, and two officers from adjoining courtrooms were needed to remove the man from the building.

Court was adjourned for the rest of the day.

He had said goodbye to Simone at the end of the day. Given her a chaste kiss on the cheek and squeezed her hand after he had walked her and Horace to the Volvo. Horace had watched this young man be a perfect gentleman to both he and Simone. He and Jason laughed and joked and talked briefly about the weather in Chicago at this time of year. They shook hands and Horace walked around to his side of the car while Jason opened the door for Simone, just as any gentleman should. While Simone and Jason innocently chatted, Horace read their faces as accurately as Mim would have done.

Those two are in love. Well, hallelujah! Babygirl has found a real man. It's about damn time she gets to be happy. That damn fool son of mine. He's an idiot. Becky, I love you, but he must have got that from your side of the family.

When William went to pick Maia up from school and was informed that she had left with her mother, Jason had tried to call Leela's cellphone, but it went directly to voice mail. Mike drove him to her sister's house, but she hadn't returned there. They drove to every place that Jason could think of in hopes that she might be there with his precious little girl. After three hours of driving around the city, Mike took Jason back to Mim's. Everyone was there, including Simone, Sly, and Ishua.

"Technically, we can't do anything as this is not a kidnapping," Ishua was saying as he walked around the living room.

"The hell it ain't?" Jason yelled.

"Technically, it isn't. Your wife is her mother. There is no custody battle, no restraining order. Are you all even legally separated?" Ishua asked.

"She did it on purpose. She couldn't even remember to pick her up when we were living together and now all of a sudden, she picks her up from school? What kind of shit is that?" Jason paced the floor like a caged lion. He turned toward Mim and continued, "You told me. You said she wasn't the type to let me be happy. It's just like you said."

He walked to the closet and took out his Kangol and jacket while mumbling to himself. "When I find her I'm gonna kill her," he said as he slammed the door behind him. To Simone's surprise, no one got up to stop him. Not even her.

Mim always told Jason that the best conversation was the one that you had with yourself. *That's the only person who really knows what you're talking about.* Jason thought of that as he rushed out of the house. He needed space and fresh air. He also needed to be away from anyone should the tears start to fall from his eyes. Mim would have told him to analyze what he was experiencing and recognize what it was, not what he felt that it was. He was angry, livid, furious but that was just masking what he was really experiencing. It was fear. Fear of what could happen to his daughter. Fear that he may never see her again. Fear that if he did see her again, she might be damaged in some way.

Oh God, protect my baby, please. Whatever you want me to do, I will. Please just protect my baby.

He headed home since he didn't know where else to go. He had been staying in the city since Tasha arrived so that Maia could get to know her aunt. The thought of being by himself was foremost in his mind. That would give him a chance to clear his head and figure out what to do next.

By the time that he arrived at his development, the sky had turned from orange to indigo. The lights were on in the mini mansions and families were settling in after work, school, soccer, and piano and dance lessons. He swallowed hard and turned on to his street towards his empty house.

The lights were on even though he couldn't remember leaving them that way. Maia was always the one who took care of turning off lights, turning down the heat, and the televisions, when they weren't being used. She wanted to protect the planet and conserve for future generations. Jason's vision went blurry as he parked the car in the driveway. He unlocked the door and stepped inside.

Maia would be pissed about the house being this warm and nobody being here.

"Daddy!"

"Baby," Jason sputtered as Maia ran into his arms.

Thank you, God! Thank you!

"I'm so glad to see you, Daddy. I was worried about you. I didn't know where you were. I would have called you, but I dropped my phone when I left school, I think. Daddy, oh Daddy, I'm so glad you're home," she said hugging him tightly around his neck.

"Are you alright?" he asked as he looked her over.

"I'm fine Daddy. I just missed you and everybody. I wondered where you were. Why did Mommy come pick me up? She never does that. Why did she do that now?"

Jason was just about to ask where Leela was when he heard her voice.

"Hey baby, ready for dinner? I fixed your favorite, roast beef and mashed potatoes. I even made a salad the way you like it. Let's eat before it gets cold," Leela turned back toward the dining room.

Maia held on to Jason's hand and looked up at him.

"It's okay Daddy, Mommy bought the food at Boston Market, so it's safe to eat."

They proceeded into the dining room as if this was a normal occurrence. Jason wondered what the hell had happened in the last five minutes. As bizarre as it was, all he could do is be thankful to be holding his daughter's hand and to know that she was safe.

Leela had set the table and was busy placing the serving spoons into the mashed potatoes and gravy. Jason sat down at the head of the table and pondered the sight of his wife displaying domestic bliss.

Three weeks ago, she wanted to divorce me, now she's trying to feed me. I'll wait 'til she eats something first.

She sat down at the opposite end of the table and smiled sweetly at Jason and Maia. Jason looked at her and remembered that her smile was one of the things that attracted him all those years ago. She fixed Maia's plate and then her own. Jason watched all of this with a look of wonderment on his face.

"Leela, how did you know I'd be home tonight?" he asked.

"I didn't, baby," she replied, "Maia needs nutritious meals, so this is what we're having for dinner. I hoped that you would come home to us, so I fixed your favorite meal. I guess I got lucky!" Another beautiful display of teeth that insurance didn't pay for.

"Leela, we need to talk," he said as he played with the food that he had dished on to his plate.

"After dinner, baby. Let's just enjoy this family time. We don't get enough of it," Leela said. "We've got the rest of the night."

Jason looked at the woman at the other end of the table and decided that she was a fucking nut.

Or maybe it's me. I'm sitting here listening to it.

He looked at Maia, trying to gauge her reaction to all of this. She stabbed a stalk of broccoli and stuck it in her mouth. She looked backed at him with eyes that said it all.

It's not you, Daddy.

Simone left Mim's about an hour after Jason stormed out of the house. She kept checking her phone in hopes that he would call. Nothing. She decided to stay at the condo since it was getting late, and she didn't have the energy or focus to navigate the interstate with all that had happened over the past few days.

After eating a sandwich and preparing for bed, she checked the phone one last time, praying that everything was all right and that Maia was safe. Why hadn't he called her?

There was a lone text message waiting for her.

It must have come while I was in the shower.

Seeing that it was from Jason, she hastily opened it.

Maia is fine. We need to talk.

The brevity and tone of the message caused Simone's brow to crease in a way that was all too familiar. She wondered what exactly had happened to make him be so abrupt.

This isn't like him. I wonder what's wrong. What should I do now?

Realizing that there was nothing that she could do tonight, she got in bed wishing and hoping that one day he might be here with her to keep her warm. With that image in her head, it was easier to fall asleep. As pleasant as it was, there was a nagging thought lurking deeper in her mind.

Morning arrived as it always did—too soon. Simone got up feeling as if she had just lied down. Her remembrance of the slightly erotic dream that she had was quickly replaced by the last four words of the text on her phone.

She picked up the phone to see if there were any other messages. Four. None from Jason.

What is it that he needs to say?

She took a deep breath and wondered if she should send him a text. It was morning and that's what they usually did. She didn't want to seem pushy so she decided just to check to see if he would be in court today.

She waited for a few minutes hoping for a response that sounded more like the Jason she knew and loved so deeply. After several minutes, the phone vibrated. She picked it up hoping to read something a little friendlier than what she received last night. She read the response.

Yes

She put the phone down and got ready for court. She wondered if this was any indication of what the day was going to be like. The text message kept ringing in her head.

Yes.

Chapter 73

The court was crowded again. The faces were familiar by this point. Karl sat at the defense table with the same look of distracted disgust that he had had for the first three days. Simone had called Horace before she left the condo to see if he would be riding with her and Sheva answered the phone.

"No, Mr. Horace said to tell you that he was busy today. Maybe tomorrow," she said.

"I understand. How is he doing with all of this?" Simone asked quietly.

Sheva was silent for a moment, then said, "It's hard for him to see one son this way and not see the other at all."

"Please tell him I'll see him later on today," Simone replied.

"I will," Sheva said.

Simone thought about all of that as she found a seat. She hoped that she could see Jason when he entered the court, so she decided to sit close to the doors at the back of the room. Jason walked in with Mike. He was wearing a charcoal suit that fit him like he was about to pose for a photo shoot. The man had presence. But in the midst of his handsome appearance, his face showed distress. Simone recognized it right away.

He said Maia was fine so what is bothering him so badly?

She was getting anxious and uncomfortable. Did he even notice that she was in the room?

Mike nudged Jason when he saw Simone. Jason turned and looked at her like she was the last person that he wanted to see. The two men exchanged words and Mike walked toward the few empty spaces in the front of the courtroom. Jason walked over to Simone with his eyes cast down.

"Good morning," he said in a very formal voice.

"Good morning. How is Maia?" Simone asked.

"She's fine. Everything is fine," he said.

Simone looked at him and realized that something was seriously wrong and saying what was on her mind wouldn't make things worse.

"Are you alright? What happened?" she asked.

"It doesn't matter. Leela has changed her mind about the divorce and has moved back home. Maia needs both of her parents…I've got to go. Trial's about to start," he turned and walked away from her.

Simone was in shock. She couldn't breathe and her heart was beating so hard that it was forcing the blood to rush to her ears. She felt lightheaded and woozy.

Did he really say what I thought he said? She moved back home? Maia needs two parents? Oh my God, he just kicked me to the curb. What just happened here?

She plopped down in the seat and stared into space.

Think, girl, think. Get a grip. The man is someone else's husband.

Get over it. You don't have the luxury to sit here and cry over it. There's a reason, there's got to be a reason...

The bailiff called the court into session. The prosecution started the proceedings, and everyone settled into what promised to be another long day. Simone sat very still and tried to hold back the tears that were threatening to overflow her dark eyes.

The courtroom door opened slightly and a few people more people entered. A young man went to the front rows of seats and sat behind Karl. A woman sat down across the aisle from Simone and smirked. She cut her eyes in Simone's direction and twisted her wedding ring. It felt a little funny after not being there for a few weeks. Leela had watched the exchange between her husband and the woman across from her. She knew there had to be somebody. There was no way that this butterscotch giant was going to take her man away from her. How embarrassing would that be? What would her friends say?

I guess I'll have to stay here and make sure lover boy doesn't slip up. I might need to go shopping this weekend. Buy some platforms and a new body shaper maybe.

The judge had decided that because the number of charges against Karl stretched over so many years that the focus should be on the most recent and work backward. Presentation of evidence in the shooting lasted until lunch break. The judge was about to dismiss the jury when the young man who came in late stood up. The judge looked at the man and started to speak when she was interrupted.

"This is for my sister Aletta. You may not have pulled the trigger, but you got her killed," the young man spoke so calmly that no one moved until he pulled out the .357 magnum and aimed it at Karl.

Chaos broke out in the court. The bailiff and Officer Cardone lunged to protect the judge while Adamian ran towards the young man. Shots flew and screams fill the room as people scurried for cover. Simone's brain couldn't process what was happening—again. More gunfire, more screaming, more people running from bullets. Hadn't she done this a few weeks ago?

Please God, protect us. Please…

Please God, let her be okay. Let me get to her… Jason had ducked when he saw the gun. Mike dove next to him onto the floor. The two of them checked to make sure that neither was injured then looked up to see if there was anything that could be done to stop the terror that was occurring in front of them.

"I got to get to her, man," Jason said.

"She's alright, man. She's in the back. She's okay. Stay down," Mike said.

Jason looked at Mike and patted him on the shoulder before he stood up and rushed to the back of the courtroom where Simone had been seated. He called her name and scrambled over the piles of people who were rushing toward the doors. He couldn't hear over the tumult, so he called out again.

Simone thought she heard his voice, but she couldn't be sure. After all, he had just walked out of her life. But if he was calling for her, how could she not answer.

"Jason!" she shouted.

He heard her and ran in her direction. He had reached the rear rows when he heard another voice.

"Jason, I'm here. Oh baby, help me! I'm so scared. Take me home. I want to go home," Leela screamed. She reached out and grabbed him around the knees. He stood there as Adamian and the court officers hauled the shooter out of the court. The young man was bleeding from his side and leg.

Jason put his hand on Leela's shoulder but looked over his shoulder at Simone. She looked up and their eyes met. He gazed at her, and she saw something in his eyes that tore her heart apart. She watched as he gathered his wife up from the floor and escorted her through the doors.

By the time the couple had made their way to the car, Leela was in the midst of histrionics. Jason settled her in the car and stood beside the door while she cried and recounted the amount of danger she had been in. He didn't hear a word that she said. He was wondering what was going on across the street. He could see people filing out of the building and police running in but he was too far away to distinguish one traumatized person from another. Then he saw someone coming closer that he did recognize.

Mike's face was tense, which caused Jason's jaw to tighten. The two friends looked each other over quickly and decided that each one was safe and sound. They hugged quickly and stepped away from the car.

"She alright?" Mike asked glancing back at the car.

"Just shook up, I guess," Jason replied.

"Did you know she was coming today?" Mike asked.

"Hell no, I left her at home this morning," Jason said.

"You what?" Mike asked.

"Don't ask, I was gonna tell you when I saw you. Did you see Simone? Is she alright?" Jason asked.

"No man, I couldn't find her. It's crazy in there. People running all over the place. I'm sure she's alright though. Only two people injured," Mike said.

"Then where is she?" Mike could see that Jason was getting agitated.

"I'm sure she's fine. It's Simone, remember? She's not like—well, you know…" Mike said looking back at the car. "She may be in shock but she's okay. She can handle shit."

Not this kind of shit. I tell her I'll be with her forever and then leave her huddled on the floor while I walk out with my arm around my wife. Nah, she can't handle that.

"Stay here. I got to find her. I'll be right back." Jason glanced at the car. "If she stops crying, tell her I left something important inside and I need to get it," Jason said to his friend.

"No problem, man. At least you aren't lying to her. Go handle your business," Mike said. He walked back over to the car, "So Leela, how's your day going?"

Chapter 74

Now ain't this some shit? You can't get this kind of drama on the premium cable channels. The real world is a helluva lot crazier than prison. Harlem sat on a bench outside of the courthouse watching the chaos. The entire courthouse had been evacuated. People running all over the place. Police and first responders tending to the wounded and those in shock. He had heard that only two people were shot but several were trampled or injured in the mass hysteria that followed. He was used to mass hysteria.

Just put the place on lockdown and bash the heads of those that don't comply. Perfectly simple. Works every time--except when it don't.

The news stations were recording everyone and everything. Screams and tears coming from women and men. Then there were the ones in shock, just staring off into space. An Ebony Fashion Fair model lookalike ran past him on his way toward the courthouse. Harlem was interested to see where this brother was headed.

Most of the time you don't see a brother running towards a courthouse.

The well-dressed man stopped at another set of benches on the other side of the sidewalk where an attractive woman was seated. Harlem looked closer because the woman looked familiar. It was the lovely listener from Big Muddy. Miss Simone. She wasn't hurt from the looks of her—at least not on the outside.

Smooth brother kneeled in front of her and touched the side of her face. Harlem squinted a little because he thought he saw her flinch just a little bit. Brother man took off his suit jacket and wrapped it around her. He sat beside her and held her hand and started talking. Fast.

Who the hell is this? It sure ain't her husband 'cause I googled his ass. Whoever he is, brother man is serious…

Harlem watched for the next five minutes as Jason talked and Simone listened. She shook her head a few times and nodded once, not that Harlem was keeping track. Jason kept stroking Simone's hair as if he had to continue to touch her to make sure that she didn't disappear. Then Jason kissed her. Really kissed her. Harlem found himself leaning forward as if to block out all the craziness that was surrounding them. He also wanted to see how Simone responded to this incredibly good-looking dude making a public display of affection and not giving a good damn who saw him—or his wedding ring.

Now ain't THIS some shit? Brother man is in love with Miss Simone. Go 'head girl! You done turned him out! 'Course you look a little turned out yourself. Wonder what hubby thinks of all of this?

In the middle of his musings, another brother walked up to the bench. A little taller than the first. More basketball player than football. The lover turned from his beloved and looked up at Basketball Brother. Lover still held her hand. The other brother said something, and Harlem waited to see what would transpire next. The men spoke in a way that made Harlem realize that they were friends. Lover helped Simone up and Basketball Brother put his arm around her in a protective hug. The two male could-be models shook hands. Lover kissed her gently this time and said something. Basketball Brother and Miss Simone, still draped in Lover's jacket, walked away. Lover did too, but he stopped and looked back a couple of times before making his way towards the street, not that Harlem was keeping track. He was deep in thought about what he had just seen.

There's a poem in there somewhere.

Love in the midst of all this

What the world has in store…

When all things seem all amiss

Still perfect at its core.

Shaky but a good start after being in a shooting. Harlem continued to take in the sights. Reporters still running back and forth. Camera people at their heels. Lyndsey Longhair was looking for someone to interview but hesitated when she saw Harlem. He pretended not to notice her and turned his attention towards the CNN cameraman and reporter.

"Don, what's up man? I was in there today. Saw the whole thing, let's go somewhere warm and I'll tell you all about it," Harlem said.

The reporter shook Harlem's hand and the three men headed towards the Starbuck's across the street.

"So, how's Frederica doing?"

Chapter 75

Court was adjourned for a week. When the trial resumed, it was closed to spectators. Even the witnesses had to be physically searched before entering the court. No one could figure out how the shooter had managed to bring a gun through the metal detectors. Someone overheard the court stenographer repeat the old adage-'Where there's a will, there's a way.' When Judge Burkiss asked the stenographer if he had said that, he responded that he wasn't part of the jury--all he did was record what everybody said. He could say whatever he wanted. Court was postponed for another two hours while another stenographer was found.

The judge and the attorneys discussed how the trial should proceed at this point and it was decided that in order to calm the jurors and help them forget the trauma of last week, they would start from the beginning, the Alayah Brittingham cold case. No harm in that.

Tasha was sworn in to give her testimony and for the first time since the trial started, Karl Dyson showed a spark of interest. It could have been because Tasha was so beautiful and poised but it had more to do with the fact that here sat someone who knew something about that night that he didn't.

After swearing to tell the whole truth and relieve herself of the guilt and burden, Tasha sat down and repeated her and her sister's story for the second time.

Simone was in the courtroom trying to focus on what was happening. Since she was a witness, she was supposed to be there each day in case she could be called to testify. She knew that probably wouldn't occur for a long time but here she sat doing her civic duty while trying not to think about all that had happened here. The holes in the walls from the gunshots had been repaired. The smell of fresh paint was strong in her nostrils. A constant reminder of how bizarre this trial had become.

She thought about how hard it must be for Tasha to relive that night. She thought about how hard it must have been for Alyetta's grandfather and brother to be sitting in jail and the hospital waiting for their own trials. She thought about Jason walking out of this room with his arm around his wife. She closed her eyes and tried not to think anymore. It was all too painful.

The prosecutor had no more questions for Tasha at this time and Cady Werman stood up to begin defending his client. He quietly asked Tasha questions as if he hadn't heard a word that she had said.

Simone forced herself to stay focused, but she kept losing the battle. When she looked at Tasha, she noticed that she and Jason had the same penetrating eyes. Their mouths might say something, but their eyes always told the truth. Tasha was telling the truth. Jason had been telling the truth outside of the courthouse after the shooting. He loved her. His daughter needed her father. There was no question about what he had to do.

That's why I love him.

The pain she had felt as she watched him walk out of the court with Leela had eased somewhat after he came back to explain things to her. As Sly led her away from the craziness, she still wondered what she had gotten herself into with Mr. Copeny. Since she had met him, her life hadn't been the same. Did she really want it to be the same as it had been?

Speak the truth and shame the devil.

Simone had heard the end of Tasha's testimony about Tisha being run down by the defendant. Cady asked what type of vehicle it was and audibly wondered why no one else had seen the alleged vehicle. Cady smiled as he finished his cross examination. He strolled back to the defense table and Tasha stepped down from the witness stand.

The next witness called to the stand was Cornelius Easterly formerly known as Langston "Harlem" Morantz. He was smiling. The bailiff asked Harlem if he swore to tell the truth, the whole truth and nothing but the truth so help you God. Harlem thanked God that he now could tell the whole truth to people who would listen and believe him. His entire life was about to change. The sins of his past could never be erased but he had learned that he could be forgiven and have a new life. A life free from guilt, a life filled with love and fulfillment. He had learned that through meeting Celestial. He had been reminded again when he saw Simone and her man on the bench. While the rest of the world was going crazy, there was still a place for what really mattered. Harlem thought about all of this as he swore before God and man to tell the truth.

"So, Mr. Morantz, please tell us how you know the defendant, Karl Dyson," the prosecuting attorney said.

"The defendant, Karl Dyson, Tyrone Jackson, and myself, pulled a train on a young girl when we were teenagers. Then Jax and I watched Karl bash her head in with a bottle and leave her for dead. Her name was Alayah Brittingham…" Harlem stopped and took a breath.

Before he could continue speaking, there was a groan in the court. Simone looked around wondering who was making the sound. Tasha was also searching for the owner of the agonized voice.

Tyreek and Shamel had been sitting together during the proceedings and seemed to have become good friends over the past several months. Shamel had moved closer to Tyreek who seemed to be in intense pain. There was the source of the sound. Tyreek was bent over grasping the back of the bench in front of him. Shamel was trying to help but didn't really know what to do. Was he hurt? Had his injuries from the shooting flared up? What was going on?

Harlem didn't know whether to continue or to stop. The prosecutor turned toward the groan. Tyreek sat back and slowly rose to his feet. Simone could tell that he still was not fully recovered from his injuries. Adamian and Ishua were on high alert, along with the other federal agents and court and police officers stationed around the courtroom.

"That's my aunt! Alayah Brittingham was my aunt! You son of a bitch! You killed my aunt! You fucked my sister and then tried to kill her. You bastard! I'll kill you my damn self. You're not going to hurt anybody else in my family--" Tyreek yelled.

"Order in the court, order in the court!" The judge banged her gavel on the bench. "Remove this young man from this courtroom until he regains his composure. Anyone other than the witness who speaks will be physically removed and held in contempt! Does everyone left in here understand me? The jury will disregard that statement! We will take a fifteen-minute recess."

The court officers escorted Tyreek from the courtroom. Shamel went with him. Tasha and Simone glanced at each other, then, both looked up at the witness stand. Harlem shrugged his shoulders and took a sip of water. He looked down at Karl at the defense table and raised his glass, imagining that it was a nice Chianti. "Cheers," he said.

Chapter 76

Jason sat at his desk staring at the computer screen as he wondered what was going to happen next. He ran a variety of scenarios through his head, each one more vivid and dramatic than the one before. In the back of his mind, he heard a soft familiar voice.

What will happen is what you expect to happen. Thinking makes it so. Hasn't the universe shown you that before?

Jason thought about it and wondered some more. Was it true? Did thinking make it so? He tested the theory to see if there was any truth to it:

Case One- He wanted real love in his life. He met Simone.

Case Two- He was tired of a loveless marriage. Leela wanted a divorce.

Case Three- He wanted Maia to have a real family…*How's that one going to work out?*

The door to his office opened and Mike walked in, uninvited as always. Maybe it was a good thing this time. It kept him from having to finish his current train of thought.

"Hey man, it's time for lunch. How about some pizza? We can go to Lou Malinata's. I got a taste for something big, hot, and thick and this time I'm talking food," Mike joked.

"You're a fool, you know that?" Jason laughed, appreciating his friend's efforts to keep his mind off of what was happening in his life. "Sly just sent a text. Seems that Tyreek went off in court," Mike said.

"Why, what happened this time?" Jason asked.

"I was gonna wait to tell you 'cause it's going to fuck you up," Mike said as he sat down in the chair in front of Jason's desk.

"What else could be any worse than what's happened already with this trial?" Jason asked.

"The girl that Karl is accused of killing was Tyreek's aunt, Alayah Brittingham," Mike said slowly allowing it to sink in.

"What did you say?" Jason asked.

"Alayah was Tyreek's aunt," Mike said.

"Shit," Jason mumbled. "Can the world get any smaller?"

"Let's hope not. If it does, you and I will be related for real," Mike said. "Come on, let's get out of here. I think you could use some fresh air. I'll drive. Give me your car keys, I don't have any gas."

Mid-day traffic in the city was as bad as rush hour and what should have taken fifteen minutes ended up taking thirty. Jason didn't mind too much since it gave him more think time. He was trying to figure out what he was really feeling since the trial started. Surprise, shock, but mostly guilt. He couldn't shake the feeling that he was somehow responsible for all the pain and suffering. Sure, he had been here before, but it seemed that he kept coming back to the same thought—if he hadn't treated Alayah that way…none of this would have happened.

His thoughts then darted to Leela. He remembered seeing her on the floor in the courthouse. How he wanted to leave her there. Making the choice to help her instead of Simone was heart wrenching. Listening to Leela cry hysterically as he tried to drive home was even more painful. It was so bad that he didn't think he could drive the distance, so he drove to William and Mim's.

When he opened the front door with Leela at his side, Mim merely cocked her head to the side and headed toward the kitchen. Tasha heard the noise and came down the stairs to see what was going on. Jason helped Leela sit on the sofa, where she immediately cried louder. It could have been because she realized where she was and had no means of escape. Tasha knelt beside the sofa and spoke to her softly.

Jason escaped to the kitchen. "Do you have a tea for that?" he asked.

"I will momentarily. Don't worry, I won't poison her," Mim said as she opened jars.

You can if you want to.

"I heard that," Mim said. "I expected you after what happened today, but I didn't expect you to arrive with your wife."

"Believe me, neither did I. How did you hear about it?"

"Tasha saw it on Twitter. Then Ishua called. This is turning into a nightmare."

"Tell me about it," Jason said as he looked back toward the living room.

"Ask Tasha to take her upstairs and get her settled, then, you take this up to her. Make sure she drinks it all," Mim said as she handed Jason a steaming cup of liquid.

Jason took the cup and sniffed it. "Are you sure it will help?" Mim looked at him without saying a word. Her eyes said it all.

"If she drinks it all, she should rest quietly for at least four or five hours. You could use four or five quiet hours, couldn't you?" she asked. "Tasha can pick Maia up from school. I will keep an eye on Leela until you get back."

He glanced down at the cup again. "And what am I supposed to be doing during those four or five hours?"

"What do you think you should be doing? I would think that today was traumatizing for other people as well…" Mim said.

"You mean Simone, right? I told her that Leela came home, and that Maia needed two parents. So…" he couldn't finish his sentence.

"And how did she respond to this revelation?"

"We didn't get a chance to talk about it really," he replied.

"Well, now you have a little time to find out, don't you?"

"So, what am I supposed to do? Run over there and ask her to marry me? I've got a wife upstairs and a daughter who needs two parents. Maybe if Alayah had had two parents things might have turned out differently. If I had had two parents…" Jason stopped speaking, realizing what he was about to say.

Mim poured boiling water into a cup. She looked at her oldest child and spoke softly. "You're right. Things would have been very different but that doesn't always mean that things would have been better. Children need two parents and I used to wonder whether choosing not to marry your father was a bad decision. He was himself before I met him, I couldn't change that. I tried. To subject you and your brother and sisters to that—no, I couldn't do it. Children need two parents who love and respect each other and want what's best for them. They need to be on the same page, Jason. You know that. Leela…Leela isn't even in the same library. You know that… so does Maia," Mim stopped talking and watched Jason's expression.

There he goes, biting his jaw.

"Do you know what Maia talks about when we pick her up from school? She talks about you and the things that you do together. She talks about how you are so smart because you answer all her questions. She talks about how you play with her and tell her bedtime stories. She adores you. You know what she says about her mother? Maia thinks that Leela doesn't love her because she forgets to pick her up and always hollers and fusses with her when Maia talks to her—unless they're doing something that Leela wants to do. She said that she wants her mommy to be more like Miss Simone because she doesn't act silly all the time and Simone listens to her and loves her more than her mother does," Mim waited for the reaction that she knew was coming.

"Why didn't you tell me this earlier?" Jason asked quietly, his jaw tightening and loosening.

"For what purpose?" Mim asked.

"Then why are you telling me now?" Jason retorted.

"You weren't making decisions then. You were in the midst of a situation, and you couldn't—wouldn't see it if I had said something. Things are different now. You're right. Your daughter does need two parents. You have the opportunity to decide what that looks like," Mim said.

"So, you're saying that I need to divorce Leela? You know that she'll try to take Maia just for spite," Jason asked.

"You know your wife," Mim replied.

"So, what am I supposed to do? I did what I thought was right. I left Simone... I told her that I was with Leela… What am I supposed to do?" his voice trailed off.

"Be patient. It will work itself out as it should," Mim said quietly placing her hand on her son's.

He smiled a wan smile. "I hate it when you say stuff like that," he said.

"I know," she replied, "but it's true and you know it."

"So, what I'm hearing is that I should let life take its course. Is that right?"

"Exactly. Don't interfere because then you mess things up, you're good at that," she said squeezing his hand. "What is it that you want, Jason?"

"I want a happy family. I want my daughter to grow up feeling loved and protected. I want someone to love and that truly loves me,"

Jason sighed. "I want what you and William have," he continued.

"I waited for that," she said.

"I know," Jason said.   They were silent for a while. The sounds from upstairs were still going strong.

"You might want to take that to her now. It should be cool enough for her to drink it all. Things should be quieter in around fifteen minutes," Mim sipped her tea as Jason went up the back steps toward the bedroom.

"Make sure that you wear a hat when you leave, it's cold outside."

Jason snapped out of his memories when Mike slammed on the brakes at the intersection.

"Damn idiot. Stop on a green light. I swear—Chicago drivers," Mike fussed.

They found a parking space and had a deep-dish Chicago style pepperoni and extra cheese pizza with Coronas and Pepsi. Jason had the Pepsi so that he could drive back. The way his life was going, he didn't need Mike to be buzz driving. He was feeling a lot better after the food and laughter that Mike usually provided. Jason thought about the things his mother said and decided to trust that things were working out as they should.

Shortly after they got back to work, the chocolate Barbie knocked on his open door.

"You have a visitor, Mr. Copeny," she squealed.

Jason scrunched his brow. "I don't remember any appointments this afternoon," he said. "Who is it?"

"He says his name is Gregory Dyson," she said.

Chapter 77

I'm going to need another suitcase of money.

Cady Werman was getting a bit concerned about the outcome of this trial and it had barely started. He had handled all sorts of bloodthirsty, murderous clients in his years as a defense attorney but never had there been such a display of hatred from so many against one person. He looked over at Karl and wondered if he even wanted to defend him anymore. But money is money and Karl had a lot of it and since when did Cady side with principle over money?

The trial had resumed after a two-day recess. Tyreek had not returned and neither had Shamel. Tasha and Simone were seated together now, trying to provide moral support for each other as both were bearing their own burdens.

The two women had developed a bond even though they had only known each other a short time. They seemed to complement each other. One was vivacious, the other was learning to be. Both were intelligent, sincere, and truthful. And Tasha could tell how much in love Simone was with her brother and that was quite alright with her. Jason had mellowed and seemed as if he was really alive instead of just going through the motions. She hadn't seen him that way since—well, she couldn't remember when.

Cady smoothed his nine-hundred-dollar tie and stepped forward to cross-examine Harlem. He really didn't want to. The original testimony had been so graphic and explicit. Nothing had been left out and it filled in whatever gaps there were in what Tasha had testified earlier. Cady wished that he had more time to find any errors in Harlem's testimony, but he wouldn't be able to because it was all true. He glanced back at Karl.

What a piece of shit.

"Mr. Morantz, or should I say Easterly since you maneuvered a new identity from the Federal government…," he started.

"Objection!" shouted the prosecutor.

"Sustained. Mr. Werman, Mr. Morantz is not on trial here and his dealings with the government do not affect his responses, as he is under oath," the judge said.

"But they do, Your Honor. How do we know that Mr. Easter— excuse me, Morantz's testimony was not motivated by a desire for release from prison where he was serving a life sentence?" Cady was pulling at straws but if he could spout enough bullshit to get through to the end of the day, he would have been successful. That would give him time to come up with a strategy that might keep Karl from ending up with a needle in his arm.

"As I stated earlier, Mr. Morantz is not on trial, your client is," Judge Burkiss said.

"Maybe he should be. If what he said earlier is true, then he is allegedly as guilty as my client. There is no real evidence to back up anything that has been said so far," Cady said hoping that the judge would get sick of him and adjourn for the day.

"Mr. Werman, watch what you say and cross-exam the witness or lose the opportunity," the judge warned.

Cady smoothed his tie again and faced Harlem who was thoroughly enjoying the lawyer's antics.

If I had had a sleazy lawyer like this, I wouldn't have ended up in prison for life. Five to ten maybe….

"Mr. Morantz, after the terrible events of that night, what did you do?"

"What do you mean, what did I do?"

"What did you do? After the alleged rape and hit and run, how did you respond?"

"It wasn't an alleged rape and hit and run. It was real, every single bit of it. I know dammit, I was there. We hurt that girl, we used her like she was nothing. When me and Jax came to our senses and tried to help her, he bashed her face in with a forty. Blood everywhere. Then he runs down a little girl on purpose and laughs about it. He chased her down. Did I tell you that? He drove around looking for her instead of getting the hell out of Dodge. Speaking of Dodge, that's what he was driving, a black Dodge Challenger with a four-fifty Hemi. You know how much power that is? You know how that engine sounds when it's revving up to smash into a little girl?" Harlem was leaning forward and foaming at the mouth.

The judge banged her gavel. Harlem caught himself and sat back. His hands were trembling as he reached for the glass of water beside him. One of the jurors coughed. Another reached for a tissue and wiped his eyes. Several just stared at Karl. Harlem recovered quickly and continued before anyone stopped him.

"So, you want to know what I did after that? I got the fuck away from here. That's what I did. I was scared. After he hit the girl, me and Jax wanted out of the car. He dropped us off by the grocery store. It was late and it was closed so nobody was around. He just looked at us and laughed. Said that we had so much pussy that we must have turned into one. I'll never forget it. He was swinging Alayah's gold necklace around on his fingers. He snatched it off her neck after he hit her with the bottle. She had matching earrings too," Harlem said. Then he added, "She had looked so pretty…before we hurt her," he stopped speaking.

"So, that is a tremendously moving story, Mr. Morantz. But there is no evidence to back up anything that you have said. True, someone attacked Miss Brittingham that night. You admit that you were there. We saw the photos of the outrageous and unspeakable things that were done to her. There is no necklace, no earrings, no car. So, what are we to believe—that my client did these things or that it was you, Mr. Morantz, since you have admitted to it under oath? If what you say is true, Mr. Morantz, then there should be some proof, some shred of evidence to convince this jury that you aren't accusing an innocent man just to fulfill your desire for revenge because Mr. Dyson became an upstanding citizen while you ended up in prison serving a life sentence for unspeakable crimes, such as what you have described to us today. Isn't that right Mr. Easterly—oh, I mean Morantz?"

Simone was speechless. She jumped out of her seat and hurried from the courtroom. Tasha watched her leave but couldn't raise herself from the seat. She was spellbound by what was occurring in the front of the courtroom.

Simone stood by the windows and stared down onto the street. People coming and going. Jason out there somewhere. Ronjai in the hospital. Greg—

"Hello, Dad. How are you?" she said into her phone.

"I'm fine, baby girl. good to hear your voice. How are you doing?" Horace responded.

"May I come over later on? I need to talk to you."

Chapter 78

Don't interfere because then you mess things up, you're good at that.

The words rang clearly in the back of his head. As much as Jason wanted to tell Chocolate Barbie to inform Mr. Dyson to kiss his black ass, he refrained.

"Send him back, please. Thanks, Mimi," he said.

Mimi smiled at Greg and pointed down the hallway. "Mr. Copeny will see you now. He usually doesn't see people unannounced but he's willing to see you. You must be special," she said with a smile. Greg smiled his best 'I got this' smile and confidently strode down the hallway. Mimi thought she heard some sort of, but she wasn't sure. The man seemed familiar to her, but she couldn't place him. *Maybe YouTube?*

 A knock on the door announced Greg's arrival.

"Come in," Jason said as he sat back in his chair. Greg entered and slowly looked around the office. Nowhere near as plush as his or as lavish. Not the digs of a man making two hundred thousand and change. A few pictures, all of a lovely little girl at various stages of life, bamboo, and a money tree on the bookshelf behind his desk.

Obviously, it wasn't working.

He recognized the plants because Simone liked that type of shit too. What did she see in him?

Besides the incredibly good looks, tight, toned physique, and fierce left hook?

"Have a seat. What brings you here today, Mr. Dyson?" Jason asked as casually as possible. Now was a good time to use everything he had learned from Simone. *Seek for understanding.*

He noticed that Greg looked different from the last time he had seen him. Thinner, older somehow. He was still impeccably dressed, keeping up the image. Cashmere polo and wool trousers.

Probably from the same tailor that his brother used. Wedding ring all shiny and bright.

"I'm here to talk to you about your relationship with my wife," he said.

"I think that type of conversation requires a degree of privacy. Please shut the door and have a seat," Jason said as he pointed to the chair. After closing the door, Greg sat down across from Jason. He struggled to contain the sound developing deep in his throat.

"What exactly do you mean when you say my relationship with your wife?" Jason hoped that he had worded that correctly.

Isn't that how Simone does it? Keep the focus on him and his needs.

"I mean what is going on between you and my wife? She says that she's filing for divorce, and I think that you have something to do with that," Greg said sharply.

"I think that if your wife is filing for divorce, it has more to do with your relationship with her than it does with mine," Jason was imagining his fist making contact with Greg's jaw and breaking it this time.

"We were fine and then she started working with you on this…case and now she wants a divorce. I think that you are at the bottom of this," Greg said trying to sound forceful and in control.

Jason almost laughed but thought that Simone wouldn't approve. "Help me understand what you mean by fine. From what I understand, your wife found out about your infidelity from your lover while she was mediating your lover's case. And then she had to decide whether to save your lover's life or watch her die. That could take its toll on even the best marriage, I would think," Jason said.

Good job. Simone would be proud of me.

He watched Greg squirm in his seat.

"You seem to know a great deal for a co-worker," Greg snarled.

"I follow social media. It's amazing the things that pop up on there. And yes, I am your wife's co-worker and if she is affected by… situations that occur in her personal life, her co-workers are affected as well," Jason answered. He was beginning to enjoy fucking with Mr. Dyson.

"As her husband, I would like for you to stay out of her personal life," Greg leaned forward as he spoke. "What happens in a marriage is private between husband and wife."

"Well, you should have thought of that before you went outside of your marriage with your subordinate. In the legal profession, that could be interpreted as harassment. Your wife is my friend and I care about her well-being. If she needs me, I will be there for her—like you should have been," Jason finished speaking and waited for Greg's reply.

"Are you sleeping with my wife?" Greg yelled as he stood up and put his hands on the desk. Jason watched him, waiting for signs of more aggressive behavior.

He's about to go off and I'm gonna have to shut him down. Come on with it. Give me a reason.

"That is the second time that you have disrespected your wife in my presence. You remember what happened last time. That was just a warning. I think it's time for you to leave my office. Can you make it on your own or do you need some assistance?" Jason stood up and took a breath. He waited for Greg to decide how he was going to leave the office.

"Are you sleeping with my wife?" Greg asked again.

"You don't get it do you? Your wife doesn't want to be married to you because you are an unfaithful bastard. You have an amazing wife who loved you and all you could do is cheat on her and treat her like dirt. She should have left your ass a long time ago, but she put up with your shit until she couldn't take it anymore. Get out of my office."

"You love her, don't you? You're in love with my wife!"

"Simone is my friend and I care very deeply about what happens to her. So, you need to get used to that. I'm not going anywhere. On the other hand, you are going to leave my office," Jason said as he walked around the desk to the door.

"Stay away from my wife," Greg sputtered as he walked out of the office. His breathing was jagged and sweat was forming on his forehead.

I've lost her. I've really lost her.

He was so wrapped up in his thoughts that he didn't hear Mimi tell him to have a nice day. Where did he go wrong?

How about when you started screwing everything that moved?

He got in his 750i and sped out of the parking lot.

Jason had sat back down when Mike appeared in the doorway. "Was that who I thought it was? What did he want?" Mike asked.

"I have no idea," Jason said. Mike looked at him and the two friends burst into laughter.

"Did you clock him again?" Mike asked.

"I should have. Why?" Jason asked.

"The way he sped out of here, I thought he was blind in both eyes," Mike said. He looked at Jason's face and saw what Greg saw—eyes filled with love for Simone Dyson.

He probably couldn't see for the tears.

Chapter 79

Chevy opened the door for Simone and gave her a quick hug. Simone returned the hug and stepped into the warm house. The smell of some sort of pie was wafting through the hallway.

"Let me take your coat. Would you like a slice of apple pie? I just took it out of the oven. Mr. Horace says it smells right so I'm dying for someone to try it," Chevy said. Simone was surprised with how healthy and happy she looked. She had lost at least ten pounds which Simone attributed to the weight of the makeup she used to wear.

"No thanks, I'm fine," Simone said.

"Hey babygirl, come on in here. You sounded serious on the phone. What's up?" Horace asked from the living room. Simone looked apprehensive to have this particular conversation with Chevy in the house. Horace seemed to sense that.

"Chevy is on her way to the drycleaner. Do you want her to pick up anything for you while she's out?" he asked. Simone shook her head and watched as Chevy put on her coat and proceed out of the house.

"Sit down and talk to me, honey. What's going on? Something about the trial, isn't it?"

422

Simone shook her head and wondered how to begin. After a deep breath, she started to explain everything that had transpired earlier that day. As she talked about the car, she could see Horace's features start to tighten.

"I remember that car. It was a gift on his seventeenth birthday—had belonged to his uncle. I restored it myself. He loved that car. Thought he was a big man driving it around town and then one day I didn't see it anymore. I asked him what happened to it, and he said he sold it. Got a real good offer from somebody out of state, he said."

"He didn't sell it, Horace. It is in one of the storage units in Joliet. Two people who were there the night that Alayah was attacked, and Tisha was run over described a car that looked just like it," Simone said.

Horace sat silently for a while. He stared at the fireplace and seemed to get lost in the crackling flames.

"Do me a favor, honey. Call Franklin and tell him what's going on and to get over here. Then call whoever needs to be called to tell them about the storage unit," Horace said as he put his head in his hands and wept.

Lord, forgive me.

Simone did as instructed and made a pot of coffee for Horace and Franklin. She could only imagine what the conversation would be like once he arrived. The patriarch of the Dyson family sat stoically in his favorite chair and gazed at the glowing embers of the fire as it started to die down.

"I always liked fires burning like this. Reminds me of my Becky," Horace began. "Did I ever tell you I met her when she wasn't nothing but a little bitty girl couldn't have been more than sixteen." He smiled at the memory. Simone shook her head and listened closely. She loved his stories and wished that this one had been prompted by better circumstances.

"I was about eighteen, nineteen years old and chopping wood for the widow lady Hawkins. She didn't have any children of her own. Husband had died in the war before they had a chance to start a family…Well anyway, I was chopping wood and throwing it in a pile so I could stack in up by the house later. Well low and behold, this group of noisy teenage girls walks by all giggly like they get and I get distracted and turn around to talk to them. They were pretty and all, so I think 'why not?', so I turn to talk to them and toss the log I'm holding behind me towards the pile—I thought. End up tossing it right towards this little bit of a thing—Rebekah Omega Tate. She spelled her Rebekah like the one in the Bible. She was a good woman too…I'm glad she's not around to see this." He took a sip of his coffee and stared back at the fire. "We didn't have much at first, but we always had a fireplace. She said I needed to cut wood for my own fireplace not somebody else's…Now I just have it delivered…." His voice trailed off.

The doorbell rang and Simone was grateful to get up to answer it. She couldn't stand seeing someone she loved so dearly in so much pain.

"Hello, Mr. Franklin, come in. Dad is in the living room," she said.

"It sounded really bad on the phone. How is he?" Franklin asked, concerned about his friend.

"I'm glad you're here. He really needs someone to talk to," she replied, escorting Franklin to the living room and closed the French doors behind her. She went in the kitchen and sat in her favorite spot near the bay window as if that would bring back happier times.

She wasn't sure how much time had passed before the French doors opened but she had been watching the sun set when Franklin said, "You can call the authorities now. They won't be able to do anything until the morning. Would you mind going with them to show them where it is?"

"No, that's fine," she said.

"After you call, could you cut us a piece of that apple pie? Horace said Chevy worked real hard on it and it would break her heart if somebody didn't try a slice tonight," Franklin said and walked back through the French doors.

Simone called Ishua and told him all that she knew. He said he would call his brother as soon as he said goodbye to Tisha. They would meet her in the morning at the storage facility with the forensics teams and a tow truck.

She hung up the phone and took the dessert plates out of the china cabinet and washed them.

He's right. The pie looks lovely. It would be a shame not to have some while its warm.

She cut two oversized slices and carried them into the living room.

Chapter 80

The flight from Geneva had been a bumpy one. The turbulence over the Atlantic had been horrendous due to the polar vortex that was wreaking havoc on the weather across most of the United States. But it wasn't enough to keep Florian from flying into Chicago on the red eye. He had been checking the news feeds from CNN and other U.S. news services about the Dyson trial. Even though he and Tasha spent hours on Skype every day, he still felt that she wasn't telling him everything and that frightened him. When he saw her on Skype she was as beautiful as ever, but something was different. She seemed pensive and tired. Oh, so tired. But there was something else, as if a burden that she had been carrying for a long time wasn't as heavy. He wondered what that burden was exactly and why she never chose to share it with him. He would have helped her to carry it. He would carry it all by himself if that's what it took to relieve her of her suffering. He would do anything for her, and he hoped that she knew that. He wanted nothing more in life than to make her his wife and to grow old with her with their children and grandchildren close by.

He wondered at times what their children would look like. Smooth skin like their mother's, the color of light brown sugar with kinky blond curls all over their heads. He liked that idea. He always hated the straightness of his own hair. He hoped that the first child was a little girl—beautiful, just like her mother. He looked forward to learning how to comb and braid her hair…

He sat watching the sun rise. The captain requested that passengers fasten their seatbelts, as they were entering another patch of turbulence as they approached the east coast of the United States.

Florian tightened his seatbelt again. He would cross hell or high water for this beautiful woman. He snickered at this thought as he gazed out on the glistening ocean ten thousand feet below him.

Tyreek and his grandmother had been on a vigil at the hospital for the past five weeks. The doctors had decided that the fetus was viable outside of the womb and the caesarean would be performed tomorrow morning. The words sounded like a foreign tongue to Ronjai's grandmother but she understood the ominous tone. As the cohort of doctors explained everything, Mrs. Henderson glanced at Tyreek in hopes that they might be saying something besides what she thought they were saying, anything that might postpone the inevitable.

"Gramma, they're going to deliver the baby tomorrow," Tyreek said softly as he tenderly held his grandmother's hand. He knew that he could surely lose his grandmother as well as his sister in the next twenty-four hours. Would she be able to stand the loss of another one of her flesh and blood?

As Tyreek sat there with his grandmother, something inside of him gave way. A space within him opened that he had previously been unaware of. In his search for an understanding of warfare, he had inadvertently stumbled on true understanding. At that moment, he understood what his grandmother had been muttering and crying and praying about all of his days. Life is precious. Life is short. Life is not promised. Appreciate it. Love it. Live it. But most of all, be grateful for it, because once it is gone, it cannot be replaced.

What profits a man if he gains the whole world and loses his soul?

He could hear his grandmother saying that over and over again after he returned home from a very profitable night on the corner. He didn't get it then. He would just look at her, suck his teeth and 'pity the old woman' on his way to add to his stash. Now, here he sat, more money in his stash than he could spend in a year and he still couldn't save his sister's life.

He tried to muster up hate for the perpetrator of this tragedy—the kid who shot Ronjai and tried to kill him. But that little boy wasn't the perpetrator—Karl Dyson was…*wasn't he?* And if he killed Karl—

It won't bring my sister back. No amount of money, or prayer, or specialists can do anything for my sister. She's gone and she's never coming back. Killing Karl will only mean he's dead too. He only did what I gave him opportunity to do. If I had stayed away from him, he would have stayed away from us. So, who's really the perpetrator?

Tyreek felt the hardness in his heart start to soften. His jaw started to quiver and his hands started to tremble. It was if he was hearing a new voice for the first time. Tyreek knew that somehow that Karl would be accountable for his actions without his help. He also knew that the same standard would apply to him.

What profits a man if he gains the whole world and loses his soul?

"God, forgive me," Tyreek muttered, "I didn't understand."

"What'd you say, baby?" his grandmother asked.

"Gramma, I'm sorry," he said with tears in his eyes. "Let's go see Ronnie for a while. There's something I want to tell her."

Chapter 81

The storage facility was blocked off with crime scene tape and the employees sent home except for Harlan Robinson, the poor man who was in charge of records. He was a meticulous little man who had been working there for the past thirty-two years. He was old enough to retire but couldn't think of a reason to. Since his wife, Hanna, died of leukemia ten years ago, he was grateful to get up every day and have something else to think about besides how much he missed her. Harlan was not only meticulous; he also had the memory of an elephant and an inquisitive nature. Hanna used to say that he was just plain nosey.

"Mr. Robinson, is it possible to pull up the files of people who entered the units on your computer?" Adamian asked.

"Yes, sir. I can do that, but it has only been computerized since 2001. We didn't want to switch over until we was sure that the Millenium scare wasn't going to harm our recordkeeping. You're too young to have had to worry about all that, probably. You must be what? In your early thirties maybe?" Harlan asked.

"So are there files for before 2001?" Adamian continued.

"Yes, sir. Mr. Dyson likes everything in order and that's what I do. Keep everything in order. Mr. Dyson is a good man and a fair man. You know what he did? When my wife was real sick and the doctors here couldn't do nothing for her, Mr. Dyson paid to fly us to the cancer center in Dallas, Texas. Yes he did. And paid for me a place to stay while she was in the hospital getting treatment. If that wasn't enough, he still gave me a salary while I was away from work. He's a good man. Anything I can do to help him, I will. What is it you need me to tell you?" Harlan looked over the top of his glasses and waited for Adamian's request.

"I need any information on the comings and goings from unit 4-R," he said.

"For how long?" Harlan asked as he got up from his chair and walked toward the records room.

"Let's start with 1994," Adamian replied.

While Adamian waited for Harlan to scour through twenty years of records, Ishua stood in front of 4-R with a warrant. The tow truck operator had sent a text saying that he was stuck in the morning traffic along with thousands of other commuters going into and out of the city. He'd wait to open the unit until the truck arrived. He thought about going back to the car and sit but he realized that he was enjoying the fact that he could stand without pain. The thought brought a smile to his handsome face. He had made up in his mind that getting shot was the best thing that could have happened to him. He would never say that to his brother or to anyone that he worked with at the Bureau, they would recommend indefinite leave for psychological reasons.

The past few years had been very hard for him. The case before the Dyson assignment had taken its toll on him emotionally. Adamian always said that his heart was too soft for this line of work. After the last case, Ishua agreed with him.

Watching your partner and three kidnap victims executed before your eyes might take its toll on anyone...but you don't say that to your older brother or the psychiatrists who sign your release papers so you can get back to work.

After this shooting, he somehow felt as if his guilt had been lifted. He couldn't explain it, but he no longer had the feeling that he should have died that day too. He smiled again as he thought about how easy it had been to open up to Miss Mim while he was in rehab. He sometimes pretended that his mother would have listened to him that way if she had lived. God, how he missed her. Even as a grown man, he somehow felt an emptiness. Mim seemed to fill that void.

He wiggled his leg and felt no pain, only the cold. He could live with that. Mim had suggested that he try alternative treatment for his injury in addition to the physical therapy he endured each day. What could it hurt, she had said. Ishua was skeptical but when he looked at how well Tisha was doing, considering the extent of her injuries and the time she had been in the nursing home, he thought that Mim might be right. Seven acupuncture treatments later, he was walking without a cane and standing in the cold waiting for a tow truck. Amazing woman, Miss Mim.

Even more amazing daughter.

How was it that a woman, in a wheelchair, who could not speak except for a few whispered syllables had touched his heart so? Maybe he hadn't fully recovered from his own trauma. Maybe he didn't want to. Tisha was special. She had the same deep haunting eyes as her mother, that spoke volumes even if her voice couldn't.

He remembered the first day that he had met her. Mim was pushing his wheelchair back from the sunroom because his pain was so intense that he no longer felt comfortable enough to stay. She suggested stopping by Tisha's room for just a minute to introduce her to someone new. Ishua hadn't wanted to see anyone or anything except his own bed so that he could deal with his pain alone. But what's a man in a wheelchair to do?

Mim introduced them but said nothing about her being Tisha's mother. The three sat and talked. Mim and Ishua holding the verbal part of the conversation, Tisha adding the smiles and nods and questioning glances. An hour passed, then another and before long, Ishua was telling the ladies about his childhood and sharing the favorite memory that he had about his mother, the lullaby she would sing to him and his brother each night. He sang it for them, something he had never done for anyone. Not even the woman he thought he had wanted to marry. When he opened his eyes at the end of the lullaby, he looked at Tisha and saw a single tear making its way down her lovely cheek. His heart melted as he looked into those haunting eyes. He tried to smile and play it off, but he was transfixed. He reached out to wipe the tear away and said, "I am so sorry. I know my singing isn't the best but I didn't mean to make you cry."

Tisha closed her eyes at his touch and slowly shook her head from side to side. With a monumental effort she formed a word and whispered it while he was close. "More," she whispered. He sang to her for another hour.

He looked at his watch wondering how long this escapade would last. He wanted to get back in time to have dinner with Tisha.

Chapter 82

The trial had been postponed until the preliminary findings were available to both sides. From that point, additional time would be provided for counsel to do any further investigation necessary so that justice was fairly served.

Acadius Werman was questioning himself about whether any more suitcases of cash would change the inevitable result. His client was beyond guilty. He was unpardonable and even Cady wasn't sure how to make all of this go away.

He had been enjoying a power lunch at the Four Seasons when he received a call from the judge to be in chambers in an hour. He had laughingly told her that he was in the midst of a seven course luncheon with a client and was laughingly told to put his other four courses in a doggy bag.

He sat in chambers with the judge and three of the seven prosecutors listening to the forensics report on the car and the storage unit in Joliet. The car matched the description of the one used in the hit and run. It also had damage consistent with a hit and run. Fibers and human hair were recovered from the damage on the outside of the car that matched hair taken from the victim, Tisha Copeny, at the nursing home two days ago.

Cady was grateful that he hadn't finished his lunch because he would have lost it when he realized that was only the first page of the report. Over the next hour, the forensics team showed photos and analysis of everything that they discovered. Fingerprints on the steering wheel were a perfect match with the registered owner of the car, Karl Dyson. Prints throughout the car matched Langston Morantz, the deceased Tyrone Jackson, and Karl Dyson. Underneath of the driver's seat, was a gold necklace shaped like a queen of hearts playing card that was a perfect match to the earring Alayah Brittingham had been wearing when she was found by the dumpster. The matching earring had been stored in a small wooden jewelry box at his father's house. The housekeeper had found the box while cleaning and it had been turned over to the team by Mr. Dyson's sister-in-law, Simone Dyson.

The analysis of the fibers went on and on. The color of the fibers was consistent with the color of the track suits that Tasha had testified under oath that she and her sister had been wearing that night.

At the request of the forensics team, DNA samples had been taken from Karl and Langston to match against the DNA found at the scene of the crime. The advances in twenty years had made it possible to determine that the DNA found in Alayah's body was definitely that of Karl, Langston, and possibly two other individuals.

Cady felt his temperature rise along with the food in his stomach. This wasn't going to play well on CNN or any other news feed. Maybe he could spin it on Fox—justice served after twenty years.

Black on black crime does NOT go unpunished.

He didn't know yet, but he'd figure it out. Eventually, the forensics team took a deep breath and sat down. Cady stood up and looked at the judge. "My client would like a plea deal," he said.

"Don't you have to talk to your client about that before you make a decision for him?" she asked.

"There's very little to talk about. Two counts of manslaughter are much better than two counts of first-degree murder. Don't you think? And this is just the first charge. I think he'll go for it," he said as he retrieved his briefcase and headed toward the door. "Not that it's going to make much difference by the time it's all said and done," he muttered.

"Mr. Werman, it seems that you are a bit disturbed at the moment. Is something wrong?" the judge asked.

"No, Your Honor," the attorney responded.

"Are you able to defend your client in a fair and impartial manner, Mr. Werman? Mr. Dyson is entitled to fair and just representation under the law," she said.

"Yes, he is, Your Honor. And I will provide that for him," Cady replied. He tried to smile but turned away quickly from the eyes that were watching him so closely. He left the judge's chambers and headed out of the courthouse wondering how he could give Karl his money back.

Chapter 83

"I love you," Jason said as he looked down at the beautiful face lying in the bed. He smiled and felt the joy in his heart rush to the surface. He had to contain the tears that threatened to spill as he looked down at her.

"I love you too, Daddy. I feel better now," Maia said. "You can go."

"Gee thanks," he laughed. "Just like that, you don't need me anymore," he said.

"I'll always need you, Daddy; but I don't need you right now. Does that make sense?" she giggled. Maia looked at her father and realized that he was obviously too old to understand without her help. "My bad dream is gone now. I know it was a dream and when I called for you, I knew you would come and fix it, like you always do. So, I'm good. That's why I know that you're always there when I need you," she said. She snuggled closer to her father.

"What's wrong, baby?' he asked.

"Who's there when you need somebody?" Maia asked.

Jason didn't respond because he didn't know how to. After a moment, he said, "Your mommie, Mommie Mim, Poppi, Uncle Mike, and you, of course."

Maia didn't respond for a moment. "What about Miss Simone?" she asked.

Jason was too surprised to speak.

What about Simone?

"Daddy, are you and Mommie going to get a divorce?"

"Where did that come from?" Jason asked, afraid to hear the answer.

"I was just wondering. You aren't happy anymore and Mommie is… well…Mommie," she said in a quiet voice.

"I'm happy because of you. Mommie and I love you very, very much and we're a family. You don't need to worry about things like that," he said as he held his daughter tight. "Things are just like they used to be," he said.

"I know," said Maia. "I liked it better when they weren't," she said. She leaned up and kissed Jason and said, "Goodnight, Daddy. School tomorrow. I've got a science test. I need to go to sleep. Miss Simone had taught me a trick to remember the color spectrum. I need to remember it, so I need some rest. She also said that if you get a good night's rest before something important, you will do better."

"Miss Simone knows a lot," Jason said.

"Yup. She's a smarticle. Just like us. 'Night, Daddy."

"Sleep tight, baby girl," he said as he tucked the covers around her.

Leela softly padded back to the bedroom.

Jason entered the bedroom as quietly as possible. He had a cup of coffee after the conversation with Maia. He needed time to think about what she had said—and what she didn't say. He smiled. She definitely was her grandmother's descendant. Very intuitive to be so young. Jason on the other hand was just beginning to understand on the level that the women in his family seem to be born with. What was it that Maia was thinking? How do you have those conversations with a ten-year-old?

Same way you have them with anybody else. Be quiet and listen.

He glanced over at the bed and it seemed that Leela was asleep. He left the door ajar, just in case Maia called out again. He took off his socks and climbed in the bed careful not to wake his wife. He lay there as still as possible thinking about Maia's comments. Leela rolled over and snuggled up to him putting her head on his chest and her arm on his stomach. He could feel the artificial nails through his t-shirt.

Talons.

"Hey, baby. I thought you'd never come to bed. It's lonely in here without you," she purred.

Since when? What does she want?

She pressed her body into his and kissed him on the neck. He lay still. She continued her ministrations for a few more minutes without getting any response. He could tell that she was starting to get frustrated because what had started as playful and effortless had become love for hire.

"Don't you like it? We haven't been together for a long time, and I miss you," she purred again.

No, you don't. You just want to keep me in check. This isn't the way to do it.

He took a deep breath and said, "Leela, it's late. I just got Maia back to sleep and I want to be able to hear her if she needs me again."

"Oh, so what your daughter needs is more important than what I need? Why didn't she call for me?"

'Cause she knows that you won't come. Please get off me.

"I don't know, Leela. Why don't you ask her in the morning. Now, let's get some sleep," he said as calmly as he could.

"Why don't you want me, Jason? Is it her? Is she who you want?"

Yes.

"Leela, stop it," he said.

"I won't stop it. I'm your wife. I'm right here. Why don't you want me? I've got exactly what she has, so what's the problem?"

The problem is that you are a selfish hussy who only does what is in her best interest and you think that having sex with me will make me stay. It doesn't work that way and that's what women like you don't understand. Having sex doesn't fix things. A man can have sex anywhere with anyone if that's all he really wants. It doesn't have to mean a thing other than he got some. Kind of like having a beer with the boys. Take it or leave it. That's why there are so many fatherless children in the world. Women trying to keep men that don't want to be kept. I want—need more than that. I'm not going to settle anymore. I'm tired of settling.

Jason peeled her of him and turned his back. "It's late and I have to get up in the morning." He lay there for a moment thinking about what Mim said about not doing anything to mess things up. Then it hit him. He got up and went into the bathroom and shut the door. He opened up the medicine cabinet and found the little pink container that held Leela's birth control pills. Never in the eleven years they had been married had he ever even touched them, let alone do what he was about to do. He opened the case and looked at the pills. They were all there. It was the middle of the month and she hadn't taken one pill. He put them back on the shelf and looked in the trash can. Pro-Act Ovulation kit.

Well, I'll be damned. Maybe I got some of that Copeny intuition after all.

Chapter 84

Every day in the Copeny-Anderson household had been a celebration since Florian's arrival. Tasha was glowing and the happiest that Mim had seen her since she was a child. She had noticed that about the three of her children she had access to. They were all experiencing some of the happiness that comes from loving and being loved. She sometimes wondered what was keeping Byron away from home, but she knew in her heart that would work itself out as well.

Florian fit right into the family. Both he and William were fans of real football and Florian could explain the intricacies of curling, something that had baffled William for years. Mim had a field day reading his face. He asked her to the first morning that he was there. She was surprised by his enthusiasm, and she looked at Tasha, who just shrugged her shoulders and held his hand.

"High forehead means that you are very intelligent. Could have been a scientist if you had wanted to be. The end of your nose suggests that food is very important to you," she said.

Florian shook his head and laughed. "Very much so. I would love to make dinner for everyone tonight if you would allow me. I would be so honored," he said.

"Sounds good to me," William said. "I'm pretty sure we don't have what you need, which is meat. I'll take you to the finest butcher in Chicago. Hot dang, I get to eat some meat tonight. No disrespect baby, but every now and then I like something that used to moo or baa or something. Get your coat Florian. Let's go."

The two men left together, happily discussing Messi's injury and how it might affect Argentina's chances in the World Cup.

"He's quite nice, Tasha. Suits you well. Very deep philtrum, I noticed," Mim said.

Tasha didn't respond but her eyes seemed to glaze over.

"What's wrong, Tasha? Doesn't he want children?" Mim asked.

"He does. He talks about it all the time. As soon as we get married, he wants to start a family," she started to cry.

Mim knew not to say anything. If she waited long enough, her daughter would fill the silence. It took much longer though than she had expected.

"I came home for two reasons. One was to testify at the trial," Tasha said.

"The other?" Mim prompted.

"To see a specialist because I can't have children," Tasha replied.

Tyreek stood at the nursery window, looking at his niece. She was so small and fragile-looking hooked up to all those machines. He thought it funny that she was fighting so hard for her life and her mother had lost that battle. He wanted to be sad about the loss of his sister, but considering her condition, she wouldn't have wanted to continue that way. She was one of the two people on this earth that he had ever loved.

He really didn't know his mother. She had been locked up when he was very young. Killed his dad or Ronjai's dad, or something like that. His grandmother never talked about it, so neither did he. Another woman, plagued by bad choices and leaving children behind to fend for themselves. He didn't want that for his sister's little girl—his niece.

Simone had been with him and his grandmother when the baby was delivered. His grandmother had cried profusely, her joy and pain intermingling in strains of unrelenting tears. Tyreek watched the tenderness that Simone showed to his grandmother and was glad that his sister had a woman in her life that had made her feel special and not like another piece of meat to be used at the whim of some no-good man.

Which is what happened anyway. But at least Ronnie started to feel better about herself. If she just had more time, she would have gotten it right. I know it.

Child Protective Services had been sniffing around the Neo-Natal Unit for the past week and Tyreek suspected that it had something to do with his niece. What would happen to her once she was big and healthy enough to leave the hospital? He wasn't sure but he had an idea that if he didn't do something, he was going to lose another member of his family.

Ponder and deliberate before you make a move. In war, practice dissimulation, and you will succeed. Move only if there is a real advantage to be gained.

He went to the waiting room and pulled out his cell phone. He scrolled through it until he found Mike's number.

"Hey Mr. Mike, it's Tyreek. Sorry to bother you but I was wondering if you had Miss Simone's phone number? Yeah, I got to ask her something."

Since Tyreek's phone call, Simone had been on edge. She had hoped that things were quieting down since the discovery of the car and the delivery of Ronjai's daughter. That had been a hard day for everyone concerned. The baby girl was so delicate and perfect that the sight of her made Simone's heart ache. How much more so for her family? Simone was trying to block these and so many other thoughts out of her mind by focusing on the cases piled up on her desk.

She didn't look up when she heard the rap on her office door. "Come in," she said. The door opened and Jason entered, closing the door behind him. Simone looked up, not at all expecting to see him standing by the door. They hadn't spoken much since that day at the courthouse and the few conversations that they had were strained, not at all the way that they used to be. She chalked that up to him being a father…

And a husband. So why is he here now?

"Hey, baby," he said as he opened his arms and stepped forward. Simone's body didn't know how to respond. Her first impulse was to rush into his arms where she so desperately wished to be, but her brain refused to cooperate.

Why was he here? What new shocker does he have to share with me this time?

Whatever it was, she wasn't sure that she could take it. She didn't have a big red S on her chest. She was only human, and her humanity couldn't take any more.

"What can I do for you, Jason?" she asked.

He dropped his arms and looked at her. "Whoa, I was hoping that you would let me hold you for a minute since I haven't seen you for a while," he said quietly.

"No, you haven't seen me in a while, so that's why I'm asking what

I can do for you," she said.

He put his hand to his mouth in an unconscious effort to keep his jaw from tightening. It had little effect. The room was silent for a moment before he continued, "I know that I haven't called much recently. Things have been kind of crazy lately," he said.

Yeah, a wife can do that to you.

"I'm sure they have," she replied.

"How have you been?" he asked.

"Busy," she said. He looked at the folders spread all over her desk and agreed.

"Why are you here, Jason?" she asked.

"May I sit down?" he asked as he pointed to the chair in front of her desk. He had wanted to sit in the one beside her desk hoping that he might hold her hand but thought better of it. She nodded and sat back in her chair as if she were bracing herself for what was coming.

"Your husband came to see me the other day," he began.

"My husband," she repeated.

"Yeah, your husband," he said.

"What for?" she asked.

"Your husband said for me to stay away from you," he answered.

"So here you are. Sitting in my office," she said. Jason made no reply. He wasn't sure how to reply or what was happening here, but he didn't like it. Simone started to chew her lip and he watched a dark spot start to develop between her brows. Mim had mentioned that happening to people when they were holding back intense anger, but he had never actually believed it to be true; and he was beginning to wonder if once again his mother was correct.

Simone shook her head slowly and looked at him, her eyes smoldering. "So now, he's my husband. Anytime you've ever mentioned him before, he's been Greg but now, all of a sudden, he's my husband. And now, here you are, after my husband tells you to stay away. Why, Jason?"

'Well, he is your husband, right? You are still married," he heard himself say it even as he wished that he hadn't.

"We're separated, which is more than I can say for you," she snapped. "You are quite married. You proved that a few weeks ago. So, I'm asking you again, why are you here? Are you having some sort of pissing contest with Greg or what? I am not a prize to be handed to the one with the most testosterone. You're at home with your wife and you're commenting on the state of my marriage? I'm at home alone at night, sleeping alone every night," she said.

Jason swallowed hard. He couldn't believe his ears. He had never seen Simone like this. She had always been so levelheaded and calm and now her eyes were slits and he could see that she was trembling. He leaned forward putting his hands on her desk. She drew back in her chair. He froze in his. He was at a loss. All he had wanted was to see her and hold her, to gain strength from her to deal with everything that was going on at home, talk to her about it so that he could make sense of what to do. He never imagined that she might have problems of her own. She was right, she was alone. He had promised her, right here in this very office, that he would always be there for her and within a matter of days he stood right in front of her and chose his wife over her. She had a right to be wary of whatever came out of his mouth.

You've really fucked up. She's through with you. Done. And you can't blame her. You're in bed with Pillsbury dough girl and you're here dogging her 'cause she's not divorced yet. Can you say hypocrite?

He stood up slowly. "I'm sorry, baby. I'm sorry. I wanted—needed to see you and I used Greg as an excuse instead of being a man and being honest. I fucked up. Please—please don't turn your back on me. You don't deserve me throwing my shit off on you. I'm sorry. I do love you, I do. I just don't know what I'm supposed to do…" he stopped speaking.

Simone took a deep breath and wiped a tear before it felt down her face. "Neither do I Jason, neither do I," she said quietly. She rubbed the scar on the back of her neck. Jason noticed that she did that when she was really distressed. She looked at her watch. "I think you better go now. Your family is probably waiting for you," she said.

Chapter 85

"There's too many people in this house," William said as he kissed the top of Mim's head and ran his fingers through her thick waves. "I love having Tasha home and her elf. And Maia, and J, and that wife of his, but damn, can't a man get any quiet time with his wife?"

Mim slapped William on his shoulder, "I hope you didn't call Florian that to his face. Why would you say such a thing?" she said.

"Yes, I did. He laughed and agreed. He looks just like the arrow shooting elf in those movies Maia loves to watch. Got the whole set right over there. Every time she's here, she wants to start from the beginning and watch all three. Nine hours of dwarves and elves. Blond hair down his back, skinny, ears, that's him," William laughed and hugged Mim closer to him. They were downstairs enjoying the moment. Tasha and Florian left early in the morning for an appointment at the Chicago Medical Center. Maia was at school for the first time in six days due to the snow. It was what both of them had always dreamed of—peace, calm, and most of all, love and commitment.

"So, what's going on with Tasha and Florian? They were antsy this morning," William said.

"You could tell? They tried to hide it," Mim said.

"It didn't take much to tell something is going on," William said as he stroked Mim's shoulder.

"Tasha thinks she is sterile," she said.

"So that's where they're going today. Doesn't that concern you?" William asked.

"Not really," Mim replied.

"Hmmph… I noticed you said she thinks she is. What's up with that?"

"You know how people think they can't have children and they try and try. Then, as soon as they adopt, they end up pregnant. I think Tasha might be in the same category. She's been experiencing pain, guilt, and regret for so long that she can't move on or produce. Now that she's coming to terms with all of the past, and seeing that Tisha is doing well, things might change, that's all," she said.

"I guess you have a flower for that too," William joked.

Mim turned to him and said, "Actually, there are some that…"

William placed his lips on hers until she closed her eyes. "Do you have one that will keep them out of the house for a few more hours?"

Simone hadn't had a good night's sleep since her last conversation with Jason. The word last stuck in her head like a dagger. What if it was the last one?

Then it was the last one. You'll survive. Call it a learning experience. You learned to stand on your own two feet and that you deserve to be treated decently. And whoever can't get with that, can get to steppin'. Husband, friend, dog, cat…

She smiled a weak smile and wished that things had turned out differently between her and Jason. She realized that it couldn't turn out any other way since they both were married. But she really loved him, and she was grateful that she had the opportunity to experience love even if she had lost.

It was nice while it lasted. Really nice. It would have been even nicer if I had a chance to...

She rolled over again in her king-sized bed and noticed the red light blinking on her phone. She picked it up to see what new problem was waiting to be added to her list.

I'm worried about you—about us. I know I messed up. Please forgive me.

Yes, you did. And there is no us and I'm going to be just fine.

She read the message two more times expecting it to change. She sat up wondering how to respond. If she responded from the heart, she would say there was no need for forgiveness, that's what friends do. If she responded from her head, she would say there was no need for forgiveness, that's what friends do. Since she wasn't trusting either her head or her heart, she plugged in the charger and turned the phone off. She knew that he would understand the tone no matter which part of her wrote it.

Even a fool seems wise when they choose not to speak.

She got out of bed and went to the kitchen and turned on the kettle. It was looking like it was going to be another long night....

The next morning arrived the same as always, early. She couldn't remember what time it was when she finally climbed back in the bed. She reached for the phone to check her schedule hoping that she had nothing pressing waiting for her. Feeling relieved that there was nothing that needed her immediate attention today, she took a deep breath and checked her text messages. Nothing from Jason.

Even a fool seems wise...

There were two missed calls from her husband.

Oh, hell no. Haven't I had enough drama to last me a lifetime? Hey, maybe that's where the name for that TV channel came from. Why hadn't I thought of that sooner?

Bizarre thoughts were running around in her head due to another night with hardly any sleep. She startled at the soft chimes of the doorbell. Her eyes narrowed as she wondered who would be at her door at this time of morning. Not Jason. He would never drive out to her house without her permission. They had only seen each other at the condo.

No, he would never. Then who?

She put on her hoodie over her t-shirt and zipped it up.

God, please, no. Don't let this be who I think it is. Please, please, please.

She looked through the glass side panels of the mahogany door, took a deep breath and pondered whether she should open it. "Hello, Greg. What can I do for you?" she said.

"May I come in? It's really cold out here," he said as he blew into his cupped hands.

That's what gloves are for.

"What can I do for you, Greg?" she repeated.

Is this déjà vu, ground hog day, or what? Is this going to turn out as badly as the last time?

She thought about it and stepped aside.

Not if you don't want it to.

"Come in," she said as she pointed to the foyer. "Have a seat." Greg noticed that she didn't offer to take his coat or lead him any farther into the house. The foyer was as spacious as some living rooms with comfortable bench seats that he had never sat on—until now. She sat on one of the benches opposite his—waiting for him to announce why he was there.

"How have you been? You look good, but then again you always look good," he said as he mustered a smile. Simone watched him carefully wondering what was going through his mind.

Why is he here so early? I'm barely out of bed...that no good bum, he thinks Jason might be here, so he gets here at the crack of dawn trying to catch me....

"What's wrong? You okay? You're face looks funny. You feeling alright?"

"I'm fine. I just got up and I'm wondering why you are here so early," she said as she tried to unscrunch her eyebrows.

"I just wanted to talk to you for a minute. Is that alright? I am your husband still," he said.

Nobody is willing to let me forget that. If I hear that one more time...

"Are you sure you're alright? Did somebody do something to you at work or last night?" he asked with a concerned look on his face.

Simone closed her eyes and took a deep breath.

Here we go. This is it. If you really want to be through with this man—here's your chance.

"Yes, Greg. Someone did do something to me. You did something to me. You show up here at the crack of dawn uninvited. I'm having a hard time understanding why but the conclusion that I have come to makes me incredibly angry and you need to explain yourself so that I can let go of this anger or you need to get out of my house," she said as she stood up and stepped toward him. He sat back on the bench feeling his back press against the wall.

"I wanted to have a civil conversation with you, but it seems that someone upset you before I got here," he said.

How long have I been married to this ass?

She rubbed her eyes and laughed out loud. Greg cocked his head to the side and looked at her as if she was possessed. She looked down at the floor and sat back down. She leaned forward and placed her elbows on her knees and closed her eyes. Greg began to wonder if she was praying.

"Okay, Greg, what do you want to talk about?" she asked calmly.

Wow. Prayer does change things.

He took a deep breath and chose his smooth 'I got this voice', the one he used to use on her when he was planning to step out for recreational purposes.

"I realize that we have had some problems recently and I wanted to let you know that I'm willing to put all that behind us—chalk it up to midlife crisis on both of our parts—and move on from here… together," he crooned.

Simone heard the words he said, and they sounded sincere and well chosen. The problem with his speech was it sounded exactly the same way it used to sound when he was lying about where he was going to be for the next two days and nights. She could hear those times so clearly in her head.

I realize that I've been away on business a lot recently but in a position like mine—it just comes with the territory…

She sat back and raised her eyebrows, waiting him out. *Breathe in, breathe out, breath in…*

"Simone, I love you. I know that now and you know that, right? I want us to stop this and act like married people. This isn't good for anybody. How do you think it looks?" he sputtered.

It looks like you're finally getting yours is what it looks like. It looks like appearances are still the only thing that matters to you. It looks like you don't have your trophy wife to make you seem less like an asshole.

She shook her head. She really hadn't had enough sleep. She needed to hold her tongue before all of that came rushing out of it. She didn't have the energy or inclination at this time of the morning to try too hard, but what good would it do her to ride the arch of anger with someone who clearly didn't have her best interest in mind?

"So, you love me, and you want us to act like married people because this looks bad. Is that right?" she asked.

Don't do that mediation shit to me!

"Baby, I miss you. I know I've made some mistakes. We both have but I want to work this out, don't you?" he hesitated before continuing. "We were good together once. We can be again if you'll just give it a chance. I know you're angry and hurt and you probably want some sort of payback, I understand that. So, you've had your fun, I get it. It doesn't feel too cool…" he said.

"So, this is all a big joke to you. You think I am trying to pay you back for hurting me, is that right? Please tell me that I'm not hearing you correctly," she said, her voice starting to tremble with disbelief. "Because I don't want to be married to you and somebody else might notice that I exist, you think that I'm trying to punish you? Are you nuts? I'd have to care about you much more than I do to put that much effort into it. Greg, let me make this as plain as possible for you," she paused.

Lord help me, then forgive me.

"I don't care about you, don't care to be with you, and really don't care what happens to you anymore. I'm through, I'm done, and it's over. It should have been over a long time ago, but I was too weak and afraid of being alone. I'd rather put up with your shit than to think that I wasn't good enough to be loved by somebody. Well, guess what? I am good enough. Finally, I realize that I'm good enough because I love me and that's all I really need. And I'm not afraid anymore. So, thank you for being such a good teacher but the lesson has been learned. I don't need you and I don't want you. <u>Do</u> you understand that?"

Her heart was pounding and the blood was rushing to her head like a tsunami. Greg looked at her and for the first time in their marriage saw what a powerful woman she truly was. He had always known it but never thought that she would figure it out, and to think that he had been the cause of her 'awakening' made him sick to his stomach.

"I'd better go," he murmured. He stood up and gathered his coat around him.

What was I thinking? She's even fiercer than I thought she could be.

He walked to the door, the sound of his shoes on the marble tiles echoed throughout the foyer. She followed him to the door and waited for him to open it—for the last time. "Whatever you plan to do, could you please wait until after this whole trial fiasco is done? Let things calm down a little bit first before…well…before…," he said.

"I can do that. Dad is going through enough without having to deal with one more mistake that his sons have made. You might want to visit him some time. Call first though, Sheva might want to leave early that day," Simone said as she shut the door behind him.

Chapter 86

The trial was winding down. It was still the flavor of the day and Karl had had his and plenty of other people's fifteen minutes of fame. Cady was proving just what a phenomenal lawyer he was because Karl was still free on his own recognizance, even after all of the charges had been addressed. The weeks had turned into a few months and the new normal had kicked in and everyone was adjusting as much as possible.

The round booth reserved for special events at DiTaglio's was filled with happy faces. The first time in what seemed like ages these particular faces had anything to be happy about. Tasha and Florian, Mrs. Henderson, Tyreek, and Simone raised glasses of non-alcoholic champagne in a toast to the wonderful news.

"Our little girl is almost big enough to leave the hospital," Florian said as he held Tasha's hand. "We want to thank you all for making it possible for us to become parents and to help us choose a name beautiful enough for our daughter." His eyes were moist, and his voice filled with emotion. "We've been looking for a furnished apartment so that we'll have a place of our own until she's big enough to go home. Mim and William don't need a baby crying at night and we have to get used to doing all the things a baby needs and…" Tasha touched his cheek and he realized that he was rambling.

"He gets like that sometime. He's trying to say…we're trying to say thank you for allowing us to adopt her. We can never, ever, thank you enough. You all will have to come visit her and watch her grow up. You are her family, and she needs to know, all of you," she said as she looked at Simone. "We are all family now."

They talked and ate a fabulous meal that impressed even Florian. By the time dessert was served, they had decided on a name. Pia Gisele, and Simone had offered her condo for as long as the new family should need it. Tasha was in tears and grabbed Simone's hand and dashed off to the restroom to compose herself.

As they were about to leave the restroom, Tasha said, "You need to talk to him." Simone had no idea why she would say that, she and Florian had a wonderful conversation during dinner. "He is really messed up and it's only going to get worse if you continue to ignore him." Now Simone understood. It surprised her that she could go a couple of days at a time and find that she wasn't dwelling on how much she missed Jason.

But I do miss him even though….

"I'm not ignoring him. What am I supposed to do? He's got a family. Not just a daughter but a wife, he made that really clear," she said, hoping that she didn't sound bitter or resentful.

"In name only. He and Maia still spend almost every night in town. You didn't know that did you? That's another reason that Florian and I were looking for a place. Leela stops by and tries to get J to come home at night, but he always comes up with a reason to stay with Maia. And Maia, poor baby, wants to be wherever her daddy is, so it's quite a mess," Tasha said as she smoothed her dress.

"Why are you telling me this? He made a choice, what can I do about that?" Simone asked as she stared at her reflection, watching it turn from happy to sad.

"Yes, he made a choice. But you're looking but not seeing," Tasha said sounding very much like her mother.

"What do you mean?" Simone asked as she shifted her gaze to her friend.

"Yes, he made a choice, and it wasn't you. He didn't choose Leela, he chose Maia, don't you understand? He chose the only other person he loves more than you," Tasha said.

Simone stood there thinking about what Tasha had said. Tasha hugged her and gave her a kiss on the cheek. "Take your time, I'll eat your dessert," Tasha giggled as she walked out of the bathroom.

Simone walked toward the front door of the restaurant for a breath of fresh air and a moment to think. As she stood there looking across the street at the Hilton, she recognized the mountain of a man that was getting out of the taxi. It was the nurse from the hospital.

He could rival Shaq…

He held the door open for a woman who came up to his elbow. She was fawning all over him and making a spectacle of both of them as he paid the driver. Simone watched the PDA and wondered what it would be like to do something like that. She looked closer and thought that the woman looked familiar.

Maybe one of the participants in the hundreds of mediations I've had done.

She looked again and it hit her where she had seen the woman. Simone had been on the floor of the courthouse huddled behind the benches looking up at the woman as she clung to her husband, Jason. She watched the couple walk into the hotel.

The check had been paid and Tyreek was helping his grandmother put on her coat when Simone made it back to the table.

"Are you alright? I was about to come back to look for you. You look like you've seen a ghost," Tasha said.

Simone shook her head, sat down, and reached for a glass of water.

I wish I had. I would feel much better.

Chapter 87

"Why don't you come with me and Sly this weekend. Chicago is playing in Minneapolis, and you know who's gonna win. Don't you want get outta town for a few? From the looks of you lately, it might be a good idea to have a change of scenery. Besides, then you can help with the gas. Cheaper divided by three," Mike said.

Jason sat at the bar nursing his third Corona and eating wings to absorb the alcohol. It wasn't working as well as he had hoped. He heard Mike and was still clear headed enough to realize that he was trying to provide a distraction. That wasn't working either. Time was supposed to heal all wounds so maybe a substantially larger amount was needed because he wasn't feeling any better about the last time he had been with Simone. He had sent her a text asking for forgiveness and he got no response. He checked the phone two or three times a day hoping for something, even if she just told him to drop dead. At least he would know that she felt something. This silence meant that she didn't care enough to respond.

Or her phone was broke. Or the 4G network tower was down. Or a bird flew into the satellite. Or sunspots….

"Another beer, please," he said to the bartender. She glanced at Mike before giving Jason another frosty mug. Mike just nodded.

"So, what do you say? Guys weekend. God knows we deserve it. All the shit that's been going on recently… oh, I'm sorry man. I didn't mean you and….well, you know…," Mike took a deep gulp of his Coors and wiped his mouth. "Too much to drink. I don't know how either one of us is getting home tonight," he said.

"It's okay. Don't have much to go home to. At least I don't. Maia's in town so no worries for her. I need to be straight enough to say goodnight though, so I need to stop after this one," Jason said.

"Man, I know it's none of my business, but you really need to talk to Simone. I don't know what happened with ya'll, but you been a real mess for the past few weeks. It can't be just work that's got you so fucked up and Sly says Simone isn't herself recently either. What did you do, man? It had to be you 'cause only you can fuck shit up without trying," Mike said.

Jason looked at the big brother he never had and laughed. Mike was relieved to see that his best friend was still in there somewhere.

"You're right, I did it. She trusted me and I screwed her over and expected her to sit there and wait for me to decide whether to shit or get off the pot," he said.

"So, what are you gonna do? Stay on the pot acting constipated or what? You know that can kill you? That's what happened to Elvis. He should have known his situation before he sat down. Then he could have done something different…," Mike took one of the wings sitting in front of Jason and bit into it. "Not that your Elvis or anything," he said between chews.

Jason shook his head and grabbed another wing that he was paying for before they were all gone.

"Maybe I will go with you guys. Give me a chance to do something different. Maia will be fine with moms and pops, just like always, so it's all good. Nothing I need to go home for. God knows that's the last place I want to be. It'll give me a chance to clear my head," he said.

"Yeah, 'cause you're full of shit, and the Kaopectate you're using ain't working. Bartender, he'd like another order of wings, please. And this time could he have fries with that?" Mike said as he licked his fingers so he could text the good news to Sly.

The rest of the week was uneventful and passed quicker than Jason expected. He was almost looking forward to hanging out with Mike and Sly. He only hoped that the topic of the Simone didn't come up. Then again, maybe in some sick and twisted way it might make him feel better to be able to talk about it and hear other people say her name. He thought about that and smiled as he remembered her explaining about the mental masturbation that a person gets from hearing their name or the name of someone they love.

Simone Simone Simone....

They picked Sly up immediately after lunch on Friday and hit the interstate before traffic slowed their progress. Mike had been right for once, the laughter and conversation and talk about the game did make Jason feel a little more like himself. For the first time in a month, he felt as if he didn't have any worries. He could even take a deep breath. How long had it been since he had one of those? They were making good time, another two hours of driving and they would be in the Twin Cities.

"Maybe we'll check out Paisley Park after the game. His Purpleness is still the man around there. A good game and good music after— what more could you want?" Sly said.

"Maybe one of those left over Sheila E, Apollonia wannabes would be nice," Mike replied. They laughed and talked while Jason stared out the back window. He was glad to not have to ride shotgun with Mike this time.

As he tried to relax and enjoy the moment, his cell phone vibrated. His first thought was about Simone and then he thought again. She wouldn't just text him out of the blue after all this time, would she? He reached in his pocket and pulled out the phone, secretly hoping and praying it was her and not something to ruin his trip. He checked the ID and it wasn't who he hoped it would be. In fact he couldn't figure out why Leela's sister would be texting him. Had something happened to her?

Do I really care?

He tried to curb the enthusiasm of that thought and opened the text. It looked like she had sent him pictures. That was nice but if it didn't say Leela was dead or dying then he didn't have to deal with it right now. He'd look at photos of Leela's family later. Right now, he was feeling pretty good and he didn't want to mess that up.

Chapter 88

The weekend had been good, real good. Chicago won by twenty-three. They would need that win because they would be on the road at Miami in two days. Paisley Park had been all that he had ever heard it was. The Mall of the Americas proved to the perfect place to find perfect gifts for Maia. Sly volunteered to drive back so Jason resumed his spot in the back seat. He was good with that. It had been a relaxing and quiet weekend. Free from drama and the hint of impending drama that he usually had when he was at home.

At least Leela hadn't messed up this trip.

In fact, she hadn't called or texted him the entire time.

God is good.

Jason got dropped off at his parents' house to an excited and happy Maia.

"Daddy, Daddy, I'm so glad your home! I missed you. I'm glad you got to play with your friends. I know that it's important to have a sleepover with your BFFs but I'm still glad you came back," she said.

"I'll always be back, baby. You know that. Come here and give me a big hug. I missed you too. Did you have a good time while I was gone? What did you do?" he asked as he scooped her up in his arms.

"Well, Auntie Tasha and Uncle Florian took me to the movies, then, we had pizza and went bowling. It was so much fun. Mommie Mim taught me how to make bread. Poppi watched movies with me, and we ate popcorn and stayed up late. It was fun!" she said.

"What did you and Mommie do?" he asked.

"Nothing. She hasn't been here since you left. I guess she was occupied," she said.

"Occupied? Where'd you learn that word?" he asked.

"I'm a smarticle, remember?" she said proudly.

"Yes, you are, baby. Yes, you are," he said. "Let's get you settled. Then I will come up and let you read me a story so I can sleep well tonight," he said.

"So, you'll be here tonight?" she asked.

"Right down the hall, just like always," he said.

"Good. Put me down so that I can practice your bedtime story. I'll call you when I'm ready," she said.

Twenty minutes later, Maia read her favorite book, The Velveteen Rabbit, for the hundred and twelfth time. Jason tucked her in after saying their prayers and headed down the hall to his bedroom. He emptied his pockets and lay down on the bed. He looked at his phone and remembered that he had postponed checking the text that Leela's sister sent two days ago. He really didn't feel like it but… what the fuck.

He opened the text and enlarged the photo so that he could see… *what the fuck?* He looked more carefully at the picture to be sure that he saw what he thought he saw. The zoom only went so far but it didn't change the images that he saw in front of him. He immediately sat up and texted Leela's sister.

We need to talk.

The response came immediately.

What took u so long? I've been waiting 2 hear from u. Meet me at SoulPub. I can b there in 30. I have more

Jason almost choked. He got up and checked on Maia. She was sound asleep. He got his coat and hat and left the house as quietly as he could. This was one time that he didn't want to have to share why he was leaving the house in the middle of the night.

He drove downtown carefully, making sure to fully stop at signs and lights. No need getting arrested for traffic violations when he had something more serious in mind.

SoulPub was fairly crowded, which was normal for a Sunday night. People wanting to get their groove on one more time before the work week started. He looked around until he saw Krystal sitting in a booth by the kitchen.

How appropriate.

She looked up as he sat down. Her eyes were swollen, and her hair was completely disheveled. Very un-Krystal like.

"How could they? My own sister! After I took her into my house and fed her and put a roof over her head! What was she thinking? What are we going to do?" she cried. She ran her hands through her hair and Jason could see how it had ended up the way it was. On the table was an envelope. He picked it up and dumped the contents on the table. Several photos landed face down but from what Jason could see of the ones that were face up, the others could stay the way they were. He thumbed through them while Krystal sat with her hands over her mouth.

"How did you get these?" he asked.

"I hired somebody," she whispered through her fingers.

"What made you do that, Krystal? What happened?" he asked as gently as he could. Krystal had been the one member of Leela's family that had any sense. He could see her pain and he hurt for her.

"I got this feeling one day. I came upstairs and saw them outside of the bathroom grinning at each other. He was helping her tighten her towel after she got out of the shower. They were just too close and grinny, you know? It didn't feel right—the way he was touching her. And after that, I'd see her looking at him and watch her switching through the house like she was in heat or something. So, I went online and found a private investigator, and this is what I got. I've got more on my phone but these are for you," she said as she slid them closer to him. "What am I supposed to do, Jason? I can't afford to leave him. It's the same thing if I put him out. The kids are almost ready for college, and I can't pay the mortgage and all the bills by myself. I knew that he had…tendencies but I never expected with my own sister. I worked two jobs to help him through nursing school. If I had known that this was going to happen, I could have worked two jobs to save money for myself. What am I supposed to do?" she asked again.

"Do they know about these?" he asked as he pointed to the pictures. She shook her head unable to speak. "Do you have any idea where he is now?"

"He worked a double tonight. At least that's what he said," she said.

"Go home, Krystal. It is your home. Go be with your kids. Can you make it okay? Do you need me to drive you home?" he asked.

"No, I got here. I can get home. Thanks, Jason. I'm sorry to spring this on you but I thought you needed to know too. What should we do now?" she asked.

"I don't know yet. Go home and I'll call you tomorrow morning. I need some time to think. It's going to be okay. One way or the other, it will work out," he said. He helped her with her coat and squeezed her hand and walked her to the street where he hailed a taxi. He watched the taxi pull off and heard Krystal's words in his head.

What do we do now?

He'd have to think about that later because right now he was having difficulty remembering where he had parked.

Once he finally found the car, he sat in it for a long period of time wondering what he should do now. He couldn't tell his parents about it just yet. Mike wasn't the person to talk to either. That 'I told you so' look would be on his face even if he didn't mean for it to be. He couldn't burden his sister with this. There was no one for him to call—no one for him to talk to. He wanted to talk to Simone but that was out of the question.

You sure? She would listen. Even if she doesn't love you anymore, she'd still listen because that's what friends do, right?

Jason wasn't even sure that she was his friend, so he started the car and drove to wherever the car took him.

It took him to his house. He parked outside and saw that the garage door was open with the Buick parked inside. He walked through the garage and into the house. The lights were off downstairs, so he figured that Leela was asleep.

Which might be a good thing right now.

He had his phone in one hand, the photos in the other. He couldn't seem to let go of either. He went up the steps as quietly as possible not wanting to awaken her while he was in the state of mind that he was in. He wondered why he had come back here at all.

'Cause it's my damn house…and there's nowhere else to go….

The light was on in the bedroom.

So, she must not be asleep.

He took a deep breath and headed toward the open door trying to figure out what he should say. When he got to the door, he didn't have to say anything. Two bodies were facing him on the bed. Shaq's twin brother's eyes were closed and his tongue hanging out as he forcefully thrust himself into Jason's wife who was on all fours with her face buried in a pile of goose down pillows. They were so caught up in the moment that they didn't notice that he was there until the flash went off as he took a picture. Leela recovered first and jumped off the bed grabbing for clothes that she had dropped earlier. Shaq was too far gone to be able to recover and kept thrusting until his body gave him permission to stop. Jason took a picture of that too.

A picture is worth a thousand words.

"J baby, what are you doing here?" she squealed as she stood in front of him with nothing on but an attitude. He couldn't respond so he just threw the pictures on the bed. By this time Shaq had finished his gyrations and was trying to decide whether to reach for the pictures or for his drawers. The look on Jason's face said it all. He put on his pants, then picked up a few of the pictures sprawled all over the rumbled bed.

"Your wife gave me those," Jason said. Leela had stepped closer to Jason and looked up at him. She reached out and put her hand on his chest as if she wanted him to finish what Shaq had started on the bed. The man in front of her and the man behind her looked at each other and then at her.

"Baby, it's not what you think. You were acting all crazy like you didn't want me and I needed to feel that there was nothing wrong with me and…." She started to cry and stepped closer to Jason as if she wanted him to hold her. He took a step back. She noticed and stepped back as well. "What, I'm not good enough for you?" She turned around and pointed to her lover. "He sure thinks I am. What's wrong with me Jason? You used to think I was good enough!" Jason turned his back and walked away. She was still ranting when he came out of the bathroom and put her robe around her shoulders.

"Leela, I'll give you until tomorrow to pack your shit and be out of here." He looked at Shaq. "I suggest that you call Krystal before she calls the hospital looking for you." He turned around and walked toward the hallway.

"What do you mean, be out of here? Where am I supposed to go? What am I supposed to do?" Leela cried, her tone changing quickly from the haughty vixen she was five minutes ago.

"I really don't care Leela. Go with him… Just stay away from my daughter and get out of this house," he said. "And don't take anything with you that you didn't pay for."

Jason put his phone in his pocket and left the same way that he had entered. The rage he was feeling was causing his temples to throb and he knew that if he had stayed a moment longer someone would have been seriously injured. He couldn't figure out what it was exactly that had him so enraged. It was obvious what it should have been but that wasn't it. He was angry that he hadn't been man enough a month ago to make a different choice. He did have choices, he just had realized it at that moment. He had lost the one he truly loved.

And for what?

In his misguided effort to give his daughter the type of family that he never had, he lost his chance to have the type of family that he truly wanted. It hit him like a ton of bricks how much he wanted Simone and that he was willing to do anything he had to do to be with her. He had been weak and stupid, and now he was angry. He walked back to the garage and looked at the Buick.

She's not taking anything that she didn't pay for.

He picked up a cinder block that was beside the wall and launched it through the driver's window. The shattered glass went all over the garage.

I pay the payments on this and everything up in here.

He picked up another cinder block and threw it through the windshield.

And I pay the insurance…I dare Mayhem to say shit to me right now.

It didn't.

Chapter 89

The sentencing phase of the trial was to start next Monday. The jurors had done their civic duty and been released to continue with their lives. If they had believed their lives to be dull and uneventful before the trial, they were more than thankful to have those kinds of lives after the trial. Now, the judge was the one to carry the weight of justice in deciding the type of punishment to be meted out to the now infamous Karl Dyson.

Cady was concerned, that based on the verdict, Karl might be fortunate to be sentenced to multiple life sentences without the hope of parole. The only other option that existed was…well…not much of an option. He knocked on the door of Karl's condo in the sky and silently prayed that he wouldn't answer. The policeman stationed outside of the door stood up and approached it after the fourth unanswered knock.

The door opened slowly, and Karl stepped aside, allowing his lawyer to enter. Karl shut the door behind him and walked over to the wall of windows. He picked up his glass of scotch and sipped, "You know it's good that these windows don't open. One misstep and bam! Flying through the air with the greatest of ease. Might be a better possibility than what's waiting for me." He took another sip and continued to stare out on the city.

Cady watched Karl to see what type of prank he was pulling this time but nothing about Karl's demeanor or body language revealed that he was anything other than sincere. Cady knew sincerity when he saw it in Karl because he didn't see it very often.

"What are you here for, Cady?" Karl asked without turning around. Cady wasn't sure how to answer. He had been planning to inform Karl of what would probably happen at the sentencing next week but now he wasn't so sure that was the best idea.

"I just wanted to see how you were holding up, see if you wanted anything," he replied.

"Last meal and all that, huh?" Karl mumbled.

"Why would you say that? It's only Tuesday," Cady said, trying to make a joke.

"Who needs to wait 'til next Monday? Done is done, no matter when it comes, you know?" Karl said as he finished the scotch. "Well, if that's all Cady, I'm really tired and I want to get some rest. I didn't know how tired I was until today. I'm so tired of it all. All the scheming and lying…. Thanks for everything though. You did good there for a while. I almost thought I might get off …'til…well, you know, you were there, right?"

Cady didn't know what to say so he didn't say anything except, "You're welcome." Karl made no effort to escort him to the door, so Cady let himself out. After he left, Karl poured another glass of scotch and went into the bathroom and opened the medicine cabinet and started reading the labels on the prescription bottles. He found one Vicodin and one for Oxycontin that he had filled for pain from the root canal last year. The dates had expired but he figured it didn't really matter. It would suit his purposes just fine.

CNN was on the flat screen TV with the sound turned down just the way he liked it. It was almost time for Frederica to do her thing.

Who needed to hear what was being said anyway? The scrolling commentary made it easy to catch up if you got distracted while doing other things like ringing up customers or restocking shelves.

AMIATT was really busy this week. Shetrator Aria, the best new author of the year—according to Oprah, was doing a book signing today and tomorrow and everybody and their brother had been buying the book. And that really included brothers.

And they say we don't read. If more people wrote stuff like this, more of us would read.

Cornelius thought about all the reading that he did during his former life. He snickered a little because it had saved his life *on so many levels.* He remembered when he first got locked up. A gray-haired old lifer, must have been close to a hundred then, was reading the novel, *Native Son.* Harlem looked at the man and said, "Why you reading that shit, old man? It ain't gonna get you out of here!"

"Youngblood," the old man replied, "If I had read this shit, I wouldn't be in here. Maybe you should heed the lesson."

"Shut up, old man. I ain't got time for no books," Harlem said with much bravado.

"Youngblood, all you got is time. Put it to good use," the old man said as he returned to his book. Harlem watched the man day after day, always reading something. James Baldwin, Homer, Alex Haley, Thomas Payne, Alexandre Dumas, Arthur Conan Doyle, Leo Tolstoy…the list went on and on.

"Old man, why you read so much? Don't it bore you?" Harlem asked one day.

"I'd rather be in here," the old man said pointing to the book, "than in here," he continued, looking around the prison block. Harlem thought about what the old man had said, and the next day picked up a book from the library cart when it came past his cell. *The Spook Who Sat By the Door.* He picked it up because of the title. He finished reading it because of the message. He was so excited about what he had read that he scoured the rec space looking for the old man. When he saw him, he and his book were sprawled out on the floor, surrounded by a group of spikey haired Aryan wannabes with swastika tattoos all over their arms, necks, and chests.

One of them was talking loud when Harlem approached them, "This old coon can't read. Bet he can sing though. You know what they say, if you want a blackie to know something, put it in a song. If you want to hide something from 'em put it in a book." The wannabes laughed and walked away. Harlem etched the face of the loudmouth into his brain for future reference. He picked up his friend and carried him back to his cell—along with his book, *The Prince*, by Machiavelli.

Two weeks later, Wannabe was flown to shock trauma and never returned to Big Muddy. The story was that he had been found in the shower bleeding profusely from the mouth. When someone tried to ask him what happened, he couldn't speak. Seemed his tongue had been severed with a dull blade and cut into little pieces and left on the tile floor beside him. It was the talk of the prison for the next month. Harlem showed the appropriate amount of shock when he heard about it.

Bet he won't say nothing else about black folks reading books.

Machiavelli would have been proud.

Cornelius was a little concerned about the serious look on Frederica's face and then he saw the bright orange headline 'Breaking News' flashing across the screen. He stopped to read the subheading.

Well, I'll be damned... what has Karl gone and done now?

Chapter 90

I don't want to live behind bars for the rest of my life and I don't want to die with a needle in my arm on display for a YouTube video. If I'm gonna die, it's gonna be on my terms, by my hand. Not somebody else's.

Karl stood in front of the bathroom mirror and stared. How did he get here? And where was he about to go? He went back into the kitchen and took the pestle and mortar from the shelf that he had picked up in Hawaii. The volcanic rock made such a smooth surface for finely crushing herbs and peppercorns—and prescription pills. It was funny how relaxing it was to stand there applying force with the pestle and seeing the fruits of your labor. If it had been under different circumstances, Karl would have truly enjoyed the moment.

The television was on the Westerns channel and just as luck would have it, the villain was sentenced to be hanged in the morning. Karl couldn't help himself so he turned to see if there would be a reprieve or pardon. He knew better. Even in fiction—the villain always paid for his crime.

So be it. Fuck you and the horse you rode in on. That's tomorrow. Tonight is all good and I'm gonna have my last fucking meal. What goes good with Vicodin?

He left the kitchen and sat on the Italian leather sofa and pulled out his cell phone and called his favorite restaurant on the Magnificent Mile, The Capital Grille. The steaks were to die for. Sad choice of words but they were incredible. He placed his order along with the most expensive Shiraz they had. Since he was feeling magnanimous, he ordered a steak for the cop outside of his door.

It is his last night after all. What the fuck. I don't want him to feel that it's been all for nothing. After he ordered and paid via credit card, he called for his favorite messenger service to pick it up.

Yeah, life is still good…at least for another few hours anyway.

There was a knock on his door sixty-seven minutes later. Karl opened it and accepted the elegantly boxed meals. He smiled at the cop and paid the messenger a handsome tip. Half the cost of the meal. Not bad for twenty minutes work.

"Would you like to join me for dinner?" Karl asked the officer.

"Excuse me sir?" the officer asked.

"Would you like to join me for dinner? I ordered two steaks, and I can't eat them both, even though I would like to try," Karl said.

"I'm on duty sir. But thank you for asking," said the officer.

"What's your name? You know, you've been out here every night for what—two months? I don't even know your name," Karl said.

"Thomas Carvey, sir," the officer said.

"Well, Thomas, you have to eat, right? And you can keep an eye on me while you do it. Come on in. I'd like some company tonight," Karl said, being as sincere as he could be. Officer Carvey entered the apartment and looked around at the plush surroundings. Karl invited him to have a seat in the living room while he fixed the plates.

"Would you like some wine? I have an excellent imported Shiraz," Karl said.

"No thank you sir, I'm…" Carvey started.

"I know, you're on duty," Karl mumbled. He was about to open the Shiraz and thought better of it. He'd save that for after dinner when he was by himself. He took out two glasses and two Pepsi. He looked at the mortar and pestle and wondered if this would be a good time to start his adventure. A little hit in his Pepsi wouldn't be noticeable. He could pretend he was just making his meal a little bit more enjoyable. The fine powder mixed into the soda completely. As Karl carried the glasses into the dining room, his cell phone vibrated. He put the glasses down and went into the bedroom to see what Cady had to say.

Carvey was standing at the wall of windows admiring the view when Karl walked back into the room. He turned around when he heard Karl's footsteps.

"Sorry, I was thirsty, so I drank mine early," Carvey said holding up his glass. Karl looked back at the table and then at Carvey.

Which glass did he pick up? I wasn't planning to kill a cop tonight.

The two men sat down and enjoyed dinner. Karl drank the remaining soda with his steak, waiting to feel the effects of the drugs.

Maybe I should have had the wine.

 After dinner and conversation with Thomas, Karl thanked him for the company. Carvey shook Karl's hand and went back to his spot on the other side of the door. Karl went to the sofa with the excellent bottle of Shiraz and waited for whatever would happen next.

Whatever would happen next was nothing. Karl felt nothing except the pleasant sensation brought about by expensive imported wine. He had felt that before on numerous occasions and this occasion was no different. And it should have been. Karl checked his watch—10:37. He was on his second Playboy Pay Per View and he was beginning to wonder if the expiration date on the Vicodin really did matter. He got up from the sofa when Bambi started to talk—there really wasn't much of a plot—so he figured he wasn't missing anything. If you've listened to one porn star, you could have listened to the toilet flush and gotten more out of it. He was on his way to the kitchen to grind more pills when he stopped suddenly and walked back toward the front door. He opened it slightly and peeked out to see

Officer Carvey slumped in his chair. Karl leaned out a little farther and squinted to see if he was still breathing. After a few moments of observation, Karl walked out and investigated more carefully.

He's breathing and he's not foaming at the mouth…so he's not dead. But he's out cold.

Karl stood there and stared at the unconscious officer. He checked his Rolex again, the shift didn't change until 7:00am. He went back into his apartment and locked the door.

Karl loved spy movies and thrillers where the heroes had so many flaws that the bad guys were afraid of them. Most of those movies taught really useful lessons such as always have your getaway bag packed and ready to go. So, Karl, being a really good bad guy, had his bag packed and ready to go should he ever need it. Tonight, he needed it. He pulled it out from the back of his walk-in closet and checked the contents—passports, credit cards and bank account information under the name of Ron J. Henderson—he'd been making large deposits and small withdrawals for the past year with no problem, so he expected that to continue in his new home— wherever that would be.

Can you say south of the border?

He loaded the duffel with a few toiletries and stopped at the wall safe in the living room for the final items. Fifty of them—packs of hundreds and twenties and a few tens for incidentals. He didn't want to draw attention. The duffel was large, so they fit quite nicely. The weight was considerable but what was that old song? *It ain't heavy, it's my money….*

 Karl made one last check of Officer Carvey before he got on the elevator and disappeared.

Chapter 91

The sentencing phase of the trial started on Monday with as much fanfare as every other part of the trial. The defendant was to be sentenced *in absentia,* since Karl had overcome the defenseless officer and drugged him, leaving him for dead. Officer Carvey had been questioned mercilessly for the past five days by the federal alphabet squad about his part in Karl's escape. When Officer Carvey repeated the same story time after time to the most advanced lie detector in existence, he was placed on administrative leave without pay pending an Internal Affairs investigation.

Officer Carvey should have been distraught over the loss of pay while under investigation, but he was an honest man and knew that he was innocent of any crime or conspiracy. And the fist-sized roll of hundreds he found shoved inside his pocket when he was revived helped a great deal. He had considered turning it over to the authorities as evidence but then he felt that God was providing for his needs since he found it before the paramedics. He had read and reread the attached note trying to make sense of it all.

I meant you no harm. Consider this a tip for your labor.

The courtroom was filled once again with all of the important players—feds, family and friends. Simone stood in the back of the courtroom trying to hold down her nausea from being in this place one more time. Had anything good happened in this room? She couldn't think of a thing.

Cady and the prosecutors were stationed at their respective tables waiting for the final round of the fight of the century. From anyone's perspective, neither one of them won the battle—although Cady won the prize. He defended the sleaziest criminal that Chicago had seen since Dillinger and people would feel sorry for him because he was duped, lead astray, used… Yeah, Cady could work with this. Maytag had nothing on his spin cycle.

Ishua sat with Tisha and Florian, and Tasha. He looked perfectly content beside her. He had transferred to the Chicago office stating that it was advantageous to his health—he could continue his therapy here. Simone smiled. It seemed that therapy was going well.

Shamel, Tyreek and Mrs. Henderson sat together toward the front of the courtroom. They talked and laughed as they waited for court to convene. Tyreek was showing Shamel pictures of his niece on his IPhone. He truly was a proud uncle.

Mr. and Mrs. Mortimeus Quick sat side by side not saying a word to each other. Each was lost in their own worlds. Occasionally, Yolanda caught Morty glancing over toward the very pregnant young woman sitting with the little boy in the wheelchair.

Morty feels so bad about that poor boy and his family. I know he wishes there was something he could do…

Morty snuck another peek at Rakeetah. He couldn't get over the change in her appearance since she was awarded custody of her nephew. She looked more like an Eddie Bauer soccer mom than the babies' momma that she had been three months ago. He wasn't sure he liked it.

She looks like Yolanda…like she doesn't need me anymore.

Simone was deciding on her seating arrangement when she felt a presence behind her. "Hello," is all the voice said. She took a deep breath and swallowed. Turning around slowly she saw who the voice belonged to.

"Hello," she replied.

"How have you been?"

"I've been fine," she said.

Liar.

 "How are you?"

"It's been a little crazy lately, but I've filed for divorce and Maia and I are adjusting," Jason said.

"You did what?" Simone asked.

"It's a long story and you don't need to be bothered with that. I can't be with the woman I love if I'm married to someone else. Simone, I love you and I want you to be my wife and Maia's mother if you want us—want me. I was wrong to say those things to you. I was trying to blame you when all I was really doing was making excuses for not being man enough to handle my own business. I'm so sorry," Jason said.

"What made you come to these conclusions now?" Simone asked.

Jason looked at her and wondered that himself. "Moms would say that sometimes the universe gives you a second chance and that everything that looks bad is really the best thing that could happen to you," he said.

Simone just looked at him, not knowing how to respond. He shook his head and gave a dismissive wave. "Never mind, it's not important anymore," he said. They stood there for a moment, not touching. He held out his hand tentatively. Simone took it and he smiled the same smile that he had on the first day that they met.

"Hear ye, hear ye. This court is called to order, the Honorable Judge Burkett presiding," the bailiff boomed from the front of the courtroom. The judge entered and took her seat at the bench. Simone and Jason sat down and held hands, fingers intertwined as they listened to the fate of the defendant, if and when he ever materialized.

Chapter 92

Today

Minnie knew it was going to be a good day. The possibility for drama on the floor was at an all-time high. If she played her cards right, she would be right in the midst of it. Miss Thing was being released at high noon and Minnie had already checked her schedule and made the adjustments necessary to have lunch at one so that she wouldn't miss a thing. That fine ass Mr. Copeny would probably be there—he's been there every day since she was admitted.

Some people have all the luck. Why can't I get one like that?

She threw her crochet braids out of her eyes and pressed the elevator button to the fourth floor.

When the door opened, the oversized over friendly nurse she referred to as The Sears Tower was leaning against the railing. "Hey boo," she said tossing her head innocently. "How's it going?"

"I'm fine," he replied.

"Just starting your shift? I'm here all day…get off around seven."

Hint hint.

"No." he looked at his watch. "I get off around noon if I'm lucky. Got things to do at home," he said.

"Oh," Minnie said. "I thought we could hang out like we used to, you know? Well, how about lunch? I get lunch around one."

"No, I'll be gone before then. I really got to get home. Thanks, though. We're working the same floor, so see you around," he said as the elevator doors opened and he exited quickly.

Hmmph. Wonder what put a burr in his butt? He used to have time to talk to me.

She went to the employee lounge to check her makeup and hair before starting her shift. She was humming to herself and thinking about the sight and smell of Mr. Copeny as he walked down the hallway. Minnie couldn't grasp why she was still calling him Mr. Copeny after six days. Ordinarily, she was on first names basis with the husbands and friends of the female patients after the first hour, but no, not this one.

She must be the bomb diggity. And I bet her smooth-talking hunk of a husband will be here too….

"Today's a good day," she sang. "Gonna be a good day…"

"Daddy, Daddy, wake up! You have to wake up!" Maia tugged and yanked on Jason's goatee.

"Ouch baby girl, what's the matter? Are you okay? What's wrong?" he asked as he jumped up in the bed. Maia pounced around on the bed. Then she popped up and went to the closet and started searching for just the right shirt and pants for her father to wear.

"I'm fine Daddy, but you need to get up because today is the big day and we've got things to do," she yelled from the closet. "You will look nice in this Daddy" she said as she held up her selection.

"Baby, it's only eight o'clock. We've got plenty of time before noon. What's the rush?" Jason asked rubbing his eyes. He hadn't slept much last night. He was too excited that Simone was getting out of the hospital today and he had a surprise for her. Maia came back out of the closet and pounced back on the bed.

"No, Daddy, we've got a lot to do, and I don't want to be like the white rabbit," she said.

"The white rabbit?" he asked.

"Yeah, you know, the white rabbit in Alice in Wonderland. "I'm late, I'm late for a very important date," she sang.

"I promise we won't be late," he said.

"We better not be. I don't want her going home with somebody else," Maia said as she kissed him on the top of his head.

Neither do I.

"Okay baby, I'm getting up," he said.

"Good, and don't forget to shave your head. It's bristly. We don't want Miss Simone to think you're bristly. What do you want for breakfast? I can make Eggo waffles," she said.

"That sound fantastic. I had a taste for waffles this morning," he said as he made up the bed.

"If I fix breakfast, you have to do the dishes," she said.

"As long as I don't have to dry the silverware, you got a deal."

Chapter 93

Simone stood in the bathroom looking in the mirror. The swelling had gone down considerably over the past three days.

It's amazing how wonderful it is to be able to go to the bathroom by yourself and hold a fork and see out of both of your eyes. Life is good and oh so precious. I need to remember that for as long as I have it.

She was about to pull her hair into a ponytail, but she changed her mind and bent over and tossed her head this way and that until she was dizzy. When she stood up, so did her hair. She shook it once, twice, perfect.

If they love me, they'll love my hair…more importantly, I love my hair. If they don't, fu…

"Good morning," came a man's voice through the door. Simone opened the door and walked across the room to the chair. In a way she was grateful that she had been injured so badly, that allowed her to have a private room.

Along with Jason's whining that I needed privacy to recuperate.

There stood The Sears Tower, Shaq's twin, whatever his name was. He didn't know Simone, but he knew that his ex-brother-in-law knew Simone and he wanted to be done his rounds before Jason showed up. He'd been avoiding him for a week. Simone still didn't know the details and Jason had never shared, but it must have been an explosive situation.

"How are you feeling today? You must be happy to be going home," he said as he checked her vitals. "Your hair looks pretty that way."

"Thanks. I am really happy, and I feel good. You're here early today. Busy day for you too?" she said.

"Yeah, my wife and I are taking our oldest to visit Morehouse this weekend and we need to leave today. We're driving so it's going to take a while," he said.

"That sounds wonderful. You must be really proud," she said.

"We are. It's been an…interesting year and this is a good thing to have happen," he said. He finished checking her blood pressure and started to take her pulse.

"It's good when things are going well," she said.

"Yeah, ain't that the truth. Sometimes you don't appreciate things 'til you almost lose them," he said.

"True, your health and family are everything," she said. He finished up and smiled at her in agreement.

"My wife and children are all I have and all that matter to me. Takes a while to figure that out sometimes. I mean I've got other family, but they have their own families, you know? My wife only has me and the kids," he said.

"She's an only child?" Simone asked innocently.

"She has a sister but…they don't speak anymore," he said quietly.

"Well, it sounds like your wife and children are in good hands. They're lucky to have you," she said.

God, you can still talk out both sides of your head. No brain damage it seems.

"No, I'm the lucky one. I know that now. I've got to finish my rounds so I can get home. You take care of yourself and be careful out there," he smiled again and disappeared out of the door. Simone could have sworn that he peeked down the hallway before he stepped into it.

Chapter **94**

Dr. Ansula signed the discharge papers and handed them to Simone. "Any questions?" he asked. Simone shook her head and folded the papers.

"You will continue to need bed rest when you get home and return for a check-up in two weeks. I'll set that up for you," he said as he shook her hand and walked toward the door. He stopped, turned around and said, "You are a very lucky lady. I've seen several accidents that were not as serious as yours with much worse results. You must be well watched over. Consider yourself very blessed," he said as he walked out of the room.

Simone did consider herself blessed. From what she had been told, her car was totaled and unrecognizable. The insurance company didn't squabble or fuss. The agent had delivered a check for the full amount of replacing her car one model year newer than the one she owned, which meant that she was getting the latest model of whatever she chose. She checked her watch—twenty minutes before she could legally roll out of here. The nursing assistant that had been so helpful this week, had stopped in to let her know that she would help with her flowers and belongings when she was discharged. Simone thanked her and had a suspicion that little Miss Nursing Assistant had a crush on Jason. Every time she saw him she twisted strands of hair around her fingers and flitted her eyes.

Poor baby, another one bites the dust. You can twist all you want. That one is taken.

Simone glanced around the room at the cards and gifts and flowers that were everywhere. It made her feel good that so many people cared. She tried to decide which ones to keep and which to donate to the hospital. Maybe someone's stay would be easier with something beautiful to gaze upon. She was going home to someone beautiful.

"See Daddy, we're going to be late. Auntie Tasha couldn't twist my hair but so fast and now we're going to be late! Do you think Miss Simone will wait for us? What if she doesn't wait for us?" Maia was checking the clock on the wall at Mim's.

"It's all good, babygirl. I promise. Everything is going to be just fine. Trust me," Jason kissed her cheek and looked at Mim holding her youngest granddaughter.

"So everything is set at Mr. Dyson's right?" he asked.

"Yes, Jason. You've asked that three times in the past hour. William and I will be on our way there as soon as I bundle up Pia. Florian and Tasha are there already with Chevy, taking care of the food. Ishua is bringing your sister. Mike and Sly are doing whatever it is that Mike and Sly do…his words, not mine. He also said that he is picking up Mrs. Henderson and Tyreek. Mr. Dyson is a very nice man, you'll like him. He really wants to get to know you. So, everything is fine. Relax, she'll love the surprise," Mim said.

"What if it's too much excitement for her? What if…" Jason started.

"Boy, shut up and go get your woman before your daughter has a heart attack. See you in a few hours," William said as he wrapped his arm around Mim and the baby. "Give grown folks some privacy for a minute."

"Okay, Mrs. Dyson, you're sure you only want to take these? That's a lot of flowers and balloons to leave behind," Minnie said as she placed the flowers that Simone wanted to keep on a cart with her personal belongings. Tyreek had sent a magnificent Zen garden complete with bamboo and orchids. Sly sent a beautiful three-foot-tall lily in full bloom. He said it would look perfect in her office.

He was right, it would. He knows me so well.

Jason, at Maia's suggestion had sent roses, strawberries, and a teddy bear family. The three of them had eaten the strawberries and named the teddy bears. Maia had taken one of the bears home with her. It had been a perfect day in the hospital.

Minnie took the flowers out of the room to the nurse's station. Simone hoped that the patients would actually get the benefit of the flowers; she could hear the nurses discussing which flowers would look good on their coffee tables. She took a deep breath and looked out the window of her room on the parking lot below. She wondered where Jason was parked and would she be able to see him if he was down there. She thought about all that had happened since she met him, how her life had changed. Was it better? Was she better? The answers would take a little bit more thought but she had an idea.

"Okay, Mrs. Dyson," Minnie squealed, "It's time to get you on your way. I have to push you out in the wheelchair. Hospital policy. Is someone coming to pick you up?"

"I certainly hope so," Simone casually answered as she sat in the wheelchair.

"Well, let's not keep him waiting," Minnie said.

"Yes, let's not do that," Simone replied with a grin.

It was a bright and sunny day that would have driven a vampire back to its grave. Simone hadn't seen the sun for six, no, seven days. She wasn't sure anymore. All she knew was that it was perfect. Everything was perfect because she had another chance at life.

So many people don't. Thank you, God. Let me live it the way it was meant to be lived. Boldly, fully, completely. Free from fear. Please God, help me get it right from now on.

Minnie pushed the wheelchair down the access ramp and on to the sidewalk. Cars were pulling up and other patients were rolled toward them. Simone looked and saw no familiar faces. She felt her shoulders tighten and she immediately forced herself to breathe deeply and acknowledge the tension she was experiencing.

It's alright. There's a reason. Everything is fine…

She put her hand up to shield her eyes from the sun and saw a familiar face walking across the parking lot with a bouquet of the reddest roses she had ever seen. The tension in her shoulders was beginning to be more than she could control. The closer he came to the hospital, the more Simone's grip on the wheelchair tightened. Out of the corner of her eye, she saw something else. Not as calm and collected as the other image before her eyes but one that made her loosen her grip.

Greg was walking toward her holding the roses up in front of him, smiling as if he was about to win a prize. His stride was smooth and sure. His dress indicated a man of refined taste. Everything about him screamed confident.

Jason and Maia were jogging toward the hospital. Her hair was blowing in the breeze and her hand was tightly gripping her father's as she dragged him along. She was carrying a teddy bear in her other hand.

Oh yeah, here we go. This is gonna be even better than I thought. It's on now. She gonna have to decide and whoever she picks the other's gonna wanna fight and then the little girl will start to scream if her pretty ass daddy gets hit and then...this is gonna be the bomb diggity!

"So, Mrs. Dyson," Minnie said, with the emphasis on the Mrs. "Which way?"

Simone looked at her handsome husband and thought about all of the years they had spent together and all that they had accomplished. She looked at Jason and his little girl running up the sidewalk. Simone looked back at Greg one more time. She pointed.

"That way," she said, without giving it a second thought.

Epilogue

"I guess you won't be needing those roses, huh?" Minnie asked as she pushed the wheelchair towards Greg. She didn't want him to faint and hit his head on hospital property.

"Excuse me, what did you say?" he snapped out of his daze and tried to focus on her.

"Looks like you won't be needing those roses," she said again.

"So, what? Do you want them?" he asked. She twirled her hair around her finger and flitted her eyelids.

"Do you want to give them to me?" she asked.

"Maybe, over dinner," Greg replied. He knew a come on when he heard one. Since he had nowhere to go tonight and no one to go with, why not? It was better than being alone again. He looked down at Minnie. She was attractive in a boyish kind of way.

Definitely not Simone but who is?

He watched her twirl her hair.

Very juvenile and immature. She's way too young and probably way too stupid but it beats being alone right now…I wonder if all that hair is hers?

"I get off from here at seven," she said.

"I don't ordinarily give roses to women whose name I don't know," he said.

"I don't ordinarily accept roses from men whose name I don't know," she answered.

"My name is Greg. Nice to meet you," he said as he placed his hand in front of her. She shook it.

God, I hate it when they shake your hand like you've got fleas.

"Hi Greg. Nice to meet you. My name is Caprice," she said. Twirl twirl.

"Caprice, like the car?" he asked.

"Exactly. My parents say that that's where I came from if you catch my drift," she giggled.

Greg shook his head.

What am I getting myself into? Why don't you just leave the roses and walk away?

He hesitated for a moment and said, "So I'll pick you up at eight, Caprice. I think I can remember that."

"Yup, just think of me as a high maintenance Chevy," she said.